THE

A Novel by

Lindsey S. Frantz

THE LACING Copyright ©2022
Line By Lion Publications
www.pixelandpen.studio

ISBN: 978-1-948807-41-8

Cover Art: T.J. Brandt
Editing By Dani J. Caile

LINE BY LION
PUBLICATIONS

Prologue

Finn

GONE. Erilyn was gone.

Finn felt like he was going to implode.

The light that had tied them together had violently snapped. Some part of him had been torn away—roots ripped from soil. Like he had a gaping hole inside his chest.

The tremendous pain he'd felt at first had receded and been replaced with something far worse.

Emptiness.

He'd been hollowed out and left to rot.

Desperate, Finn closed his eyes and gripped his shaggy hair, pulling hard in the hopes that the pain might help him focus. He thought back to the golden light that had surrounded Erilyn when she had been trapped by Morrigan, tried to feel that light somewhere inside himself.

But it was gone.

No golden light. No warm comfort that felt like home.

No Erilyn.

Beside him, Cillian hovered, waiting for an explanation, but Finn didn't have time to explain. The tether had snapped, which meant Erilyn was in trouble. She needed him. With all the strength he could muster, he lunged for the iron gate that served as a cell door and shook the bars, screaming at the top of his lungs.

Chapter 1

"Ringol"

Erilyn

THE wavy window glass was foggy. Beyond it lay the wylden camp. The weight of the long, difficult road it had taken to get here rested on my shoulders like a yoke. Only a few weeks ago we'd been tucked away in our winter cabin, but it felt like so much longer.

Zeke, the wylden alpha, stood beside me. He was a tall man with dark skin and the most beautiful teal eyes I'd ever seen. His relaxed expression and stance almost made me forget that until an hour ago, he'd been intent on breaking my spirit and tying my will to his. If I hadn't forced myself into his aura and fixed the cracks, just like I'd done for Fia, I wouldn't be *me* anymore. I shivered and fought the urge to step away from him.

Sensing my eyes and thoughts on him, he leaned toward me. I took an involuntary step away and his neutral expression shifted to a glower.

I didn't trust Zeke. Not yet. It had been only minutes since I'd healed his cracks. He was in control now and could shield his thoughts and feelings from me if he wanted, but he didn't. I could feel his desire for me to help his people as I'd helped him, but I could also feel his desire for me. Like Cillian and Roark, he wasn't used to taking no as an answer. If I wanted to make it out of this room and make it back to my friends, I had to tread carefully.

With measured breaths, I relaxed my muscles and met his teal gaze. I would not be intimidated by him, and I knew that his newfound wholeness and subsequent morals would not allow him to force anything from me.

Zeke's shoulders slumped a little as he asked, "Now?" He nodded toward the window and the wylden people on the other side. He could read me as easily as I could read him.

"We'll need help," I said, standing up straighter and pushing past my exhaustion. "To help your people, it's going to take more than just you and me." I tried to do as Fia had taught me and pictured what I meant—pictures as well as feelings. He nodded once then left the building, the door slamming behind him.

My shoulders slouched in relief at his absence. I wrapped my arms around my stomach and squeezed. Without Zeke looming over me, I could let myself think. And let myself panic.

Before I'd had a chance to mend Zeke's aura, he'd broken the tie between Finn and me. I'd felt it snap like a bone and I wondered if Finn had felt it too. I felt utterly empty and I hoped that because Finn didn't have abilities, he hadn't felt it, because it had *hurt*. Arms tight against my belly I curled in on myself and squeezed my eyes shut.

Where was Finn? Was he okay? I'd thought our tie had been unnatural, a mistake, but now that it was missing I couldn't help but think that I'd been wrong. Without it I felt exposed, like some vital part of myself had been ripped away.

With a shaky breath, heart in my throat, I let my senses expand in the hopes that I would sense Finn or one of the others. I knew Finn's aura more intimately than even my own, and I could sense it! I wanted to reach for it, to see if he was okay, but the door opened and I pulled my awareness back, shielding myself as much from Zeke as I could as he stepped into the room. He'd been *right there,* but I couldn't risk searching fro him now.

Zeke walked in, a scowl on his face, and I knew he'd felt what I was about to do. But then Fia walked in just behind him like a fresh breeze on a stagnant day. Her face broke out into a grin as she gripped both my hands. Her relief at finding me whole poured into me through her fingertips. She gently probed my mind as one might prod a bruise, looking for damage. I showed her that I was untouched and whole, then, doing my best to shield my thoughts from Zeke, I let her see my memories of what I'd done to Zeke.

She spun away from me, eyes wide, and stepped toward Zeke. He didn't react as she crouched and moved closer. She circled him and I opened up my sight enough to see their auras—hers a midnight-blue, his a vivid teal— swirling around each other like oil poured into water.

After a long, tense moment, Fia straightened and turned toward me. She smiled, showing off her yellow-brown teeth, and put her hand on her chest. "Like us," she growled.

I nodded and exhaled. "We want to help all of your people." I stepped closer to her and took her hand so she could read my intent more clearly. "We want to bring peace between the people of Sunnybrook and—" I paused. I didn't know what this town was called and I let her feel the question in my thoughts.

"Ringol," Fia said, an almost proud look on her face. "Home."

"And Ringol," I said, the word foreign on my tongue. "But to do that, we have to help as many wylden as we can. Make them like you and Zeke."

"All," Zeke growled, then cleared his throat as if hearing the almost inhuman nature of his voice for the first time. "All," he repeated more clearly.

"All the wylden." As overwhelming as that was, the thought of the wylden being like Fia—curious and loyal—gave me a renewed sense of purpose. If the wylden were all like Fia, there could be real peace. I closed my eyes for a moment as I imagined a world like that, but when I opened them, Zeke's expression—fraught with tension—brought me up short.

"Soon," Zeke said, eyes once again on the cloudy glass window. "Close."

Now that I was paying attention instead of focusing on my own worry and fear, I could feel his anxiety at the edges of my awareness like the sharp smell of a skunk somewhere deep in the woods.

Fia's hand in mine was warm. I looked at her, waiting for clarification. When Zeke took my other hand in his large, calloused one, I jumped, but he didn't try to invade my mind again. Instead, I felt my mind join with theirs as equal partners. With painful clarity I was reminded of the children and our walks together through a different forest as they tried to teach me how to use my abilities. The pain of their absence was a deep, dull ache, only rivaled by the absence of Finn.

"Close," Zeke repeated, ignoring my own inner turmoil to show me what he needed me to see.

I closed my eyes and let the two of them take me to *see* what was making Zeke so anxious.

Our *vision* moved so quickly, everything was a blur. It was faster than I'd ever traveled and I wondered if it was because of Zeke. Joined like we were, I could feel that his power was a deep, almost bottomless well. With a shock, I wondered how I'd been able to heal it. There was so much. This amount of power, of boundless energy, should have swallowed me whole.

I didn't have long to think about that, though, as we abruptly stopped. Under normal circumstances, I would need to take a moment to orient myself and overcome the dizziness that always accompanied my *sight* traveling outside my body, but Zeke wasn't patient. It was as if he took my head in his hands and shoved my face toward what he wanted me to see. It was jarring, but before the disorientation was gone I could see that we were in a cave. The walls sloped in above our heads and I could smell the tang of earth and stagnant water through whoever's senses we had latched onto.

We were spying on a group of cave dwellers. Never had I seen so many of them in a single tunnel. As a people, the population of Citadel tended to stick to small, quiet groups. When they were gathered in larger packs like this, it was always in bigger, open spaces and never for very long. There were more people than I could count and they were all moving forward, silently, but with a palpable purpose.

Zeke and Fia helped me *see* and the cave dwellers' auras flared into crystal clarity. Where once the tunnel was dark, it now was bright with an array of colorful aura-lights. They pulsed in a way I'd never seen before, all together, as if to the rhythm of a single beating heart. There was a rainbow of colors, but as I looked more closely I saw that a few of them were starting to fracture like the wylden's. Like Morrigan's.

The people of Citadel were taking vitium. It was like being dunked in a tub of ice water.

Zeke and Fia jerked us back to our bodies. I stumbled as they released both my mind and my hands and fell back into a wall, gasping as if I'd just run very far. Fia looked apologetic, but Zeke looked unaffected.

"Okay?" Fia asked as she stepped toward me, her hand gently finding my shoulder.

"I'm okay,." I pushed off the wall to stand and her hand fell away. I looked at Zeke and exhaled heavily. "So what we just saw—those people from Citadel are coming here."

He nodded once, then turned back to the window. "Close."

My head was swimming with what that could mean. Fia, gentler than Zeke, touched my arm again and images slowly appeared in my mind. After our connection moments ago, it stung a little—a muscle not quite ready to be used again.

People from Citadel beneath the earth, their auras pulsing.

Their base camp—not Citadel itself, but a large cavern below Sunnybrook.

Sunnybrook full of pulsing lights, all moving toward us.

"That's why you were attacking Sunnybrook," I whispered. "You thought they were in the city, but they weren't. They were *below* it." I swallowed heavily. I grew up in Citadel. Everything there was subtle. Quiet. So much wasn't as it seemed. "They tricked you so you would attack the upworlders."

Zeke's shoulder were tense as he nodded. When he turned back, his expression finally showed some of the desperation he was feeling, which permeated the room.

"All," he said. "Help. *Now.*" His voice was back to its insistent growl, but I could hear a subtle shift voice that hadn't been there before. He was afraid of what was coming and was worried for his people. That alone pushed me toward my decision.

"Fia, will you help me?" I pictured us together, healing auras side-by-side, and she stood straighter. She nodded, long, matted strands of her hair swaying forward. With trepidation tingling in my fingertips, I wet my lips and took a deep, shaky breath. I wanted to ask for Finn, but Zeke's desire to do this now had to come first. If Finn seemed like an obstacle or a distraction, I woudln't put it past the wylden alpha to kill him. To help Finn, I first had to help Zeke.

I faced him, trying to mimic Fia's newfound confidence with my own posture. "Who first?"

Zeke softened as he smiled broadly, his teeth as yellow as Fia's. He looked toward the door with a new, hopeful light in his vitium-colored eyes. I felt a shift in the air as he communicated with someone outside. It didn't surprise me this time when only seconds later, the door opened.

Chapter 2

"Isolation"

Finn

THE bars didn't budge even after Finn shook them as hard as he could. Exhausted, he stumbled back. He knelt on the ground, mind whirling around the vast emptiness in his chest.

"Finley," Cillian said forcefully, "what is going on?"

"I don't know," Finn said, desperation and determination filling up the painful emptiness inside of him. "But I have to get to Erilyn." With a deep breath, Finn rose to his feet again. He looked around, searching for any possible exit.

Still sitting on the ground a few feet away, Lowell—the upworlder they'd met after being tossed in this cell—laughed darkly. "There's no way out of here," he said before coughing and pressing his hand into his belly as if it hurt. "You think I haven't tried?"

"There has to be some way," Finn said, crossing back to the cell door and giving it another firm shake. "I have to get to her."

"Will you please just stop and tell us what's going on?" Cillian asked. His tone was sharp with frustration, though the tight lines around his eyes suggested that he, too, was worried.

"I don't know—" Finn moved from the cell to the other bars that ran from the ceiling to the floor, shaking each in turn in the hopes that one might wobble. He spoke to Cillian without looking at him directly. "I felt something. Like—" He made his way around the small cell and shoved at the final bars angrily, then shoved his fingers into his hair and pulled again in frustration. "Like something inside me *broke*." Finn looked at Cillian, eyes wild. "Erilyn and I were connected." His words couldn't do justice to the gaping hole inside him where she'd once been.

Cillian exhaled slowly through his nose. "Yes, I'm aware." He crossed his arms over his chest. "Hold on," he said, settling his feet a little further apart and absently wetting his lips. His eyes lost their focus for a moment as he looked at Finn, but then he gave his head a slight shake and he was back. "It's gone," he said with a nod. "The vitium I've taken has almost completely worn off or I could try and see what happened. But that alone was much more difficult than it should have been."

"It doesn't matter what happened. I *know* she needs me," Finn said, hands balled in fists at his sides as his heart pounded a frantic rhythm inside his chest.

"The only way you're getting out of this cell," Lowell said from his pile of rags in the corner, "is if those monsters take you out. And trust me, you don't want them to take you out." He sounded bone-weary and hopeless, but his words gave Finn an idea.

"I have to get to her," Finn said directly to Cillian.

Cillian opened his mouth—maybe to talk him down or ask him questions—but Finn didn't wait to find out what he was going to say. Instead, he rushed back to the bars of the door and grabbed the cold metal in his hands.

With the children, he'd practiced hiding inside his thoughts. Now he tried to do the opposite. He screamed at the top of his lungs and tried to think of things that would make them come—he thought back to his first interaction with wylden, when he'd snuck into their camp and considered, for a moment, killing one of their children. It was a horrific moment and one that he was deeply ashamed of. He hoped it would be terrible enough, a strong enough memory, that they would think he was a threat. Would come and take him. If they took him out of the cell, he had a chance of escaping and getting to Erilyn.

Cillian pulled him off the bars. He hooked his arms around Finn's chest. "Finley!" he yelled right into Finn's ear. "Stop!"

Finn elbowed Cillian, chest heaving, and shoved him back, intent on staying at the gate and screaming until someone came. When Cillian came at him again, ready to pull him away from the bars, Finn reared back and punched him without a second thought. Cillian stumbled back and grasped his jaw, but Finn was already back at the bars.

Erilyn. The pressure he felt in his chest to get to her increased the longer he was disconnected from her. He picked up a piece of stone that had come loose from the once-solid floor and used it to beat against the metal bars. Thinking of the wylden child hadn't helped. Instead, he pictured the wylden man he'd killed in Erilyn's clearing.

He forced himself to remember the cold air and his need—as desperate then as it was now—to find her and protect her. The wylden man had been on top of her, pinning her to the snowy ground. He remembered picking up the knife. Remembered the way it had felt in his hand—heavy and cold—as the man had rushed him and impaled himself on the blade. His memories were getting away from him, moving on their own now, and he could almost hear her scream in his ears as she'd felt the blade entering the wylden's chest. Felt him die.

Finn screamed, frantic to get to her now as the fear of the unknown mingled with the pain of those memories.

Cillian slunk toward Lowell to distance himself from whatever fate Finn was going to bring about for himself. His jaw was already darkening with a bruise and he wasn't the sort of man who would sacrifice himself for another—at least not someone like Finn.

Finn's voice grew raw from screaming, but then the outside door opened and pale morning light poured in.

Two wylden men—big and muscled—stomped in. Their eyes were narrowed in anger. One wore a snarl that showcased missing teeth.

Finn felt a wave of something cold—they were trying to calm him as Erilyn had done before—but his fear for her was so strong that he somehow managed to shove them out.

"Let me out of this damned cell!" he screamed at them. He brought the impaled wylden to the front of his mind, holding the image of his blood soaking the snow in his head. He just needed them to open the door and he could get away. Get to her.

The wylden men regarded him silently, then turned as if they were going to leave. In a final moment of desperation, he gripped the piece of stone he'd used to beat the iron bars with and threw it at the men.

The shard hit one of them in the back of the head with a dull thud, but they both spun as if they'd felt the sting. Their eyes locked on him and Finn felt like icy water had been dumped over his head as they crossed the space to the cell door.

One of the wylden unlocked the cell door with a rusted skeleton key. The door scraped as it opened, passing over a deep groove in the stone floor—the results of years of use. Before Finn could make it past the doorway, the wylden he hit with the rock grabbed him roughly by the throat and dragged him out. With the two wylden distracted, Cillian rushed the door in his own escape attempt, but the second man shoved him back and slammed the door shut.

Finn clawed at the hand that gripped his sore throat, but the wylden man's grip was as hard and unyielding as the impenetrable bars had been.

As the man dragged Finn outside, his vision grew blurry. Before they pulled him outside, he saw Cillian gripping the bars, jaw clenched and eyes wide.

Finn's toes dragged the ground as he fought against the wylden's grip, but he might as well have been trying to dig through rock with his bare hands with the good it did. The harder he fought, the tighter the wylden squeezed. His vision started to go black around the edges, but he kept scrabbling against the iron-like fingers gripping his throat. Cool sunlight fell on his reddening face as he was dragged down the dirt-packed street.

Finn fought the dark pull of unconsciousness. He was trying to see where they were, trying to orient himself, trying to remember where they'd separated him from Erilyn. But his vision blurred more and more from the pressure on his throat and all the buildings they passed were little more than blurred shapes that pulsed with the heavy beat of his heart.

Erilyn, he tried to call out in his mind. He couldn't contact her, but maybe she was *listening*. Maybe she was reaching out for him too. But the chasm in his chest echoed in return.

Angry, pain-induced tears filled his eyes. He tried to take a breath only to gag with the pressure on his windpipe.

Erilyn! he called one more time, focusing on the memory of her warm, golden light. He expected the echo. He expected nothing, but then he felt something—a tickle in his mind.

The wylden holding him growled and tightened his grip around Finn's throat again. Pain rippled through his throat, his lungs constricted, and everything went black.

FINN awoke sometime later in a pitch black room. His whole body ached as if he'd been beaten. Maybe he had. He was lying on the cold, hard ground, curled around his knees like a baby. With cramped fingers he touched his tender throat, which hurt more than any other part of his body. It felt like a deep bruise and he wondered if any permanent damage had been done.

With a groan, Finn used one arm to push himself up to sit on the cold, hard floor. His head throbbed with each painful beat of his heart and his mouth was dry. Even though he couldn't see in the blackness, the room felt like it was tilting and spinning. He closed his eyes and pressed his palms against his closed eyelids to try and steady himself.

After a few deep breaths the room felt more stable, and he was able to open his eyes again. His first assumption, that there was no light at all, had been wrong.

He could now see a door outlined in pale gray light. There were no windows, though, and when he reached out to see how big the space was, he could touch all four walls from where he sat on the ground. The room he was in was no bigger than a storage closet. Despair settled on him like a wet blanket.

Clumsily, he stood to stretch his cramped muscles. He reached for the rectangle of light, hoping to find a doorknob, but there wasn't one. Where a doorknob had once been he found a hole patched with something that felt like straw and mud, hard as a rock. He pushed at the door, but it barely jiggled. It had to be heavily bolted from the outside.

He was trapped with no way out. He'd made the same mistake again–just like when he'd run headlong into that wylden camp all those months ago, he hadn't thought this through. He'd been impulsive and stupid and now he would pay for it. He only hoped that until he could figure a way out of here, Erilyn would be okay.

With a huff, he fell back against the wall and slid to the floor. He extended his legs and pressed the bottoms of his feet against the door. The space was so small he wouldn't even be able to lie down.

Fresh panic welled in his chest and he forced himself to think of Erilyn. What she would do if she were here. She would take deep breaths. She would listen. She would wait.

So that's what he did—he closed his eyes, deepened his inhales, and listened. There were no noises outside the room, so he assumed the wylden had thrown him in here and left. He was alone. He wasn't sure if that was better or worse than them waiting right outside.

Finn's head fell back and hit the wall with a thump, his concentration gone already. He thought back to his wild and pitiful attack on the wylden camp all those months ago. He'd gone there, intent on attacking them, to prove to Morrigan that he was the kind of man that she told him he should be—someone brave and reckless and strong. It had been stupid, especially given what he now knew about Morrigan's control over him, but he couldn't regret it because it had led him to Erilyn. If he hadn't made that ridiculous choice, he might never have met her, and that was a reality he couldn't fathom.

Even though he felt hopeless, trapped in this closet, he soothed himself with the knowledge that his first stupid choice had led him to Erilyn. He had to believe that this second stupid choice would as well.

Chapter 3

"Harem"

Morrigan

THE scent of unwashed bodies assaults your nose and you sneer in disgust. Through the stink you smell other things—fear, despair, sadness—and you can't help but hate the women that surround you.

Arms still tied, you manage to roll to one side and rock yourself up to sitting. No one offers to help you, but you don't expect them to. You are used to doing things on your own. As the vitium in your body fades your muscles twitch, trying to dislodge the imaginary ants that you feel all over your skin. You grit your teeth and try to ignore it. The auras of the people around you are so faint you can barely see them. If you don't dose soon, you won't be able to see them at all.

It's been so long since you've gone without vitium, you can't even remember what it feels like. To be without your *sight*. Without your *gifts*. You don't want to remember what it was like to be the girl you were before.

The feeling of marching ants intensifies and starts to prickle and pinch, like a limb that's gone to sleep and is waking up, but worse. It itches and burns and you want nothing more than to shake yourself until the feeling is gone, but you know it will only make it worse.

"Morrigan," says the nightcrawler woman, her voice soft. You'd forgotten she was here and refuse to look at her. "Would you like some water?" You consider biting her hand as she reaches for you, or at least saying no, but then she's there in front of you, materializing like a pale spirit and the cup of water reminds you of how thirsty you are. You can't see her aura at all, and you panic until you remember—she can hide her aura and she can hide others. A useful ability. One you could use to your advantage, if given the chance. Better not bite her just yet.

You nod and she tilts the cup to your lips. The water washes over your mouth, cool but gritty, and you drink greedily.

"We should tell her where we are," the nightcrawler says, pity in her voice as she looks over her shoulder. You follow her gaze in the dusky room and see Lucy, a scowl on her freckled face. You meet her eyes and smile without warmth.

"Why?" Lucy holds her arms crossed tightly across her chest.

"Because it's the right thing to do," the nightcrawler says. *Aiyanna.* Her name comes to you from some foggy memory of when these people kept you asleep. You grind your teeth as the memory of being trapped resurfaces—hot and painful—but try to keep your anger hidden. For the moment, these people are all you have. Resources that you can't afford to lose.

Lucy stares at Aiyanna for a moment longer, then her eyes lock with yours—cold anger burning deep inside. "We're in a harem," she says. No pretense. No gentling of the words. "For wylden men."

The smile falls from your face and you look around, really taking in the people around you now. Unwashed bodies. Fear. Despair. Sadness. Some of the women you see are wylden. Others are not. All are broken and your own fear washes through you like a flash flood in a storm—sudden and wild.

A small, cool hand touches your shoulder and you jerk away from it as your heart thumps against your ribs. Aiyanna, on her knees beside you, tries to comfort you and you shift further away. Reflexively, you *look* at her, forgetting she can hide herself from you. As you *look,* the prickly feeling in your limbs ebbs away to nothing and with it trickles the last of your power.

The girl in front of you fully solidifies—no longer an apparition—and you know that the vitium in your system is spent.

You look around again, the flash flood of panic swelling like waves inside your chest.

No auras.

The colors of the room are dull—browns and grays in the hazy light.

It's like you're looking at everything through fog. The waves of panic rise and crest as sweat beads on your face.

But then, just as quickly, the waves settle into a stagnant well of water. You are empty.

Something in your expression must change, because the look on the nightcrawler's face says she pities you. "We should untie her hands," Aiyanna says to Lucy. You grow unreasonably angry with her kindness. "I don't think—" she turns to look at you again, her eyes squinted the smallest bit. "I don't think she can use her abilities anymore."

You physically curl in on yourself, fighting the urge to attack her, to hurt her for exposing your weakness, but her expression only becomes softer.

"She's still dangerous," Lucy says, coming to stand behind Aiyanna almost defensively. You are grateful for that. You are grateful that there's no pity in Lucy's eyes. Grateful that she, at least, sees you for the warrior you are.

"How dangerous can she be in here?" Aiyanna whispers as she gazes up at the younger girl.

Lucy hesitates for a long moment, her green eyes shifting from Aiyanna to bore into you like knives, but she doesn't scare you. Nothing scares you anymore. And then, her hard look turns to pity as well, and she nods.

Aiyanna touches your shoulder again and you flinch away, fighting the urge now to bare your teeth in warning. "I'm going to untie your hands. All right?" Her voice is soft, calm, as if she's speaking to an animal caught in a trap. You hate her for this, but you also need these bonds removed if you ever plan to escape. You force the angry expression from your face and offer her your wrists.

With the lightest of touches, she undoes the intricate knots. The ropes fall away and you roll your shoulders, then spread your fingers wide before you curl your hands into fists. You rub your wrists where the ropes had rubbed, expecting pain, but finding only a mildly unpleasant ache. The ropes weren't so tight that they injured you. You know that means Cillian tied them. He would have been the only one who didn't want to cause you pain.

Cillian. Just the thought of him forces unwanted emotions to well up.

You force the thought of him away. The thought of his face. His hands. You have more important things to focus on and the thought of him will just hinder you.

Lucy takes Aiyanna's hand and pulls her up and away from you. You notice the way their fingers stay woven together and you fight a snarl. First, Finn fell prey to a nightcrawler, and now Lucy. They're barely human. Seeing them leech onto an upworlders disgusts you, but that's something else you have to keep hidden down deep if you plan to use them to escape.

"Thank you," you say instead of voicing your anger, your voice barely a whisper. You look up and meet Aiyanna's eyes, then Lucy's, hoping they can't see through your false sincerity.

Lucy nods once, then adjusts her grip on Aiyanna's fingers as if she might fly away.

With newly freed hands, you untie your ankles and stretch out your legs. Aiyanna and Lucy move to a far wall and sit on a low bench, shoulders pressed together, fingers tangled together, leaning toward one another.

No one else in the harem speaks, but their silence is loud in your ears. With stiff muscles you push yourself from the floor, wobbling only a little as you stand. The other women—wylden and upworlders alike—shift away from you, but you don't care. They mean nothing. You find a free seat and lean back against the wall.

Eyes closed, you remember what you'd felt when you were first dropped in here—the roiling energy of people moving beneath the earth. In those moments of watching them, you'd felt their anger, their hatred. The nightcrawlers are coming to this wylden stinkhole. You fight a smile with the thought of the carnage they promised to bring.

When they attack, you can escape and find more vitium. When they attack, Erilyn could be killed—you know she won't be able to stand idly by and just watch—and then you won't have to worry about her anymore. When they attack, you can return to Sunnybrook and say that the wylden have been destroyed. That you were the one who destroyed them.

All you have to do for now is *wait*.

You fight to keep the smile from your face as you close your eyes and wait as patiently as you can for the battle to come.

Chapter 4

"Healing"

Erilyn

I wasn't sure what I'd expected when the door opened, but seeing two of the large, muscled wylden who had captured us and brought us here hadn't been on the list. My muscles tensed, ready to run as I remembered the feel of their rough hands on me, but then Fia was there, slipping her hand into mine and giving it a squeeze.

In my mind she whispered, *Safe. Loyal.*

Hand-in-hand with Fia, I watched and tried to regain my composure. How was I going to do this if the sight of every wylden sent me into a panic?

One of the two men shut the door and they both looked at Zeke. Though one of the men was larger than Zeke, he commanded their respect with his demeanor. The two men waited for the span of a single breath, eyes going a little wider as he communicated with them silently, then they both laid on the ground in the middle of the room, eyes toward the ceiling.

Zeke looked at me from behind the curtain of his long, dark, tangled hair, his teal eyes bright with apprehension. I could feel it as clearly as I felt Fia's hand in mine and I bristled. The way he communicated with me felt *intimate,* and that was not something I'd signed on for. With a grunt, he pushed his long dreadlocks back over his shoulders and pulled back.

"Show." His voice was gruff as he nodded toward the two prone men. In my mind I saw myself kneeling between the two of them, a hand on each of their chests. Zeke and Fia crouched, mimicking my actions. I was to be their teacher.

I didn't want to open up to Zeke, didn't want to experience the intimacy it would require, but for this I would have to. With a deep breath, I let myself open up to him a little more. Zeke's anxiety was palpable and I realized that these two men weren't only loyal to him — they were his friends. The fact that he had chosen them to go first was his way of showing that he trusted me.

If he was willing to show me that much trust, I had no choice but to do the same in return.

Still, I wished Finn were here with me, or Luna. I looked at Fia, my friend, and she gave me a small smile, her aqua eyes bright in the dim room.

I looked back at the two men and thought of my friends. I wondered if they were okay. I wondered if Rosemarie and Seraphina were being treated kindly. I hoped Aiyanna and Lucy had been kept together, because I knew they would watch each other's backs. I needed to believe that Finn was fine, and that Cillian was on his side, so that he wasn't alone. But I had a feeling that until I did this—helped Zeke help his people—I would be left wondering.

With a deep breath through my nose, I knelt between the two wylden on the uneven wooden floor. One of them—the one with a scar on his face who I'd met first when we were captured—clenched his hands at his side. They were doing this for Zeke, because they trusted him. They wouldn't hurt me, because he didn't want them to.

Pushing my fear aside, I put one hand on each of their chests. I braced myself for the onslaught of feeling that came with touching another person, but it never came. Unlike upworlders and cave dwellers, wylden feelings weren't wild and uninhibited. They were tightly controlled—a complex and beautiful language that they wielded even more clearly than upworlders wielded words. I smiled at the irony—these wild men and women with such strict inner control—then let my eyes drift closed. I could feel Zeke's eyes on me and needed to concentrate.

I took a moment to slow my breaths. Just like my morning meditations, I needed to be in the right mental state for this to work. I felt Zeke and Fia join me as I centered myself. In my mind, Zeke and Fia waited. I had to carry them through these rivers of light to where things must begin, show them what to do, and then let them try to heal these new wylden men. I would be the guide, but they would do the work. If it worked, the three of us could begin to work in earnest.

The wylden man on my right, the scarred one, had an aura that was a deep scarlet—almost maroon–and for a moment I felt my own aura shying away from it, as it reminded me a lot of Morrigan's. But I took another steadying breath and made myself really *see* it. The maroon light was broken, like all wylden auras, but not as broken as some of the other wylden I'd encountered, which surprised me. He was so big, and his scar showed that he had fought. The man on my left was completely still. His aura was a vivid, cracked, pale yellow that reminded me of spring flowers whipping about in a thunderstorm.

On the other side of the maroon wylden sat Zeke, his eyes and awareness on me. He wanted me to help them heal both of these men at once–something I'd never done. It felt like a test, like he needed me to prove my strength. I'd never been asked to split my focus, my essence, like this before, and doubt washed over me. If I failed here, the fragile alliance I'd built with Zeke could shatter.

Even though I needed to focus, in my doubt I thought of Finn. If he were here, he would give me that smile that he saved for only me and tell me that he believed in me. He would take my hand and I would be able to feel his faith in what I could do.

I exhaled with renewed purpose and focused on the two men beneath my hands. I could do this.

The yellow wylden seemed more open than the other, seemed softer, so with Fia tagging along I traveled into the man's aura. The pale yellow light was broken and sparked like flint on stone as we moved along the fractured tributaries toward his center. Working together we reached the rich, pale yellow center quickly. Unlike the rest of his aura-light, it was calm there and pulsed gently with each beat of his heart. I settled myself in, extra careful to simply float in the light and not tie him to me by mistake. This was the first time I'd done this without being under duress and it was easier to keep myself apart.

I could feel Zeke waiting for me. I had to somehow be in two auras at once. In the yellow aura, Fia settled beside me, around me, and it helped me feel stable. I used her as an anchor as I allowed part of my consciousness to split away and travel back along the broken yellow light to myself.

I could feel myself surrounded by soft yellow. I could feel both hands on the mens' chests. I could feel Zeke anxious for me to lead him in as well.

Disoriented, I squeezed my eyes tighter and zeroed in on the other wylden's aura. The brilliant maroon startled me and I was taken back to the suffocating blood-red that was Morrigan's aura, but then Zeke was there, his vitium-blue light a strangely comforting beacon at my side.

Without waiting for my fear to get the better of me, I dove into the maroon light. Part of my brain expected resistance—Morrigan's aura had fought me with all it had—but of all the wylden auras I'd experienced, this man's was the least broken and I moved along it easily.

His scar, his scowl, his anger as he'd taken us captive—I couldn't find any of that here. Instead, this rich, maroon aura-light—almost a deep purple in some places—allowed us to travel along its streams to its center where the light moved in soft waves. We reached the end of the path quickly and settled.

Using Fia and Zeke as anchors, I floated in the auralights, and yet I could feel the strain of splitting myself like this. I was surrounded by both yellow and maroon, essentially in two places at once, and I wondered why I wasn't coming apart at the seams. It felt like I should be.

Beside me, Zeke settled into the purplish maroon light and grew still, waiting for me to guide him.

It felt like being in the eye of a storm. I braced myself to work on both men at once, trusting Fia and Zeke to rally quickly and take over. Zeke might be strong enough for something like this, but not me.

My hands were sweaty against the coarse fabric of their ragged shirts. I focused on the center of their aura-lights—the pulsing, solid light that I'd always thought of as being where a heart might be. From there, I gathered their light toward me, careful to stay separate, then pushed it out along the tributaries that were broken, like shoving water forcefully through a clogged pipe. I pushed it out toward the cracks and fragments and watched as the thick, pure light filled in the gaps.

It was exhausting trying to heal them both at once, even for these few seconds, and I wouldn't have been able to do much more on my own, but then Zeke and Fia began to work. I felt them move ahead of me and watched as they each gathered light toward them and with a dazzling burst of light, moved it away from them, down the broken tributaries. With a zing of panic, I saw Zeke's teal light leak into the maroon. I wanted to warn him, but I could sense his acceptance of it. They moved away from me, navy and teal drifting further into yellow and maroon, and then I was alone, drifting in two different seas of light.

I felt unsettled, floating in yellow and maroon alone. Without any idea of how to do it, I tried to gently move the two halves of myself back together. Instead, it was like a band of taught rope had snapped. I was jerked back to myself, the two halves of my aura colliding and merging in a single breath-stealing moment. The recoil was so sharp I felt like I might fall, but Zeke and Fia were still there, hands on my shoulders, and they steadied me even as they worked.

Breathless, I opened my eyes and watched the men beneath my hands change. Zeke and Fia were doing the work, but I was their conduit. At least for now.

Zeke's vitium-colored light surged through one of my arms and into the scarred man while Fia's navy light enveloped my other and mingled with yellow. I watched, transfixed, as the two men slowly became whole.

When it was done, Fia and Zeke released me. Their auras retreated back up my arms and faded away until I was entirely myself again.

Drenched in sweat, though I'd personally done very little, I stood to distance myself from the two men who still lay prone on the ground. The air was cool, but I felt overheated. I longed for a breeze or a dip in my pond.

My back pressed against the far wall, I stood in silence. It was long moments later that the two men started to stir.

The yellow-aura'd man woke first. His eyes opened and he stared at the ceiling for a few breaths, his chest rising and falling with exaggerated purpose. Then he sat, eyes wild, until they landed on Zeke.

"New," he said in a broken whisper, his voice lighter than I'd expected. Zeke nodded once.

The other man awoke a moment later. Unlike his friend, he popped up into a crouch, head snapping from side to side, his fear a thick tang in the air as soon as his eyes opened.

My immediate reaction was to calm him, as I would for Finn or the children, but Zeke beat me to it. He was there in less than a breath, crouching, eye-to-eye with his friend. The maroon wylden stared at him, his own vitium-blue eyes wide as he stared into Zeke's. Neither man moved, but slowly the scarred man softened.

"Safe," he said, his voice so smooth and normal-sounding, it startled me. I'd become accustomed to the gravelly quality of wylden voices.

Zeke nodded. "Safe."

The room grew quiet again and I wondered what it was they were all sharing. I was reminded of my time in the snowy woods with the children, being shut out as they communicated and I bristled with irritation and sadness. Then, Fia looked at me and I felt an opening. If I wanted to join in, I could experience their conversation, their feelings, along with them. I was tempted, but something held me back. I wanted this closeness with the children, whom I loved, but not with these wylden who I barely knew. I shook my head and she gave me a soft smile as that invitation faded away.

They were all still, all communicating silently, and then they weren't. I started, pressing myself further against the wall while Zeke and the others moved suddenly and with purpose. They moved the meager furniture around the space, laying scraps of blankets on the floor and stacking the rickety tables and chairs in the corners to make as much space as possible.

Once the floor was clear, Zeke approached me and I stiffened my spine. They were all healed, but I wasn't foolish enough to believe that made me safe. I was still an outsider.

"Time—" he said, grimacing and stopping as if to find the words. "Time for others?"

He was asking me, not telling. Whatever test he'd set for me with these two, I must have passed, and when he communicated with me now, I didn't feel that intense desire from before. Instead, I felt respect.

The other men were looking at me as well, waiting, and I felt the weight of what was happening settle on my shoulders. This was so much. It felt like *too* much. But now that we'd started, we couldn't stop. I'd chosen my path.

I looked back at Zeke and in spite of my exhaustion, I nodded. Relief passed over his features and the door opened. Outside, wylden were amassed, waiting. Three of them walked in and I thought I recognized them from our capture, but I wasn't sure. I only really recognized the scarred man. Of these three new people, one of them looked angry about being called in, but like the others he lay on one of the mats on the floor, regardless of his feelings.

The pale yellow wylden joined Fia and the maroon one joined me while Zeke moved toward the angry man. I was glad I wasn't going to have to work on his aura. A quick glance told me it was terribly fractured. One of the worst I'd seen. I wasn't even sure I could heal an aura that broken.

I glanced up at the man with the maroon aura, the one who'd captured me and brought me to Ringol. He was exceptionally tall and broad, but he smiled down at me, his lips pressed together, and I couldn't help but think he looked kind. I wondered what his name was, but before I could ask, he answered me.

"Dill," he said in his too-smooth voice.

"Erilyn," I replied, and he smiled again. Like Zeke, he was quite handsome—all raw muscle and sharp lines— but unlike Zeke I found his presence to be soothing.

Fia and the other wylden were already working. Zeke seemed to be fighting to calm the third. I had the brief urge to help him, but then Dill shifted so that he was between Zeke and me as he laid his hand on the chest of the man in front of us. My job was to teach him. Zeke and his seemingly endless well of power could take care of himself. I placed my hand beside Dill's and gave him a nod, then together we dove into this new wylden's pale pink light.

Chapter 5

"Hallucinations"

Finn

TIME passed slowly inside the small, dark room. Without sunlight, it was hard to tell how much time had passed and the light around the door changed so irregularly he knew it had to be light from a fire or candle rather than the sun.

When the door opened for the first time, Finn wasn't prepared. He blinked stupidly as the light assaulted his eyes. Two things were dropped by his feet and he jumped like a scared cat. He recovered from the shock and pushed himself toward the open door just in time for it to close in his face and knock him back. He heard the bolt lock but gave it a firm shove anyway, more in frustration than because he thought it would actually move.

His eyes needed to readjust to the dark after the sudden influx of light, but once they had, he squinted at what they had brought him. There was a small, chipped bowl with some water in it–most of it had spilled on the floor when it was plopped down–and a dented, metal bucket. Finn wrinkled his nose as he realized what it was for.

He was hungry, but after a winter of eating the bare minimum, he knew he'd be fine. He sipped the water in resignation and sat back again, eyes locked on the door, determined not to miss it the next time it opened.

WHEN the door opened again, some hours later, Finn was tired, but ready. The light that poured through was bright, but he kept his eyes on the floor so he wouldn't be disoriented. As soon as the door moved he grabbed it, wrenched it open, and barreled past the person holding it. He made it a few feet before thick hands grabbed him and jerked him back. His feet flew from under him, but he had been ready for that, too.

He twisted in the wylden's grasp and swung wildly at the large man's face. Finn's fist made solid contact with meaty flesh, but the wylden acted as if he hadn't felt anything. Finn swung again and the wylden grunted and dropped him. Before he could get back to his feet, the wylden's fist connected with Finn's cheek and he went sprawling back toward the closet.

Finn looked up in a daze as a second fist smashed into his eye. The ground seemed to tilt away from him. He tried to stand, but before he could figure out which direction was up, rough hands gripped him and he was thrown back into the closet, knocking over the crude bowl of water and spilling what was left of it all over the floor. The door closed and Finn was once again left in the dark. His head throbbed and he could feel the flesh around his eye beginning to swell. Pain rebounded in his skull with every beat of his heart.

Head in his hands, he fought against the feeling of hopelessness that pressed in around him.

HOURS passed. Finn's head hurt worse and worse and he was afraid to doze off, worried they had damaged his brain and he might not wake up.

The next time the door opened, Finn didn't try to rush out. It wouldn't do to try the same stupid thing twice. They were tense and ready for him, but when he didn't make any move to rush them again, they relaxed a little. The room outside his prison was lit by moonlight that seeped in through a cracked window, as well as the light from a low burning fire in fireplace. There was one door, in addition to the window, but it was closed. He couldn't see much else past the massive guard, but he was shocked to realize how similar this space was to the apartments in Sunnybrook. It was dirtier and in need of repair, but other than that remarkably similar.

Wylden were supposed to be wild. They lived in caravans out under the sky. None of this—the town, the prison, the closet, the room beyond—made any sense.

One of his guards removed his waste bucket away and dropped in a new one, which was good because the first was starting to smell. He was just grateful it hadn't been knocked over when he'd been thrown in here like the water bowl had, but he'd had enough foresight to put it against the corner. They refilled his water bowl from a roughly hewn clay pot, sloshing some on the floor in the process, and left him again in the dark.

Finn let his head fall back against the wall with a painful thump, his headache from before rebounding into his eyes. He did it again. And again, only stopping when his swollen eye started to throb and it became difficult to think past the pressure in his head.

One window. One door. A locked door between here and there. The only way he was leaving this prison was if his captors allowed it. It was painful to realize that he should have listened to Cillian. He had tried to pull Finn back, to get him to stop and think, but Finn hadn't listened. His only focus had been getting to Erilyn, and in his impulsiveness and stupidity, he was stuck.

Finn took a sip of his water, then set it on the opposite side of the small closet from the waste bucket, hoping to hold off on using the latter as long as possible. He squeezed his eyes shut, even though it hurt. He wished he could do what Erilyn could do. What the children could do. If he had their abilities, he could break out of here, or at the very least be able to tell if they were all okay. Instead, he was stuck in the dark, feeling useless.

He sighed and chewed on the inside of his cheek. He gnawed on one spot until he felt the skin break and blood started to seep into his mouth. The sharp pain and iron tang were welcome distractions from his brooding.

Erilyn. He let his head fall back against the wall as he pictured her face in his mind—her blue-gray eyes that reminded him of stones in a riverbed, the way her cheeks reddened anytime she had a strong emotion. Finn thought back to the moment they'd found Erilyn and the others and he'd seen her aura—a deep, burnished gold.

That aura had been connected to him until it snapped. It had been part of him. He tried to remember what it had felt like before it broke. He'd felt settled. He tried to picture it, tying the two of them together. Like a child trying to will something into existence, he kept his eyes closed tight and imagined it connecting his heart to hers. In his mind, he could imagine her gentle smile that she reserved only for him.

As he drifted toward sleep, with Erilyn's face firmly in his mind's eye, light bloomed behind his eyelids. It was a golden light—bright like dandelions in spring, like summer sunshine—and he knew deep in his soul that it was Erilyn. It was brighter than the light he'd seen when she'd been connected to Morrigan, but still, he knew it was her.

He focused on the golden light with every bit of himself. There were other lights in his periphery all around him, but he couldn't take his eyes away from her light—brilliant, beautiful gold. The light condensed until it took human shape. He could just make out the shape of her nose when she turned to the side, and could see how she held her arms pressed against her stomach. He longed for the dream to show him her face, but it didn't. She was a silhouette of the most beautiful golden light imaginable. All around her were other light-forms, some crouching, some lying down, some standing, but his attention was fully on her.

Erilyn, he thought, his heart aching for the feel of her hand in his. The form in his imagination turned, as if toward him. A tear dripped down his cheek in the dark as he imagined her stepping into his arms.

Finn?

He heard her voice in his mind and he squeezed his eyes shut even tighter, in spite of the pain of his bruises. Her voice sounded so close.

Surely he was asleep, but it didn't matter. Seeing her, hearing her, even in this way was better than being cramped in his closet-cell.

He would have stayed with her until he woke up if he'd had the choice, but the dream changed. One moment he was looking at Erilyn's golden form and then next it was as if he were being pulled by a rope. He flew through walls made of insubstantial shadows so fast he felt dizzy. The shadow walls glowed faintly teal.

But as quickly as he began moving, he stopped. He was in a room filled with thin, watery lights made up of barely more than shadows.

There were two that shone brighter than the rest — one vivid pink, the other deep purple — and they called to him almost as strongly as the golden light had. He'd never seen any aura except Erilyn's, and yet without a doubt he knew these lights were Sera and Rosemarie. While all the other forms in the room were vague and indistinct, these two were so crisp and clear that, like Erilyn, he could almost see their features. The purple one, Rosemarie, was rocking back and forth as she cradled someone iridescent and small. Other tiny, shadowed lights crowded around her like moths hovering around the edges of firelight. Only Seraphina—as brilliantly pink as a spring flower—stood alone and off to the side. Her aura was bright and rippling and he had the sudden ridiculous urge to shield his eyes as if the light might blind him.

But then, without his consent, he was moving through the shadowed walls again. When his vision came to a stop he was overwhelmed with the urge to leave, but he couldn't make himself move.

The space was oppressive. Over to one side was a group of barely flickering lights that were so dim they all blended together into an amorphous mass of dingy gray. Compared to these lights, the ones he'd seen surrounding Rosemarie had been vivid. On the other side of the space, set apart, were three more vivid lights. Two caught his eye—a soft lavender and a minty green. Bits of purple and green twined together, swirling around one another, but never mixing completely. It was beautiful, like a field of purple wildflowers.

But it was a third light, red as blood, that made him want to run. It looked like a piece of broken pottery that had been crudely put back together, filled with gaping black cracks. The red light snapped and crackled, and as he watched it, unable to tear his gaze away, it turned toward him and set his heart racing. He recognized this lightform as easily as he'd recognized the one belonging to. Erilyn.

It was Morrigan.

His heartbeat was frantic as the red light leaned toward him, but then he was off again, swiftly passing through blue-green walls without feeling them.

In the next room were two light-forms. One was light pink, and the other a silvery gray. Something about the shimmery, neutral nature of the light made him think of Cillian. Unlike the other gray lights he'd seen, this one shimmered like the backs of silver maple leaves underwater.

As he watched, fascinated by the shimmery silver ripples, a third light joined them. This light was faint and watery like so many of the others, and after a moment the silver and pink slowly moved toward it.

Withot warning, an invisible rope seemed to tug him around the middle and drag him back into his closet-prison. No more lights. It had all felt so real, like maybe he was actually seeing auras as he'd imagined for so long.

Finn's eyes flew open, his chest heaving as if he'd just run a great distance. His mouth was dry and sweat dotted his brow. With shaking fingers, he drained the last of his tepid water.

Mouth still dry, Finn pulled his knees against his chest. When he closed his eyes, he could still pictured the colors. His dark closet felt all that much smaller now. He squeezed his eyes shut and let his thoughts drift back to the golden light he'd seen first—Erilyn.

Chapter 6

"Alone"

Morrigan

YOUR eyes are cloudy and your ears are muffled, as if they're stuffed with cloth.

It feels like you're half-dead as you sit in filth. Surrounded by filth.

You see the soft glances Lucy and Aiyanna share, their fingers woven together, the way they lean into each other. As if their misguided version of love will save them from becoming breeding stock for the wylden monsters. An orphan and a nightcrawler and you hate them.

You can't *sense* their hope—not having your abilities is like having your arms tied behind your back—but you can see it in their faces. Their naïveté makes you so angry you struggle to keep the rage from showing on your face.

A day passes in this shadowy hell. You wait, conserving your energy, moving only to relieve yourself. The wylden women here—barely alive—offer you scraps of their food. They have only a small store of food and you wonder why they're giving you, any enemy, any of it. Proof of how foolish they are. If they would hoard it among the strongest, let the weakest fade away, they would survive a bit longer. Stupid animals. If you had vitium, if you could dose, you would just take it from them and kill any who stood in your way.

Feeling helpfless, your rage grows until it is an inferno and you squeeze your eyes shut to try and contain it.

Deep breaths and focus. Even without your vitium, you know you're *more* than these creatures.

You need a distraction—the surge of anger moving toward this place puts a smile on your face.

But then it falters, flickering away like a candle's flame. They should have been here already. You start to second guess yourself. Maybe you'd been wrong and they weren't coming to attack the wylden.

But no.

You *saw* them.

They're coming. They have to.

You close your eyes and try to focus, try to *see*, but there's nothing behind your eyelids but endless black. Anguish wells inside until—

There. Behind you. Something new. A surge of fear.

You whip around and look over your right shoulder. There's no one there, but you can almost *see* something. The faintest whisper of green light. It feels familiar, but it's gone as quickly as it came. A whiff of smoke.

It feels like you should *know* what it was. Frustrated and confused, you look back at Aiyanna and

Lucy, still sitting against the wall. Aiyanna is asleep with her head on Lucy's shoulder. Lucy's cheek is pressed to the top of Aiyanna's head.

Their contentedness in the face of all this misery burns the memory of the green smoke away. Your eyes are open, but your mind is somewhere else as again, without warning you are assaulted with memories that steal your breath.

Finn's warm arm around your waist, his fingers splayed over your hip as you watch the sun set with your head on his shoulder.

Cillian's lean body curled around yours. His sleep-heavy breath in your ear. The thick blanket draped over your bodies, cocooning you together. The fireplace casting flickering light across your face as Cillian pulls you against his chest in his sleep.

Finn's lips, soft and tentative, as he kisses your cheek for the first time. His own cheeks crimson when he pulls away, shy, and takes your hand. Later, the way his mouth responds to yours as you kiss him for the firs time. Your chest, warm and full.

Cillian's lips against your skin as he whispers kisses into your hair and across your cheeks, your nose, your lips. The soft way he possesses your body without ever truly taking the control away from you.

Finn's eyes — hollow and pained — as you break his heart. Feeling him leave. Feeling his intentions as he races away from Sunnybrook, taking some part of you with him. Inside, you beg him to stay and fight for you. Inside, you hope he never comes back.

Cillian's eyes, his radiant silver glow, as you join, vitium pulsing between you. Feeling your auras—silver and crimson—crashing together likes waves on a shore. Wishing this feeling could last forever. Knowing it will have to end.

With a pain-filled gasp you break free from your memories. They make your chest ache and you don't want it. You don't want any of it.

Eyes open, you realize you've been pulling at your hair so hard your scalp aches. Lucy's worried eyes are on you and you drop your hands to your lap and scowl as you will your heartbeat to slow.

"Are you ok?" she murmurs and you glower and turn away from her.

Memories don't serve you. Emotional ties are nothing more than weakness. You have to focus on here and now if you want to survive this.

The nightcrawler attach—you are sure it will come. You don't have your gifts right now, but when the pale cave dwellers arrive and wreak havoc on these wylden beasts, you'll be ready and you will get your gifts back.

Chapter 7

"Reunited"

Erilyn

We healed auras for hours, one after another, until I could no longer keep my eyes open. I'd curled up in a corner to get some sleep, but when Fia gently shook me awake, it felt like I'd only been there a few minutes. My eyes were blurry and my muscles ached as I stood and stretched my cramped muscles.

Dill sat in front of me, posture slumped. He'd stationed himself between me and the others when I went to lie down. Since he'd been healed, he'd scarcely left my side. He'd been my shadow as we we worked, and when my exhaustion had become too much, he'd led me to the corner and taken up a spot between me and the fray.

I yawned as I blinked over and over, trying to clear the film from my eyes. My back cracked as I stretched and my joints ached. Fia approached, a cup of water for each of us, and smiled.

"Almost done," Fia said, her spoken words clearer than I'd ever heard them. She smiled at me. "Tired," she said with a nod toward Dill, who was still sitting in his guard position on the floor.

I looked down at him. His eyes were bloodshot and barely open. He let me feel how protective he was of me, though I wasn't sure why.

"Dill," I said, touching his arm. His red-rimmed vitium-blue eyes popped wide and he straightened. "Please, rest." With my fingers on his arm I gently nudged him back toward the corner where I'd slept. "Just for a bit." I pictured him reclined there, eyes closed, breaths even.

He looked up at me as if he might argue, then sagged and nodded once. He scooted back against the wall and was asleep almost instantly.

"How many wylden are left?" I asked Fia before yawning again.

"Few." She motioned toward the cracked door. Outside, only a handful of wylden still waited.

"How long did I sleep?" I rolled my neck and shoulders to alleviate the stiffness and ache.

"Hours," Fia said with a soft smile. "Needed it."

I looked out the door again and thought back on the now countless wylden that we'd healed. So many men and women with aurs that were now unbroken and pure.

I ran through as many as I could remember in my mind, and with a start I realized that in all the people we'd worked on, we hadn't healed wylden who were very old or very young. Fully awake now, I braced myself for an answer I wouldn't like and asked, "What about the children?"

Fia's eyes popped wide, then she furrowed her brow and spun toward Zeke so suddenly that her dark, tangled hair flew around her in a wide arc. He met her gaze, his vitium-blue eyes narrowing. She took a step toward him and he growled low in his throat before nodding and turning away again.

"Coming now," Fia said, her cheeks red with anger. "*Forgotten,*" she spat, staring daggers into Zeke's back.

I stared at Zeke's back as well, wondering how someone who seemed to care about his people as much as he did could forget about their most precious population.

Attuned to the wylden after hours of work on their auras, I let my awareness spread among the new arrivals. I'd never healed a child and needed to get ready if I could. But I stopped when I felt something painfully familiar. In less than a heartbeat I'd crossed the room and pushed through the door, out into the sunlight. A group of at least fifty children had arrived, along with a handful of elderly women. At their very center, carrying two small children in her arms, was Rosemarie, followed by a very tired, very angry Seraphina.

My heart ached and tears sprang to my eyes as I stepped toward them. Rosemarie saw me and a tired smile lit up her dirt-smudged face.

I was ready to run down the steps toward her, but then Zeke stepped onto the small porch and I hesitated. His arms were crossed oer his broad chest as he looked at the smallest and oldest of his people with a scowl. He wasn't hiding his feelings—he felt like they were a wasted resource.

Anger hot and thick in my throat, I faced him with my feet planted wide. "We're helping them."

He scowled down at me, but I wasn't so afraid of him anymore.

My jaw set, I said, "*All*. Remember?"

He stared at me for a long moment, as if he might argue, this his shoulders fell slight and he gave a single nod before he walked back inside. His attitude would have angered me if I hadn't known the reason was the coming attack. He wanted his people ready to fight and children and the elderly didn't factor into that.

But it didn't matter. We were going to heal all of them. Relief filled me up as I looked out over the sea of tiny, filthy faces. Some of the smallest children were held by some of the biggest, but they all were gaunt, dirty, and scared. In their faces I saw Galen, Asa, Noah, and Jubal reflected back at me. My heart cracked open.

Hands shaking, I went down the few steps, ready to help, but the children nearest shied away from me. I could hear Rosemarie murmuring reassurances and they settled a little, but instead of coming toward me they all pressed more tightly around her. I stopped at the bottom step and sat. Their fear—of me, of what was happening, of the wylden milling around town—was palpable. Each child would be afraid as I healed them, and I couldn't bring myself to put them through something they didn't understand. They'd been scared enough in their lives already.

I closed my eyes and let myself *see* them in the hopes that I could figure out an alternative to dragging them away one by one. They were all clinging to one another, and their auras blended together in a rainbow. Their auras weren't as broken as the adults' auras had been. Just as they held onto each other's bodies, their lights flowed into each other like a single body of water. It reminded me of how Seraphina and the younger children often looked when they were together. Within the ocean of light before me, only Sera and Rosemarie's lights stood apart—stones in the colorful sea flowing around them.

I watched the pale rainbow of auralighs ebb and flow for a long moment before I had an idea. I opened my eyes and turned back toward the buliding.

"Fia!" She was outside in an instant. With feelings and images I showed her my idea. A smile lit up her face and she nodded with enthusiasm.

"Rosemarie," I said, my voice shaking as I turned toward her, more glad that I could verbalize that she was here and okay. I wanted nothing more than to go and wrap my arms around her, but that had to wait a bit longer. "Can you keep the children together? I want to help them, but they have to stay close."

She nodded and adjusted her grip on the two babies in her arms, pressing a kiss to one of their temples before she knelt down in the dirt. The children watched her, little vitium-blue eyes wide, then did as she did. She smiled at them as they all scooted in close, all touching shoulders or knees or hands. The older women—all wrinkled and hunched—stood stoically by, but pressed in a little closer as well, surrounding the circle of children like a protective wall. Unlike the children, their auras were nearly shattered, but they were also connected to the ocean of light like broken twigs on the edges of a pond.

Seraphina stood behind Rosemarie, arms crossed over her chest, eyes focused off to the side. *Sera,* I called in my mind, but she didn't turn. I couldn't tell if she had shut me out or was just ignoring me. "Sera," I repeated aloud, willing her to just look at me for a moment. I longed for the little girl I'd found all those weeks ago who had clung to her siblings. Who had clung to me, at least for a little while. "I need you. Will you help me?" I held out my hand toward her and her eyes met mine for a split second before she looked away. I felt some part of my cracked heart fracture even more with her refusal. "Fia," I whispered. I would have to mend my relationship with Sera after I mended the auras of these children.

Fia nodded and stepped closer to my side. My eyes drifted closed as my aur found hers. Together, we moved into the rainbow cloud of light. There, Rosemarie waited. She was our anchor and I let myself bask in the soft, coolness of her deep purple aura before we began. In her arms were the two tiniest babies. Their auras were the least damaged of all of them. I had to look hard to see any cracks at all. The babies shared a light blue aura—twins.

Delicately, Fia and I entered the pale blue light of the twins. The gentlest light I'd ever sxperienced surrounded me and tears welled in my eyes and dripped down my cheeks. I couldn't imagine anything more pure than this.

I breathed in, careful to keep myself apart, and with a light exhale I pushed their soft blue outward.

Like dropping a stone in a still pond, the light of each aura rippled out away from the twns, solidifying as it moved through each child. When it reached the elderly women on the fringes, the momentum carried it forward and effortlessly healed them as well. The prism of colors rippled and overlapped, then receded back to themselves until the ripples stopped and all was still again. The ocean of light that connected the children and the older women with them was now whole.

It was so much easier than I'd expected, even with all of these children to work through. So much easier than with any of the adults.

I opened my eyes, tears still trailing down my cheeks, and looked out at them. The older children stood a little straighter. Smiles were slipping onto their faces like light at sunrise. The elderly women with them seemed confused, but not unhappy. As each child acclimated to what just happned, their fear trickled away.

As the fear disappated, it was like a storm cloud had blown away to reveal bright, warm sunshine. Rosemarie stood, the babies still in her arms, and other healed wylden came out from where they'd been watching and offered children their hands. One or two at a time, children paired up with adults and walked away. The last two to go were the tiny twins. Rosemarie kissed each of their foreheads once as she handed them to a woman no older than me.

When it was only Rosemarie and Sera left, I surged down the stairs and hugged Rosemarie, holding her as tightly as I dared. Even though I knew she wouldn't like it, I couldn't help myself and I reached for Seraphina as well. She reluctantly joined us, letting me hug her with all that I had in me, though she didn't hug me back.

"I'm so glad you're both okay," I breathed into the space between us.

"Are you okay?" Rosemarie asked, stepping back to take my face in her hands. "He took you. We thought—"

"I'm okay," I whispered, grabbing her fingers in mine and holding them tight. "He tried to—" I looked at Sera, not wanting to share this horrible thing with her, but she simply rolled her eyes.

"Tried to tether you," she said with venom. She was thinking of what I'd done to Finn. I was glad she hadn't picked up on the other things Zeke had planned for me—things I'd only caught glimpses of in his mind that I couldn't bare to give words to.

"But I didn't let him. He—"Somehow, telling them that my connection to Finn had been broken felt like sharing something very intimate. It was only between him and me. "He tried to tether me, but when he tried I was able to fix the cracks in his aura instead. Just like I did with Fia." Nearby, Fia stood tall like a sentinel, reminding me of how Dill had guarded me throughout the night. My wylden friends and protectors.

"You've been healing them?" Rosemarie asked, a soft smile on her face, and I nodded.

"Almost every wylden here," I said, my voice cracking as the gravity of what we'd accomplished settled on me. We'd almost done it. After we were finsihed, I could ask for the rest of my friends. For my family. For Finn.

Zeke chose that moment to come back outside, a tired smile on his rugged face. "Done," he said, his voice rough with exhaustion. Relief washed over me.

"Zeke," I said, approaching him with all the confidence I could muster. "My friends—" I pictured Aiyanna and Lucy, then Cillian, and finally Finn, knowing that of all of them, he was in the most danger if Zeke had changed his mind about a forced match with me. "Will you bring them to me now?" I swallowed heavily and clenched my shaking hands, pressing them against my hips, knowing it was no use to try and hide how anxious I felt.

Zeke's eyes widened and he let me feel his shock and turmoil at my request. He'd expected me to forget about them in favor of the wylden I'd helped. Expected me to choose to join him after all the work we'd done together.

As much as he'd changed in the span of a day, he still didn't understand what it meant to be an individual. The wylden were all connected, all tied and blended in ways I was only beginning to understand, and I needed him to understand that my friends were that for me.

Finally, after letting him *see* and *feel* everyone else, I showed him Finn. I let him *feel* my need for Finn, my sadness, my hope that he would be brought back to me. And finaly, let him *feel* the love I felt for him, even after our tether had been broken.

He stared down at me for a long time, but eventually, he sighed and noded. He motioned with his hand for me to follow him back into his home. I held my hand out for Rosemarie and Sera to join me—I wasn't willing to be parted from them again—and together we went inside to wait.

Inside Zeke's home, wylden milled around us. Some offered yellow-tooth smiles while pulling Zeke's furniture back into its previous positions. Others came in only to communicate with Zeke—who was standing in the middle ofmm the room, arms crossed—and then left. He reminded me of a queen bee surrounded by workers.

Rosemarie, Sera, and I stood back against a wall beside Dill, who still slept. I smelled smoke waft in from somewhere outside, followed by the smell of roasting meat. My stomach growled at the thought of food.

Moments later, a young wylden woman walked in holding a dented piece of metal as a tray. On it were charred, crudely ripped hunks of meat.

Even though my stomach was screaming for food, I couldn't eat that. I'd eaten meat a couple of times when I was younger and the experience had been horrible. With each bite of food I had felt the echoes of the animals' deaths in my bones.

Before I had a chance to think of a response that wouldn't offend the kindness this wylden was offering, Fia stepped in. She stopped the woman by standing between us, chin lifted. "Plants," she said, the word sounding foreign on her tongue. The woman looked confused as she looked at Fia and then at us behind her. Zeke approached with narrowed eyes. "*Plants*," Fia repeated with more vehemence. Even though her voice didn't get any louder, her intent did.

Beside me, Dill blinked his sleepy eyes open before he sprang up and joined Fia. He looked back and gave me a smile, the scar on his face pulling his eye down a little. Seraphina looked at him with narrowed eyes, then gave me a cold, withering look.

Zeke sighed as he also looked at Dill, then at me, his gaze heavy with disappointment.

The wylden woman nodded, left the tray of meat on the floor, and left. Before the door could fully shut, it was pushed open again. Aiyanna and Lucy were ushered inside by a small group of wylden men, along with a handful of underfed-looking upworld women with haunted expressions.

I picked up the tray of freshly cooked meat and handed it to one of the women. Her eyes filled with tears. I turned to Lucy and Aiyanna and pulled them both into my arms and I felt another bit of pain melt away.

If they were here, surely Finn would be soon, too. I looked over their shoulders toward the door, anxious to see his face, and felt like I'd been doused with icy water. My eyes met Morrigan's—more hostile than ever—just as the door closed behind her.

"It's okay," Aiyanna said, pulling away from me and moving so she was between Morrigan and me.

"Her power's gone," Lucy said, her voice dark as she tugged Aiyanna a little closer to her side.

They'd brought me my friends, and Morrigan, and a host of wylden women who had shadows under their eyes. When wylden men walked too near them, they curled in on themselves and shied away. My heart pounded a painful, angry rhythm as I pieced together what these women had been used for. I clenched my fists and took a deep breath. For now, they were safe. I would make sure they stayed safe.

The women were huddled around the tray of food, crouched and tense. The room was filled with many people and I looked around for someone to take these women somewhere safe. My eyes landed on Dill, who watched the women from a few feet behind me. Even though he was scarred and huge—when I'd first seen him

I'd been afraid—he was by far the gentlest wylden I'd come across so far. He would be able to help them and keep them safe from others, but they would be afraid of him, too.

I locked eyes with Fia, all of this passing between us in an instant, and she smiled. With a straight spine and sure steps, she took Dill's hand. His cheeks went ruddy as they walked together toward the upworld women. As Dill approached, they gripped their hunks of scorched meat tighter and leaned toward one another.

"Help," Fia said, her own voice soft.

The women didn't seem to hear her as they all stared up at Dill with wide, terrified eyes. Dill, face still red, let go of Fia's hand and croched down with his head bowed. Together, he and Fia let the women—and the rest of us in the room—feel heir calm, protective intent.

"Here to help you," Fia said, still standing between Dill and the women. She pointed reached back and put her hand on Dill's shoulder, then pointed towad the door. After a moment, the women relaxed enough to stand, one at a time. Fia led them outside and Dill stood. He shot me a shy smile as they left—a gentle giant.

"Where are Cillian and Finn?" Lucy asked in a hushed tone as I joined them again. Aiyanna's arm was around Seraphina's shoulders in a protective stance.

"Erilyn doesn't seem to care," Sera mumbled, and I jerked back as if she'd slapped me.

I clenched my teeth, unsure of what to say, as Sera stared daggers at me. From across the room, where she waited by the door, Morrigan smirked at me.

"Erilyn?" Lucy asked again, her arms wrapped around her middle.

"I'm not sure," I said, my voice wavering with the weight of Sera's accusation. "I asked Zeke to bring everyone and—"

As if on cue, the door opened again and I spun, heart racing. Disapointment like cold rain fell over me as Cillian, not Finn, walked in. As usual, his posture was straight and he carried himself as if he were the one in charge. But when his eyes landed on Morrigan all pretenses fell away. His eyes widened, his lips parted, and he strode to her with long, sure steps and wrapped her in his arms.

Morrigan went stiff, but then her arms slowly crept around his waist and she tucked her face against his chest. He held her as if she were someone precious.

I watched with baited breath as, hehind Cillian, two other men walked in, one supporting the other with an arm around his waist. Neither were Finn.

My heart hammered in my chest as the seconds stretched into eternity, but the door didn't open again.

No.

"Cillian," I said, voice breaking. He kept one arm around Morrigan as he turned to me, expression neutral again. "Where's Finn?" I took an involuntary step forward, hands in fists at my side, as if I could will him to appear.

His expression turned remorseful and my stomach clenched with worry. "They took him away," he said. "Yesterday. I don't know where."

Rage filled me up. I spun and crossed the room to Zeke. I let the full weight of my anger, my fury, my fear, pour into him and he leaned away from me in spite of the fact that was I was nearly half his size.

The room went quiet. Power crackled in my fingertips as heat welled in my belly like boiling lava.

As clearly as I could I pictured Finn in my mind. I allowed the full weight of the emotion I felt for him to pour into Zeke. If my feelings had been water, they would have drowned him. Even though I didn't need words, I used them. I spat through gritted teeth, my voice a growl. "Where is he? Where is Finn?"

As clearly as I shared my emotions and thoughts, Zeke shared his. He hadn't called for them to bring Finn with the others. He still hoped I wold choose to lead the wylden with him.

The rage in my gut grew until I was sure I would catch flame. The others in the room pressed themselves against the walls as I prepared myself to do whatever I had to get Fin back.

Chapter 8

"Release"

Finn

FINN woke to the sound of boots clomping outside his door. He sat up, his back aching, but when the door opened this time, he didn't try to move.

The light outside wasn't overly bright, but still Finn winced. The only light he'd seen had been the colorful auras he'd dreamed about.

The wylden who opened the door stepped in and Finn gritted his teeth, braced for pain. But it never came. Instead, hands grabbed him firmly by the arms and hauled him up to his feet. He stumbled, knocking over his water bowl, and the wylden righted him. The grip wasn't painful, but still Finn didn't try to jerk away. Getting beaten to a pulp wouldn't help him get back to Erilyn. He would wait and see where they were taking him and hope it wasn't to some grisly death. With one hand on Finn's arm, the wylden led him outside where Finn took painful gulps of the fresh air.

The injured man that had been brought to their shared cell, Lowell, had said upworlders were used to train the younger wylden men how to fight. Finn braced himself for this as they walked, his thundering in his chest.

The sunlight was bright and the air was growing warmer, reminiscent of spring, but it did little to calm his anxiety. He didn't know where the wylden were trained to fight, so he wasn't sure what he was looking for. When they stopped in front of the building that Erilyn had been taken into, he stared dumbly at it. Surely the training didn't happen here. The sun shone, the wind blew, and the dented metal sign that hung by the door creaked.

A shout from inside made his heart leap. The words were muffled, but he would know Erilyn's voice anywhere. She sounded angry, not hurt, and his fear of fighting a group of wylden was replaced with a surge of hope. His first instinct was to rip free of the wylden man's grasp and dart inside, but this wylden had brought him this far and he didn't want to risk more injuries when he was this close to her. Instead, he took a deep breath and waited, even though every nerve ending in his body vibratd with the desire to move.

The door swung open and for a moment he saw her—standing toe to toe with a wylden man, hands in fists at her side, cheeks crimson. *"...where he is, now!"* was all he heard before Lowell walked out, supported by another man Finn didn't recognize, and the door shut securely behind him. Lowell slowly made his way down the steps. Dazed, Finn wondered how he'd gotten free.

"You're alive," Lowell said, and Finn nodded.

Without a word, the wylden holding Finn's arm let go. Finn looked at him, ready to fight, but he walked away without a backward glance.

"You might want to get in there before she loses it and tears the place down," Lowell said as he motioned back toward the building with a nod of his head.

Finn, heart in his throat, limped up the short steps and pushed the door open and stepped into the tense room.

As the door swung shut behind him, Erilyn spun. All traces of anger vanished as soon as her gray-blue eyes met his.

He didn't remember crossing the room, but she met him halfway and everything around them vanished. All he could feel and hear and see was *Erilyn*. Her arms were around him, squeezing, and in spite of the pain in his ribs he squeezed her back, not caring if it hurt, only wanting to be as close to her as he physically could. He would feel this pain for eternity if it meant keeping her here in his arms. She was crying unintelligible words into his shirt and he pressed his lips into her hair over and over. He couldn't tell if she was shaking or if he was.

"You're alive," she breathed as she calmed down, her voice a whisper against his chest.

"Are you okay?" he asked, pulling back just enough to see her face, to see that she was well and whole. He cupped her face, tucking strands of dark blonde hair behind her ears.

She reached up and brushed her fingertips across the bruising around his eye. Fresh tears spilled over her cheeks as she looked down at his bruised throat. Her thumb traced his bottom lip where it was split.

With a shaky breath she took a step back, still holding onto his arms, and looked at him from head to toe. Her expression darkened as she took in his injuries. She met his eyes again and he saw the fury flickering in those gray depths. Erilyn let go of his arms and moved beside him, then gingerly slipped beneath his arm. Her hand rested above his bruised ribs, featherlight, as she tried to support some of his weight.

"I need some things," she said, her voice low and menacing in a way he'd never heard. She faced the large wylden man who'd taken her, but she didn't seem afraid. He wore a scowl on his dark face. Finn lifted his hand to Erilyn's shoulder and gripped it tightly. He wouldn't be separated from her again.

The wylden man had long, dark, gray-streaked hair that hung in thick clumps around his face. His skin was dark and smooth, but his eyes were a startlingly bright blue-green. As he stared at them, Finn felt a shiver pass over him and the hairs on his arms stood at attention. The large man's eyes bored into Finn, but Finn refused to react.

"Zeke," Erilyn barked and the large man's gaze shifted to her. As he stared at her, the shivery-feeling in the air intensified, then disappated like smoke.

The man—Zeke—exhaled with a growl and turned away. Erilyn relaxed beneath Finn's arm and walked Finn over to where he now saw the others waiting. She eased him onto a stool and took his hand. Everyone smiled at him except Seraphina who wouldn't meet his gaze.

"Glad to see you alive, Finley." Finn turned toward Cillian who was standing a few feet back. Cillian had his arm around a young woman with wild hair and filthy skin. It took him a moment before he realized the woman he was looking at was not a wylden, but was Morrigan. She looked pitiful and her eyes on him felt hungry. He quickly looked back to Cillian.

"You too." Finn nodded before he turned away.

"Zeke showed me what happened," Erilyn said, holding his hand delicately. He relished in the feel of her warm skin against his and brought her hand to his lips to press a kiss there. "I'm so sorry I didn't come get you sooner," she choked out, voice breaking. "I didn't know. I—" She swallowed heavily as two fat tears slipped down her cheeks.

"I was stupid," he said, swallowing painfully past his bruise. "At this point, I should know better than to take on wylden by myself." He smiled at her with one side of his mouth, fighting a wince as it pulled at the bruises on his face.

Erilyn smiled the smile she saved just for him. "Hopefully you've finally learned your lesson."

Finn nodded and adjusted his grip on her hand so that their fingers were twined together. "Definitely." His split lip ached when he smiled, but now that he was with her, he couldn't help it. The door opened and shut again and Finn craned his head to see, fully taking in the room for the first time. "What's going on here?" he whispered.

Erilyn blushed, but before she could answer, Aiyanna did. "Erilyn mended the wylden auras," Aiyanna said her voice soft but proud. "They're not a danger to us anymore."

Finn looked back at Erilyn, who shrugged one shoulder self-consciously. "It's what took me so long to get you out," she almost whispered. "Fia and Zeke—" she motioned toward the big wylden, "and some others—we've been working on healing their auras." She shrugged again and he gave her hand a squeeze. "And now, they're all—" her eyes traveled around the room until they came back to Finn. "They're all better." She sighed as if a great weight rested on her shoulders. "But I couldn't get any of you until we were finished. Zeke needed to make sure I'd stay until the end." She swallowed and dropped her head as if she were ashamed.

Finn thought back to his hallucination—Erilyn's golden aura surrounded by a pale rainbow of light—and wondered if it had actually been real.

He gripped her hand a little tighter. "It's okay," he said, his voice husky. She met his eyes—stormy grey—and the ache in his chest that he'd felt back in cell throbbed. "But—" he glanced at the crowd around them, all watching their conversation, and he cleared this throat.

"Could we talk for a minute? Just you and me?" He leaned toward her and adjusted his grip on her hand.

Her hair, dirty from so long on the road, fell in front of her face like a curtain as if she were avoiding his eyes. "After we get you better."

The door opened again and Fia walked in carrying a tray with various things on it.

"Finn," Fia said gruffly, a smile on her face. He returnd her smile, strangely glad to see her.

"Thank you," Erilyn said as she released Finn's hand to take the tray, which held a bowl filled with leaves, a ragged strip of cloth, and a small decanter of water.

"Food," Fia said to the group, standing tall and proud. She nodded toward the door, where a large man with a scar on his face stood, holding it open. Finn thought he remembered him from when they were taken from the woods and his muscles tensed. If the scarred man noticed, he didn't react other than to smile and duck his large head "Plants. For you," Fia said and the scarred giant nodded.

"You all go eat," Erilyn said as she sat the tray on a small table nearby and poured water into the small, clay bowl. "We'll join you soon."

The others exchanged glances with one another, huddling in a little closer than they had before.

"They'll leave you alone," Erilyn said. "I promise." She bit her bottom lip. "Fia, Dill, will you stay with them?"

The scarred man holding the door nodded again, the smile never falling from his face. It tugged at his scar, but he didn't seem to mind.

"Fia can take you to the food and Dill will make sure no one bothers you," she said to her friends as she stepped to Finn's side again.

"We'll be right outside," Rosemarie said, touching Erilyn's shoulder, then Finn's, as she passed.

The wylden in the room left with Fia and the others. Sera was last and looked back at them with a pained expression on her pale face, her eyes lingering on Finn before she stepped out, the door clicking shut behind her.

In the new silence, Erilyn mixed herbs into the water while Finn waited, his heartbeat loud in his ears. She soaked the cloth in mixture, then sat on her knees in front of him and gently pressed it to the cut on his lip. He sucked in a breath, expecting pain, but was met instead with a cool sensation followed by some mild relief.

"Rosemarie used this mixture on me when I was little. After she found me in the woods. It helped with the pain from the sunburn I had," she said, dipping the cloth in the liquid again before gently dabbing at other small cuts on his face he hadn't realized he had.

"How did Fia know what to give you?" he asked, his voice rough. Now that they were alone, he just wanted to hold her, to kiss her, to tell her he loved her, but the words wouldn't come and he couldn't make himself move. So instead, he just watched her as she focused on his injuries.

"I *showed* them," she said, chewing on her bottom lip as she worked up his face toward his swollen eye. "So much has changed in the last couple of days, Finn," she said, finally meeting his eyes. He was taken aback by the intensity in her gaze. "So much."

She pulled her hand away from him to soak the cloth in water again, but he caught her hand in his to stop her. "You told me about a tie between us. A connection. But, it's gone, isn't it? I felt it. Here," he said, pointing to his chest. "It hurt."

Erilyn ducked her head and closed her eyes in shared pain, but he tilted her chin up and she looked at her, her expression heartbroken.

"What happened?" he whispered.

"Zeke," she said, her words coming out broken. "Their leader. He—he *broke* it. Snapped it. He was trying to tether me to him and couldn't unless the tie between us was gone." She took a shuddering breath. "It's why I didn't find you sooner. I was afraid if I pushed for you too hard, he'd kill you." She swallowed. "He still thinks, deep down, that I'll *choose* to stay here with him instead of leaving with you."

"Did he—" the words died in his throat as he thought of all that could have happened to her while he was trapped in his cells.

"No," she said quickly. "I stopped him. I'm okay."

Relief spread through him as if he'd dipped his entire body in the medicinal bath she'd been using on his wounds.

Erilyn went to dip the cloth back in the medicinal bath again, but he stopped her. He took both of her hands and slipped off the stool so that he was right in front of her, on his knees as well. He held her hands and stared into her eyes, unwilling to waste any more moments on indecision.

Before they had been captured, Erilyn's biggest fear was that Finn only thought he loved her because she had accidentally tied them together. But there was no tie now, nothing in the room but him and her, and without any tie or abilities or anything else, Finn knew that he loved her.

"There's nothing tying us together now," he said, releasing one hand to cup her face. Her eyes drifted closed and a tear trickled down one cheek. "You said you needed to know how I really felt." Still holding her cheek, he leaned forward until his lips were almost on hers. "So know this—I love you," he whispered, his breath brushing against her lips. He wanted nothing more than to kiss her, but she was the one who had ended things between them. He knew how he felt, but not how she did. So he pressed his foreahed to hers, letting his thumbs brush her cheeks, the leaned away.

Erilyn opened her eyes and stared at him for a brief moment before she closed the small gap between them and pressed her lips to his. The cut on his lip ached, but he didn't care. His hand slipped into her hair as her arms slid around his neck and something in his chest—something that had been angry and afraid and wild since Erilyn was taken—settled. Her lips on his were soft but insistent and Finn had the thought that he could stay here, pressed against her, forever and that would be just fine.

Erilyn pulled back and smiled the smile she reserved only for him. "I love you, too," she said, and he laughed at how shy she sounded, wincing when his eye ached with the movement.

The door opened, but Erilyn didn't pull away. Fia brought food for both of them. She smiled as she sat the bowls beside them, then left without a word.

Finn looked down at the food that the wylden had made for them—charred nuts, raw greens, and some sort of thick, mashed root. It didn't look very appetizing, but his stomach was screaming for it. Erilyn scooted back and handed him one of the bowls. A few tentative bites proved that it wasn't half bad.

"The wylden made us dinner," he said as he took a second bite. "Things really have changed."

Erilyn smiled and nodded, but her smile fell away as she ducked her head. "There's something else." She clenched her hands in her lap, her own food forgotten. "Something I haven't told the others yet." She took a deep breath and met his gaze, fear plain on her face. "Cave dwellers—ones with abilities like mine—are coming here. It's why I agreed to help Zeke. It's why we were working so hard to heal all his people so quickly." She swallowed heavily. "The people of Citadel are coming for a fight."

Chapter 9

"Shift"

Morrigan

CILLIAN hasn't left your side. It's hard to concentrate on what you need to do with him so close. He is a distraction, flooding your mind with terrible, wonderful things. Like sinking in mud, you slip into memories. Your hands cling to his body as you struggle to pull yourself back to the present.

Stars shine overhead. Together you drink vitium and discover who can see furthest. You win, but his hands distract you as they paint constellations across your skin.

From the shadows you watch Cillian whisper in Erilyn's ear, his silvery aura prodding her gold. Your jealousy burns so hot you know he can feel it.

His lips on in his office in front of the fire place. His mouth erases your guilt, erases Finn from your mind, and stokes your need for him.

You told him you'd been with Finn while he was off with Erilyn. His face, angry and red. His hands on you, both rough and gentle as he tried to make you his again. As he kissed you, you realized that he now, finally, belonged only to you.

And now, you add to the litany the newest memory—his face, hopeful and open, when he saw you in that filthy, wylden room and pulled you to him as if you were the most precious thing in the world.

"I'm so glad you're okay," he'd whispered brokenly into your hair as his big, warm hands spanned your back. His warmth soothed you and you hated it. Hated how vulnerable it made you feel, as if you needed it. Needed him. You missed your patrol leathers, the ones you burned. Your clothes now let you feel his warmth, feel how is muscles move under hs skin, and you feel yourself leaning into him, wanting more. Too weak to resist.

"You need to eat," he says, pulling you from your memories and offering you a charred nut.

You wrinkle your nose at the smell. "Is there meat?" you ask, your stomach growling. You want to see if you can hear the whispers of the animal. It always made you feel strong to feel the life you consumed.

"This is all there is for now." He grasps your hand and you melt as his smooth palm glides over you skin. You want to run your fingers through his. You want to rip your hand away. "Please, Morrigan," he says, leaning his head toward you, his blonde hair falling over one eye.

You reach up to brush it back, a habit, before you realize what you're doing. He turns his face to press a kiss to your palm. You hate the way your stomach flips at the touch of his lips against your skin. Hate how badly you want him to do it again.

You pull your hand away and take the charred nut he offers. It's burnt and coats your tongue in ash, but Cillian smiles.

He turns to speak to Lucy on his other side, and your eyes drift toward the building where Erilyn and Finn still are. The thought of the two of them makes you simmer with rage. They brought you here. They took your vitium. They should suffer. You will them to come out so that you can—

"Morrigan?" You spin, nostrils flared in anger, but it is just the little nightcrawler girl. Seraphina. "I brought you some water." Her voice is almost a whisper as she holds out a bowl half-filled with clear water.

You lean away from Cillian to accept the water. He looks to you, worried, until he sees the girl. He relaxes and goes back to the conversation with his sister. Keeping your eyes locked on the girl, you drain the bowl and hand it back.

"Thank you, Seraphina," you say, your voice smoother than it's been in a while. With a nod, the girl returns to her seat beside Aiyanna. The older nightcrawler looks at you, then pulls Seraphina tight against her side as if protecting her.

You smile at her and she looks away, cheeks pink. With no eyes on you again, you look back toward the building, once again willing Erilyn and Finn to come out so you can finish this once and for all.

Chapter 10

"Break"

Erilyn

ONCE we'd finished the humble meal Fia brought us, I made a makeshift pallet on the ground. As soon as Finn was lying flat I lifted his shirt so that I could see his abdomen. I sucked in a sharp breath when I saw the bruises striped across his ribs.

"It's not so bad," he said as my hand hovered over his purple and green stained skin.

I lightly let my fingers rest on the affected area and he winced. "With the cave dwellers coming, we need to get you bandaged up. We have to leave and you have to be able to move."

"Leave?" Finn asked, his eyebrows shooting up toward his hairline.

I laid the cloth drenched with the medicinal wash on the bruised skin to let it soak in. "They're coming to fight the wylden. Not us. We can head back through the forest, back to Sunnybrook. We should be safe there. But if you're too sore, we won't be able to move very fast."

Finn stared up at the ceiling taking shallow breaths. "What you're doing is helping," he said, looking at me from his one good eye, "but couldn't you do what you did before and heal all of it?"

My heart stuttered as I thought of the last time I'd healed Finn—his blood gushing out of the wound from Morrigan's knife, coating my hands in heat as he went cold. Figuring out how to knit him back together. Realizing I'd tied him to me by mistake.

I'd helped heal a lot of auras since that moment, more than I could count, but I wasn't sure I trusted myself to go back into Finn's. I wasn't sure I ever would. His aura was almost as familiar to me as my own and I wasn't sure I could keep them apart.

As if he could read my mind, he said, "I trust you." His hands were steady as he took mine and placed it flat on his chest. He held it there with a gentle pressure.

"I—" my voice caught as I felt his heart beating beneath my fingers. I couldn't—*wouldn't*—tie him to me again, but I also couldn't leave him like this. The medicinal herbs would help with the pain but he would still take a long time to heal. The bruising was deep and who knew what other injuries he had inside. Bandages wouldn't be enough.

"Erilyn, I trust you," he repeated, his voice soft as his hand continued to press mine flat against his chest. His heartbeat was strong and even.

With a haggard breath I let myself *see* his aura, careful not to touch it with my own. In the beautiful green light there—light that filled me with both a deep, primal longing—I could see mottled spots where his injuries were, where the green was so deep it looked almost black. My aura reached for his, desperate to heal him, to twine with his light, but I pulled back, breathing shallow and quick. Finn watched me, a soft expression on his face devoid of judgement.

He trusted me. But I didn't trust myself. I wouldn't let myself make the same mistake again.

Fia, I called, heart pounding painfully inside my chest as I pulled my aura in, further from Finn's. *I need you.*

She came moments later and without a word settled on her knees on Finn's other side. He looked up at her, looking awkward.

I *showed* Fia his injuries in my mind. Her brow furrowed as she openly wondered why I needed her for this. "Can you help me heal him?" I asked aloud while silently *showing* her my fears—the pull of his aura, the way my own had tangled with it, my fear of trapping him again, all colored by my immense guilt.

I expected that to clear things up, but she still looked confused. Her head was cocked to one side as her eyes darted back and forth between us.

"Will you please help me?" I whispered. Finn's hand, which still held mine one his chest, closed warmly around my fingers.

"Eri," he said. His beautiful blue eyes were wide and locked on me. "You can do this. *I trust you,*" he said. He pulled my hand from his chest and kissed my palm, making my heart ache. "I love you," he said, and tears sprang to my eyes.

I could feel his love as clearly as my own, but it didn't convince me to do this on my own. If anything, his love was the impetus that allowed me the strength not to. I wouldn't risk tethering him against his will again.

I shared all of this with Fia, but her confused scowl only deepened. With a flood of joy and serenity, she showed me the tangle of gold and green that she'd seen in us as if it were beautiful. If she'd shown me this in the moments after Zeke broke the tether, I would have agreed with her.

But not now. Finn didn't have a choice in this. Not really. It may be the wylden way, but in those pairings each person made a conscious choice to join. I wouldn't force that on Finn.

With a sigh and a nod, Fia placed her hand on Finn's shoulder to help me, but he kept his eyes on me. I smiled, my lips trembling. With a slow exhale I closed my eyes and his aura came into focus.

The beauty of his auralight brought a fresh wave of tears and he squeezed my fingers where he held them. There were points where the deep green of his aura pulsed—his injuries—but the rest was a strong, vivid, summer green. Unpolluted by gold or red or any other color. With the tie between us broken, he was whole and he was beautiful.

I could have stayed here, floating, basking in his lovely verdant light, but I knew if I stayed too long, I would slip. I could feel my own aura longing to joing with his.

With a stiff resolve, I got to work. Fia and I worked well as a team. I showed her how I'd healed her leg, how I'd healed Finn's knife wound, and she mimicked what I'd done with ease. I watched the bruised light brighten as the swelling and bruising receded, and along with it I felt his pain dissipate. He had no broken bones, so it didn't take long. With one last longing look at the sea of green, I pulled back.

When I looked at his face again, some of the tension I'd been carrying evaporated. His bruises were gone and he blinked, testing his previosuly bruised eye, as he looked up at me.

My hand slipped from his chest as he pushed himself up. He winced in the expectation of pain, only to smile broadly when there was none. "Thank you," he said to Fia as he reached for my hand beside him.

She nodded at him, then cocked her head to the side again. She met my eyes and I immediately saw what she saw—Finn's hand in mine, his green aura and my gold reaching for one another.

I wanted to explain why I wouldn't tie us together again—his agency had been taken away by Morrigan and by me—but before I could form the thoughts the door slammed open and Lucy charged in, eyes wild.

"Something's happening," she said, her voice low and strained.

The three of us were up in a flash, Finn's hand firm in mine as we darted outside. I'd been so focused on Finn, on his feelings and my own, that I hadn't *felt* any of the chaos we walked into.

Our friends were huddled together near the edge of the porch while wylden darted all around, using guttural words that I couldn't understand with my ears, but their emotion filled the air like acrid fog—they were terrified.

"The cave dwellers are close," I said as we reached the others, catching snippets of images and individual emotions from the wylden we passed. Everyone's eyes went wide except Morrigan's and Seraphina's. Morrigan met my gaze and smiled. "I'm sorry I didn't tell you all sooner. I thought we had more time to—"

"You've put us in danger *again*," Seraphina spat from beside Rosemarie. Her aura was a vivid, hot pink and flickered like a freshly fed flame.

"It's not her fault," Finn said, moving to stand slightly in front of me, still gripping my hand. Seraphina rolled her eyes, but her aura seemed to stutter with sadness.

"It doesn't matter now," I said as the collective fear of the wylden seeped into me and made my feet itch to run. "We have to go. Now."

"We're leaving?" Aiyanna asked.

"The people of Citadel are coming to fight the wylden. They've taken vitium," I said, letting that sink in for a moment. "We can't be here when they arrive."

"How do we get home?" Rosemarie asked, pulling Seraphina closer as if that alone might protect her from what was coming.

"Through the forest." Finn's hand twitched in mine.

Seraphina scoffed. "We barely made it through the first time," she said, pulling away from Rosemarie and putting her hands on her hips to face me. "We should stay and fight." Her aura flared again.

"Anyone without abilities—and without *training*—won't stand a chance," I said, frustration making my words sharp. "The forest is our best chance. We made it through once, we can do it again. We'll just have to—" I felt Zeke approach and spun, my nerves on edge from Sera's anger, which was directed entirely toward me.

Zeke's eyes were sad as he stpoped a few feet away, giving my friends some space as they all tensed in his presence. "Path," he said. "Secret." He stared at me for a long moment, his vitium-colored eyes sad and afraid. In my mind I could see the path he meant—through the woods, safe from the dangers there. In that moment, he wasn't shielding anything from me. My heart constricted with the weight of what he shared, what he felt, and I felt my heart fracture.

Zeke stared at me for a moment longer, his expression tight, and then walked away. All around us wylden were building barricades out of broken furniture and loose stones. I could feel the children and the elderly hiding in the buildings on the edges of town. The upworlders who'd been in cells weren't anywhere in Ringol. Zeke had let them go. It was these considerations—for the people he saw as weak and useless—that made my decision for me, even as it broke my heart a little more.

My friends weren't going to like what I had to tell them. I took a moment, a few beats of my heart, to get my own emotions under control, before I spoke. "Zeke showed me a safe path through the forest," I said, voice quiet as I turned back to my friends. Finn let go of my hand and pressed his palm to my lower back. "Until now it's been a wylden secret, but he's given it to me so we can get away before the fighting starts."

"Then let's go," Finn said, stepping closer, his fingers gripping the back of my sweater as if he could sense what I was about to say. "Let's go now."

"Sera," I said, voice cracking. She was angry with me, she blamed me for everything that had happened to us so far, but she was the only one I knew for sure I could share the path with.

Sera scowled at me still, but I offered her the path in my mind like a gift. Her eyes went wide as my feelings of sadness accompanied the images. A hint of the little girl I'd met all those weeks ago returned to her face for a single moment—soft and sweet—but then it was gone, her expression closed off once again.

"Fia, will you take them to get a few supplies? Whatever can be spared?" Fia nodded, her eyes sad. She knew what I intended to do. When Morrigan and Cillian started to follow them, panic spiked in my chest. "Not you Morrigan." My voice was hard like stone and Morrigan spun toward me. "You aren't leaving. You can't go back to Sunnybrook."

Her eyes flared angrily and she took a step toward me, only getting as far as Cillian's reach. "You just expect to leave me here alone with the wylden?" she spat. Cillian pulled her back to him, his jaw tense and his eyes hard.

"No," I said, voice cracking. Finn stepped closer to me and I braced myself as my heart fluttered against my ribs. "You won't be alone, because I'm going to stay, too." I swallowed past a lump in my throat. "I'm going to help the wylden fight."

Chapter 11

"Futility"

Finn

ALL around him was movement and voices, but all of it faded away as Erilyn's words echoed in his ears. He stared down at her, but she looked anywhere but at him. Anger and fear bubbled up inside. He forced himself to listen as the others spoke.

"You have to come with us," Lucy said, her voice strained with anger. "What are you thinking?"

"It's not safe here," Rosemarie pleaded, reaching for Erilyn with her fingertips.

"You can't make Morrigan stay," Cillian spat, pink tinting his tanned cheeks as he tightened his grip on the wild woman's shoulders. Never had Finn seen the usually neutral man so agitated.

"The children need you," Aiyanna interjected, an edge to her voice.

Finn wanted to add something. If anyone could convince Erilyn to come with them, he thought it might be him, but his jaw felt glued shut as his heart beat a painful cadence in his veins

"What do you think about this, Finn?" Seraphina asked, acidic and sharp. Guilt weighed heavily on him with the sound of her voice. He'd barely given her a thought during his incarceration and it was clear that the last two days hadn't been kind to her. Her clothes were dirty, her face too pale, and she wore a mask of anger that hadn't been there before. In forty-eight hours she'd become a different child. A different woman.

"I think—" In spite of the anger he felt that Erilyn was once again making a choice without him, a choice that separated them, he took his hand away from her lower back where it had been resting and threaded his fingers through hers. He cleared his throat. "I think you all need to get some supplies and I'll talk to Erilyn about why she needs to come with us."

Finn had never been a leader, but his quiet words urged the others into action. Fia motioned for them and they followed her. Cillian held Morrigan against his side as if she were something fragile and forced her along with him. Sera glowered and threw a glare over her shoulder, but Finn barely noticed. He was focused on the slight, powerful woman beside him.

"Finn—" Erilyn's voice broke as she continued to look away from him.

"No," he said, giving her hand a gentle squeeze. "No. We need to talk about this. You can't make this decision all on your own. Not this time." He squeezed her hand again and wet his lips with the tip of his tongue. "If you're going to do this, I at least need to know why."

After a long moment, she looked up at him and nodded slowly.

The wylden still swarmed all around, so Erilyn led Finn to the alley beside a building. Behind the building was a wall of natural stone. It reminded Finn of the quarry behind his small cabin and made him think Ringol must have once been a mining town. Ringol was more broken down than Sunnybrook, but really not that much different than Finn's home.

The air in the alleyway smelled dank where the snow had melted and revealed piles of dead vegetation, but there were no wylden or people around to overhear them.

The noise from the barricades being built was more muffled back here and Finn could almost pretend that they were alone. As he looked down at her now, he was taken back to their last conversation like this—when she told him, in no uncertain terms, that she was leaving Sunnybrook and he had to stay behind. He remembered she'd been distant that day. At the time he hadn't understood why, but now he knew she had been putting distance between them because she felt guilty that they were tied together.

But the tie was gone now. There was no reason for her to stay behind and every reason for her to come home with them. He had to make her see that.

The sun didn't quite reach where they stood and Finn felt chilled in the shadow of the building. Erilyn finally met his gaze and opened her mouth to defend her decision, but before she could say a word, he cut her off with a kiss.

He half expected her to pull away, but she softened against him immediately. Encouraged, he lifted her onto the tips of her toes to deepen the kiss, holding her flush against his chest. Even without blended auras, he had never been more sure of the fact that he was meant for her and she was meant for him.

Their kiss was hungry, lips dancing together, breath mingling, and he felt something settle inside him. Like when he'd imagined her aura before, he thought he once again saw golden light, except now it was in front of him, calling to him and drawing him close. It felt good. Felt right.

But then she slowed their kiss, her lips soft as she pulled away, and the golden light vanished. He was left, chest heaving and filled with a deep longing.

"You can't stay here," he said before she could speak, and her peaceful expression shifted to despair. "You can't, Eri."

"They need me," she said, putting her hands on his chest to push away from him, but he kept his arms around her waist, unwilling to let her go.

"Why?" He inched closer and leaned down so they were nearly eye-to-eye. "This town is full of strong, fierce, *dangerous* wylden. They're more than capable of handling whatever's coming." He took a deep breath, then exhaled heavily. "They can't need you more than I do," he whispered, and her face crumpled with sadness.

Erilyn stared up at him for a long moment, before she leaned into his chest instead of pulling away. His sweater was clenched in her fingers and he found his heart beating a painful rhythm.

"If I don't stay and hep, we risk losing the peace we've found with the wylden." She gripped his sweater tighter. "I don't want to stay," she said, her voice low. "I don't want to be without you. Don't want to send you away. But I'm responsible for them being changed." Her eyes were wide, willing him to understand. "I've learned so much about them, and I think—" she pressed her lips together. "I think they're afraid of what's coming. They can think more clearly now. Can assess the danger and the risk. Before, they were nothing but instinct and desire, but now—" her voice broke and she adjusted her grip on his shirt, stepping even closer to him. "Now they can think about what could happen to them, and they're so afraid," she whispered. She bit the inside of her lip. "I upended their lives. I have to stay and make sure they can do this. I owe it to them."

Finn looked down at Erilyn. Her slate-blue eyes burned with determination and sadness and again he felt that pull in his chest that told him that being with her, being near her, was precisely where he was supposed to be.

"I need you, too," she said before he could respond. "More than you know. And I wish there were another way, but I *have* to do this." The pain in her voice dissolved any resolve he had to fight her choice.

He sighed and leaned his forehead against hers, pulling her closer in the process. This wasn't how this was supposed to go. "You should let us stay. At least a few of us," he breathed. It was a statement, not a question, but she shook her head all the same.

"Only Morrigan. She has to stay," she said into the space between them. "If she makes it back to Sunnybrook, she'll get her hands on vitium. And then..." she trailed off.

Finn nodded. His stomach clenched painfully.

"I should stay with you," he breathed, fingers splayed wide across the back of her ribs, his breath moving the little hairs around her face.

"The children still need you," she said. She pressed her cheek against his chest and he kissed her hair.

The last time they'd had a conversation like this, she'd felt like she was a million miles away. This time, she was right here with him. His pain was her pain and it was going to make letting her go twice as hard.

She turned her face, squeezed her eyes closed, and pressed a lingering kiss right over his heart. "I promise to come find you as soon as I can."

Finn was quiet for a long moment as he thought. His hands trailed soft patterns over her shoulder blades and lower back.

When he had been with Morrigan she'd always complained that he never took charge. He knew part of the reason Erilyn didn't want him to stay was because he couldn't fight. It made him feel like he had with Morrigan—like he wasn't enough of a man. Insecurity roared forth and for a moment he considered telling Erilyn that either she was going with him or he was staying with her, regardless of her feelings. It's what Morrigan would have wanted. But that fleeting thought vanished as quickly as it had come, because unlike with Morrigan, he had nothing to prove to Erilyn. More than anything he wanted her to come with him back to Sunnybrook, but he also knew that this was important to her.

He loved her. He trusted her. If she needed to do this, he had to accept that.

His voice was gruff as he said, "You promise you'll come back to me—"

"As quickly as I possibly can," she finished for him, her voice muffled by his sweater. He hugged her tighter as tears gathered in his eyes, then braced himself for what he knew came next—leaving this strange, broken place without her hand in his.

Chapter 12

"Hope"

Morrigan

CILLIAN'S hand in yours is firm and sweaty. As the others stuff decrepit supplies into their packs, he looks at you, a soft smile on his face and sadness heavy in his eyes. Then his eyes move away from yours and he answers a question his sister asked. Without his eyes on you its like a spell is broken and all you can think about is running away and finding vitium.

It's been too long since your last dose. Your skin is itchy, your mouth dry. You can't stop wetting your lips and trying to *see.* But it doesn't work. Your vision is blurred, your movements wooden. Cillian's hand in yours is too hot. Too sticky. You want to jump out of your own skin.

You have to get away.

Your vitium liquid is gone, but you think there is raw vitium close. You can feel it calling to you, thrumming in the earth beneath your feet. But it's hard to tell exactly where, because without a dose already flowing through your veins your ears feel stuffed with moss and your eyes feel covered by shadow.

But then Cillian looks at you again, a smile on his handsome face, and everything comes into focus. You feel yourself smile as he pulls you closer, arm warm and safe. He's talking to the others, but what they're saying doesn't matter. You lean into him, a sigh on your lips, content to stay right here. It feels a little like falling asleep.

But then it hits you. Why does a simple look from him make you calm? Why does the warmth of his arm make you feel so perfectly content? Is he trying to tether you? Your skin tingles in warning and you tense.

You have to get away.

Things move in and out of focus around you. Cillian's hot, sticky hand. His cool, soft eyes that draw you in. And outside of him, the little nightcrawler girl flitting around you like a dying moth—never close enough to get burned, but circling. Curious.

On alert again, you look over your shoulder toward the building where Finn and Erilyn disappeared behind. You can't *hear* or *see* them, and you grit your teeth so hard your jaw aches. They've been gone a long time. They probably left without you. Abandoned the group in its weakness. It's what you woud have done.

Your heart is racing and you focus on this. This anger. This betrayal.

You remember Finn before Erilyn came—soft and pliable. He would have done anything you asked. He was weak, but he was yours. But Erilyn has poisoned him beyond hope. She is a tumor that you will remove once you get your vitium back.

Cillian looks at you again, his eyes darting over your face, and you grow soft and forget Finn for another moment. He slides his fingers between yours and your stomach clenches pleasantly with the friction of his skin against yours. Visions of all the times you were together — all heat and breath, dominance taken in turns — fill you up and you can't focus on anything but him. Cillian smiles and kisses your forehead, his lips dry and cool, and you think back to the time he took you in the snow, the heat of vitium coursing through your bodies so hotly that the snow around you melted.

You have the thought that he might be tethering you now, but it feels so good you allow it, at least for a little while.

"I won't let her leave you here," he says to you, his voice a whisper against your forehead. He kisses you again, his lips lingering.

The illusion of warmth and memories is broken as you remember — *Erilyn*. You turn away from Cillian's lips back toward the building where she and Finn disappeared. Still gone.

You stare at that spot, willing them to emerge, knowing they've already left. You can still feel Cillian against your side, still feel his sticky, hot hand on your arm, but you ignore it. The shadow beside the building seems to grow as you watch it and you know they've left. Finn is gone.

But just as you are about to turn away, anger boiling in your stomach, they emerge and it's like a rug has been pulled from beneath your feet.

Finn holds Erilyn's hand just like Cillian holds yours, but unlike Cillian, Finn's grip on her fingers is light. Cillian holds onto you like an animal on a rope—keeping you at his side through sheer force of will. Finn holds her like a butterfly, trusting her to stay, willing to let her leave.

The fire of your anger grows white hot and you bristle.

The others, all talking quietly, grow quiet as they approach, waiting to hear their decision, but even without abilities it's clear to you. Erilyn has convinced Finn to do what she says, which means you are stuck here. Unless you can figure out a way to escape, you aren't going back to Sunnybrook.

Chapter 13

"The Last Time"

Erilyn

FINN squeezed my hand as we approached our friends. He loved me enough, trusted me enough, to let me make my own choices. That made the choice I'd made even harder, but I'd felt Zeke's fear. I had drastically altered the fate of his people, and while I believed it was for the best, I owed it to them to stay through their first major trial.

Morrigan stared daggers at us, but without her vitium, I was no longer afraid of her. Seeing her like this, she was nothing more than a broken girl. I just had to keep her here, away from liquid vitium.

"You're letting her stay, aren't you?" Lucy scowled and crossed her arms over her chest.

"I'm not *letting* her do anything," Finn responded, eyebrows furrowed. "I want her to come with us more than any of you—" his voice was harsh. "But I trust her to make her own choices. And you should too."

Lucy's scowl deepened, amd Aiyanna stepped to her side and pressed a pale hand against her lower back.

"If I stay, we may be able to have real, lasting peace with the wylden." I swallowed heavily. I could feel all their eyes on me, which made me want to hide behind my hair, so I looked at Rosemarie—the one person who had always watched me without judgement. "If I leave them and this fight with the people of Citadel goes badly, the peace we have right now may not last." I took a deep breath. "Zeke trusts me, but that trust has limits. If he's killed during this fight, or simply gets angry that I left—" I let the possibilities hang in the air as I kept my eyes locked on Rosemarie's.

She nodded, eyes sad. "I understand." Her voice was warm like honey. "We all just want you to be safe." I was taken back to so long ago when Rosemarie had coated my burns in cooling, medicinal rags and whispered that I was safe over and over as I shook through the night.

Tears threatened, but I held them back. If I started to cry now, I wasn't sure I would stop. "As soon as this fight with the cave dwellers is over, I'll come straight to Sunnybrook to join you."

A bark of laughter erupted from Morrigan's lips. "The people of Sunnybrook hate you," she spat, her voice barely more than a growl in her throat. "If you go back, you're as good as dead."

"That's not true," Lucy interjected as she stared at Morrigan.

"Cillian can clear her name before she gets back. Right?" Finn adjusted his grip on my hand as he turned toward Cillian. Something had changed between them after they'd been taken away.

Cillian looked from Finn to me. He released Morrigan's hand and draped his arm over her shoulders, then pulled her close. "Is Morrigan returning with us?" Morrigan squirmed in his grasp and her face darkened. Cillian didn't see, but I did.

"No," I said, stomach clenching. Without Cillian's support, Sunnybrook might never be a safe haven for me. But even if that was the case, I couldn't let Morrigan go back. At least not yet.

Cillian's face fell. "I would clear your name if I were returning to Sunnybrook, Erilyn, but I won't leave here while Morrigan stays." He looked down at her and his face softened. "I've spent enough time pretending—" His mouth opened as if he wanted to say more, but instead he only sighed and looked back at me, his eyes weary. "If Morrigan stays here, I stay."

"You can't do that!" Lucy stepped forward and exclaimed, causing more than a few wylden to stop their preparations and turn toward us in surprise. Her anger and fear poured off her like oily smoke.

Aiyanna took Lucy's hand and a wash of cool air seemed to blow all the smoke away. One look at Lucy's face told me she was still angry, but Aiyanna had shielded her feelings. The wylden lost interest and turned away

"Cillian," Lucy pleaded, "Sunnybrook needs you. If you stay here, we'll be without a leader." She bit the inside of her cheek and I could see her fighting with herself before she said, "And I need my brother."

Cillian's face softened with Lucy's plea and hope flared in my chest, bright and hot, but then he looked down at Morrigan, still pressed against his side, and exhaled heavily. I didn't have to be looking at his aura to see that his mind was made up.

"The council can lead until we get back, just as they've been doing since I left." He looked at Lucy, and his voice grew soft. "I'm sorry, Luce."

Lucy's face fell as she looked from Cillian to Morrigan and h er aura-light—deep orange like the sun just before it disappeared beneath the horizon—grayed.

"Just come with us," Lucy said looking for Cillian to me. "We can all just leave together." She swallowed heavily and tears welled in the corners of her eyes. "Or we should all stay. One or the other." Her chest was heaving and Aiyanna's grip on her hand was tight.

"I can't make any of you leave," I said, "but I can't guarantee I'll be able to protect you if you stay. What's coming—" The anger I'd felt coming from the cave dwellers still echoed in my bones. "It's going to get really bad and I would never forgive myself if any of you were hurt."

"Protect us?" Seraphina asked, face screwed up in a snarl. "We're in a town full of wylden who could crush you with a *thought* if they wanted. You can barely *sense* the animals around you, Erilyn. How are you supposed to be helpful here?" She rolled her eyes and crossed her arms.

But past her angry exterior, I could see her worry, buried so deep I wasn't even sure she was aware of it.

"A lot has changed, Sera," I said, voice low. Different shades of pink flashed and flickered like a flame within her aura. "It's important for me to stay. You're going to have to trust me on that." Sera's expression didn't change, but her aura flashed brightly.

Rosemarie put her hand on Seraphina's shoulder and Sera wilted. "How long do we have?" Rosemarie asked.

"You need to leave as soon as possible," I whispered, heart breaking. Finn squeezed my hand. "You all have to be away from here when the cave dwellers arrive."

"From one danger to another," Morrigan rasped. No one looked at her.

WE walked in silence until we reached the path at the edge of the Dark Woods . Even in the full light of day, the forest felt ominous. But Zeke had shown me that the path was safe. The wylden used this path to traverse the forest.

"Sera, you know the way." She nodded stiffly, arms at her side, but I hugged her as tightly as I dared. I kissed her hair and caught the faintest sense—a whisper of a thought—that she wanted me to come with them. Next I hugged Aiyanna and Lucy, who both hugged me alittle tighter than they ever had before. Rosemarie's arms around me were firm and I tried to pour all the love I'd carried for her over the last four years into this one embrace. Too soon she was pulling away.

I turned to Finn last and he took my hand.

"Give us a minute," he said, voice gruff.

As he gently pulled me to the side, Lucy released Aiyanna and stepped toward Cillian. I watched as she hesitated for only a moment before she stepped into him and hugged him around his waist. His arm fell away from Morrigan as he hugged her back. By choosing to stay behind, I was ensuring that Morrigan, and therefore Cillian, stayed behind as well. I was almost tempted to change my mind and go with them, just so they wouldn't be split up, but a single look at Morrigan strengthened my resolved to stay. She couldn't go back to Sunnybrook without me. Just like the wylden, she was my responsibility. If she got her hands on the children, or on vitium—

"Erilyn," Finn said, disrupting my racing thoughts and drawing my attention back to him. Even though we weren't alone, I focused all my attention on him. He took my other hand and wet his bottom lip with the tip of his tongue. His bright blue eyes—the color even brighter than usual because of the sky blue sweater he wore—were on me and I was overcome with tenderness.

"I know you're doing what you have to do, and even though I want to, I won't try to talk you out of it," he said, his voice low so that only I could hear. "But I need to know you'll come back to me when this is over." He wet his lips again. "Not knowing where you were, if you were okay—I can't do that again. So, I'm going to ask you something and I need you to answer."

"Alright," I whispered, feeling as if I were standing on a precipice.

"I know what it feels like to be without you," he said. "I know how it feels to lose you." He adjusted his grip on my hands so that he was holding my fingers and rubbed my knuckles with his thumbs. "I never want to know that feeling again. So when you come back—" he stared so deeply into my eyes it felt like he was seeing into my soul. "When you come back, I want you to marry me." His expression was open and vulnerable.

I still wore the wooden ring he'd made for me and it pressed comfortably into my finger. Warmth bloomed in my belly and spread through my limbs. This wasn't the warmth that caused earthquakes or concussed the air and trees. This was the warmth of a dream I'd never allowed myself to have.

"There's no tether making me want this," he said when I didn't answer right away. "There's just you and me." He stepped closer and his breath caressed my lips. "That's all I want after all this, Eri. Just you and me. So, please, say yes?"

Pure, bright love poured into me through our joined hands—like warm honey and a soft breeze. My knees felt weak even and my heart fluttered wildly.

"Just you and me," I whispered as tears welled and fell from my eyes. I was sure he could hear my heart, racing in my chest, but it didn't matter. "That's all I want, too."

His relief washed over me like summer rain and a beautiful smile stretched across his face.

"That means we won't split up like this again. Okay?" He let go of my hands to cradle my face and I leaned into the warmth or his palms.

"Okay," I breathed as I turned my head just enough to brush my lips again his palm, relishing in the feel of his callouses against my lips.

Hands warm on my cheeks, he pulled my lips to his. His fingers slipped back into my hair as my arms went around his waist. I didn't voice it, but I wasn't sure I would survive what was coming, so I didn't hold anything back from this kiss in case it was our last.

I wanted to tell him that I didn't want to be away from him. That I loved him more than I ever thought I could love anyone. That he was the best person I knew. But I didn't say any of those things and instead tried to pour those feelings into our kiss.

His lips on mine were insistent and soft, and I felt our auras begin to swirl around us. For the first time, the feeling of them reaching for one another didn't scare me. They weren't tied together, weren't being forced to tangle. This time, it was like they were dancing around us, wrapping us up like two blankets, surrounding us like shields.

Our kiss ended too soon—my lips, my body, my aura pulling away from his at the same time. As I stepped back, hands shaking, I went cold from the inside out.

Finn was going back to Sunnybrook without me. He needed to. Needed to make sure that the others were okay. Make sure Luna had made it when I sent her away.

"If you see Luna—" I said, my voice cracking. I hadn't let myself think about her because I'd had to focus on so much—on surviving, on saving my friends. I'd sent her away to save her, but she'd never been on her own before.

"We'll both be waiting for you in Sunnybrook when this is over," he said as he tucked my hair behind my ear. He spoke with such confidence that I had no choice but to believe him.

There were so many things left to say, but the storm of emotions raging inside me and the impending danger for my friends kept the words inside. Instead, all I could do was nod and squeeze his hand. I leaned forward to kiss him one more time, his lips warm and pliable, then stepped back and let him go.

Cillian had his arm around Morrigan again, holding her to his side, and I joined them as Finn joined the others. I could feel Morrigan's eyes boring into me, but I didn't care. I wouldn't take my eyes away from my friends in case this was the last time I saw them.

Heartaching a little more with each step they took, I watched Sera lead them into the Dark Woods . Finn brought up the rear. He looked back at me, a sad smile on his face, then put his hand on his heart for just a moment. My promise—to join him in Sunnybrook and marry him—stretched between us—as he turned and follow the others, disappearing into the shadows of the woods.

Chapter 14

"The Dark"

Finn

THE woods were darker than Finn remembered, but maybe they just seemed darker because Erilyn wasn't here with him. He looked back again, hoping to see her for a second longer, but they'd already been swallowed up by the twisted, dark trees. He thought he could still feel her—a shining golden beacon—somewhere behind him. It felt like walking into a snow storm and leaving the warmth of the fire behind, and the ominous feeling of these woods didn't help.

He tried to focus on the others in front of him, on the path that only Seraphina could see, but he couldn't keep his thoughts from Erilyn and what was happening back in Ringol. Had the cave dwellers reached them yet? Was she alright? He could still feel the echoes of her lips on his, and had to fight the urge to run back to her.

But he couldn't do that. He'd made a promise. He had to trust that if something happened to her he would know. He would *feel* it. Or if not, Seraphina would.

He looked behind them again into the dark tangle of trees and sighed. He wished that they were still tied together. She had called it a tether, but to him it had felt like a lifeline. If it were still there, he knew he would be able to tell if she was okay. Finn walked in silence, heart sick, as they moved deeper into the woods.

"Can we take a break?" Lucy asked some time later. The path they were following wasn't a physical one and they had all been navigating around fallen branches and forest litter for hours.

"We need to keep moving," Seraphina said without looking back, her voice flat and lifeless. Rosemarie walked beside her, holding Seraphina's hand, and she glanced back at Finn. Worry creased her brow.

"The path is safe, just like Erilyn said—" the bitterness in Seraphina's voice was undeniable, "but if we stop now there's a chance the animals in these woods will find us." She stumbled over something in her way and Finn could just imagine her scowl.

Aiyanna walked with Lucy in the middle of their party. Her voice was quiet and strained as she said, "I'm not allowing the animals to see us, and there's something about this path—it's hiding us a little, too—but if we stop, I don't know how long I can keep us hidden." She looked over her shoulder at Finn and in the dark.

"If we can just keep going, we should make it out by nightfall." Sera never looked back.

Lucy's shoulders slumped and Aiyanna shifted closer, making Finn ache with longing. He glanced behind him again and was met with darkness.

The air was thick with shadows and the only sounds were of breaking twigs underfoot and their labored breaths filled the air. Thanks to the darkness, off in the distance Finn saw a pale, green glow. He was sure it was the starlings' pond and he was grateful they weren't moving toward it. He could still imagine the fumes from that toxic place and feel the gazes of the giant starlings prickling along his skin.

He turned away from the light and focused on the twisted trees. The tree trunks were thick, the branches gnarled and barren, the bark unnaturally dark with moss and moisture. He'd spent his life in Sunnybrook, exploring the woods around the city, and never had he seen a place like this.

"Why are these woods like this?" he asked, breaking the silence, his voice swallowed up by the bulbous tree trunks around them.

Lucy started at the sudden sound and stepped closer to Aiyanna.

Seraphina's voice from the front of the small group was quiet when she answered. "I think it's the vitium." She paused and looked around before slipping to the right, just between two particularly large trees. "There are huge deposits of vitium in the earth here. I could feel it in Ringol too, but it's especially concentrated here. It reminds me of the vitium caves in Citadel where I grew up, but darker. Almost like it's been mixed with something else, but I'm not sure what." She shivered.

Finn didn't need special abilitiesto feel the darkness Serapina mentioned. Again he looked back, knowing he wouldn't see anything, torn between following his friends out of these woods and running back through the woods to the girl he planned to marry.

EVEN though they were all exhausted, they walked through the rest of the day. When night started to fall, the silent forest came alive. Calls and cries that he didn't recognize rang out from the darkness.

Animals squeaked and squealed. In the distance, Finn heard what could only be described as a roar. They all picked up the pace. Only when moonlight started trickling down through tree branches did he knew they were almost out. The branches were thinner and less gnarled and each breath came a little easier.

After what seemed an eternity, the five of them spilled out into the moonlit field. The darkness of the woods had squeezed them like a narrow cave might and Finn gulped the fresh, open air.

"There's a stream closeby," Seraphina said, voice ragged. "The one we were following when all this started."

When they reached the water's edge, they each dropped to the ground. They weren't safe yet, but they were closer. Closer to the younger children and hopefully to Luna. Finn didn't look back at the treeline they'd just left. Instead, he looked at his friends.

Sera stared out at the small stream, her eyes hard. Besides her, Rosemarie filled water skins in shaking hands. Lucy and Aiyanna sat, shoulder to shoulder. Then he looked to his side, where Erilyn would be, and his breath caught. If Erilyn were here, they wouldn't feel so disparate. So fractured. He closed his eyes and sighed, but all he could see was her face. He hoped with everything he was that she was okay.

"It was her choice," Sera spat into the silence, startling everyone into looking at her. Finn opened his eyes and she was looking directly at him. "Erilyn *chose* to leave us and go after the wylden, then she *chose* to stay with them and send us away." He was surprised to see tears in her eyes, to see her lip quiver the smallest bit.

"I know." Finn tried to be gentle, hoping to help cool her ire, but his admission only seemed to make her angrier.

"I don't understand—" she said, voice trembling, "how she can keep making the wrong choices, but you keep choosing her."

There it was. the thing he'd worried about for weeks, spoken into the night as plain as day. It was a if the earth had fallen out from under him. Even though she was just a child, just barely on the verge of adulthood, Seraphina wanted him to choose her over Erilyn.

"Sera," he said, wanting to reach out and comfort her, but knowing that would only make everything worse.

"No. Forget it," she said, pulling her knees to her chest and hiding her face in her arms. "Forget I said anything." Her voice was once again that of a little girl and he had no idea what to do that could help.

Finn looked over Sera's shoulder to where Rosemarie stood. The tired, wrinkled woman shook her head. Her eyes drooped with exhaustion and sadness as Seraphina huddled in front of her, her pale hair glowing bright in the moonlight.

"We should camp here tonight," Aiyanna said, drawing Finn's gaze. Her expression was soft. "Will you please get some firewood, Finn?" She smiled with tight lips, eyes darting briefly to Sera.

With a heavy heart, he walked along the stream to find kindling for a fire while Aiyanna, Rosemarie, and Lucy comforted Seraphina. When he returned long minutes later, Seraphina wouldn't look at him, but she wasn't hiding anymore and he had to assume that meant things were at least a little bit better.

He gave the wood he'd gathered to Lucy, and Aiyanna squeezed his arm lightly. This was as good as things were going to get for now, but at least he and Aiyanna had finally found an equilibrium. It was a small victory, given the state of things, but he would take it.

Unwilling to say anything that might shatter this brief bit of almost-peace, Finn tried to focus on their next steps. Tomorrow he would be back in Sunnybrook with Asa, Galen, Jubal, Noah, and hopefully Luna. Just the thought of all of them gave him a renewed sense of purpose as he lay on the earth beside the fire. He stared up at the stars through the tree branches, the moon filtering down through the clouds, and he sent up a silent hope that all of them—the children, his friends, Erilyn—were going to be okay.

Chapter 15

"It Begins"

Morrigan

CILLIAN'S arm is an iron band around your shoulder as you follow Erilyn back toward the stinking hole that is your newest prison. *Ringol.* The name is as simple and distasteful as its people.

"You'll need to find somewhere safe to hide," Erilyn says to Cillian. She won't address you. Won't look at you. Now that she's alone, she's too afraid of you and your bare your teeth.

Cillian's hand spasms on your arm and Erilyn sighs, "I know you don't like this, Cillian, but—"

"Whatever gave you that impression?" Cillian spits, his hand a heavy, hot weight against your arm. You have to fight the urge to squirm away. His hold on you keeps you prisoner as much as Erilyn's intentions.

Erilyn stops—the poor excuse for a town just within sight—and turns. Her eyes are red as if she's been crying and you want to slap her. She's crying over Finley, ueseless as he is. She's so weak. So stupid.

"She's unstable," Erilyn says as if you aren't standing right here. "Look at her," she says, gesturing toward you, "the vitium is out of her system and she's still—still *wild*." She looks at you for a moment, nostrils flaring, before her eyes dart back to him. *Erilyn and Cillian in his study, leaning toward each other, sharing meals.* You want to claw her eyes out for looking at him now. "I'll figure out how to help her," she says, her voice and face going soft in a way that makes your blood boil, "but to do that you have to keep her safe right now, which means you have to *keep her here.*"

Cillian is quiet for a long moment. His muscles are rigid against your side, but just before he speaks, they soften. "All right," he says, dejected. It is like a punch in the stomach. She's poisoned Cillian, just like she poisoned Finn. Did she tie him to her as well? Without his vitium dose, would he even know if she had?

"But we aren't locking her up again," he says, sliding his hand down your shoulder to grip your upper arm. "I won't let you do that. I'll keep her with me." He looks down at you, eyes shining with emotion, but it feels far away. You think you may have felt that way for him once, too, but at this moment it's nothing more than a hazy memory, burned away by the fury you feel toward the monstrous girl beside you. "I'll keep you safe," he murmurs, but you can only stare.

You say nothing as you're taken back into Ringol against your will. You have no abilities to read the auras in the town, but things are different than they were when you left less than an hour before. Wylden no longer rush about. Instead, they are stoic, standing silent and still, pieces of rusted metal and fragments of stone in their hands as weapons. *Pitiful.*

"Zeke," Erilyn says as a large wylden—a man with his dark skin and bright eyes who might have been attractive had he been human—approaches.

"Time," he says, his voice a growl that sends shivers down your spine. "*Now.*"

There is a long pause and you wonder what he is sharing with her in that silence. You crave that knowledge and find yourself leaning toward them as if that might help you *hear* and *feel* and *see* again. But there's nothing. Smoke where there should be clean air.

"You can hide in Zeke's rooms." Erilyn turns back to Cillian, expression grim. "The cave dwellers are here. Zeke's felt them." Her voice shakes with fury as she looks at you and you know what she's going to say before she says it. "They have liquid vitium," she spits. "This is your fault."

"She didn't do this," Cillian says before you can speak. You don't like to be spoken for. Don't like to be silenced. "I was the one who maintained the vitium trials. I had the choice to stop them when I was appointed, but I chose to keep them going." He stood taller, his hand on your arm twitching as if with guilt. "I was the one who ordered the capture of Rosemarie—" Erilyn's expression hardens, "and made her work on the solution. Morrigan was brought in after that. She was assigned." His voice—

usually so strong and self assured—is weak and it turns your stomach.

Erilyn looks back to Cillian, full of barely suppressed fury. "It doesn't matter now," she grinds out between her teeth, hands in fists at her side. "Just stay hidden. And keep her with you at all times." She turns as if to leave, but slowly looks back. "I'll come get you both as soon as it's over and—" she pauses and looks at you for a long moment. Her fury seems to seep out of her like steam. "And we'll all head back to Sunnybrook, together."

The image of Rosemarie's cell flashes in your mind, except now you are being held behind the bars. Did Erilyn put the image there? Is it from your own mind? You want to accuse her to assess her guilt, but it's too late. Erilyn is gone, following Zeke toward his pathetic group of armed wylden. You would have followed, would have demanded to know, but Cillian is there, pulling you into the stinking room where Erilyn altered so many wylden and turned them into something less.

There are stairs in the back of the room, hidden behind a door that hangs on a single hinge. Cillian opens it and takes your hand to pull you up behind him. The stairs lead to a narrow hall. Two doors in the hall are jammed shut, but the third opens and Cillian pulls you into what must be Zeke's bedroom. There is an ancient mattress on the floor, covered in scraps of rags and old blankets. The room is littered with artifacts from past generations—a clay pitcher with faded flowers on one side, a chipped cup, a dented metal sign that looked like it was once green and a few letters still visible—*R I N G O L*.

The room stinks like an unwashed body and you wrinkle your nose while Cillian moves around, touching each strange item as he goes. Then he turns to you, hands in his pockets, and sighs. You know that sigh. You've heard all of his sighs at one point or another and can recognize most of them for what they are—sighs of anger, of passion, of frustration, of sadness—but this one is new.

Outside, you can hear noise that suggests the battle will soon begin, but the window is boarded up, so all you can do is listen using only your ears. You feel drawn to the fray about the begin and bristle at being trapped in this stinking room. Cillian walks up to you and gently takes your hands in his.

You start to pull away, anxious to press your ear to the boarded up window to hear something, anything. But then your gazes meet and for a moment the fight leaves you and you get lost in his silver eyes.

Chapter 16

"The Nightcrawlers"

Erilyn

FURY from Cillian's admission coursed through my veins, but it would have to wait. Zeke and I walked toward the frontlines through wylden who watched us with wide, vitium-colored eyes. This close to so many people, I couldn't keep their feelings from washing over me. But I used what I'd learned in my time with the wylden to determine how much I saw and felt instead of letting it overwhelm me as it once would have. I focused on their auras and saw a rainbow of pure light, pulsing and rippling with fear and nervous energy. Their auras ebbed and flowed together without mixing, but all of them were touching and unblemished, and I was caught up in how beautiful it was.

My mind drifted to Finn, to the way his green light had looked when Fia and I had healed his injuries, and I wondered what it might look like for his aura to ebb and flow with mine like this—free and untethered.

Distracted by my thoughts, I was caught off guard with a sugged surge of nager off to the side. Zeke continued making his way through the crowd, but I stopped. A group of wylden stood together, weapons ready like all the rest, but their auras were spiraling and spinning with unspent anger. A deeper look showed something shadowed swirling inside their auralights.

Sensing my eyes on them, one of them looked at me and his anger struck me like a fist, making me stumble back. I threw up the walls that I'd used since I was a child to protect myself and nearly ran to Zeke.

When I reached him, he was moving between wylden, silently sharing support and encouragement. I touched his arm and showed him what I'd seen. The darkness seemed to originate in their centers where Finn's light had been the strongest.

Zeke sighed. He patted my arm and attempted a smile. "Not worry," he said with a nod toward the group. "Good fighters."

They were ready to fight, that much was for certain, but their anger had felt too big for this one battle and I worried about what would happen after. But this was his fight, is people, and I nodded and followed him to the very front of the line to wait.

The moon rose, bright enough to see by, but it would be our other senses, our abilities, that allowed us to meet the cave dwellers when they came.

We stood at the mouth of an old mine, just outside of town. It was pitch black inside but the darkness wouldn't be a hindrance to the people of Citadel. My only solace was that with the wyldens' heightened senses, the darkness wouldn't hinder them either. In this fight, I was the only one at a disadvantage.

A knot of fear formed in my gut. Maybe Sera had been right—maybe me staying behind was foolish. I was risking my life, my future, in this fight which didn't belong to me.

But then I felt Fia and Dill nearby, their auras brushing against mine as if they were squeezing my shoulder for support, and my nerves calmed. I was here to help them—these wylden who were now my friends.

We stood for a long while in the moonlight, listening to the wind whistle over the mine's mouth. The wylden seemed calm, almost content as they stood and waited, but anxiety prickled at my skin like a limb waking up after falling asleep. With each moment that feeling grew until I felt something in the air shift.

And then they appeared.

Garbed in dark clothing, uncharacteristic for the people of Citadel, the group of cave dwellers walked almost silently into the moonlight. They weren't afraid of the moonlight as I'd expected them to be, or of the wylden in front of them. Instead, they marched with purpose. I could have convinced myself these were different cave dwellers than the quiet people of Citadel, but there was no mistaking the man who led them—Aiyanna's father, Chief Roark.

Roark was a large man, at least for a cave dweller, with a full white beard and ropey muscles that spoke volumes about the amount of food he was allotted. Most cave dwellers were small and light, like Aiyanna and the children, so a man like Roark stood out. Anger surged in my chest at the sight of him. This was the man who'd kept me, kept the children, in vitium caves to try and breed soldiers. The man who'd beaten Aiyanna when she was small.

I hated him.

The cave dwellers with him pooled around the sides of the mine entrance, but Roark approached us. Heat swelled in my gut as he got closer and I had to take a tight rein on the power inside me. Just like when I'd shaken the earth after the death of my glowworms, my feelings wanted to let this power out. This man was a danger. It was because of him that I could do what I could do, but the process to get here had nearly killed a whole cave full of children and many others since.

I felt the heat spread into my limbs and beside me Zeke tensed. Why was I holding it back? This was the one time nnot being in control would achieve a goal. I'd nearly died when I'd run from Citadel because of Roark. He was why I'd escaped to the upworld, why I'd suffered weeks of burns. If it hadn't been for Rosemarie—

It was as if I'd been splashed with frigid water and the heat in my finger tips receded back to my core. Roark's abuse had led me to Rosemarie. To Luna. And eventually, to Finn. The fire in my belly shrank until it was nothing more than an ember. Zeke relaxed and gave me a quick nod as Roark stopped just in front of us.

I could *see* the vitium-fueled energy flickering inside him, and inside all the people with him. Their skin was artificially darkened with what had to be the same cream we'd found in the cabin and used on Aiyanna and the children. If it weren't for their white hair and pale eyes—all in varying shades of blue and pink—they might even pass for upworlders.

Roark looked at Zeke for a long moment, appraising him, then his gaze flicked to me. His eyes widened in momentary surprise, then they narrowed.

"Erilyn," he said, his voice low and menacing. The energy around us crackled and made the hairs on the back of my arm stand on edge. He was letting me see his power in order to cow me. I wasn't sure if that showed his arrogance or his fear.

"Chief Roark," I answered, happy there was no vitriol in my voice. Zeke was at my side, tall and strong, and I could *feel* Fia and Dill nearby. I wanted to punch Roark in the face, but he couldn't know that. Not yet. I would give nothing away that he might exploit later. I had to be strong as I faced him for both the wylden I was with as well as Aiyanna.

"Ah. Is my daughter with you?" he asked, as if he could read my thoughts. Then he smiled at me, his lips turning up in a way that was almost feral. I'd pictured Aiyanna's face too *loudly*.

"She's gone," I said, putting everything all of my energy into shielding where they'd gone, and his face darkened. If he thought she was dead, all the better.

Maybe he wouldn't look for her if things in this fight didn't go our way. If nothing else, maybe I could protect her from him.

"No matter," he said as he rolled his shoulders as if to relieve a pain. Behind him, the cave dwellers were silent. I *looked* at them and *saw* their fear, their hesitancy, but that didn't mean they weren't still dangerous. What had he done to make them come here? I'd grown up in Citadel and I knew that most cave dwellers were content to stay beneath the earth. I had been the outlier, anxious to leave. He had to have done or said something to them to bring so many of them upworld.

"Are you in charge here?" he asked me as he sneered at the wylden gathered behind us..

"No," I said. I saw Zeke straighten and lift his chin. Compared to Zeke, Roark was pitifully small. "But I'll speak for them." Zeke shifted toward me, his teal aura a comfort for the first time in the long days that I'd known him. I looked at Roark's people—at *my* people, whose auras flickered like recently fed fires—then back to him. "How have you gotten these abilities, Roark?" I whispered, unable to keep my curiosity at bay.

Roark's smile made my skin crawl. "The people of Sunnybrook gifted their solution to us," he said. I felt a shiver of fear as It hought of Finn and the others—if Sunnybrook had allied themselves with Citadel, it would mean that I'd sent Finn and the others straight into danger. Zeke felt my panic and his mind joined almost softly with mine. With our shared power I was able to look into Roark's mind to *see* the truth behind his words.

"Not all of Sunnybrook," I almost sighed. In Roark's mind I'd seen the patrolmen who'd met with him, felt their trepidation, as they'd delivered the liquid vitium solution in exchange for rare stones. Roark's face hardened. "It was only a few people. A few disgruntled members of the patrol."

Roark stepped back with a sneer and shoved me from his mind. His aura—a bright, sickly green that reminded me of the toxic pond in the Dark Woods — flared.

As his aura pulsed with a display of power, it wavered. Unlike the wylden, who held their auras steady and full, these people were only strong because of the liquid vitium they'd ingested. Just like Morrigan. But unlike her, they were untrained. Unused to the effects of the solution.

The wylden behind me exuded a variety of emotions—fear, anger, sadness, anxiety—but they were all secure in their abilities. It was as much a part of them as their hands or feet. I couldn't stop my smile as I realized we had the upper hand.

Roark glowered at me. He had no idea what his peoples' limitations were and my pity for him outweighed my hatred. But he was arrogant and brash, he would push his people past their limits. Even though I knew we were stronger, there would be unnecessary bloodshed tonight. I wanted the wylden to win, but I didn't want anyone—wylden or cave dweller—to die.

"What do you want, Roark?" I asked and Zeke shifted toward me.

"Fairness," he said, his voice gruff. "For my people."

Zeke growled low in his throat, but I was reading his intentions as quickly as he experienced them. "Then why did you come prepared to fight?" I asked.

Roark scoffed. "Too long we have been imprisoned in darkness beneath dirt and rock." He motioned upward toward the open sky—the bright stars and full, white moon. "We aren't ignorant of the ways of the upworld," he sneered. "To gain this, we know we have to *take it.*"

"You don't." I shook my head, but he only laughed—a dark sound.

"Then what of this?" he asked, motioning toward the army of wylden behind me. "Is this your idea of a peaceful welcome?"

"We felt you coming," I said, hands balled in fists at my sides. "We felt your intention—your anger and aggression!"

"It doesn't matter." He took a single step back toward his people. "The people of Citadel will get what is rightfully theirs."

I'd been so focused on Roark and Zeke. I wasn't paying attention to the other cave dwellers. So without warning, there was an explosion of sound, images, and lights in my mind from the wylden people around me. A group of cave dwellers had tried to sneak into Ringol and collided with the wylden with shadowed auras. The clash of auras and steel and fists rippled through our ranks like a wave and the other wylden and cave dwellers sprang into action.

Pain and anger raged around me like a wildfire in dry grass as the fight began. We'd been spearated in the fray, but Roark darted toward Zeke. If he died, the future peace between the wylden and upworlders would be over before it began. I threw myself between them, hands outstretched, but a cave dweller tackled me to the ground before I could do more than inhale, a sharp knife raised above me. I *shoved* him off and scrambled up. Zeke was still standing, in the center of the fray and holding his own against Roark and a few others. Fia was at his side, hair flying around her, as she fought, her hands and feet lightning quick.

Chest heaving, I looked around. Again I had the thought that it had been foolish of me to stay behind, as if my presence could turn the tide of this battle. I should have gone with the others. Should have stayed with Finn. But it was too late for that.

The fight continued and the wylden were pressed back into Ringol. I was helpless to do anything except move with the tide and do my part against the invading cave dwellers.

It was so dark, even with the moonlight shining down. Everyone moved so fast that it was hard to tell individuals apart using my eyes. The children had taught me to *feel* them as they hid, and I used that now. Eyes closed, I *looked* at all the people around me. The wyldens' auras glowed brighter and more steadily than the cave dwellers. And on top of that, they *felt* different. They were familiar. Sweeter.

I'd fought before and no matter how I did it, each time I hurt someone I felt their pain echoed back inside me. But this time, it wasn't just me. I was part of the ocean of aura-light that was the wylden people and together we pressed on.

The heart of the fight moved deeper into Ringol, into the streets where my friends had stood only hours before. The elderly wylden were hiding with the children in a building on the edge of town and I could feel their fear through my connection to the wylden. I could feel Cillian and Morrigan too, hididng in Zeke's rooms, and even though I was angry with them, even though they'd caused me no end of pain and grief, I wouldn't let the cave dwellers find them. I'd told them I'd keep them safe, that we would all return to Sunnybrook, and I intended to keep that promise.

I was so focused on Cillian and Morrigan that a cave dweller caught me off guard. A knife sliced through the arm of my sweater and blood poured from the wound, soaking the fabric at an alarming rate. Volcanic heat filled me up and I shoved my hands toward the woman, throwing her. She flew through the air and bowled into a clump of people, knocking them all to the ground.

The pain in my arm shocked me back into the present. All around bodies and auras collided. The air was rent with the sound of clanging metal and screams that ripped through the night. I covered my arm wound with my good hand and focused on the pain, on knitting the wound back together. When blood sopped pouring through my fingers, I wiped my blood on the hem of my sweater and looked all around. I couldn't turn the tide of this battle, but I could find my friends. I could try and keep Fia, Dill, and even Zeke safe.

Eyes closed again, I *reached* until I felt them—Zeke's thick teal liht battling Roark's malignant green, Fia, pulsing navy alongside Dill's cool maroon as they circled each other together like a single mind. They were all okay, so I let my awareness expand more, into the light that connected the rest of the wylden. They were angry—lifetimes of an instinct to survive no matter what roaring forth— but thanks to the work we'd done, their auras were stable. They were holding back instead of giving in to that animal part of them that said to rip and shred until they were the only ones standing.

The cave dwellers' aura-lights jumped all around like water poured into a hot pan. They weren't used to this much power and it was causing them to behave recklessly. They were burning through their vitium without any regard for the damage they caused. It was a painful, violent stalemate—the cave dwellers pushing, the wylden holding their ground.

The children had tried to teach me how to be part of a whole and I used that knowledge now and kept my feelings wide open, listening and watching through the auras of all the wylden. I felt the tide turning in our favor as the cave dwellers started to flag. I was part of the wylden and they were part of me. I floated among their auras, watching, listening. Because of this, when the first cave dweller was killed, I felt the hot spray of blood from their slashed neck as it soaked into the earth. I fell to my knees in the dirt and a scream tore from my throat. But I wasn't the only one who felt it. The group of wylden who worried me came alive. One of them held the bloodstained knife—I could see it through his eyes—and as the cave dweller's heart pumped it's last, their shadowed auras sang for *more*.

I forced my eyes open and stumbled to my feet. Stomach heaving, I vomited into the dirt.

No. We'd been winning. No one had died, but now, all around the dead cave dweller the pitch of the fighting increased and it was spreading through the rest of the ranks. Fresh fear blended with an almost insatiable rage. It was too much. All of it.

Heart smashing against my ribs so hard it felt as if they might crack, I ducked behind an old, broken water barrel and pulled my knees against my chest. The pain of the cave dweller's death echoed through the marrow of my bones and I couldn't stop my body from trembling in shared pain and despair. It had been naive to think there would be no death here. I squeezed my eyes tight, trying to will it all to stop. But out in the street the battle raged as their fervor grew.

It hurt so much, so I did all I could and hid—like when I'd hidden beneath the roots of my tree, like when I'd hidden in the caves as a child, like I'd hidden all my life.

But I had stayed behind in Ringol to help. Not hide.

Heart in my throat, I gripped the edge of the barrel and looked out into the fray. I found the wylden man who'd killed the cave dweller straight away. Dark blood splattered his face and hands and in the moonlight he bared his bloody teeth and let out a war cry. His aura, and his companions' auras, swirled with shadow.

I needed Zeke. He could stop them. Contain them. Using my eyes and my *sight*, I looked for him. I spotted Roark quickly—taller and broader than the rest of his people, white beard spattered with dark blood—but he wasn't fighting Zeke anymore. Panic flared white hot in my chest. Without Zeke, the bloodthirsty wylden would run rampant. I stepped wanted to come out of hiding to look more effectively, but I couldn't risk getting distracted by a fight of my own. I searched, pouring all of my energy into finding him, and finally I *saw him*. He was engaged in another fight, but he was alive.

It would not be easy to get to him—he was surrounded by cave dwellers who were coming after him hard. I stepped out from behind the barrel, intent on heping him, when the next person died. And then another. And another. It was like a chain reaction had been set off and Ifelt rooted to my spot as their agony and fear washed over me.

It was too much. Each death was one too many.

This had to stop, but I needed help. I couldn't do it alone. My mind was reeling from all of the pain I was absorbing and I couldn't think. I needed—

"Help," Fia gasped as she broke through the colliding bodies, shoving people aside as if they were made of cloth. She grabbed my arm—wincing when she felt the echoed pain from my knife wound—and pulled me to a crouch with her in the darkness. "Needed me," she panted. Her lip was split and her clothes were torn, but she was here. She was okay. I pulled her into a hug, my whole body shaking with relief.

As I held her, grateful for her heartbeat and her labored breaths which showed me that she was alive, I shared with her my fear—the shadowy wylden on a bloodthirsty rampage, destroying any chance at peace, killing the cave dwellers without mercy.

Fia pulled away, eyes wide, and looked toward where the first man had died. Death didn't affect the wylden like it affected me, but now she was seeing it through my eyes.

"I don't know what to do," I croaked, gripping her arms with claw-like hands.

"Push," she said after a moment, her voice low. Her vitium-blue eyes almost glowed in the moonlight. *"Push below,"* she growled. In her mind I saw us joined, pushing the desire to retreat into the minds of the cave dwellers, doing it all at once, just like we'd done with all the wylden children. The cave dwellers wouldn't be expecting it. They didn't know how to influence others with their emotions. We could catch them off guard and end this quickly.

"Can we do it alone?" Icy fear slogged through my veins at the thought of this failing, of more people dying.

Fia shook her head. "Not alone." She took my good hand, laced our fingers together tight, and closed her eyes.

Together, we dove into the collective pool of the cave dwellers' auras. It was all too big, too massive to shift, but before I could give into my despair I felt other wylden join us—first Zeke, then Dill. Then others. It wasn't all the wylden, but it was many. We were an ocean of light.

Fia squeezed my hand. Just like when I'd led her and Zeke through healing the auras of her people, it was my job to lead us here. My empathy would be our guide. The wylden were the power behind the throw, but I was the head of the spear. I let my power pool in my belly and within it I felt it being fed by the power of all the wylden with me. Once I felt so full I thought I might burst, I pushed a thought into all their minds at once, so gentle it was like urging a child to bed.

Time to go home.

I held my breath as I waited. Nothing happened at first and I felt the heavy weight of hopelessness settle. In the periphery of our shared awareness, I felt more deaths—diluted through the countless wylden auras joined with mine—but still I winced as that pain settled in my bones like an old wound.

There had already been too many lives lost. This had to work.

I doubled over in pain as I felt a new death—a knife in someone's belly. It felt different than all the others and I had to fight to catch my breath around the pain. While they other deaths had felt like echoes, this one felt as if it were happening near me. To me. My heart beat an uneven cadence as tears sprang to my eyes. I took a steadying breath as I pushed past the pain and focused on getting these people back to their home beneath the earth.

Home, I thought again, tears in my eyes as I pushed a little harder. I pictured Citadel as it looked in my memory, painted in the faint light of glowworm lanterns. The scent of rich, wet earth. The warmth of their beds in the dark. The quiet. *Home.* Though I had no great desire to ever return there, I knew what it felt like to want to go home and I let that feeling infuse all the rest.

The shift happened quickly. Cave dwellers backed away, confused, and the wylden fighting them allowed them to. Those not joined with me could feel what we were doing and added their auras to the *push*. Only the shadowed wylden kept attacking at full force, their rage a stifling black cloud around them. Zeke and Dill, still connected to me, moved between the angry ones and the cave dwellers who had begun to retreat. In the distance, I could see Roark, angry, confused, looking all around in confusion as his people were moving back toward the mine instead of further into town. He was shouting orders—I'd never heard a cave dweller shout so loudly— but they weren't listening. The cave dweller's auras were flickering now, their vitium-fueled abilities nearly spent, and as the last few passed by Roark, I felt the defeat settle across his shoulders like a mantle. He stood on the edge of town, looking back toward us. His power was still bright, still strong, but without his people with him, he was as good as powerless.

Zeke and Dill held the wild, angry wylden at bay as Roark, with a last, longing look at Ringol, gave in to my *push* and left as quickly as he'd come.

Chapter 17

"Loss"

Morrigan

CILLIAN smiles down at you and you remember the first time he smiled at you like that. He was so beautiful and so powerful that he made you feel beautiful and powerful, too. Made you forget about Finn.

But that was long ago—before vitium, before wylden, before you'd tasted *real* power.

"Are you okay?" he asks as his hand cups your cheek. His warmth seeps into your flesh and you hate how much you crave that feeling.

"Yes," you respond, though you aren't sure that's true. Is he tying your will to his and making you say this? Or are these feelings yours? You think you might want to kiss him, so you do, and he softens against you as his lips mold to yours. When you pull away you grip his shirt and say, "Cillian, I need you to help me get away from here." If he were tethering you, you wouldn't have been able to say that. Empowered, you try to push him to comply before you remember that your abilities are gone.

"We should stay until the fighting's over," he says, brow creased in concern. His thumb drags over your cheek and the friction makes you shudder with longing. You wonder if Zeke's bed is clean enough to lie one and fight the urge to kiss him again. "I need to keep you safe," his whispers, his breath ghosting over your damp lips.

Conflicting emotions rage inside you. Something soft and hopeful blooms in your chest while bitterness roils beneath it. Sweet and sour. You feel torn down the middle.

"Cillian," you say, stepping closer to him. Your hands are flat on his chest and his hands find your waist. "Please." You say it as a whisper and press into him slightly.

His pupiles dilate and his breath catches.

"We can run away," you say, as you look up at him through your eyelashes. "Just you and me." You meant it as a bribe, an enticement, but as the words leave your mouth you find that you want that, too. You imagine being with Cillian off somewhere in the wild—making love under the stars, living on your own terms—and for a moment it feels like you are filled with liquid sunlight.

But then a noise outside—someone crying—pulls you back and the images in your mind are replaced with Erilyn. All that liquid sunlight is washed away in red as you envision yourself driving a knife into her throat.

"Morrigan," Cillian says, voice gruff. His hands leave your waist and find your cheeks. He brushes your unruly hair behind your ears and looks down at you as if asking for permission before softly kissing your lips. His mouth banishes the image of Erilyn for a moment and you let yourself float in the soft warmth of his touch.

"I love you," he says, resting his forehead against yours for a few beats of your heart before he leans back. "I'm sorry I—" he searches your eyes, his hands on your cheeks suddenly too warm. "I'm sorry I haven't been better about showing you that."

Flashes of memories tinged with sadness fly through your mind—they feel silvery and cool, and you know that somehow, even without vitium, you're seeing into his mind.

Erilyn entering Sunnybrook and Cillian's guilt-ridden pang of desire to tether her. How he'd secretly enjoyed the thrill of trying to tame her and make her his.

You in your patrol leathers, sunlight bathing your skin, and Cillian's desire which is so strong you feel dizzy. His guilt as he puts distance bteween you and him in public so his feelings for you—so intense they hurt—don't jeopardize what you're both trying to acomplish.

You grit your teeth as his memories invade your mind. It feels like you're seeing them, but not like he's consciously sharing htem. Almost as if you've managed to sneak in and see the things he most wants to keep secret. Maybe he has tethered you, maybe not, but now that you know exactly how he feels about you, you have the upper hand.

"It's okay," you say as the memories fade. You take a breath. You still want to kiss him, but you feel more in control that you have in a long time. His warmth no longer lulls you. Instead, you want to scream. Want to claw his face and run—for wanting her, for not wanting you enough to make you properly his—but you need him to get free. And some part of you still wants him to run away with you, to make him yours in every way that you can.

The battle outside still rages. If you're going to leave, now is the time. You know if you stay, regardless of what Erilyn promised, she will make you stay here with the wylden, powerless. Or she'll kill you.

Cillian looks toward the boarded up window and you see the moment he makes the decision to help you. "We can slip away in the fighting," he says, a newfound fire in his eyes. He squeezes your upper arms and his palms are warm through the sleeves of your shirt. "We can make it back to Sunnybrook before Erilyn. " He stares down at you and you're struck by the sudden urge to kiss him again, so you do. He sighs against your lips, then takes your hand, lacing his fingers through yours. He is leading you by the hand, but you know you are in control now. You let him pull you back out into the narrow hall.

You are trembling with anxiety to be away from here, but even more than that, anxious to find more vitium. You are tired of feeling like you're only half awake, of feeling like you are at the mercy of those around you. Cillian will help you find some. He'll take it with you and together you'll be unstoppable.

Cillian pauses at the front door and turns to you. He kisses you again, slow and deep, and you let yourself get caught up in this moment. Once you leave here, you'll be running and there won't be time for this. And while your goal is to get away, you want to make time for this. For his mouth and hands and breath. When he pulls away he smiles at you, tucks some hair behind your ear, then pulls the door open and tugs you through.

The shock of the fight is exhilarating as you step into the open air. Wylden and nightcrawlers battle all around and your fingers itch for a blade.

Cillian's grip on your hand tightens as he pulls you down the broken steps and pulls you between two buildings. He's surveying the area, looking for a clear path. You think it's foolish to stay here—you should be putting fast distance between this stinking town and yourself, using the fight as a distraction—and you are a moment from telling him that when a nightcrawler appears. His chest heaves and he holds a long, curved knife in his pale hand.

Cillian steps between you and the danger. He shoves you back and you stumble. He glances at you to make sure you're okay, afraid he's hurt you. You want to scream at him, but he spins back around just in time for the nightcrawler to plunge the wicked blade into his stomach.

Time slows.

Cillian seems frozen there, knife sticking out of his belly, dark blood seeping into his stained shirt, and you forget to breathe.

Then time kicks back in like the rebound of a slingshot and Cillian falls back. The nightcrawler holds onto the knife as it slips from his belly, slick with blood, and Cillian lands in the dirt at your feet.

You lunge forward, heart in your throat, a scream tearing from your throat. The nightcrawler lifts the blood-slicked blade toward you and hisses the word, *"Beast!"* But you barely hear. Barely comprehend. Inside your chest liquid fire roars fourth. It fills you like molten metal and blasts away from you, sending the nightcrawler flying back into the fray. His shoulder clips the wall and a small pouch he wears tied to his arm falls to the ground.

Your blood is calling for his. You want to go after him, to hurt him, *to kill him,* but Cillian grabs your ankle and you stop, ice replacing the fire inside you. You see him, see his blood-soaked shirt, see the darkness dribbling from the corners of his mouth. You fall to your knees and press your hands to the wound, but blood pours from between your fingers, hot and horrible.

"I can fix this," you whisper.

Cillian coughs up blood. His teeth are stained dark with it. You close your eyes and search for that power you just felt, the power that filled you up and exploded from you, the power that you know can save him, but there's nothing except dreadful emptiness. "No!" you scream, pressing your shaking hands into the wound harder to try and staunch the flow of blood. "No no no."

"Morrigan," he says, coughing again, and you're back to yourself. His face comes into focus and you feel hot tears racing down your cheeks. "I'm sorry."

"I can't—" You keep pressure on the wound as you search for words, for help, for something. "I'm sorry, Cillian. I can't do—"

"I love you," he says, his lips grotesquely pink, even in the darkness. His eyes are going dim and you know if you could see his aura, it would be too—silvery light evaporating like smoke. *I love you.* His lips move without any sound.

"I love you, too," you say, though you aren't sure you know what love is.

But Cillian smiles like he believes you, his eyes locked onto yours. You can't stand the look you see there—trust and love—so you lean forward and press your lips to his. He tastes like iron as his last breath slips past your lips. When you pull back, the light is gone from his eyes.

"Cillian." You say his name as if that might change something, but it doesn't. "Cillian," you choke out, voice ragged. You pull your hands away from his belly and stand. You expect his eyes to follow you like the always have, but they don't.

Cillian.

Heart trying to escape your chest, you dart toward the corner, the taste of tears and blood on your lips. You cough as vomit threatens your throat, but you hold it back. Your foot bumps something and you look down, trying to see through the tears in your eyes. You blink and blink until you can see again. It's the pack that fell from the nightcrawler's arm when you threw him.

With numb fingers, you pick it up. Open it. Inside are several small, glass jars, wrapped in leather. They make your fingertips hum and you lift one up to the moonlight. Your heart skips as the dark blue liquid sloshes against the glass.

Vitium.

Cillian is forgotten for a moment as you remove the cork from the first bottle and down the bittersweet liquid without a second thought. There's a beat of nothing, a breath, and then the world around you explodes with sensation. You take a shuddering breath as you *see* and *feel* and *sense* where everyone and everything is.

It's like taking a breath after being held underwater for too long.

Senses roaring forth you identify the nightcrawler that killed Cillian heading away from Ringol. You try to take in everything at once. You want to go after him, to punish him, but you can also sense Erilyn. Sense her *pushing* the cave dwellers out of this putrid town.

With a sudden burst of hope, you turn and your eyes find Cilian's. You search for an aura, for any wisp that you could grab onto to bring him back, but it's gone. He's gone.

The nightcrawlers are leaving. Erilyn is pushing them out of town through the sheer force of her will. And all you can think is that she didn't push them out quickly enough. Cillian is dead, and it's her fault.

Cillian's blood is cooling on your hands, but all you know is you need to find her. You need to kill her while you can, before she realizes you aren't waiting like a chained dog in those stinking rooms. But you look down again and at Cillian's lifeless eyes. His hand is open as if asking you to take it. To follow him away.

You feel frozen. How can you leave him here? How can he be gone?

You are standing in the shadow of the building, frozen with indecision, when Erilyn approaches and your choice is made for you. You are grateful for the darkness as you duck behind some old crates and hide your aura from her eyes and mind. The fresh vitium courses through your veins and you push away the pain of Cillian's death to focus on the power at your fingertips.

Anger simmers in your chest. She's coming to check on you, to make sure you're still a penned beast. Your eyes dart to Cillian and something in your heart contracts painfully.

You clench your fists but force yourself to remain hidden. She steps up to the door to Zeke's home and stops when she sees it's ajar, then turns toward the alley where you are hiding. Where Cillian fell for the last time.

As if she already knows what she will find, she walks slowly, shoulders curled, and when she sees Cillian's body she stops. Her yellow aura grows pale with sadness.

This is your chance. She's alone. Distracted. Exhausted. *This is your chance.*

Power wells inside you, ready to burst forth and end this, end her. But then she kneels beside his body. It feels like your blood has crystalized in your veins. You want to knock her away when her hand moves toward him. To scream that he doesn't belong to her, that he was always *yours*, but all she does is put her hand on his unmoving chest, her aura watery as if it were adulterated with actual tears, then reach up and gently close his eyes.

"Wherever you are," she says, pulling her hand back as she stares down at his face, so handsome even in death, "I hope you find peace."

Unable to move, you watch as she stands and steps back. She looks toward the alley's opening, and even though you can't read what she's thinking—if you tried, she might sense you—you know she's calling for someone. A moment later, two wylden approach and deftly, but gently, lift Cillian's body and carry it away.

It's quiet where you're hidden and the air is growing colder.

You're alone now.

Alone.

You think about Cillian—his soft lips and warm hands—and about Erilyn's kindness to him in the end. She'd wished him peace. After all he'd done to her, to Rosemarie, she'd wished him peace.

It takes everything in you not to scream as rage explodes in your chest. After that kindness to him, you aren't sure you'll be able to kill her.

It's her fault he's dead, you tell yourself. *She didn't purge the nightcrawlers from Ringol in enough time. She didn't let you both leave with the others. It's her fault Cillian is gone.* But she'd also made sure you were safe in Zeke's rooms. You were the one who'd dragged Cillian from the safety of that space into the fight. Toward his death.

It's your fault as much as it's hers.

So, you can't kill her. At least not now. But you also can't forgive her for his death. You can't forgive her for taking Finn away and turning him against you.

Finn. With Cillian gone, Finn is all you have left. She stole him from you, poisoned him against you, but maybe you can get him back. You feel like you have to get him back.

If you leave now, you can beat Erilyn back to Sunnybrook. *It'll be easier without Cillian,* you tell yourself. You'll move faster. And now you have a reason to go back. To get to Finn. To make him love you again.

You stare at the bit of earth stained with Cillian's blood for a long moment before you move. It's easy to hide with so much vitium racing through your veins, and you have the rest secured to your arm—a calming weight.

Sticking to the shadows of the rickety buildings, and then the shadows of the trees, you *search* for the dark forest. Aiyanna is hiding Finn and the others are hidden from you, but you don't need to find them to get back. You aren't afraid of the woods, of the birds, of the toxic lake. In this moment, you are all power. You are infinite.

Pushing Cillian from your mind, you run toward Sunnybrook and toward the only thing that might lend some peace to your fractured life.

Chapter 18

"Tension"

Erilyn

I'D never held any great love for Cillian, but it didn't make it any easier to watch two wylden men carry his body away. He'd lied to me, tricked me, tried to control me, but even with all of that, deep down I thought he might be a good person. Or at least, not an inherently bad one. I put my hands on my stomach where I'd felt that pain before, the same place Cillian had a wound. The contents of my stomach threatened to come up. I'd felt him die, and I hadn't even realized it was him. I'd been too caught up in what was happening with the cave dwellers, and because of that, he'd been alone.

The wylden burned their dead, but they were going to bury Cillian. I wanted Lucy to be able to come back and say goodbye. My stomach cramped with guilt. I'd sent her away and her brother had died. I was leaving a path of destruction and death in my wake.

But I couldn't worry about that. At least not yet. As much pain as Cillian's death had inflicted upon me, there were other things I had to deal with first.

Like the fact that Morrigan was, without a doubt, missing. I *looked* for her in Zeke's rooms, but I knew she wasn't there. Cillian wouldn't have left without her. Everything seemed to be falling apart.

Saturated with grief and worry, I went in search of Zeke. More people had died than I'd realized—both wylden and cave dwellers—and the bodies were being separated. I found Zeke along with Fia as they oversaw the loading of cave dweller bodies into the back of one of their rickety wagons.

"Where are you taking them?" I croaked. I hadn't realized so many had died. After that first, painful death, I'd hidden myself from the pain of the others. Now I wished I hadn't.

"Caves," Zeke said, face solemn. I could feel his intention now as easily as Fia's—I was surprised to find I didn't find it at all distasteful now that he wasn't trying to convince me to join with him—and he showed me the cave where they would take the bodies, so the cave dwellers could retrieve their dead. I knew, from my time living in Citadel, that the dead were taken far from the city and buried deep in the earth. Burning them would be an insult, and Zeke knew that.

Along with this knowledge, I could feel Zeke's sadness as well as his confusion. He'd never felt this sort of pain over the loss of life. I tentatively let my awareness expand to *feel* the other wylden around us. I was shocked to feel similar sentiments from everyone nearby. And while it was painful to share in this new set of emotions, and I hated that this happened at all, their newfound empathy it removed any reservations I still harbored about healing, and aligning myself, with them.

Dill was there as well, silently moving bodies, lifting them gently onto the wagon. He really was a mountain of a man, but when he lifted the cave dwellers—so much smaller and more delicate looking than him—I couldn't help but admire his gentleness. I reached out and nudged his mind, and he looked at me, his face a mask of grief as tears slipped silently down his cheeks. They left trails in the dirt and blood spatter there and I imagined wiping them away as I might for one of the children.

Fia stood off to the side, statuesque, but her eyes never left Dill as he moved through the bodies. I took her hand and gave it a squeeze. Even though her expression was blank, inside she carried a deep well of sadness that made me catch my breath. But I didn't let go.

With Dill in charge of the rest, Fia, Zeke, and I headed back toward town. Fia's hand clung to mine.

"This can't happen again," I said as Fia leaned into my shoulder the tiniest bit. Cillian's eyes, devoid of life, flashed in my mind. "The cost was too high."

Zeke hummed in agreement, but said nothing else. The wylden were a people of few words.

We made it to Zeke's rooms and walked up the few steps, the heaviness of the past day weighing us down. "We need to stop this from happening ever again."

I wanted to get back to Sunnybrook, back to Finn and my friends, but I couldn't leave while the wylden were in such disarray. The entire population—all except for that small, angry group—were low. It was as if the feelings of the few were leaking into the rest. We were floating in an ocean of sadness.

"Lace," Fia said. She looekd at me first, then let her gaze rest on Zeke. "Upworld, crawlers, and Ringol." The raspy quality of her voice was gone and had been replaced with something soft and almost sweet.

"What does that mean?" I didn't know the word, but her tone of voice made my hands tingle.

"Lace," she repeated, then pressed her palms together and slipped the fingers of one hand between the fingers of the other. "*Tie.*"

She met my gaze again and I was overwhelmed with the images and feelings she shared with me.

Tendrils Finn's aura braided together with auras of my gold. Both auras—gold and green—pulled toward each other.

Then, the children—vivid pink, sky blue, violet, dusty rose, pale yellow—their auras were also connected. I'd never noticed before becuase there was no braiding, no tendrils, they all just ebbed and flowed into one another in a sea of light, just like all the wylden I'd seen.

My vision was blurred with tears as she showed me Finn again—lying on the floor of Zeke's home, his aura reaching for me along with his hands. Me, my golden aura held so close, pulling away from him so much, that it was almost hidden.

As Fia showed me these things, as my heart ached for Finn anew. As I let Fia's feelings wash over me, I felt Zeke's guilt. He'd broken that connection.

I had been wrong about my tie with Finn. So very wrong. A person could forcefully tether an aura to theirs, as Morrigan had done, but that was not what had happened between Finn and me. It wasn't what had happened between Sera and the other children. Not what was happening between all the wylden. Tears coursed down my cheeks and I clutched my stomach as the absence of that connection truly hit me for the first time. As I saw how beautiful it was for the first time.

Fia cocked her head to one side as she waited for me to process. "Lace all people." She *showed* me groups of wylden, cave dwellers, and upworlders, all connected, their auras a singular, multi-colored ocean of light.

Zeke's vitium-blue eyes were bright. His previous guilt shifted to fierce hope and determination.

"A truce?" I asked, my voice rusty. Fia nodded and Zeke smiled.

It sounded wonderful, almost too goo to be true. "What about—" I *pictured* the group of angry wylden, the ones who'd drawn first real blood and called for more after the fight had ended. "Will they agree to this?"

Zeke's smile fell away and he growled low in his throat. I expected more conversation, but without any other warning he left us as he went out into the night.

The door shut behind him and Fia pulled away from my mind, the lovely feelings of lacing slipping away with her. The room was dark, lit only by moonlight from the window. Without anything to distract me, real life rushed back.

"Cillian died," I said into the quiet, needing to voice it to someone. "Morrigan's gone." Fia stood silent. I looked at her in the dark. "I need to get back to Sunnybrook. to the kids." I thought of their beautiful auras all laced together, and even though Fia had never met them, I knew she would *see* and understand. Finally I whispered, "I need to get back to Finn."

"Lace again," she said, a sad smile on her angular, lovely, face. *Again*—the word itself sparked hope in my chest.

"It can happen again?" I whispered. I'd assumed that when Zeke had broken our connection, it was permanent. "The tie—I mean, the *lace* with Finn?"

Fia nodded, her eyes still a little sad. "Strong lacing," she said.

I had so many questions for her—why she was sad, how she knew our tie was strong, how e we were supposed to do it again—when we heard a loud scream from outside.

The two of us darted out the front door. In the middle of the street stood six wylden, vitium-blue eyes shining, teeth bared. It was the same group, the ones with shadows in the auralights, that had frightened me before.

Zeke and Dill—both big and imposing—stood in front of them.

"Fight!" the wylden in front shouted. His voice was a deep growl that was almost unrecognizable as human.

I looked at his aura—choppy and frantic like a bolt of electricity that wouldn't dissipate. Shadows still swirled within the light, though it wasn't jagged and broken like before. His gaze shot to me and his eyes narrowed. "You," he growled, and then he lunged toward me. His intent to kill me was thick and sour like curdled milk.

I gasped as he forcefully joined his mine with mine, the connection like broken glass digging into my skin. He let me see his people as he saw them—their aura-lights dim, strength gone, broken and ruined.

He only made it a few steps before Dill and Zeke were between us. Dill shoved me behind him, his maroon aura flaring with fury.

"Nico!" Zeke screamed as he shoved my attacker, his voice loud and imposing. He stood over the wylden man, now prone on the ground, his chest heaving. "No more death," he said, his words dripping with power. Other wylden had gathered around with the noise and power like moths to a flame. The other five angry wylden clustered around their fallen friend as he stood in their midst.

"Lace," Zeke said to all those gathered. "Grow." He held his hands out as if in invitation.

Fia took my hand. Through the connection that all the wylden shared, I saw wylden, upworlders, and cave dwellers, all together, auras blending and flowing into each other in a sea of light. It was all saturated with a feeling of cool peace. Through the wylden bond—the lacing of their auras that seemed as natural to them as breathing—I felt their amost universal acceptance of this plan. They'd all changed so much in the past few days.

Only the shadowed me remained apart. The man who shoved me—Nico—got in Zeke's face, breathing heavily, spit flying from between his teeth. He growled and clenched his muscles, but Zeke remained still. Nico's anger grew as he stepped back and spit on Zeke's feet. His companions were behind him, half-crouched, ready to fight. His eyes darted past Zeke and locked with mine. *War. Destruction. Power. Death.* That's all he held inside. I did my best to keep my face as neutral as Zeke's was, but the hairs on my arms stood at attention.

Nico looked from me, to Zeke, then spun in a slow circle and looked at all the people gathered. He called to them through their laced auras and asked them to join him. His chest was heaving, his eyes alight with his plea, but no one stepped forth. When he realized he and his few companions were alone, his aura flared.

"Go," Zeke said, his thick voice sad. The moonlight was bright, but the wyldens' vitium-colored eyes were brighter. Like animals' eyes when they reflect firelight. "We will lace with them." He enunciated each word slowly, using a complete sentence as if to make his point.

The six men in the center bristled. A hum of threat hung around them as they readied to fight. But there were only six of them, and many more wylden ready to fight for Zeke.

After another breath that was thick with tension, the six men turned and ran from Ringol. The wylden parted to let them through.

Zeke's shoulders slumped in relief and exhaustion and the other wylden slowly drifted away, back to their homes. Everyone was so tired and the pain of the fight, of losing so many, of all that had changed, made every breath feel like a chore.

I swallowed a lump in my throat as Zeke rejoined us. Dill still stood in front of me, protecting me even though the threat was gone. I put my hand on the ropey muscles in his arm and he relaxed and stepped back.

"Lace," Zeke said, his voice tired. "Ringol and—" he paused, cocked his head to one side, then said, "Sunny-brook." He nodded. "After, crawlers."

"Citadel," I said, and he nodded.

"Tonight, we burn." His voice broke. His face was tight with strain. "Tomorrow, Sunny-brook."

I wouldn't be going back alone. To lace our people, we needed it couldn't just be me that returned.

"We'll go together," I said, fear and excitement weighing equally in my chest. The people of Sunnybrook were going to be hard to convince that the wylden weren't a threat anymore, but I knew if I could just show them how they were now, it could work.

"Together." Zeke put his heavy hand on my shoulder and I didn't flinch away. We would go to Sunnybrook together and I would speak for them. Just like with Roark, they would be the power, but I would be the head of the arrow.

Chapter 19

"Clear"

Finn

DAWN crested the horizon and trickled through the winter-trees and Finn and the others woke. Achy and cold, Finn covered the cooling embers of their fire with damp soil and they left their campsite in almost complete silence. Just like the day before, Rosemarie stayed with Sera, Aiyanna with Lucy, and Finn was left to walk alone. He wouldn't let himself think of Erilyn. After Sera's reaction the night before, thinking of her would only lead to strife. Instead, he focused on getting home and what to expect when they arrived.

They'd only been gone from Sunnybrook a matter of days, but so much had happened in that time it felt like much longer. He was anxious to hug each of the children again and hopefully to find Luna with them, safe and sound.

As they walked, Finn tried to figure out how far from Sunnybrook they actually were. He felt lost out here. Their initial journey from Sunnybrook to find Erilyn had taken a complete day of walking with almost no breaks. The path Zeke had given them through the Dark Woods had been in a different direction, and Finn wasn't sure if it would be closer or further from the city wall. Thinking about it made his head hurt.

"It's about the same," Seraphina said, looking back over her shoulder and meeting his eyes before quickly looking ahead again. "The distance, I mean. We should make it to Sunnybrook by nightfall."

Normally, a slip like that—thinking so loudly that she could hear him—would have made him feel embarrassed and probably a little angry. But now, after all they'd been through over the last few days, he was just grateful she was talking to him again.

With all of his concentration, he focused on how he felt, so that if Sera was still listening she would understand. He let his love for her—pure and strong, though in no way romantic—be his main focus. He wanted her to know that no matter what, he would always be on her side. He wasn't sure exactly how to convey that with just emotions, but he tried his best, and when she looked back at him and gave him the smallest of smiles, he thought he might have succeeded.

"So, what are we going to do when we get back?" Lucy asked as they stopped briefly to rest and drink some water from their waterskins. "Without my brother, it might get dicey, especially with Aiyanna and Sera with us. " Her hand found Aiyanna's and their fingers laced together.

"All we can do is share with them the truth," Rosemarie said as she pulled rations from her pack. She always seemed to have more food in her pack than the others and Finn wondered how much she was eating herself if she had so much to share.

Lucy's gaze locked on Rosemarie. "So we're just supposed to waltz up to the gates, ask to speak to the council and say, 'We're back, and we brought some cave dwellers with us. Oh, and by the way, Cillian's off with Morrigan, who's crazy now, and with Erilyn, who you all think told the wylden to attack us. They're with the wylden as we speak, but don't worry, because they're nice now?'" Lucy's voice grew louder and louder until the apples of her cheeks were red. Aiyanna wrapped Lucy's hand in both of hers and squeezed, but Lucy seemed unaffected.

"No," Rosemarie said, her voice soft and patient as she handed Sera some of the food the wylden had given them. Seraphina wrinkled her nose at the charred nuts, but ate without complaint. "But we should tell them about how the wylden have changed, and that Cillian is with them to work toward peace."

"All right," Lucy said, still scowling. "So, a half-truth. But how do you propose I explain, not only Seraphina and Aiyanna, but you—a person long thought dead—and Finn, who they all assume was killed by Erilyn months ago?" She looked around at all of them and seemed to deflate. Aiyanna watched Lucy with unblinking eyes. "We just haven't thought this through." Lucy sighed. "None of you understand. You weren't there. The wylden attacks made everything in Sunnybrook so much different than it ever was before. The people—we—we were afraid, and fear is powerful."

Finn tried to think of what Cillian would do in this situation. He didn't know Cillian well, but he thought he knew him well enough to figure out how he would spin this. "We'll ask to talk to the council," Finn said from where he sat off to the side. "Cillian's with Erilyn. The fact that he stayed with her, that he trusts her, has to count for something. And as his sister, they'll listen to you, Luce."

"And the wylden?" Aiyanna asked as Lucy clenched her teeth. "We've seen that they've changed, but I don't think the people of Sunnybrook will blindly believe us when we say they're not a danger anymore."

"Having you there will help," Rosemarie said, her voice warm. "You can speak for your people, Aiyanna. Many in Sunnybrook don't even believe cave dwellers exist. Hearing you will give credence to what we say about the wylden."

"But I don't speak for my people," Aiyanna said, her voice unusually harsh. Now it was Lucy's turn to try and calm her with soft looks and a squeeze of the hand. "My father—" She exhaled heavily through her nose. "I want nothing to do with him, and so I want nothing to do with them." Finn would have believed her, had her voice not broken at the very end. She may hate her father, but she loved her people.

Rosemarie nodded and absently stroked Seraphina's hair. "Even so," she said, her voice gentle.

"You can represent them. And I—well, I will stand for the wylden." She swallowed heavily. "Darling—a wylden man that Morrigan set to guard me—was my companion for some time. She left him to die, but before that we found a sort of equilibrium. And after my time with all the little ones in Ringol..." she trailed off. "I can speak for them."

"Will you tell them where you've been?" Seraphina asked, her voice soft as she looked up at Rosemarie, all of her newfound hostility gone. "What Cillian and Morrigan did to you?"

A sad smile crossed Rosemarie's weathered face and she pulled Sera into her side and pressed a kiss to the top of her tangled hair. "No. At least not yet. That will just cause more division. What's done is done and we need to set the stage for peace, not invite more confrontation." She kissed Seraphina's hair again.

Finn watched Lucy's face as her ire drained away. There were dark circles under her eyes and for the first time he really noticed how worn down they all looked. He'd been so focused on finding Erilyn that he'd stopped noticing the way the others' shoulders slumped or the way their eyes were always half-closed with exhaustion.

Their exhaustion weighed heavily on him, as if it were somehow his fault. He wasn't sure when Erilyn would come back—surely the fight was over by now, or maybe they'd been able to avoid it altogether—but instead of focusing on that, as he couldn't be sure either way, he decided he would use his time for other things. Erilyn was strong and smart. She would take care of herself, and while she did that, he would take care of the others.

He looked up from his thoughts and caught Seraphina watching him. Her eyes wide, but her expression was blank. He smiled, again focusing on how much he cared about all of them, not just Erilyn, but she looked away.

"We can be in Sunnybrook by this evening," Rosemarie said as her eyes darted between them. "Right Sera?"

The young girl nodded, then shivered. Rosemarie tightened her arm around Seraphina's shoulders. Each day was warmer than the last, but drifts of snow still dotted the landscape and the air still held onto the last vestiges of a winter chill.

"Let's build a fire and have some pine tea, then rest a bit while we come up with a more solid plan." Rosemarie looked at Lucy who nodded reluctantly.

"Finn, will you get some firewood with me?" Aiyanna asked. She squeezed Lucy's hand. Finn nodded and followed her into the woods while the others gathered pine needles for tea.

For a few minutes gathered wood in silence— enough for a small fire. But when they were far enough way for the others not to hear them, Aiyanna stopped and faced him.

"I know you haven't always liked me," she said, voice as quiet as always but now more self-assured than it once was. "And we both know why that is."

Finn felt his heart stutter. He'd never thought they'd have this conversation, had never wanted to. But they were alone in the woods and he owed it to her to hear her out. He nodded, but his lips felt glued shut.

"I never meant to fall in love with Erilyn," she said, her voice forthright. She stood a little taller, though her cheeks flooded pink. "And whether you believe me or not, I never deluded myself into thinking that she'd ever love me back."

Finn narrowed his eyes. "That didn't make it any easier for me to stand by and watch," he said, surprising himself with the bitterness in his voice. He cleared his throat and exhaled heavily, letting go of as much of that animosity as he could in the face of Aiyanna's forthright honesty. "She never saw it, though, I don't think. Never realized how you felt."

Aiyanna smiled a small smile and shook her head. "She didn't. And I'm glad she didn't. I wanted—no, I needed you to know that I don't feel that way about her anymore." She ducked her head for a moment, then looked back up at him again, the tiny frayed braids she wore in her hair swinging with the movement. "I needed to clear the air, to lay it all out on the table, because I need to talk to you about Lucy," she said quietly. Finn felt the last of his anger toward Aiyanna—something he hadn't realized he stilled carried—slip away.

"She's like my little sister. Finn adjusted the sticks in his arms.

"Well, I don't feel the same about Lucy as I did about Erilyn." She bit the inside of her cheek. "With Erilyn it was almost like, by loving her, I could erase all the horror of our shared past." She blinked rapidly to hold back tears and looked up at him. "I tried to kill her once, you know," she breathed. "When we were children."

Finn nodded, but held his tongue, giving her space to speak.

"I *wanted* to kill her," she whispered as her eyes went unfocused. "For knowing what my father had done to me, I wanted her to suffer like I had." She bit her top lip so hard it left a divvet just below the bow. "I hated that anyone knew my shame. So when I met her again all those years later, I think that I needed to *love* her to make up for how I'd felt them." Her eyes glistened. "And I do love her, but not—not like I love Lucy." A few tears slipped down her pale cheeks, each lifted in a soft smile. "I love Lucy because she's—she's temperamental and passionate and kind and—" She trailed off and shrugged, then used her shoulder to wipe a stray tear from where it dripped from her jaw. "I just needed you to know that. Because we're friends now and—and I know you care about Lucy, too."

Finn sighed. "I'm happy that you and Lucy found each other," he said with a small smile. "And for the record, I like you now, Aiyanna." His smile turned into a smirk. "But I can't say I'll miss the looks you used to give Erilyn."

She smiled and ducked her head, her pale cheeks once again pink. "Well. You can watch me give those looks to Lucy from now on." She gave him a smirk of her own. "We should gather more wood," she said as she shifted the small stack she carried in her arms. Finn laughed and nodded.

Back with the others, Sera lit the small pyre, just as Erilyn usually did. With only the sound of the fire crackling, Rosemarie made some hearty pine tea from their gathered needles. Finn reached into his pack and pulled out a cup—an old, dented, metal cup with people painted on the side. It had been Erilyn's when he'd met her and she'd told him she'd always hated it, but holding it now made him feel closer to her.

He glanced over at Aiyanna, who smiled bashsfully as Lucy whispered something in her ear. Near them, Seraphina had her eyes closed as she rested her head on Rosemarie's shoulder. Her face was smooth and young-looking without the new scowl she wore most of the time.

Almost content, Finn sipped the hot tea, spicy pine washing over his tongue. The flavor reminded him of Erilyn's clearing. She would join them soon, and then things would finally exactly as they were supposed to be.

THE pine tea revived and refreshed them and the rest of their walk back to Sunnybrook went quickly and smoothly. Aiyanna had a new lightness to her step as she trekked beside Lucy. And while Seraphina was still quiet, she too seemed like she carried less than when they'd left Ringol.

When they reached woods he recognized, Finn sped up, no longer needing Seraphina to guide him. They were close to home, which meant they were close to the children and hopefully to Luna. Once he was back with them, they could all wait for Erilyn to return together. Only then would he let himself worry about the proximity of the Dark Woods to his home.

When the wall around Sunnybrook came into view, it was all he could do to not run to it. He needed to get into town to find Mehri's apartment so he could make sure the littlest children were safe and sound.

Finn had wanted to sneak in through breaks in the wall, just as they'd left, but Rosemarie had talked him out of it. If they wanted this peace with the wylden to be taken seriously, they had to be as forthright as they could. So they made their way to the gate that stood between two large, white trees. They approached slowly, hands held out so that it was clear that they weren't hiding anything. As expected, members of the patrol drew weapons—bows and arrows—as soon as their small party was within sight.

Finn and Lucy stayed in front of Sera and Aiyanna while Rosemarie stayed to Sera's side. The two cave dwellers were in more danger than the rest of them. But when the patrolmen saw Lucy, they lowered their weapons and smiles lit up their gaunt faces.

Haggard looking, the patrolmen waved their group through the gate, which hung crookedly from half-broken wooden hinges.

"Your brother's gone," one of the patrolmen said to Lucy as he descended the ladder that led to the landing beside the gate. "He's been gone for days." His face was tight with tension. "We looked for you when he disappeared, but you were gone too, and—" he was young and his eyes were wide as he sighed. "We're just glad at least one of you is back."

"Cillian was with me," Lucy said, straightening to her full height. She'd always been tall—almost as tall as Finn. "He was detained." She didn't look around, but Finn thought he saw a slight blush infused the skin between her freckles. "He should be back soon."

"That's all well and good, but what are we supposed to do until then?" the second patrolman asked. He looked even younger than the first—barely a teenager.

"Surely the council—" Lucy started.

"The council just fights and fights. While they fight about whether we should hunt the wylden down or reinfornce the walls to hide, the rest of us just wait." The younger man sighed and pushed his unwashed hair away from his face. "Food's been rationed while they decided and everyone's afraid and hungry." He scrubbed his hand over his face. "We can't keep going like this, but with you back..." he trailed off, raw hope in his eyes.

Lucy was just over seventeen, but she straightened further and nodded. She reached back without looking and took Aiyanna's hand. So far, the patrolmen hadn't given Aiyanna or Seraphina a second look and Finn wanted to keep it that way. The sun cream disguised their skin and extra shirts wrapped around their heads like scarves hid their snowy hair, but they were still strangers.

"I'll talk to the council. They should elect someone to stand in Cillian's stead until he can make it back." Her eyes darted to Finn and he took an involuntary step back. That was not a role he wanted.

The older patrolman, who looked close to twenty, said, "But you're Cillian's sister. It should be you." Relief tingled along Finn's skin.

Lucy opened her mouth to protest, cheeks red, but Rosemarie stopped her with a wrinkled hand on her shoulder.

"Can you call a town gathering, young man?" she asked. Even though she wore dirty, ripped clothes, her voice held an edge of authority. The older one nodded. "Wonderful. Have them all ready this evening and Lucy will address the people. The meeting hall should be big enough, I think?"

He nodded, looking more relaxed now that someone was calling the shots. "We're glad you're back," he said as he looked back to Lucy, a shy smile on his narrow face, and then he and his partner were off, running into the town to let people know there was going to be a town meeting.

"A speech for all of Sunnybrook?" Lucy asked, voice shrill as she rounded on Rosemarie. "What am I supposed to say?"

"You're going to stand in for your brother and tell your people, *our* people, what's been happening." Rosemarie nodded, lips pursed together. "Tell them *all* of it. We have to get them ready. If I know my Erilyn as well as I think I do, she'll be coming soon, and I doubt she'll be alone. She's healed the wylden—an impossible feat—and I would wager her next move will be to try and bring peace between them and us. If the people of Sunnybrook aren't ready for that, it could get ugly very quickly."

At this, Lucy sobered. "Okay," she said. "Alright." She turned to Aiyanna, fingers still connected, and her voice went quiet. "I don't know what to say."

Aiyanna smiled softly up at Lucy. She was quite a bit shorter, and a few years older, but they fit together just right. She brought Lucy's hand to her lips and kissed the tips of her fingers. "We can figure it out together."

They were all safely inside the gate and they had a plan. Finn couldn't wait any longer. "If you all have this," he said, drawing the eyes of the others. "I'm going to go find the kids. I'm sorry. I have to know if they're okay, and I'm not sure I'd be much use with a speech anyway."

Lucy looked over his shoulder, then back to him with the first real smile he'd seen from her in a long time. "Looks like you'll have an escort."

Finn's heart stuttered as he spun around, and a smile just as broad as hers split his face. Luna bounded down the street toward him. He knelt just in time for her to skid to a stop. Her paws landed on his shoulders and he wrapped his arms around her, almost falling backward as she gave him her best approximation of a hug. She purred loudly and butted her head under his chin and against his cheek, long tail whipping about, paws heavy and warm on his shoulders.

"I'm glad to see you, too," he said, voice thick with emotion, as he scratched between her ears. She rubbed her cheek against his, her thick whiskers trailing along his skin. Her fur was soft and warm and relief washed through him at finding her healthy and whole. She mewled and looked around. "She's not here," Finn whispered as he continued to stroke her fur. "She'll be here soon though." Luna head butted his chin again. "Can you take me to the kids?" He pictured the four little ones anyway, walking away with Mehri as he'd last seen them. He had a feeling Luna could sense more than he realized.

He stood and she sat in the dirt in front of him. The injuries she'd suffered days before had healed beautifully thanks to Seraphina. Luna chirped and went back the way she'd come.

"Coming with me, Sera?" He turned to the young girl who had her arms crossed over her chest. She reminded him a lot of Erilyn, bu he did his best not to share that thought. After a brief pause she nodded, and with a wave to Lucy and the others, they silently followed the large white cat through the streets of Sunnybrook.

It was strange walking through Sunnybrook in the daylight, Sera at his side, but it also felt right. As if she and the others had always belonged here.

Mehri's apartment was in a building near Lucy's. Finn used to live close by as well, but that seemed like a lifetime ago. He wondered if his things were still there, though he'd taken most of it to his workshop when they'd been here before.

Luna walked straight to Mehri's door, which was on the ground floor, and put her paws up on the wood, stretching her muscles as she did so. The door swung open and Luna dropped back to the ground.

When Finn had seen Erilyn for the first time after his confinement, it had felt like seeing sunlight after being in the darkness for far too long. When he saw the children now, the feeling was remarkably similar.

Sera darted into the room before he could step a foot over the threshold and he watched as her four siblings—not by blood, but by choice—surrounded her. Even without abilities he could feel their love like a tangible presence in the room as they silently held each other.

He walked inside and closed the door behind him. Mehri was off to the side, a cup of tea in her hand, which she offered him.

"They told me you were on your way," she said, smiling at the quiet reunion. "They're such special children."

"They are," Finn said. He took the warm cup of tea and nodded in thanks.

The five children were huddled and silent, for a while. He knew they were sharing things that he couldn't hear or see, but this time he wasn't jealous. More than anything, he was grateful that they were all together again. He sipped his tea and waited, able to breath for the first time in days.

After a bit, one by one they drifted away from Sera and came to him. He sat his tea down and crouched as they hugged him, four sets of tiny arms finding places to cling as he did his best to hold them all. Relief rushed through him with the feel of their little hands and arms, followed swiftly by grief that Erilyn wasn't here, too.

"Eri will be okay," Galen whispered against Finn's cheek and he pressed his eyes closed.

"Are you all okay?" Finn asked, pulling back to really look at them. "You all look bigger." He couldn't keep a smile from his face as he took all four of them in.

Asa stepped back, standing tall with a proud smile.

Tea back in hand, Finn sat on one of the overstuffed pillows Mehri had for chairs. Galen went to Mehri, who lifted him onto her hip. Noah and Jubal each grabbed one of Sera's hands and pulled her onto a second seat, while Asa scooted onto the cushion until she was sitting pressed against Finn's side. In the middle of it all, Luna lay on a rug in the middle of the room, watching Finn with big, expectant eyes.

"Mehri has been giving us a *lot* of food," Jubal said, smiling as he lay his head on Sera's shoulder. "We probably have grown!"

"Luna *showed* us you'd been taken," Noah murmured, her eyes big as she held onto Sera's hand. "We were afraid for you."

"I'm sorry about that," Finn said, putting his arm around Asa's shoulders as she snuggled contentedly into his side. "But we're all okay. Rosemarie's in town with Lucy and Aiyanna, and Erilyn will be back as soon as she can. Everyone is excited to see the four of you."

"We'll see them at the meeting," Noah said with a yawn.

Mehri looked puzzled, but before he could explain, a knock sounded on the door. Mehri handed Galen to Finn and then answered the door, making sure to keep it mostly closed so whoever was out there wouldn't see the congregation of children inside. The patrolman who'd knocked spoke softly, and as the door closed, they could hear him knock on the next door down.

"We're all to go to the meeting hall in half an hour," she said, and Finn nodded.

"The children will need sun cream," he said as he started to dig in his pack. "And hats or scarves to cover their hair.

Mehri nodded. Together, they covered the children in the skin-darkening cream and protective clothing, then headed into town to hear what Lucy, Aiyanna, and Rosemarie had decided to say.

Chapter 20

"Run"

Morrigan

THE wylden are distracted and you escape so easily it's pathetic. They are carrying the bodies of their dead to a nearby field to be burned. The field is rich with vitium. They are nearly silent as they work, but you can be silent too. Besides, they are broadcasting their broken hearts big and wide and aren't looking for you as you slip past them.

They are weak and they are stupid. Before Erilyn neutered them, they knew better—to stay quiet, stay hidden, stay fierce. Now they are nothing more than screaming voices and shining lights just asking to be destroyed.

You sneak past them, past the wailing inside their heads and the dull, painful beats of their hearts, and enter the Dark Woods where all of their sound vanishes as if it never existed at all.

Startled, you stop and let your awareness expand. The wylden are *screaming* so loudly you should be able to hear them for miles. The woods are so *quiet* after the cacophany of Ringol that it's disorienting. The woods are dark—the moonlight barely penetrates the branches—and with each step the light dims. As you adjust, you start to *hear* and *feel* the things in the forest, though you still cannot *hear* the wylden outside of it.

Far in the distance are the starlings that you'd hoped would kill Erilyn. Around them are other animals that you didn't sense before—massive cats, strange wolves, so many others that are too small to tell apart. They all feel twisted. Dangerous. But you aren't afraid.

Ignoring the animals, the birds, the potential for danger, you take off at a good pace, trusting your instincts to guide you and if need be, to protect you. You have to make it back to Sunnybrook. To Finn. You struggle to remember why you ever gave up on him. He needs to know that you can be together again, because without Cillian—

Cillian's pallid face. Blood on his lips. The taste of iron after you kiss him.

His warm hand holding you against him. Keeping you with him.

You trip on a root and sprawl across the ground as Cillian's face and hands and essence invades every part of your mind. Your senses are overwhelmed with the memory of him and you feel a wail rise up in your mind and in your throat.

His hot breath on your neck as his lips trail kisses from your shoulder up to your lips.

His eyes are molten as he says, "I love you."

I love you.

The scream bubbles up inside you, but you don't let it escape. It echoes inside your head and for a moment you understand the wylden and their cries. For one brief, blazing moment, you are one of them, mourning, screaming with every fiber of your being at the injustice and pain of having lost him. For a moment, you don't care who hears you. All you care about is Cillian. That he's gone. That you are without him and your insides feel like they may burst into flame from the pain you feel.

The animals in the woods stir, called by your silent cry, and with monumental effort you stop. You shove the anger and pain back down until it's nothing but an echo reverberating in your skull.

Chest heaving, face wet with tears you don't remember falling, you push yourself out of the dirt. The woods are so dark you can't tell what time it is. But it doesn't matter. You can find your way to Finn no matter what. He's all you have left. A beacon in the endless night.

Under control once more, you put one foot in front of the other. Without your emotions in the way, you keep part of your mind locked on the animals that you alerted to your presence with your cry—strange, dark lights, slinking through the forest toward your pain.

In the distance, a wolf howls, followed by the howling of others. Their voices blend in dissonance until it sounds like a single voice. You stop to *listen* and hear twigs snap. There are big cats—bigger than any cat should be—stalking you. The big cats stalk you, but they aren't close enough to be a danger yet. They are tracking you from too far to be using only their natural senses, and you put forth some energy to *hide*.

With part of your *senses* tracking the animals who hunt you, you let your mind drift back to Finn. How you'll get him to come with you. You can't tether him again—Erily somehow ruined that. It will have to be his choice. You'll have to convince him that you're better for him. Remind him of why he loved you. All before she returns to Sunnybrook and infects him again.

He loved you first. Before her. Before the world broke apart at the seams. Before Erilyn showed up and destroyed it all.

Hot, sticky anger coats your tongue as you realize you missed your best chance to kill her. In a moment of weakness you let her live. Because of her treatment of Cillian's body—

Blood seeping from his mouth. Light seeping from his eyes. His hand reaching for you.

Pain rebounds in your chest, your breath hitches, but it's only for a moment. You keep it in. You push the pain back again and keep moving. You could have killed her, should have killed her, but you didn't.

You have to do something to slow her down, to give you more time with Finn in Sunnybrook where all of this began.

The wolves howl again in the distance and you stop to listen. There are so many noises and *sounds* to pay attention to. When you came through these woods the first time in the middle of the day, aside from the starlings, everything had been quiet. The animals must wait for the dark. You can feel their dark, pulsing energy in the woods all around.

If Erilyn is going to return to Sunnybrook, she will have to come through these woods. She will wait for day, but you have a plan. You stop looking for Sunnybrook and instead *find* the starlings' pond and head straight for it. As you move, you find veins of vitium beneath the earth and draw from its power. It *feels* different than vitium normally does, but you drink it in, the vials of liquid vitium still a comforting weight against your arm. You grow stronger as you move and with conficence you reach out to the wolves, the ig cats, and call them to you as you run.

If Erilyn can command a single, pitiful white cat, you can command these creatures. You're stronger than she is. Better.

You run until you can see the green glow of the pond. You stop just outside the light of the pond and methodically build a small fire. You have time and you need the advantage of the heat and the light.

Once it's crackling, the flames struggling in the damp air, you sit on the putrid forest floor and wait. Eyes closed, you let your fury—that Finn chose Erilyn, that you've lost control of Sunnybrook, that Cillian is dead—fill you up and surround you like armor. Some of the animals—small, twisted rodents and reptiles—sense you now that you aren't hiding anymore and take off, running away from how brightly you burn. But a few are curious and approach with caution.

They stop outside the ring of firelight and you open your eyes. Even in your revulsion you smile. A cat stands in front—massive, hairless, black as ink with thick, ropey muscles covering its frame. It's so dark, only the light of the flames reflecting off it's dark eyes and shiny skin allow you to see it with your eyes. Behind the cat are two wolves. As if in opposition to the cat, the wolves have an abundance of black and gray fur that fluffs around their faces. They're smaller than normal wolves, but their teeth are sharp and drip far past their lips. And finally, the starlings—the large, oily black birds that live near the polluted water—have strayed from the safety of their pond and wait above you in the trees, bending the tree branches they sit on with their abnormal weight.

They all watch you, watch your aura, as you continue to burn. You'll have to bind them to you for your plan to work. They are probing you, trying to figure out what you are. They haven't realized you're a person and before you do, you'll need to bind them to your will.

You think of Darling—the first wylden you ever tethered—and remember how empowering it felt to tie his will to yours. He had bent to your will like wax warmed by the sun.

You take a moment to prepare, to steady yourself, and then dive into all of their minds at once. You do not hesitate. Do not hold back.

The cat screams, the wolves cower, the birds spread their wings as if to take flight, but you're fueled by necessity and anger and before they can do anything more you have them roped like wild horses.

It only takes a few seconds. When you come back to yourself, they've all settled. They bristle only a bit as you tighten your reins. The cat adjusts first and approaches the fire. It blinks and turns its face from the heat. You cringe at the sight of it—black, hairless skin shines in the firelight, and thick muscles distort its proportions. If you couldn't *feel* it, you might not even be able to tell it is a cat. The wolves stay at the periphery of the firelight and watch you. You can see them more clearly now and are only a little bit surprised to realize they are attached at the shoulder and side. The birds are the only ones that still seem agitated, though they have settled enough to stay in the trees above you.

You take a satisfid breath and ignore the putrid air as it fills your lungs. Erilyn has her little cat, but these creatures are yours. They will keep Erilyn away. You *show* them Erilyn, show them what you need to do. You compel them and they accept your directions—they have no other choice.

In control, you relax a little as the exhaustion from the last few days catches up with you. Before you travel to Sunnybrook, to Finn, you need to rest. With a yawn, you lay down beside your tiny fire and close your eyes. The big cat lies a few feet away, eyes on the first. The wolves and prowl around the periphery of the firelight. A smile graces your lips as you fall asleep. You aren't afraid because your new pets will protect you. They have no other choice.

Chapter 21

"Obstacles"

Erilyn

DAWN was near when the last of the bodies were ready for the funeral pyre. All the people of Ringol had gathered. I stood off to the side with Fia. It was eerily quiet in the field.

Funerals had been quiet in Citadel, too. Whenever someone died, the community would surround them and sing, glowworm lanterns in hand. Their song was barely a whisper, but it called other glowworms from where they rested in the nooks and crannies of nearby caverns. By the end of the dirge, the whole space was filled with bright blue-green light as all the worms pulsed in rhythm with the melody. Then, when the song ended, the glowworms would crawl away. The glowworms in the lanterns would go dark, and the whole space would be absolutely dark. It was only after that that their bodies were taken far into the earth the be buried.

While almost everything about this was different, there was soemthing in the air that felt the same—the bodies in the field, surrounded by the survivors and the sound of wind rustling through the damp, dead grass carried a similar melancholy.

We stood in the field until the sky started to lighten from blue-black to a deep orangey-gold. As the sun's light started to stain the sky, I heard a sound that resonated in my head and chest. A deep hum. A vibration. It was the wylden, humming low in their throats. What began as a single, low tone started to shift and change as different voies took up the song. I couldn't sense a pattern, there was no discernible melody or rhythm to the vibration, but it was beautiful.

When the sun crested the horizon, the vibration shifted. Sunlight seeped into my skin, the cold from the night was banished, and through tears I saw the bodies on the funeral pyre begin to shimmer. The sunlight dripped around them like honey and the shimmer intensified.

I was unprepared for the flash of light as the pyre ignited. I drew back and shielded my face, but when no sudden blast of heat came, I returned my attention to the fire. The flames that engulfed the bodies burned steadily in a rainbow of colors—like their auras were burning away. I waited for the smell of burning flesh to hit me when the wind shifted, but it never did.

The fire grew at an unnatural speed. A fire this size should have damaged the surrounding woods, should have spread, but it stayed contained. As the sun rose further, the fire grew.

The sky lightened to gold, and then a bright, pale, blue and the fire died away as quickly as it started, leaving a large pile of ash. Together, the wylden moved away from the pyre, toward the edges of the field. As we moved, the wind shifted and lifted the ash. As if guided by an unseen hand, the ash hung suspended in a fog over the field, only to float down and cover the dead grass like the finest layer of black snow.

Throughout all of this, the hum had remained a steady presence in my ears, and vibrating in my chest. One by one, the voices started to fall away. The vibration lessoned until all that was left, again, was the sound of the wind rustling the branches of trees and stalks of dead grass. And yet the ash on the field remained where it lay. When the last voice faded away, the wylden turned, silent once more, and headed back toward Ringol. With one last look at the ash-covered field, I followed.

BACK in Zeke's rooms, the air was thick with sadness. Dill sat on the floor, head in his hands, while Fia stood a few feet away watching Zeke pace back and forth. He locked eyes with me as the door shut behind me. Their auras— Zeke's vitium-blue, Fia's navy, Dill's maroon—were watery and thin.

"I'm sorry about your people," I said, my voice feeling like an intrusion.

"Gone," Fia said, her voice gravelly with grief. My heart ached along with hers as she showed me the gaps in the ocean of light that made up the wylden people.

"I can't bring back those you've lost, but maybe we can heal these wounds by lacing our people together." I looked at Fia, then at Dill, who'd returned his head to his hands. "Back in Sunnybrook."

Dill's head snapped up, his teal eyes sharp at the mention of me leaving. Fia placed her small hand on his massive shoulder and he slumped again.

"I care about you," I said. "But until there is peace between your people and the upworlders, none of us are safe." I wanted them to *feel* how the people of Sunnybrook felt about them. To know why this was important.

"They know how you *were*, but not how you are now." I addressed Zeke, who watched me with hooded eyes. "I know we can find peace, but that can only happen if I go back to Sunnybrook."

After a moment of tense silence, Dill stood to his impressive full height, unfurling like a stalk of wheat in sunlight. His face was wet with tears and his eyes were bloodshot, but he looked at me and nodded, his aura thickening slightly as he moved past a little of his grief.

Zeke nodded as well, though his face was unreadable. Fia smiled, but I knew she would be with me no matter what.

"Others," Zeke growled and a few breaths later the door opened. In walked four more wylden—two women who could be twins, both with vibrant auburn hair and freckles, an older man with deep wrinkles, and a boy who had to have been around my age. I wanted to ask why these four people, but if I wanted Zeke to trust me, I had to trust him.

"With us." Each of the four nodded and bowed their heads—not to Zeke, but to me. I blushed as the air warmed around me.

IT was midday before our whole group was prepared to go. As we were leaving, Zeke went to the wylden man with the light pink aura who'd been healed along with Dill. He placed his hand on his shoulder and stared into his eyes for a moment, then the other man nodded gravely. I thought Zeke's shoulders dropped a little as we walked away.

"Lead," Zeke growled as he joined me.

The wylden who were coming with me had tried to mimic the way I looked with their clothing. Their faces were mostly clean and their clothes, though tattered, were as neat and tidy as I'd ever seen them. Their long, stringy hair had been tied back with bits of string. They still didn't look quite like upworlders, but they no longer looked like the wylden they had been. Our group was meant to be a bridge between Sunnybrook and Ringol. They watched me, their faces blank, but their auras swirling with pent up fear, excitement, and anxiety.

"No matter what happens in Sunnybrook," I said, addressing them, feeling the weight of another responsibility settle on my shoulders, "I'll keep you all safe."

There was no answer, but I hadn't expected one. My arm had been healed by Fia, and my sweater replaced by the only other one I'd brought with me—one we'd found in our winter cabin. With my freshly filled pack on my shoulder, I led our small party toward the secret path through the Dark Woods .

As we crossed the threshold into the forest, right where Zeke had shown me the day before, my blood sang with warning. I hesitated, afraid, but the wylden at my back seemed unaffected so I made myself move further into the darkness. So many bad things had happened in these woods and this time I didn't have my friends with me. My fear was catching up with me. That was all.

We moved through the near-darkness, the wylden footfalls even quieter than my own. I tried to focus on my breathing, to calm my racing heart, but the deeper we went into the woods, the more my skin tingled with the threat of danger.

The branches above us were thick and tangled, but a small bit of daylight still filtered its way through to the damp ground. I kept my eyes on the shifting patterns of light to keep myself from spiraling into a panic. If I hadn't been watching the shadows and light dance together, I might not have seen the starlings move until it was too late.

Two of the birds swooped down from the canopy of tree limbs as if materializing from nothing and dove right for our heads. Their auras were swirling black voids and had been hidden from me, but now that I knew where they were I could see the emptiness where their auralights should be. The warning I'd felt since we entered the woods screamed anew inside my skull.

Behind me, the wylden scattered. These starlings shouldn't be here. When we'd met them before, it was clear that they stayed near that green pond, almost as if they were tied to it. Something terrible must have forced them away from their poisonous home for them to be so close to the edges of the forest.

Sudden, fresh fear for my friends—the wylden with me and Finn and the others who'd come through before—roared forth.

"Fia!" I yelled, eyes locked on the birds as the dove at us over and over again. She ran from behind a tree and gripped my hand, her power joining with mine in less than a breath. It was a rush, feeling so much power funneling through me, and for a fraction of a moment I understood why Morrigan was the way she was. But the danger to my friends broke the spell the power had cast over me and I came back to myself.

Joined with Fia, I could sense far and wide. Zeke and the others were keeping the birds away from us with blasts of air, so I turned my attention to the woods, intent on finding what else was making me skin prickle. These few birds were just the beginning—a distraction. Around us I could feel them amassing—dozens of swirling voids up in the trees. Beyond the birds I felt others—at least three big, twisted auras—headed toward us.

"We have to leave the path," I said over the sound of beating wings. I could feel animals lying in wait on all sides as if they'd been placed there like traps. I focused on the encroaching animals, trying to *see* or *feel* anything that might help us. There was something nagging at me about all of them—the starlings included. Something familiar shimmered at the edge of what I could *see*. I thought that the wylden and I could beat them if we fought, but I didn't want to risk any lives—wylden or animal—if I could help it.

I closed my eyes—Fia would keep me safe as Zeke and Dill kept the birds at bay—and sought out our pursuers.

I found one of them quickly. It had an aura that reminded me a little of Luna. It was a cat, I thought. But unlike any cat I'd ever felt or *seen*. Instead of purple, the aura was inky blue, like the sky at midnight just before a storm. But around the edges of that dark blue light, similar to moonlight around a storm cloud, was a brilliant, blood red.

Morrigan.

"We can't hurt them," I gasped as I came fully back to myself. Additional birds had joined the first few and they swooped toward Fia and me. She pulled me down as our joined hands flew up to shove the birds back with a wave of energy. "They're not—" In my mind I showed them all the cat's aura surrounded by Morrigan's. "It's not their fault," I said as the animals crept closer. "Zeke, we need a new path."

Zeke's anger burned low and hot. This path had always been safe for the wylden and now Morrigan had used it against us. Dill took over with the birds as Zeke crouched low, head swiveling side to side. He found whatever he was looking for and then he was off. The rest of us followed him away from the birds, away from the other animals which were fast approaching in the darkness.

I kept my senses trained on the animals behind us as we crashed through the underbrush of the Dark Woods . I brought up the rear—the wylden were much faster than I was—and I could feel the animals' confusion with our sudden departure from the path. It was just a few moments, but it was enough to give us a little bit of a head start before they started chasing our scent.

A wolf howled in the distance, followed in discord by other wolf voices. Large bodies crashed through the trees behind us, snapping limps and disturbing the ragged forest litter. My heart bounded along with them as I pushed myself to move faster.

The wylden and I uprooted trees as we shot past them, desperation fueling each footfall. They fell behind us to block our pursuers, or at least slow them down.

Zeke led, so I kept my attention on the animals. The birds seemed hesitant to travel any further from their pond than they already were, and I felt their numbers thin, but the wolf howls continued and the big cat was gaining ground faster than should be possible. It was going to catch us.

"Zeke!" I screamed with my voice and my mind. We had to leave these woods. I'd never seen these types of animals outside this forest.

Joined as we were I could feel how frantic he and the others were. Something about the woods made it hard to navigate, so when Zeke found the treeline I felt his relief like a blast of cool air. My feet pounded the earth to catch up with the wylden who moved further away with every step. The trees were thick, but up ahead there was light. Each breath burned in my throat and chest, but I pushed harder. Zeke and the others broke through the treeline, vanishing into the light, and I sobbed in relief.

I was almost there, freedom almost within my grasp, when a massive, muscled body plowed into me and knocked me to the side.

The great cat was twice as big as me and screamed in my face, it's hot breath rancid. Fear and anger welled up in me and I screamed back, my hands pressed against its grotesquely muscled chest to keep it's jaws from my throat. The skin was hot and smooth and I cringed as its muscles contracted beneath my fingers.

The cat's jaws snapped above my face and I used everything in me to *push* it away. The creature flew backward and yowled in pain as its back smashed into a tree, causing the trunk to buckle inward. I scrambled up an darted for the treeline. I crashed through and fell into damp field grass, right as the cat rushed me. It broke through the trees and my stomach bottomed out, but the direct sunlight hit it before it could get to me. It screeched as it scrambled back, leaving deep gouges in the soft earth with its massive, curled claws.

Safe in the darkness again, it prowled the shadows. My chest heaved as I watched it, unable to move from where I'd fallen. Behind it I could just make out the outline of the wolves' auras—one a dark, deep yellow, the other orange—but they also didn't venture near the light. The birds were all gone.

Fia and Dill each took one of my hands and helped me to stand. All of my muscles trembled from exertion and adrenaline.

"Go around," Zeke panted as he stared into the woods.

"That will take days, won't it?" I asked. I kept my eyes locked on the animals in the woods.

Zeke grunted. Despair settled heavily in my chest.

"We need a better way," I said."These animals— Morrigan sent them to stop us. When the sunsets, they'll come after us even if we aren't in those woods. And if she sent them, that means she's headed to Sunnybrook." Bile rose in my throat as I thought of her going after Finn, or the children. I could only assume she knew Cillian was dead, but I didn't know if that made her more or less dangerous. "I need to get back as quickly as I can." I tried to show them my fear, but my heart was pounding too hard from our escape from the woods and my fear of

Morrigan was clouding my ability to think straight. Fia winced as I shared too much, too fast.

From behind Zeke, the older wylden man, whose name I hadn't yet learned, stepped forward. His skin was marked with deep grooves—wrinkles from a lifetime in the sun and wind—and his eyes were tired, but he still walked with a straight spine and a sure step.

"Caves," he rumbled, his voice rough as if he hadn't used it in years. "Old path."

My skin erupted in chillbumps. "The path that Roark used to move from Citadel, to Sunnybrook, and back to Ringol. There's a direct path *through* the caves." My heart felt like a hummingbird and my hands tingled with spooling energy.

Zeke's dark face was blank. I knew he didn't want to venture into Roark's territory after the fight we'd just had with them, but I was desperate to get back to Finn and the other and warn them about Morrigan.

"Zeke, please," I begged. Somewhere along the way, Zeke had grown to care for me. He watched me now, conflicted—angry, frustrated, and afraid. I didn't want him to feel those things, but we had to get back to Sunnybrook. Morrigan could ruin everything. I took a few deep breaths to calm my still racing heart and tried to share all of that with him. The tension slipped from his shoulders and he nodded once.

From within the shadows of the trees, the black cat made a pitiful mewling sound deep in its throat. It sounded like a frightened kitten. Behind him, the wolves whined. They were afraid. Delicately, I *touched* them auras. They recoiled, but a single touch it was enough.

They were being compelled to complete their task—stopping me. They were afraid that they would fail. My only hope was that if we could get far enough away from, the compulsion would vanish. In spite of how dangerous they were, I felt sad for them. The monstrous cat whined again, then made a sound somewhere between a meow and a growl that made my skin crawl.

If I had more time, I would try to help them. Try to break the tie Morrigan had placed, but it was too dangerous. I couldn't risk it before I made it back to Finn.

I kept my *feelings* attuned to the cat and wolves until we were too far away to feel them anymore. We walked, silent and bruised, following the older wylen man toward the old path through the earth. Beside me, shame rolled off Dill like smoke. He felt like he'd failed me in the woods. I tried to comfort him with a hand on his arm, but he pulled away and hung his head. Fia slowed a bit to walk beside us. She didn't say antyhing, but she did let her arm bump against Dill's. Only then did I feel his tension lessen.

Rock outcroppings sprung up through the earth in the rolling field, growing more and more jagged as we alked. It was as if the earth had been shoved up into mounds by some giant hand. Within one of these large piles of rock was a large cave mouth, partially obscured by tree saplings that were only just waking up from winter. If they'd been in full bloom, it would have been much harder to see.

I was ready to dark in when Zeke stepped in front of me, anger in the lines that ran across his forehead.

"Crawlers," he growled, the word was tinged with icy fear. Back in Ringol, we had numbers on our side. But under the earth, we were at a disadvantage and he was afrad.

"They're my people," I said, trying to imbue my words and feelings with more confidence than I actually felt. "The caves are my home, too. Not just theirs. I can get us through." I wasn't sure if that was true, but the caves were our fastest path to Sunnybrook. To Finn.

He looked at me with the same puzzled expression he'd given me the first time I mentioned my cave dweller heritage. I looked more like an upworlder than a cave dweller and I knew that confused him, but that didn't change who I was. I came from Citadel. Escaped from Citadel. Even if I didn't belong there now, it had once been my home.

With the threat of the animals in the Dark Woods ever pressing behind us, I took the lead and walked past Zeke to the cave entrance. The ground sloped down as it tilted away into the shadows within.

For a moment, I was somewhere else—thirteen years old, exhausted from running and running up. Toward light. Toward the threshold of the caves, which were the only world I'd ever known. Up toward the bright, dangerous upworld.

But then I returned to the present, to this cave, facing a new threshold to cross. With a deep breath for courage, I stepped into the dark.

The cavern we entered was bigger than it had looked from the outside. In the back was an opening to a tunnel. My eyes adjusted to the dark quickly. The air was cooler in here than out in the sunlight and I shivered. Fia stepped beside me.

Daylight slanted into the rocky space and over to one side I saw what looked like the remains of a very old campsite—a single, broken clay cup, a circle of stones that could have once been a small fire pit, and a tattered, element-stained cloth.

We needed to move. Every moment we waited here, the sun sank toward the horizon, which meant every moment the threat of the animals in the dark forest grew. Every moment, Morrigan was a step closer to Finn. But something about this ancient campsite kept me rooted where I was.

The wylden were silent as I crouched beside the broken cup, my heart fluttering inside my chest. I reached out to collect the cup, my fingers hovering just above it, but my eyes were drawn to the scrap of cloth. It was stained and dingy from the damp cave, but I thought it might once have been grayish blue—almost the same color as my eyes. We couldn't use this, but still I reached for it.

My fingers met the stiff, filthy cloth, and just like when Cillian gave me the blanket in Sunnybrook that had been imprinted with images of Finn and Morrigan, I was assaulted with memories.

A woman with long, blonde hair cradled a sleeping toddler. A man sat beside a small, smoky fire, his knee bandaged, holding a stick out like a sword. The woman's fear was thick as she held the child—a little girl—her face tearstained and streaked with dirt.

"Erilyn," the woman whispered, her voice a hiccup. She looked up at the man, her periwinkle aura pulsing as if with her heartbeat. "We have to keep her safe. No matter what."

The man leaned over and looked at the baby, his face full of love and sadness. He pressed a kiss to the little girl's forehead and she squirmed in her sleep. His aura flared a deep, warm gold.

"Keep her here," he said, his voice low.

In my memory, their voices echoed, drawing forth long forgotten emotions. Tears flooded my eyes and fell in rivers down my cheeks.

"They'll kill you," the woman choked. "I can't lose you—"

"Get back to Sunnybrook," he said. He lifted his hand to her face and rubbed his thumb across her cheek.

Sunnybrook. My heart stuttered. Outside the memories, I heard someone crying.

"There has to be a way for us bo—" The woman choked as a crude arrow speared her throat. She coughed up blood as she fell still clutching the small girl. When she hit the ground, her

arms went limp and the child rolled away still wrapped in a blue-gray blanket, now awake and screaming.

The crying turned to gasps and screams.

The man with the bandaged leg leapt up, his voice an agonized cry as he darted for the child, but he was too late. Something struck him as well and he fell, the clay cup beside him breaking as his foot hit it.

In the flickering firelight, the toddler wailed. Her round face was illuminated by the warm firelight, which was mirrored in her pale golden aura.

From the shadows of the cave, men emerged. In the front of the party was a young Chief Roark. He nudged the dead man with this foot, then the woman, his face impassive. Sure they were dead, he walked to the bundled baby who's cries grew in volume and pitch. He leaned over and picked her up, his nose curling in disgust. He pulled the blanket from her body and let it fall to the ground so he could look at the wriggling, screaming child. Her little back arched, her face was red, but even if she'd gotten away from him, she wasn't quite old enough to walk.

"They called it Erilyn," another voice said. Roark grunted.

"Should we dispose of it?" the other man asked.

The screaming had subsided and had been replaced with quiet sobbing.

Roark shook his head as he stared at the baby. "We've been waiting for someone to test in the vitium chamber. Who better than a child that no one will miss? She may be the key to breeding an army to rival those damned wylden," he said as he studied the screaming child held too tightly in his gloved hands. "And if it doesn't work, we can try something else."

Roark handed the child to the man who'd wanted to dispose of her, then wiped his gloves on his pants as if she were something filthy. The others pulled packs from the dead couples' lifeless bodies. Roark led, the man holding the baby bringing up the rear, as they headed back into the tunnel. The baby wailed pitifully as they all disappeared into the dark.

With a gasp, I scrambled back—away from the memories, from the blanket, from all of it. But I couldn't get away from the pain. My lungs felt tied up as I tried to breath. I felt choked on my tears.

I'd seen my parents—periwinkle and warm gold. My family. They'd been murdered by Roark. Then he'd taken me.

I felt like a trapped animal. My heart wasn't fluttering, it wasn't racing, it was trying to break through my ribs. I needed to get out of here. Get away. Get back to—

Arms went around me, locking tight, and all I could see were the men who'd taken the baby—taken *me*—into the caves all those years ago. I tried to shove them off, screaming and flailing, my tears making it impossible to see. But then Fia's calming indigo presence was there, soothing me like a cool cloth soothed a fevered brow. My panic settled into a dull ache. I gripped her arms where she held me and noticed that I was shaking.

I let her hold me as the tears continued to come, choking me. I gasped through them as Fia's grip loosened. Her arms were solid around me, but soft. "Erilyn," she crooned. "Here now. Not there."

With her help, I returned fully to the present. My heart ached with this knew knowledge, these old memories, but I could think again.

I clung to Fia and choked out, "I'm not a cave dweller."

For the first time, I remembered my parents. My mother's cornsilk hair and soft lavender aura. My father's gray blue eyes and deep gold light. *My parents.* I looked at Zeke. I felt Fia's arms. They'd already known I wasn't really from Citadel. They'd always known.

Heart beating against my ribs still, the full realization hit me. I looked back toward the campsite that had been my parents' last, let their final conversation repeat in my head. "I'm from Sunnybrook," I whispered, voice and heart breaking.

Chapter 22

"Settling"
Finn

WHEN Finn and the others arrived at the meeting hall, it was full. The people inside were restless, but Rosemarie's face brightened as she caught Finn's eye and waved them over. As soon as they reached Rosemarie, who stood against a far wall, near the front, she crouched and pulled each of the four children to her with kisses to their cheeks and foreheads. She looked up at him with a radiant smile that, for a moment, washed away the strain of the last few years. Finn was taken aback by how much she reminded him of Erilyn.

The meeting hall was full of agitated people—some sitting, some standing—and the children huddled tightly around Finn, Rosemarie, and Mehri. Only Seraphina stood off to one side, a scowl on her artificially darkened face. Rosemarie took her hand and tugged her against her side and the scowl softened. Lucy and Aiyanna were huddled together, just behind the podium.

Rosemarie leaned so that she could speak directly into Finn's ear. "Lucy's nervous, but I think she'll be okay," she whispered.

"She will be," Asa said, looking up at Rosemarie, her face partially obscured by the large magenta scarf wrapped around her pale hair. "Aiyanna's with her."

"Tied," Galen said before he turned and buried his face in Mehri's neck.

As if on cue, Lucy stepped up onto the small platform behind the podium. Her presence caused the general agitated murmur in the room to settle as all eyes turned toward her.

Her cheeks were redder than her hair, but she stood tall with her shoulders squared as she faced the gathered people of Sunnybrook. Members of the patrol were sitting interspersed with the crowd, not patrolling the perimeter as Morrigan would have had them do.

Aiyanna joined the others and flashed a quick smile. She wore a dark hood that covered her hair, but her face was visible, and her eyes were locked on Lucy.

Lucy turned, as if feeling Aiyanna's gaze, and smiled. When she turned back to the amassed people, her posture was a little less tense. She cleared her throat and gripped the podium with long, pale fingers.

"My brother," she said, her voice a little too loud, "Cillian," she said at a more reasonable volume, "should be here to speak with you." The crowd murmured it's assent, but when Lucy spoke again they quieted. "But he's gone for a good reason." She stood a little straighter. "When the wylden started to attack our city last season, we were all at a loss. We were all afraid, including my brother." She took a steadying breath. "The winter was especially hard, because we couldn't leave our walls to gather food. The threat of the wylden was ever-present and—"

"And none of that's changed!" yelled a voice from the crowd. "So where is he now?"

Lucy looked in the direction the voice came from. She took a breath before she continued, "He's with Erilyn."

Loud, angry whispers erupted and Lucy let them all talk at once, waiting until they settled on their own to speak again. She looked back at Aiyanna, and the older girl smiled and nodded in encouragement.

"Morrigan told all of you that Erilyn was responsible for the wylden attacks, but she wasn't," she said, raising her voice at the end to be sure to be heard. "Erilyn came back to Sunnybrook to help us, even though it was dangerous for her. And now, she's with my brother, and Morrigan, and they're working with the wylden to put an end to all of this."

Lucy's announcement caused an eruption. Some people shouted in anger, others clutched their neighbor and wept. Lucy stood, face stoic, with her hands up to wait for silence.

But the noise didn't diminish. It grew. Luna, who'd been hiding just outside the door, slunk in and hid protectively in some shadows behind the children. Finn wanted to help, but he wasn't sure what to do. Before he could think of anything, Aiyanna stood and made her way to Lucy.

Like the children, Aiyanna was wrapped from head to foot to hide her cave dweller heritage. Only her face, darkened only slightly with sun cream, was visible. She looked uncomfortable as she walked to Lucy's side, but her steps didn't falter. Lucy smiled at Aiyanna, her shoulders visibly relaxing, as she reached the podium. She took Aiyanna's hand and gave it a single squeeze. Aiyanna smiled up at her, took a deep breath, and removed the shawl she had wrapped around her head, followed by the scarf and gloves.

As people began to notice her, notice her pale skin and white, braded hair, the room went quiet.

For as long as Finn could remember, he'd heard about cave dwellers—pale ghost-like people who lived beneath the earth—but until he met Erilyn and went down into Citadel with her, he hadn't been sure they were real. They'd always seemed like a legend. A story for children. Even their nickname—nightcrawlers—made them seem more look boogey men than a real people.

Asa let go of Finn's hand and he watched as all five children joined Aiyanna and removed the clothes covering their heritage.

Finn looked for the nearest exit, his heart pounding uncomfortably. Who knew how the people gathered would react to cave dwellers who'd snuck in under their noses? If things went poorly, he would grab the children and leave through the door behind them. He felt Luna slink closer to him, her white fur standing out against the dark floor, a growl low in her throat. Together they could keep the children safe.

When Finn looked back to the podium, Lucy was smiling. He put his hand on Luna's head to calm her and felt her settle beside him. They would see what Lucy had planned.

"My name is Aiyanna," she said into the stunned silence. The younger children stood in front of her, but Sera stood at her side. "I'm from Citadel, the city that lies beneath the forests that surround Sunnybrook."

People in the crowd began to murmur.

"I know Cillian, and Erilyn. What Lucy says is true—they are brokering peace with the wylden. If all goes well, we can have real, lasting peace between all of our peoples." The smaller children, even Galen, were totally still. "I am the daughter of the Chief of Citadel," she continued, her voice carrying evenly across the crowd. "We have live below you, even moved among you, for generations. We didn't reveal ourselves because my father, Chief Roark, forbade it. But I am here to change that." She scanned the crowd, her chin high, as she gave them time to absorb the truth of her words.

"Through Aiyanna, we already have peace with Citadel," Lucy said, as she stepped to Aiyanna's side opposite Seraphina. Finn thought he saw their fingers touch for the briefest of moments. "My brother, with Erilyn's help, is making peace with the wylden. We've never thought that was possible, but until recently the people who lived in the caves were barely more than a myth. Yet, here they are." Lucy looked at the children and Asa looked up at her with a brilliant smile. "Once they return, we can stop being so afraid of what's outside that wall." Her voice broke at the end and Aiyanna took her hand—pale white fingers slipping between long freckled ones.

"And if your brother fails?" a man somewhere in the crowd asked. Voices murmured their assent and heads nodded. Finn kept his eyes on his friends at the podium, still ready to grab the children and run if he needed to. Sera met his eyes with pursed lips and gave him the barest shake of her head.

Sera's hand went to Noah's shoulder and each child subtly grabbed hold of another until they were all connected. The air in the room changed. Finn kept his eyes on the kids. Something was about to happen. His stomach clenched with nerves.

"If he fails—which he won't—then we have these five to keep us safe." Lucy gestured to the children. The people in the crowd snickered and guffawed, turning to whisper to one another as they pointed up toward the small stage.

There were loud shouts that all blended together.

"What are children supposed to do to keep us safe?"

"Is this a joke?"

"They're freaks!"

Galen had been clinging to Sera's leg since they removed ther scaves, but now he stepped away, his fingertips clinging to the hem of her sweater. Finn watched their eyes go unfocused and he tensed. The congregation sensed it too and went quiet again. When silence had returend, the candles and lamps lit along the room flickered, as if with wind. Then, with a bang, all the window shutters and doors slammed shut and all the candles and lanterns—except for a few right near the stage—went out.

Finn counted two rapid beats of his heart and then the windows and doors reopened and the flames relit as if nothing had happened. Galen stuck his thumb in his mouth and stepped back to Sera, who rested her hand on his curly white hair.

"These children are very powerful," Aiyanna said, stepping forward and resting her hands on both Sera and Asa's shoulders. "And they are here to help protect Sunnybrook."

There was another eruption of sound, this one less angry and more confused. It was evident that the children frightened some of them, but when Galen went to Rosemarie and asked to be picked up, then promptly lay his head on her shoulder to sleep, some of the anxiety in the group lessened.

Lucy held her hands up again and took questions, letting anyone who wanted to speak do so.

As the adults in the meeting hall talked, the other children grew sleepy as well. Noah and Jubal both sat on Finn's knees, a head on each of his shoulders. Asa tried to stay awake, blinking her eyes open wide like an owl, but after a time even she succumbed and her little head fell against Mehri's shoulder. When she was good and asleep, Mehri tugged the slight girl across her lap and covered her with a scarf.

Only Seraphina still stood, eyes and ears intent on what was being said. It reminded Finn that after all they'd been through, Sera wasn't really a little girl anymore.

By the end of the very long meeting, the community had voted—reluctantly—to trust that Aiyanna and the children would keep them safe, along with the remaining members of the Patrol, should the wylden return in aggression. They also voted—with much less trepidation—that Lucy should be in charge, at least until Cillian returned. In a single day she'd done more than the entirety of the council had done in weeks to give the people hope. The council members, who were in attendance, grumbled a bit more than the rest, but also seemed a little relieved to have the burden removed from their shoulders.

Finn and the others waited for the townspeople to file out before attempting to move the sleeping children. As people filed out, they passed by Lucy to shake her hand or simply nod. As they passed Finn, who held Noah and Jubal, their expressions ranged from curious to afraid, but Finn just smiled at each of them and held onto Noah and

Jubal a little tighter. His return from the supposed-dead had been forgotten in all the excitement from the day. It was only after the last person from Sunnybrook had left that their small part made their way back to Mehri's apartment, sleeping children in tow.

"The children can stay with me as long as they want or need to," Mehri said as she led them inside. The apartment wasn't large, but it was warm and comfortable. She went into the bedroom, where she'd expanded her mattress on the floor with additional cushions and hand knit blankets, and laid Asa down. "They all sleep in here," she whispered. The other children were laid down beside their sister. Only Sera remained awake.

Back in the living room, Mehri lit a few candles. "You can all stay," she said, moving to her small fireplace and getting a fire going with flint and kindling. "There's not much room, but there's enough."

Lucy smiled tightly and shook her head. "I'm going to make sure my apartment is still in one piece." Her eyes darted to Aiyanna and she bit the inside of her cheek.

"I'll go with you." Aiyanna smiled.

"What about you, Finn?" Lucy asked. She looked relaxed as Aiyanna took her hand again. "Going back to your apartment?"

"No," he said, shoving his hands deep in his pockets. That place carried too many foggy, anger-filled memories of Morrigan—of the time he'd spent under her control. "I'm going back to my workshop. That's where

Erilyn will look for me first when she gets back." Luna pressed against his leg and he pulled one hand from his pocket to scratch between her ears.

"Sera and I will stay here, Mehri" Rosemarie said, gently draping her arm over Seraphina's shoulders. Sera had been quiet since before the meeting. "If there's room."

"Of course," Mehri said with a smile. "Sera, you can sleep with your siblings. I've been staying out here to keep an eye on the door, so there's plenty of room for you in there." She smiled at Sera, but Sera kept her eyes on the floor.

Rosemarie rubbed Seraphina's arm and said, "Thank you," but the young girl kept her eyes trained down.

As Lucy and Aiyanna said their goodbyes, making sure Rosemarie knew where her apartment was in case she needed to find either of them quickly, Finn pulled Seraphina to the side.

"You know where I am if you need me, too. Okay?" he said as he gently gripped her shoulder, wishing she would look up at him.

She nodded, eyes still downcast. For the entirety of the meeting she'd been alert and listening, but as soon as they'd come back here, her whole demeanor had changed. Finn thought she might want him to stay here, too. But he couldn't risk missing Erilyn when she came back. And he couldn't ask Sera to come with him to his workshop, alone. He didn't want to give her the wrong impression and make things works between them.

"The other kids will be happy that you're here," he said.

She nodded again, but she still wouldn't meet his gaze.

With a sigh he said, "I'll be back first thing in the morning." He pulled her to him and gave her a one-armed hug against his side. He was surprised when she actually returned, pressing her face into his side.

"We'll be here waiting," Rosemarie said. Seraphina slipped against the older woman's side.

Finn nodded. He looked toward Mehri's bedroom where the four little ones slept, then back at Seraphina one last time. He'd come all this way to make sure they were okay and it felt strange to be leaving them so soon. But he wasn't leaving htem alone. They were Rosemarie and Mehri who were more capable than he was of caring for children.

With a sigh, he followed Lucy and Aiyanna out into the cold night.

Luna chirped at Finn as she followed him out. He waved at Lucy and Aiyanna as they disappeared into the night, hand-in-hand, then crouched beside the large while serval cat and scratched between her big, soft ears. "You should stay here," he said. She butted her head against his hand and meowed low and mournfully in her throat. "To watch over the children," he said as he let his hand rest on her thick fur. "I'll be back in the morning."

She leaned up and butted her head against his chin, which made him stumble back and laugh.

"When Erilyn's back—" he said as he ran his fingers through her thick, white fur, "the three of us will go somewhere." He scratched lightly along her spine and a deep purr started in her chest. "We'll find a place to escape all this—this—" he sighed. "This bad stuff."

Luna chirped again and licked his cheek with her scratchy tongue. With a flick of her tail she darted back into Mehri's house. Mehri gave him a last wave and then shut the door.

Hands deep into his pockets, Finn walked back to his small cabin with only the light of th emoon for company. It used to feel like such a long walk—before he'd traveled through the Dark Woods to Ringol and back.

It was strange to be alone. He hadn't been alone like this—aside from his imprisonment in Ringol—in months. When he was with the children, with Erilyn, even when no one spoke, there was a vibration that he could feel in his skin. He hadn't really noticed it when it was there, but without it he felt exceptionally lonely. This silence held only his breaths and footfalls.

When he reached the workshop, there was no smoke curling from the chimney and the windows were dark. He stepped in, disappointed Erilyn hadn't made it back yet. He'd half-hoped that he'd return and find her waiting for him.

Inside, the room was exactly as he'd left it. He went to tie the rope latch, but decided against it. The door would remain unlocked in case Erilyn returned in the night. He knew she could get it open either way, but wanted her to get to him as quickly as she could.

It had gotten cold again, and with muscles and joints that were stiff and sore—from his imprisonment, from his journey, from his loneliness—Finn built a small fire. When they'd left the cabin to find Erilyn they'd taken most of the supplies they'd saved, but he still had the blanket from his pack. Eyes on the door, he got as comfortable as he could on the threadbare rug, his back to the small fire, and covered himself with the blanket wishing she were curled beneath it with him.

The tiny cabin felt much too big. With them all here it was cramped, but he preferred that to this hollowness he found himself surrounded by now. Even the air felt empty—no vibration, no noise—so he focused on the crackling of the fire at his back and the warm light it cast on the walls around him.

Alone as he was, he didn't feel like he needed to shield his thoughts, so for the first time in a long time he let himself really think of Erilyn. He pictured her face when they shared a secret, soft and open. He imagined the way her hand felt as it slipped into his as they walked, how her fingers warmed against his skin. He thought of her lips against his, of how perfectly she fit, tucked against him when they slept. Her laugh, more breath that sound. The way her eyes blazed when she was angry. The ferocity with which she protected what she loved. The quiet way she made her way through life, and the way her face brightened when they were together.

It took some time, but Finn was eventually able to fall asleep with Erilyn on his mind and a deep ache in his chest.

FINN woke with a shiver as the morning light peeked through the curtains. He'd only been asleep a few hours, so he had a raging headache, but the fire was nearly dead. He'd told Seraphina and Rosemarie he would come back to Mehri's first thing.

He scrubbed his eyes with the heel of his hand and rolled toward the door, only to sit up with a start. Seraphina was sitting against the door with no blanket, her head drooped forward, face obscured by tangled white hair. She snored lightly, a bare whisper.

Fully awake after that small fright, Finn stoked the coals in the fire until the flame caught again, added some wood, then prepared a kettle for tea.

He turned after hanging the kettle over the fire and found Sera awake with her eyes on him. With stiff movements, she stood and brushed her hair back from her face with a shiver. Finn waved her over to sit nearer to the fire.

"You're always welcome here." He pulled some dried herbs from one of his small cabinets. "But shouldn't you be with the others?" He kept his voice light, hoping it wouldn't make her angry.

"It felt strange," she said as she pulled her knees to her chest and rested her chin on them. "I don't belong there. But they do. They fit."

Finn sprinkled the herbs into the water and stirred it with a long wooden spoon before replacing the lid. "They're your family," he said as he leaned against the counter and crossed his arms over his chest. "Just because they're with Mehri doesn't mean you don't belong with them."

"They're not really my family," she said, her voice quiet. She pressed her lips together until they turned white. "Before the others kids, I was in a vitium cave alone. Asa and the twins were brought in together, then Galen, but other than Noah and Jubal, none of us are actually related. We're not a real family." She sniffed and tightened her arms around her legs.

"Of course you are," Finn said as he recrossed his arms over his chest. "Blood doesn't make you a family." He thought of their time in the winter cabin—the children playing in the snow, Aiyanna making tea, of how he'd grown to love all of them regardless of where they'd come from before. He couldn't think of that time without thinking of Erilyn and Luna—of how he would wake up each morning, wrapped around her with Luna sandwiched in somewhere too. He tried to reign those last thoughts in, but he was too late. Her eyes snapped up to his and her face darkened and she looked away, into the fire.

Finn sighed and pulled the kettle from the fire. He poured the thin liquid into the clay mugs they'd left behind. "After we've warmed up a bit we'll head back to town and get some breakfast with the others. I'm sure you'll feel better after some real food."

Seraphina nodded, her face drawn and sad as took the tea he offered. She took a sip and grimaced. Finn took a sip of his as well and spat it right back into his mug. With a laugh he took her cup and shook his head. "Don't drink that," he said. "It's awful."

Seraphina surprised him by smiling, her shoulders relaxing down away from her ears. He hadn't seen her this relaxed since they found Rosemarie in the quarry cave.

"Come on," he said, offering her his hand to help her stand. "Let's just head back to town now. We can meet the others for breakfast and—"

"Sssh," Seraphina interrupted, tightening her grip on his hand as she stared at the door with big, frightened eyes. "I think there's someone outside," she breathed, voice barely audible as she tugged him back toward the fire. "I can't—I'm not sure." Of all five siblings, Seraphina was the most attuned to her abilities. The only reason she wouldn't be sure about something like this was if the other person had abilities and was trying to hide.

"You aren't sure?" he asked. He tugged her a little behind him. "Someone's hiding."

She looked up at him and nodded, her face paler than usual.

"Do you think it's Aiyanna?" he asked, swallowing past a suddenly dry throat. "Is she hiding?"

He stared down at her, felt her grip tighten in his, and knew what she was going to say before she said it.

She shook her head and exhaled a shaky breath. "I think it's Morrigan."

Chapter 23

"Taken"

Morrigan

FINN'S little workshop stands sullen through the leaf-bare trees. You'd had it built for him so he would be further from town—from Erilyn. Now he's exactly where you need him to be.

With a light touch you *look* inside the cabin. Rage explodes in your chest when you feel two people there. You're a moment from grabbing hold of the pitiful fire inside and sending the whole thing up in flames when you realize the second person is not Erilyn.

This person is powerful like Erilyn, but is the wrong color. Brilliant pink instead of sickly yellow. It's the nightcrawler girl. The one who was kind to you in Ringol. Seraphina. You sense a deep well of power in the girl, but also rivers upon rivers of pain. You know better than anyone how to manipulate pain. Her being here is better than you could have hoped.

They don't know you're here yet—the girl is too wrapped up in some imagined sadness while Finn pulses and glows bright like a candle. You *watch* as their auras ebb and flow together like the ripples in a pond—a familial tie. You don't think the girl is even aware of it. This tie is not like the one you used to bind Finn to you—reins meant to hold an animal in check. And it's not like it was when Erilyn held him—fingers intertwined. This connection has more give. More independence. It would be pliable if you knew how to mold it. A grin stretches tight across your face.

You try to peer into their heads, to see what it is they're talking about and why they're here alone. You can sense their feelings—the girl is angry and Finn is remorseful—but the thoughts themselves are cloudy. You used up the small vials you took from the nightcrawler on your trek through the Dark Woods and the effects are starting to wear off. After you'd tied the cat, wolves, and birds to your will, you'd needed more vitium to keep the other vicious creatures at bay.

But you'd prepared for this. Just before coming here, you'd gone to the quarry to get moreYou'd seen what was left of Darling, his feet boots sticking out from beneath some hardy bushes, and had felt a pang of something, but you couldn't figure out what that something was because the vitium inside the cave called to you.

Your water skin is now filled to the brim from the stores in Rosemarie's old cell and you take three deep gulps. Your senses sharpen into focus and a shiver of contentment ripples along our skin.

You reach for their thoughts again, but they've changed. They're happy. Laughing. It's disgusting.

Flushed with fresh vitium, you assess the two of them. The girl is powerful, and while you think you could overpower her, you don't want to waste the energy on a fight if you don't have to. There's only one door to Finn's workshop. Only one way in or out. With the two of them cornered, you'll have time to convince her. Sway her. She already half-hates Erilyn, so it should be easy.

You're ready—to get Finn back, to break Erilyn's spirit by taking the girl, too, to win. Like releasing a deep breath, you stop hiding and allow your presence be felt for the first time, your aura flowing out from you like summer sunshine.

Seraphina *feels* you and her spike of fear is delicious. Finn joins her shortly after. You bite your lip and smile as you *taste* it in the energy around them—tangy and cold. Perfect.

With a light tread you step onto the porch. Your foot touches the rough wood and an echo of memory breezes by—silvery gray, anxious, confident. *Cillian.* Pain lances through your chest and you stumble, but catch yourself.

You take a steadying breath and feel past Cillian's echo. Only Finn and Seraphina are inside. Not even Erilyn's white beast is here. You wouldn't have minded ridding the world of it.

Inside, the girl thinks she's hiding them, but she doesn't know all you can do. Your power is a never ending well that she can't even begin to imagine. You want to laugh at her ignorance, but you don't. Instead, you school your expression and push the door open. Like acrid smoke, you are assaulted with the nightcrawler's fear and regret that she didn't sense you earlier. Poor thing.

Finn stands, holding the nightcrawler girl behind him. He's angry. He's afraid of you.

He's alive.

For a moment, you see him in your memory, *lying on the ground, your blade sticking out of his bely, his blood staining the snow pink.* And then, in your mind's eye, the image blurs, and when it clears again, it's Cillian's body instead, dirty and broken on a wylden street.

You push those images away and smile. You look into Finn's angry, blue eyes. You blink and suddenly it's Cillian, not Finn. Blood dribbles from his lips and you can hear the echo of his last *I love you.*

Your smile vanishes as you close the door behind you with a soft thud.

"What are you doing here?" Finn asks, crowding the girl behind him as if he could somehow shield her from you. It would be almost sweet if it weren't so pathetic. "Where's Cillian?" he says, his voice cracking.

Cillian's eyes are blank. His body is limp. The cool silver of his aura vanishes like fog in the heat of the sun.

"Dead." Your voice is cold. "But it doesn't matter. I'm here for you."

His flare of icy fear grates against your nerves. What does he have to fear from you, his first love? You remember how smooth his skin felt against yours. How soft his lips were. You try to share those memories with him, but you can't get into his mind.

You grit your teeth in frustration. He tenses as the girl shrinks behind him. You have to play this smarter. You have to keep your head. Memories of Cillian are clouding your judgement, making you sloppy. So you force him away.

You knew you couldn't tie Finn again, but you thought you could still *reach* him. You need to get the girl on your side. You're glad you didn't come in and immediately kill her.

"I'm here for you, because—" with everything in you, you hide your true intentions. "Because the cave dwellers are coming." You fabricate images of them and bring them to the front of your mind. "Cillian died trying to come back to warn you. Erilyn—" you choke on her name and look at Finn, eyes wide, hoping he can't see past the act. "I'm not sure what happened to her." If you try to lie about her, you'll fail. A half-truth is your best option.

Finn's face hardens and you feel his worry for her swell like a flood. He takes an involuntary step forward, as if he could step out his door to find her. You fight the snarl that wants to paint your face.

"We need to leave," you say, picturing woods. Hiding. "To keep you safe. Both of you." You look at the girl, peeking from behind his back, and hold out your hand.

It's then that Seraphina steps out. You think she's going to take your hand and smile. Finn tries to stop her, but she steps around him, eyes hard and discerning. "She's lying."

Anger burns hot inside you, but you keep it contained. Your face betrays nothing. You keep your hand held toward them.

"Seraphina," Finn says, his confusion and ignorance endearing. "Can you see what really happened to Cillian?" He swallows heavily. And to Erilyn?"

You were Finn's first love and he was yours, and yet he trusts this pale little runt more than you. Your first instinct is to lash out and hurt her in order to punish him, but you're too smart to ruin this one chance.

Seraphina squints at you. She's pushing into your mind. Prying. You try to keep her out but somehow she slips in, seeing what you don't want her to see. Rage rises in your chest. The fire behind them beckons to leap from its grate and consume them.

"Cillian's dead," she says as she stares inside you, as if you were a book open to be read. You focus on Erilyn, alive and whole. If she can see into your mind, she will only see what you want her to see. "But Erilyn's alright. Still with the wylden, but okay." She looks up into your eyes and for a moment you can *see* her as clearly as she *sees* you. "She wants you to go with her, but—but she can't force you. She tried to tie you again, but she can't."

While she reveals these secrets, you look for something in her to use as leverage. She is broken from being isolated in those disgusting caves for so long. She longs for love, for acceptance, for individuality. She feels separate from her siblings and resents them for their closeness even as she longs to be fully part of it. Conflicted in so many ways. She believes that she's in love with Finn and yearns for him to love her in return. But she doesn't understand love. She thinks what she feels for him is being in love when in reality it's just the type of love that anyone with a good family might experience. But it doesn't matter what she knows and what she things, because whatever it is you can use this to twist her to your will.

The rage inside you dims to a slow, steady burn.

As she tries to pry deeper into your mind, you reach in and latch onto her misguided feelings—onto her love for Finn, her desire for his love. You're a little bit disappointed that that's all it took for you to take her. *Weakness.* Tendrils of crackling red snake their way into her warm, pink auralight and grab hold like thorns snagging soft skin.

"She's right," you say once you have hold of her with a touch that is firm, but so light, she isn't aware of it. "I do want you to come with me. I should have lied before."

"You're insane," Finn says as he runs his fingers through his shaggy hair.

The memory of your reflection in Erilyn's pond—wild and unhinged—flashes in your mind. "No. I'm not," you breathe through clenched teeth.

"I won't go with you," he says, gently taking Seraphina's arm and pulling her back to his side. Her aura flares where he touches her—hopeful and sickeningly sweet—and in her distraction you take hold of her love for him a little more tightly.

"If you don't—" you keep your voice light as you focusing on bending Seraphina to your will as you speak, "I'll go into Sunnybrook and hurt the other children." You press your lips together as if the thought makes you sad. "You don't want that, do you?"

"We can protect them," he says, putting himself between you and the girl again. "Sera and I will protect them. You won't get near them."

Never have you seen him so strong, and you bristle. This was how you'd always wanted him to be for you, but he never could be. The only thing that gives you solace is that his words are empty. Sweet, soft, naïve Finn doesn't know the little nightcrawler is yours now. There's nothing he can do. You give her a little nudge, making her think she's seeing your thoughts instead of what you are choosing for her to see. With each beat of her heart, you tie her a little more closely to you.

"We can't," Sera says, her voice cracking. "I can see—" she shudders. "She'll hurt them, Finn. Kill them. Even little Galen." She chokes out the last bit and turns to him, tears in her eyes. It's pathetic how fast he crumbles. "We have to do what she says."

"No," he says, voice hard even as his face falls. "I won't go." His eyes are wide in panic as he looks at you, then back to the girl. "Sera, come on. We can protect them.

We—*you*—can." His voice is desperate and you feel that same shiver of contentment from earlier shudder across you skin.

"Seraphina," you purr. She looks at you, past Finn, her eyes big and open. Her pale skin and hair are unpleasant to look at, but you soften your face and try to smile. "You were kind to me in Ringol. Let me be kind to you now." You extend your hand again. You take a step closer. Finn tries to pull the girl back, but she doesn't budge. "I know what you want," you whisper and her eyes grow larger.

She shakes her head and crosses her arms over her middle, but she doesn't budge. Finn's aura flares dark green in agitation.

"I know," you repeat as you take another step closer, hand extended, palm up. "I want to help you get what you want." You let an image of Finn pass between you. "I'm here to protect him. You know as well as I do that she's bad for him. Dangerous." You sift through all the memories of the times Finn has been in danger since he met her. "If he comes with me, with *us*, we can get him away and—" you trail off and watch as her childish imagination races with possibilities, filling in the blanks on her own. "But I need your help."

The air in the room shifts as you feel her bend to your will. Finn must feel it, too, because he backs toward the counter, leaving her where she is. His muscles are coiled tight.

The fire behind the nightcrawler girls jumps as her power surges. Her eyes meet yours and she stands a little taller, her pink aura settling, but still bright. You can see the tendrils of red that you've planted there, but know that she can't yet. "All right," she says and you curl your hand—extended with your palm up and open—into a tight fist.

"Sera," Finn says from the corner, but she keeps her eyes on you.

"I can't control him," you say and the girl nods in understanding as you plant the idea in her mind. Finn stares at you, then back at her. His eyes go wide as he feels the tether that the girl places snap tight.

"No," he moans, his face crumpling in sorrow. "You can't do this—" His mouth snaps shut as she purses her lips, her eyes shining with tears that she refuses to let fall.

"Erilyn's bad for you," she whispers as she looks up at him, eyes shining in the firelight. "Morrigan's right. We'll take you somewhere away and we—" Her cheeks grow rosy. "And things will just be better. For all of us. The others will be safe in Sunnybrook and you'll be safe with me." Her eyes snap to you. "With us, I mean."

Victory sings brightly in your chest as you work to maintain your composure. While Seraphina holds Finn in her tether—the little girl is stronger than you realized at first—you hold her in yours. You hold her lightly, just enough that you can influence her will without her noticing. You'll tighten it, little by little, as you go. And through her, you have them both on a leash.

"We should go," you say to her, placing a featherlight touch on her shoulder. She nods, then swipes her fingers under her eyes once, catching tears you didn't see fall.

"Sera," Finn croaks. "Please." But she turns away from him.

You step from the cabin into the pale morning sun, the girl and Finn behind you. Her steps are subdued and heavy, and her aura—so bright only moments before—has already dulled with the weight of what shes' done. Finn fights every step he takes, dragged along behind her, but a quick check shows you that her tether is secure.

The crisp air hits your skin, refreshing you. The sun is up and you take a deep breath of air that tastes like damp leaves and new groth. You smile as you lead them into the forest, away from Sunnybrook. You hide the three of you and you know the children in town haven't *sensed* you. Or if they have, by the time the reach the workshop it will be too late.

Your smile broadens as you think about Erilyn and the surprises you left for her in the dark forest. If she survives your animals, she'll return here only to be crushed when she finds Finn gone. One way or another— either by her death or her heartbreak—you've won.

Chapter 24

"Discovery"

Erilyn

MY revelation—*I was from Sunnybrook*—had brought only silence. I clutched the grimy scrap of blanket in my fingers. I could still see her face in my memory. Could still see the cool lavender of her aura. I knew without a doubt she was my mother. I'd seen my father too, his aura a darker shade of gold than mine.

Ever since I was small, I'd had dreams—shapes and voices and light—but these echoed memories made them clear in my mind. Other memories that had been locked away somewhere deep in my memory came roaring forth. I stood, Fia at my side, and let them wash over me.

My mother singing me to sleep.

Our apartment filled with all sorts of knitted and sewn things.

My father coming home smelling of fire and pungent spices.

My mother smelling of fresh-baked bread and pine tea.

I sifted through the memories like drawings in a book. I saw my crib—roughly hewn wood that had been sanded smooth—with a multicolored blanket folded over the rail. The blanket tugged at some other memory that wasn't quite ready to surface. I remembered crawling on the floor, playing with wound balls of yarn. I'd pulled myself to standing on a basket woven made of thick vines that looked remarkably like the one Rosemarie had when I stayed with her

Rosemarie. A fresh flood of memories surged as I thought of her. My knees gave way, and I felt hands guide me to the floor, but all I could see in my mind was Rosemarie. She didn't look like she did now. She didn't look like I remembered her from four years ago, when she found me near death. She was younger—her hair thicker, her skin more supple, her clothes fresh and lovely.

I sobbed deep in my throat as I remembered—

Rosemarie rocking me to sleep as a baby, stroking down the length of my nose with her pinky.

Rosemarie covering me with a patchwork blanket in my crib. Then, later, covering me with the same blanket in her cabin in the woods as she nursed me back to health after finding me in the wood.

Earlier than that, *Rosemarie kissing my mother's cheek, her purple aura reaching for the lavender of my mother's in a way that let me know that one came from the other. My mother hugging Rosemarie, looking so much like her it hurt to see, and calling her Mama.*

Like being trapped under a frozen lake and finding a hole in the ice from which to breathe, I gasped and struggled to regain myself. My eyes flew open and I gasped, hands scrabbling to find purchase. I found Fia, waiting, her face just inches from my own. She held me as I frantically gripped her arms, my senses returning. My cheeks were cold with tears and my chest felt so tight, I wasn't sure I could catch my breath.

"Rosemarie—" I croaked, heart racing. I stared into Fia's vitium-blue eyes.

She nodded once. "Laced," she said, her voice soft, as if she were talking to a frightened child. "Family." She cocked her head to one side as if in question.

I choked through a fresh wave of tears. In all the time I'd been with Rosemarie, how had I not known she was my grandmother? How had she not know who I was when she found me?

"We have to get back." I pushed myself up from the cold ground. Gritting my teeth against more possible memories, I picked up the scrap of blanket and shoved it in my pack, both grateful and disappointed when I wasn't overwhelmed with more.

Zeke looked at me and cocked his head to the side. It was a trait the children also had. His eyes widened and his teal aura flared bright. "New," he said with a nod toward me. "Full."

With my lost memories swirling in my mind—my mother's laugh and my father's scratchy beard—I nodded.

"Follow you," Zeke said. I looked outside, shocked at how late it had gotten. I'd been in my memories for hours. I wanted to apologize for making them wait, but then Dill was there, his hand a light weight on my shoulder, followed by a wave of warmth.

I wiped the tears from my face and gently reached for each wylden's aura. Once we were all together—not tied, but touching softly, almost like we were holding hands—we headed to the back of the cave, through the entrance where the cave dwellers had taken me. Passing through this opening removed something from my shoulders, some weight I'd carried all my life. It was as if I could feel my parents with me—as if they'd been waiting here for me all this time.

I'd never been able to see in the dark like the other children of Citadel. Now I knew it was because I'd always belonged in the sunlight.

The wylden trailed behind me, their footsteps so silent I wouldn't have known they were here if it weren't for their subdued aura-lights following me. I couldn't see well—their eyesight was better than mine—but I knew how to navigate the tunnels. I'd spent my childhood traversing them, often hiding from other children. There were tricks to finding your way through—the way the water moved, the way the fungus grew, often there was a pattern to them—at least the ones the cave dwellers had carved. I could find our way.

The cloying scent of mud and stone brought back more memories and I didn't fight them, trusting my wylden friend to keep me safe in the here and now.

Aiyanna's cold gaze as I gathered food with the other children. The other children ostracised me because she did. The loneliness that had crept into my bones a little more each day.

I stumbled over a rock, distracted, but I kept walking. I wasn't going to let them take control of me again, but I needed to see them. To learn more about who I was.

The nanny who'd cared for me when they brought me to Citadel rocked me, shushed me, as I cried and clawed at my eyes in the darkness. Her face lit with blue-green vitium light, and she smiled down at me, wincing as I screamed for hours on end. Her aura, a faint chartreuse, blended with the teal of the vitium around us and wobbled unsteadily.

I shook my head and refocused. Light and life ran in rivers through the earth, through the stone. These memories had woken something else in my mind and I could feel all of it with brilliant clarity. It was as if I'd been half-asleep for all of my life and had finally woken up.

I tried to take in everything around me and was shocked to see how much of the land was touched by vitium. It wasn't just the vitium caverns. Teal laced through the rock even though it wasn't visible to the eye. It touched all of Citadel. All of the earth above, stretching out to Ringol, to the Dark Woods, to Sunnybrook. I'd spent my whole life thinking it existed in pockets, that it was isolated and to be avoided. But it was *everywhere*.

I let my awareness zip through the caves and caverns, something I'd never been able to do before.

Ahead of us I sensed Citadel's city center, the people in an uproar.

The wylden and I slowed. I could feel the fear and anger of the cave dwellers in waves. The earth seemed to tremble with the ferocity of their emotions. Fia slipped her hand into mine and together we traveled through the dark corridors, racing, until we stopped in the soft light of Citadel.

We were seeing through the eyes of one of the cave dwellers who was gathered there. Above, high on a platform, stood Chief Roark. The normally quiet people murmured in angry tones as they looked up at him.

"We can try again," he said, his voice unnervingly loud in the stone space. Never had I heard anyone speak like that in Citadel. "With more of the vitium solution from the upworlders, we can go back and—"

"Our people are dead," a voice cried from the throng. "Our friends!"

"They know we're here now," another said, tears in their voice. "They'll come for us!"

"We don't need anything from up there," called a third. "We've never needed them before! We don't need them now."

"We are *trapped* here!" Roark yelled, his voice echoing around the cavern in a way that made me wince. "We deserve all that they have, and more!"

Roark's aura flared bright and broken like Morrigan's. I felt my resolve strengthen. The people of

Citadel weren't my people, but they deserved a better leader than Roark.

"As long as Roark's in charge, he'll keep coming after our people," I said once Fia and I were back with our group. While we'd been observing the assembly, Dill, Zeke, and the others had clustered around us in a sort of protective circle. "If we're going to find any sort of lasting peace—"

"Lock up," Dill said, voice low.

"Peoples' choice," Fia said. We were in a lightless cavern, but with our auras connected as they were I could see all of them like glowing silhouettes.

I'd been joined with others before, and I had felt drunk on power. But now I had more power at my fingertips than I knew what to do with, I didn't feel that way. I felt calm. Settled. In control.

"If they see any of us, me included, they won't react well." Memories of fleeing Citadel, chased by children who pelted me with stones, raced through my mind. "Your people killed theirs and I'm not welcome here. Not anymore."

"Hide," Fia said. As she thought it, I saw it, as if our minds were part of the same thing.

The people of Citadel were angry with Roark. All we had to do was sprinkle an idea into their minds—to lock Roark up until they could find a new leader—and they would do the rest.

Together, we formed a circle and held hands—Fia on one side, Dill on the other. Our joined hands were like anchors as we all went back into the frantic energy surrounding Citadel.

I didn't want to force the cave dwellers to do anything against their will—I wasn't like Morrigan—but I didn't mind suggesting what I thought the whole city already wanted. As gently as pouring cool water into a bowl, I let the idea to imprison Roark seep into their minds. I didn't push it, I didn't try to convince them, I just let the idea out so that they could *hear* it. The thought quickly spread from one person to the next like ripples in a pond and I felt their collective intention change.

The wylden and I waited. We *listened*. We *watched* from our hiding place many tunnels away.

The people of Citadel weren't attuned to one another, but together they quickly came to a consensus. When the peoples' collective desire reached Roark, he swelled with rage. His abilities were waning, his vitium solution wearing off, but even if he'd been at full strenght, he was no match for all of his people together.

"It's done," I said, feeling a deep sense of personal relief as our circle broke. Roark had been the one to destroy my childhood. He'd destroyed Aiyanna's, too. And now he'd killed people for the sole purpose of gaining power for himself. It was time for him to pay.

"Stay," Fia said. "Two will watch." Her voice was tired as she pictured two members of our party—the boy and the older man. "Messengers.."

I took a moment to sort through their feelings—something that was going to take practice. They were kind men and willing to do what it would take to broker peace. They would approach the people of Citadel and show them that there was nothing to fear. An old man and a young boy posed no threat to the hundreds of people in the city.

"I don't know your names," I said, turning toward them, even though I could barely make out their silhouettes.

"Alder," said the older man. His voice was gruff, but kind.

"Bala," said the boy. He was only a little older than Sera. Just a kid.

"Alder and Bala," I repeated, wanting to remember their names. It occurred to me that aside from the few wylden I considered my friends, I hadn't made much of an effort to get to know any of them as individuals. It was an old prejudice—that I didn't think of them as people. Not really. I wanted to change that. "When you make it to Citadel, find the elders," I said, showing them the group of men and women who were supposed to advise Roark. "*Show* them what we want, and if they won't listen—" I felt a flare of fear for them, but they exuded confidence. "If they won't listen, then get away. Protect yourselves."

Alder reached over and placed his hand on my shoulder followed by a rush of warm thanks. I felt them say goodbye to the others, and then they left, moving toward the pulsing energy of the city.

"Sunnybrook," Dill said into the strained silence, and I shook my head to clear it. I felt the loss of Bala and Alder more acutely than I'd thought I would. Dill bolstered me as a bit of his maroon aura wrapped around me like a soft blanket.

"We can reach it by tomorrow, I think. Or at least make it back to the upworld somewhere near the wall." I wet my dry, cracked lips.

I missed Finn, and now that I knew who Rosemarie really was, I was even more desperate to get back to her than I had been before. I wanted to know that Luna was okay. That they'd all made it back to Sunnybrook to the children. I longed for Finn's hand in mind, for Luna's fur beneath my fingers, for Rosemarie's gentle presence at my side.

I needed to help the wylden. I hoped Alder and Bala would be alright. And in all of this, I still didn't know where Morrigan was. My hands shook as the weight of all of it pressed in like heavy stone.

"We are with you," Fia said, her voice low. While I longed for Finn and the others, I was grateful to have these friends here with me now. It was because of Fia that I'd been able to see the wylden for what they truly were. Together we could do whatever we needed to.

"Follow you," Zeke said, echoing his words from earlier, but his voice was gentle in a way I'd never heard.

This journey—through the Dark Woods , through the earth—was changing us all.

Through his eyes, I could see myself—*helping his people, helping the people of Citadel, desperate to get back to the people I loved*—and even though he didn't need me as a mate anymore, didn't need me to help the wylden, he was still choosing to help me.

"Okay," I said, chest tight with tension and an overload of emotions. "Follow me."

Chapter 25

"The Fog"

Finn

EVERY step into the woods, Finn fought against Seraphina's hold. His limbs were cooperating with her instructions—feet stepping, arms swinging—but inside he was fighting. He screamed in his mind, hoping one of the children in town would hear him, but he knew he was too far. And even if he weren't, Seraphina was keeping him hidden.

He kept his eyes on Sera in front him, her shoulders curled in as if she were carrying something heavy. She'd betrayed him, after all their time together, she'd blindly believed Morrigan's obvious lies. He cared for Seraphina deeply, loved her like a sister, but at the moment he wanted to rage at her for what she was doing.

Whatever invisible burden she carried seemed to grow heavier as her shoulders curled in a little more.

He breathed in and out through his nose, trying to calm his racing heart enough to think this through. When Morrigan had controlled him, everything had felt hazy and sleepy. He'd been almost numb to the outside word. And when he'd been tied to Erilyn it had just felt like finally being settled. Being at home in his own skin. Sera's tie—her leash—was something in between. She wasn't forcing him to do anything other than to keep putting one foot in front of the other and keep his mouth shut. She wasn't clouding his thoughts, so he felt every ounce of his desperation to get free. And he knew she did too. Being stuck like this was worse than being trapped alone in that closet in Ringol.

In his closet cell, he'd tried to force himself out and it had only made things worse. He needed to think. With every ounce of individual will power he still possessed, he took deep, deliberate breaths. Calmer than he was, he tried to make his lips move, to convince her with the sound of his voice to stop this, but no sound passed his lips.

Sera looked back over her shoulder and met his steely gaze. Her eyes were wide with what he thought might be shame, her cheeks were tinged pink. Through her hold on him, he felt a surge of affection and longing. It was so strong, so overwhelming, that it broke through his anger.

Unlike when Morrigan had him tethered to her, he could feel Sera's emotions. If he could feel her, he knew she could hear him. He just had to make her listen.

Sera, he thought, putting all of his remaining will behind that single word. Her feet stumbled, but kept walking. *You don't have to do this.*

She flinched as if she'd been hit. She didn't stumble again, but she ducked her head as if embarrassed.

Your siblings, he said, picturing their faces. *Aiyanna and Lucy. Rosemarie. We need to get back to them. We need to get back to our family.*

Faintly, like an echo of a word spoken, Finn could feel her resolve begin to waver. The leash that held his mouth tied shut and pulled his steps forward loosened just a little.

Relief swept through him like a gust of fresh air. The muscles in his jaw released. Finn opened his mouth to speak out loud when he felt a new presence in his mind. It was thorny and made him want to shove it away, but he couldn't. His jaw snapped shut again, tighter than before.

Finley, Morrigan's whispered voice bounced around inside his skull and he recoiled from it as much as he could. He tasted something metallic and rotten as a burning pain sliced through his head. *Eventually, you'll understand.*

Seraphina, he begged as tears welled in his eyes and bile rose in his throat. *Please.* Even the words in his mind felt choked off now, as if they were being muffled by a blanket.

Sera didn't say anything else, but Morrigan's presence left abruptly and he thought maybe Seraphina had pushed her out. But then Sera was gone too. Her leash tightened and Finn's muscles went rigid. He could no longer *feel* her feelings, or *sense* her at all. But his thoughts were still his own, and he considered that a small victory.

"You're strong," Morrigan said, slowing from her position in the front of their party to walk beside

Seraphina. She stood too close. Finn tried to move, to step between them, to keep Morrigan away, but his body was not his own. Morrigan glanced over her shoulder, through the curtain of dark hair that had once been shiny and sleek but now was stringy and tangled. She smiled at him and a shiver raced down his spine. She reminded him of a wylden.

"Stronger than you realize," Morrigan said as she turned back to Sera.

"I am when I'm with the others—" Sera started, her voice soft.

"The others aren't here now, are they?" Morrigan said. She inched closer and her fingers were like claws as they curled around Seraphina's narrow shoulders. She pulled the slight girl against her side.

Inside, Finn screamed *NO!* but no one heard him. Or if they did, they ignored him.

Sera shook her head and looked up. Morrigan was nearly as tall as Finn, all lean muscle and sharp lines. For a time he'd thought her the most beautiful woman in the world, but now he could see her for who she truly was—ferocious, angry, unstable.

"No," Seraphina said after a long moment. "They're not. It's just me."

"Just you," Morrigan said, squeezing her shoulder. "And look what you can do." Morrigan stopped and physically turned Seraphina toward Finn. "You can do *whatever you want*, Seraphina. No one to tell you where to go or what you're allowed to do. You're strong enough just as you are."

Seraphina looked at Finn, her eyes open and searching. He tried to talk to her, but she was still shutting him out. He couldn't form words in his mind, so he pulled forward memories. *Asa telling them all about different plants. Noah and Jubal holding hands as they walked. Galen clinging to Seraphina's neck and falling asleep with his cheek on her shoulder.*

"You're *helping* him by bringing him with us," Morrigan said, her voice a scratchy whisper. She leaned closer to Seraphina's ear and for a moment, Finn thought he saw a hint of red flash around her body, but it was there and gone. A trick of the sun. "If you want him to stop *showing* and *telling* you things you don't want to know, just make him stop." Morrigan smiled. Her grip on Seraphina's shoulder tightened and Sera winced. "It won't hurt him. It will just make it easier for him to accept what we're doing to help him." Her grip loosened and she stroked the side of Seraphina's hair as Aiyanna and Rosemarie often did.

Seraphina looked at Finn. *Please,* he wanted to say. *Please, don't do this.* But he couldn't. The little girl he'd grown to love, who loved him, wouldn't do this. But when he looked into her eyes now, he didn't see that little girl anymore.

And then, like fog that rolled in so thick you couldn't see your own hand, his thoughts and feelings were swallowed up and quieted.

This is what it had been like to be controlled by Morrigan, except then he hadn't realized what was happening until it was over. Experiencing it happen was infinitely worse.

Finn could still remember everything—that he didn't want to be here, that he was being brought against his will, that what he wanted more than anything in the world was to get back to Erilyn and the rest of his friends—but even with all those memories still accessible, it was like he had no emotions tied to them. He was numb and cold and couldn't muster the energy to care.

"There," Morrigan said, squeezing Seraphina's shoulder again, gently this time. "Isn't that better? Now he won't feel so sad."

Seraphina didn't say anything, but she nodded. And when Morrigan turned, she turned with her. Finn followed them, no longer able to fight against his imprisonment, no longer wanting to, as they walked further and further away from Sunnybrook.

Chapter 26

"Subtleties"

Morrigan

YOU'RE proud of how well you're keeping your feelings hidden. Hearing Finn think about Erilyn—how her tether had been so much *better* than yours—as well as those other brats made you want to scream. More than once you wanted to grab hold of the girl's tether, to take control for her, but you can't. All you can do is listen and watch and it's almost unbearable. If you were in control, he wouldn't think of them at all. Ever. He would only think of you.

But you aren't in control. At least not directly. At least not yet.

You can be patient. The nightcrawler girl is young and pliable and with the right ministrations bends easily to your desires. It was simple to turn her against him, to push her to do as you wished. Given enough time, Finn will either forget Erilyn, or you and the girl will force him to.

Just the thought of Erilyn as less than a memory sends sweet chills along your skin. You try to think back to the time before her intrusion into your lives, but it's difficult, so you focus on other sorts of memories. Of the heat between your bodies as Finn wrapped his limbs around you. You relax as this memory satiates you, but too quickly Finn becomes Cillian and your skin tingles as you long for his fingertips to brush your arm, to cup your cheek. Tears are in your eyes and you are again looking down at him as his eyes go blank, as blood trickles from his mouth into the dirt of stinking Ringol. All previous warmth gone, you shove the image from your mind with as much force as you can.

A quick glance at the girl tells you that you kept all of that to yourself—a mild balm. She's too distracted by Finn to pay attetion, anyway. You try to focus on her—she's strong and easy to manipulate, which makes her the perfect weapon. Focusing on her helps you not focus on the memory of Cillian's pale, lifeless face. Helps you forget how badly you wish he were here now.

"Where are we going?" Seraphina asks after a while, her voice tired. You've been walking for hours, mostly in silence. You aren't tired, and her waekaness is irritating, but you keep yourself in check. If you want to use her power, you have to keep up her strength and morale.

"We're going to the dark forest." You keep your voice light, because you know she'll resist this. You'd hoped to be closer before telling her your plan. Seraphina stops, which means Finn does, too. "It's okay," you say, smiling broadly as you face her. "When I was there before, I explored. The animals there are just misunderstood.

They're no more or less dangerous than animals anywhere else," you lie.

"It's not safe," she says, then looks at Finn for confirmation. He nods in agreement, but his eyes are still unfocused so you know she's making him agree. How childish of her.

"For anyone else, you'd be right." You step forward to hold both her shoulders in your long-fingered hands. "But for us—" you give her shoulders a squeeze, stare into her unnatural eyes, and *push* the slightest bit, "it's safe. I *promise*."

She fidgets as if uncomfortable—fighting back—so you *push* a little harder. She can't know what you're doing, so you have to keep it small, keep it subtle, make her think they're her own thoughts and conclusions as they come to her. If you push too much, too fast, she'll figure it out and your hold on her isn't strong enough yet. She might break free.

You picture the starlings, then layer that with a feeling of serenity and in her mind the dark feathered-creatures soften. You imagine the twin wolves and focus on their soft, fluffy fur instead of their fangs, and she warms to them as well. You can't think of the cat, it's too grotesque, but the two other animals were enough. Seraphina relaxes and you move again..

"We need to get there quickly," you tell her. You take her hand as you'd seen Rosemarie and the older nightcrawler do. You'd rather not—her skin is sticky and there's dirt under ner nails—but Seraphina smiles at you and you smile back. You are figuring out more and more how to control her. She's so simple, it's sad.

Through your linked hands, you offer her a little of your energy, taken from the vitium infusion you drank, and her pace picks up.

You could take them on the safe path through the woods that you see in Seraphina's head, that's what she wants to do, but you worry that Erilyn made it through. Instead, you take the long and winding way, letting the forest call to you and guide you. Seraphina hides you, and you lead.

The Dark Woods are close—so much closer than anyone ever realized, hidden by the animals inside—but there's a stop you want to make first. Besides, you need to give your dark creatures extra time to finish off Erilyn and any wylden beasts she brought with her.

BY nightfall, Finley and the nightcrawler girl are dragging. Through Sera's hold on him, you feel the beginnings of his agitation. He knows where you are, though you aren't sure the girl realizes yet. It's part of the reason you wanted to bring him here—to see how he would react, to see how tight Seraphina's hold really is.

When you walk into the clearing where Erilyn had once lived, Finn stumbles. You see his green aura flare and fight anew against the girl's hold, even though he's even more exhausted than she is. You look around and cringe—everything is infused with Erilyn's putrid gold light, though it's faded in her long absence. You didn't notice it the first time you were here, but you were distracted then. You are sure Seraphina can see it, too. You're curious to see if she can maintain her control on Finley here where Erilyn's aura, her presence, has stained everything. If the girl can manage him here, she can manage him anywhere.

"This is Erilyn's place," Seraphina says in the middle of the clearing.

"It is." You crouch by the fire pit and start a small flame in the twigs and leaves that have collected there.

"Why are we here?" Her voice shakes and warning blares in your mind. Being here is making her miss Erilyn and causing her to second guess her trust in you.

You hadn't considered that. You hadn't considered that the girl might actually care about Erilyn, too. Her thoughts were so focused on Finn, on her teenage need for him to love her, that you'd thought she despised Erilyn. Just like you.

Coming here was a mistake. You have to tread carefully.

"I thought being here might give you both some comfort. A way to say goodbye," you say. You stoke the fire you've built and allow the flames to feed on your energy as much as the little bit of wood. "I know leaving your behind was hard. But it *is* for the best." With the small fire flickering in front of your hands, you turn to the girl. "I know you care about her—" you keep your voice soft when you want to snarl, "but that doesn't change the fact that she's a danger. To both Finn and you." You step closer to her. "If she knew how you felt about him—" the girl jerks as if you slapped her and her eyes flicker to Finn then back to you. "Who knows what she would do to you."

Because the girl is young and afraid and inexperienced in the ways of love, this lie is enough and you *feel* her calm. Your tether is secure.

While the girl battles with her own feelings, Finn looks all around, eyes wide. Sera has loosened her hold on him in her distraction.

"Can you gather some firewood?" you ask her. You need time alone with Finn. He's successfully kept you out, but maybe, through your control of Seraphina, you can figure out a way to control him a little without having to ask her to do it for you. "I'll keep Finn safe here." You smile and tuck a strand of white hair behind her ear, then lay your dirty hand against her freakishly pale cheek

"Okay," she says, looking between the two of you. "Just—" she hesitates. "Don't leave me," she whispers.

"We'll be right here." You gently swipe your thumb against the soft skin of her cheek and she relaxes. It's ridiculous how easy her trust has been to gain. You still need her, so you will keep your promise.

When she's out of earshot, when you know she's focused on finding firewood and keeping Finn calm from a distance, you make your move.

Finn's eyes go wide as you approach. His muscles tense as if he wants to spring away, but he can't. He's standing, but you're nearly his height so you don't have to look up to meet his gaze like most women would. His eyes look almost as green as his aura in the flickering firelight. You lay your hand on his cheek and ignore how the muscles in his neck tense as if he wants to pull away. Those same muscles used to tense for more pleasant reasons thanks to your touch.

"Finley," you whisper into the night. "When this is all over, things will go back to how they were. How they're supposed to be." You stroke his bearded cheek. You need to find a razor for him to shave so that his cheek is as soft and smooth as it was when you were together. Cillian's beardless face flashes in your mind, but you shove it away and focus on the man before you. "Just you and me." You lean forward to press your lips to his cheek, just beside the corner of his mouth. You are thinking of shifting just a little, of pressing your lips against his so that he remembers why he loved you in the first place, when he jerks his head back.

He shouldn't be able to move. Not even a little.

"No," he growls through clenched teeth. Sweat has beaded on his forehead as if he'd just run a great distance. You take a step back and look at his aura. It is as vibrantly green as a tree in the peak of summer, but within it you see gold, leeching into his aura from the ground. Even the waste from Erilyn's aura calls to him and his aura accepts it willingly.

Anger consumes you in a flash—lightning setting fresh dry kindling ablaze.

You lean forward so that your nose is almost touching his, your heart pounding like a war drum. "You don't have a choice," you breathe and are gratified when you see the horror in his eyes.

Seraphina is returning and you quickly move back to the fire. You smile at her as she lays down the little bit of wood she returned with, her eyes narrowed in suspicion.

"He's upset," she says, looking at Finn, her aura going milky and pale with concern.

"He doesn't understand how we're helping him. Not yet," you say, forcing your own racing heart to slow. "Help him calm down, Seraphina." You say it like a suggestion, but you also *push*. She's so focused on him, she doesn't notice.

Seraphina takes his hand—his eyes widen, but she just smiles, her cheeks pink—and forces him to calm. His shoulders sag and his eyelids grow heavy. The gold that was beign absorbed by his green slip away. Around the edges of his green are bits of almost-gold. Once you have full control of his mind again, you'll burn it all out.

Tired now, Seraphina leads Finn to the fire and he lays down. He doesn't fight her—or rather, he can't—and he is asleep, his head on his arm, in seconds.

Your lips can still feel the warmth of the corner of his mouth where you kissed him. "Well done. We'll leave at first light." The girl nods, but keeps her eyes glued to Finn's face as she worries the hem of her ragged skirt with her tiny, white hands.

Chapter 27

"Sidetracked"

Erilyn

WE walked in silence, all exhausted. I found myself straining to *hear* Alder and Bala the further we got from them, but they were hidden well. We'd traveled far outside the limits of Citadel, but we weren't yet to Sunnybrook. This land, these tunnels, were unknown to me.

As a child, I'd thought I'd been everywhere the underground had to offer. The adults had sent us in groups out to harvest food and from the perspective of a ten year old, I'd felt very important—at least for a while. I had been trusted with traveling out into the earth to gather life sustaining food for my people. But now I knew we'd never gone very far from the city center. We'd been in Citadel, close to the protection of the city, the whole time.

Using my senses now, I could see how enormous the network of tunnels truly was. Like tree roots, these tunnels began in Citadel but spread out far and wide in all directions, going miles in all directions. If Sunnybrook weren't so clear up ahead—a mass of pale lights and vibration that could only be a group of people living together—I could easily get us lost down here.

When the collective exhaustion of my wylden friends reached its peak, I stopped and whispered, "We'll need to rest here tonight." All five of them were on edge—their auras clinging to mine like little hands holding on to their mother's skirt. They were people of the sun and sky, not of dark holes and rock. "But just for a little while."

They would do as I wanted, I could feel as much, but I could also feel their discomfort at still being trapped in the dark beneath so many tons of earth.

Light. We needed light. I felt selfish for not thinking of that before. I had been so focused on my desperate need to get back to Sunnybrook, to get back to Finn and Rosemarie, I hadn't paused to consider how being down here might affect the wylden.

We didn't have torches or lanterns, but I had an idea. We needed a naturally occurring source of light.

I led our small group into a cavern that was big enough for us all to lie down. They all sat huddled together, and their auralights were nearly blending together as they comforted one another in the pitch black.

While they tried to settle, I closed my eyes and tried to think past the constant, soft noise that came with being connected to them. Unlocking my old memories and being so attached to the wylden for so long had taught me a tremendous amount about my own abilities. Separate fromor them for a moment, I let my mind drift into the cracks in the stone. There was so much more life down here than people realized—insects and fungi and burrowing rodents and snakes—but I was looking for one creature in particular. I let the vitium soaked earth carry me along like a current in a stream.

When I heard the gentle song that I knew so well, one I would forever know deep in my soul, I knew I'd found the. Tears pricked my eyes as I reached out and called them to me. These were not the same creatures I'd known in my youth, but still they came as if somehow, as a collective, they remembered me. When I heard Dill gasp, I knew they'd arrived.

I didn't expect such a rush of emotion when I saw them and I stumbled toward them without meaning to. The wylden, all seated, leaned toward the tiny glowworms as they crawled slowly from the crevices in the walls and spread out, dotting the walls and ceiling, to light the cavern. They filled our space with a pale blue-green light like so many far away stars.

Their song was cool and clear and reminded me of the glowworms that that had been killed when I was a child, and all the ones before them that had comforted me in my darkest times. As these memories joined the song in my mind, their light increased and pulsed along with each beat of my heart. Even though they had no language, they were listening.

"Light," Fia said, her voice relieved.

"They'll stay with us," I said. "I'm sorry I didn't think of it before." I, too, felt relieved to have a reprieve from the darkness.

"Stars," Dill whispered, his voice breaking. He sat on his knees, fingers extended as if he might want to touch them.

"Grateful," Zeke said, lifting his chin. Zeke's eyes, and the eyes of the others, reflected the glowworms' blue-green light. They were beautiful.

"We'll sleep for a bit before we head on," I said. They all nodded, eyes still on the glowworms above and around us. "I'll keep watch." No one looked at me, but I felt their gratitude.

After a few more moments, the wylden laid down to sleep, shoulder to shoulder. Dill fell asleep last, his eyes glued to the glowworms until he could hold them open no longer.

Only when I was sure they were all asleep and wouldn't be affected by my thoughts and feelings did I give in to the overwhelming feelings that I had been keeping at bay since we entered the earth.

Thanks to my time in Ringol, splitting my aura between more than one thing was a simple thing now. I kept watch with part of my awareness focused on our surroundings, but I let the rest of me drift, untethered, while waves of emotions from all that had transpired in the last day washed over me.

As a child, I'd been put into Citadel's orphanage. Before today, some of my earliest memories were of glowworm-filled lanterns held tight to my chest. At the time, I'd imagined I could feel warmth in the glass, could hear a song they sang to only me. Now I knew that it had all been real. Their light mimicked ther auras—a pale, beautiful aqua that reminded me of the sea in some of the picture books Rosemarie had read to me.

I had so much to process. With deep, steady breaths, I floated in the glowworm light—soft and cool. It reminded me of floating in my pond with the darting lights of the minnows all around me, the sun trickling through the thick canopy of leaves above. I could easily imagine the birds singing softly from all around while Luna sunned only feet away. It was peaceful and just what I needed to face these new memories.

I was a toddler. *Crying. Screaming. All around, the walls glowed teal. It hurt my eyes even though it wasn't that bright. My skin felt burned and raw. A woman came in the midst of my crying and lifted me from my hard bed. She cradled and rocked me as I screamed in pain and fear.* I could feel the echoes of that pain now. *The woman, my nanny, rocked me and suddenly the pain eased as I felt her for the first time—her sadness, which was cool, and her fondness for me. She made me think of my mama and daddy, of my grandma, and my tears and cries tripled.*

The memory shifted and I was now little older—maybe three. *The woman who had held me was now the one who was crying. She was holding her head, staring around at the walls and talking to herself under her breath. The light didn't hurt my eyes or skin anymore—it was almost soothing now—but her feelings did. She was confused and angry and her feelings pressed and grated against me like rough stone. She paced back and forth, pulling at her white hair, while I sat in my crib—almost too big for it now—and covered my ears in an attempt to block out her feelings. Her aura was a pale yellow, almost white, and I watched as it fractured and split.*

Another shift, like turning the pages of a book. I was still in the same room, but the woman had stopped her pacing. She was sleeping on her cot on the floor beside my crib, her presence at my side prickly as her broken aura zapped around her like lightning. As I lay there, a deep sense of loneliness settled in my young chest. I pressed my feet against the bars of the crib, but I was too long to stretch out now. So, curled on my back, I watched as glowworms gathered on the ceiling. They twinkled and their song filled my head and lulled me to sleep, washing the loneliness away.

Hot tears leaked from my eyes, but I didn't wipe them away. Just like he had with Seraphina and the others, Roark had put me in a vitium cave. I had been the first in his experimental army. My nanny's mind had deteriorated there. She'd been fine when she first started caring for me, but then she'd broken. He'd chosen children, because unlike adults, we could adapt.

It was so much. Too much. Like I used to do so often in the woods that were my home, I focused on my breath, and with each inhale I remembered all the things I wanted to forget, and with each exhale I let them go one at a time. At least for now.

My parents dying in the mouth of a cave—their main concern to keep me safe.

My nanny in the vitium cave who'd cared for me slowly going insane as she, too, tried to keep me safe.

The vitium walls pressing in on me like a heavy, painful weight.

Being alone for so long. So very long.

With those painful memories gone, at least for now, I wanted to try to get some rest. I expected to float in the glowworm light until morning. I could stay awake and still rest as the little furry worms lent me their energy through the night. But before I could drift into a restful state, something at the edge of my awareness caught my attention. It was big, but quiet, and once I *sensed* it, I couldn't pull away. I felt pulled toward it like a tide.

Curious about what it could be, I drifted closer. There were no images, no sounds, just a deep vibration that resonated deep in my bones. Never had I experienced anything like it. I moved deeper into the earth, further from my friends, but the vibration didn't seem to get any closer. So I stopped and focused to see where it was, to figure out what it might be.

I took a breath, reached out with my awareness once more, and gasped as I was jerked away into memories. Except this time, they weren't the memories of a person. They were memories carried by the earth.

Chapter 28

"Resistance"

Finn

FINN had thought if he ever returned to Erilyn's clearing he would be with her and Luna. He'd thought that maybe they would come back and stay for a while as they figured out where they best belonged, together. That maybe they could build a small house here or at least somewhere nearby.

Instead, he was again stuck in that fog that Morrigan had put him in, except this time someone he loved and trusted had put him there instead. It was a very special sort of torment.

Morrigan and Sera had gone to sleep hours ago. The fire had died down to embers and the moon shone brightly above, but Finn was wide awake. He couldn't move—Sera's hold on him, even while she slept, was strong—but her compulsion for him to sleep as well had worn off. When she'd put him under, he'd wanted to scream. Wanted to ask her why she was doing this, to show her how badly it hurt. But he couldn't. Even his thoughts had been caged since Morrigan's intervention.

But with both of them asleep, his mind was free—at least for now—and his thoughts were his own.

He stared up at the sky and watched the moon and stars inch across the sky. He'd woken over an hour earlier and had been struggling to move, even a little bit, the whole time. As soon as Seraphina and Morrigan woke, he'd be leashed again. This was his only chance to get away. Finn didn't want to leave Sera behind, but Morrigan had done something to her. His only chance to save her was to get away and come back with help.

He'd been struggling, teeth gritted, for the better part of an hour and all it had gotten him was a sense of frustration and desperation.

It was like his mind was trapped inside a body of stone. Sweat beaded on his brow as he tried in vain to wiggle his fingers or toes, but no matter how hard he strained, how loud he screamed in his mind, his body was not his own.

The only part of his body that responded to his desires were his eyes and he desperately looked around for anything that might help. His gaze landed on Erilyn's pine and fresh pain bloomed in his chest. He was grateful Morrigan hadn't suggested they sleep beneath it. That was Erilyn's place—where he'd first slept beside her. First learned her kindness as she nursed him back to health. In the moonlight now he saw the blossoms—tiny white flowers dotting the side of the tree that had been burned. In his memory he could still see the tree, limbs smoking, as Erilyn sang life back into it. She'd used her gifts to save it and to make it something new. Just like she had done for the wylden. Just like she had done for Finn.

His heart beat with a dull ache and as he remembered her singing to the tree that had been her home—her smile, her eyes bright as he held her close. He could almost imagine her golden aura surrounding them both, just as he'd seen it in his wylden cell, when one of his fingers twitched.

He was so startled by the feeling that the images of Erilyn in his mind vanished. His heart stuttered and his breaths were strained. He'd moved his finger. Rejuvenated by that small success, he decided to try again.

He thought back to how it had felt to be trapped with Erilyn inside that hollow tree when they'd been attacked by big cats all those weeks ago. Her body had been warm against his and he'd felt complete trust that she would keep them safe even though they hadn't known each other well. Before that, she'd been a stranger, but when he'd shown up here, she'd helped him heal. Her kindness had renewed his faith in humanity after Morrigan had crushed it.

Erilyn. He held her face in his mind and it was almost like he could hear her telling him to just *try*. That she knew he could do it. He pictured her, hand on Luna's head, holding her other hand out to him as if asking him to join her.

His skin tingled, like a limb waking up after being asleep for too long. With great effort, Finn rolled to one side. He was sweating, struggling as if he were being held in place with ropes, but he was moving.

On his hands and knees, he looked up at Erilyn's tree and he breathed in the scent of pine needles—a scent he would always associate with her. The little white blossoms shifted lightly in the wind reminding him of the glowworms in her caves and the joy they'd given her. His joints loosened and his muscles responded.

Each shuffle of his hands and knees hurt, but still he crawled, hoping that if he could get enough distance from them, from Sera, her hold would snap like a string pulled too tight. He pictured Erilyn's face again, the fire in her eyes when she was angry, the way her whole demeanor opened up when she wanted to help someone, and it helped him move along inch by painful inch. He pictured her lips, how they curled up at their edges just before he kissed her, and he was able to move a little faster, a little more fluidly.

With every inch, he moved a little faster. He made it to the edge of the clearing and hoped for a brief, brilliant moment, that he had made it. He could feel her hold lessening with each shuffle of his palms and knees through the crackly brown leaves. A little further and he could get up. Could get away.

But as he crossed into the woods, they began to stir. It was quiet at first, the sound of limbs stretching and breath changing. He was moving more freely now and felt his limbs loosening. He would be able to stand, to run, if he could just make it a little further. A few more feet.

But Morrigan must have felt him leaving. "Seraphina," Morrigan snapped, her voice making the blood and Finn's veins run icy.

He was moments away from freedom—he could feel it as clearly as the sun on his face—when Seraphina's invisible leash snapped taut. Inside his mind he screamed as his body went rigid.

"I'm sorry," the little girl said, voice heavy with sleep and anguish. "I've got him now."

Finn pictured Erilyn's face, imagined her calling to him, but his limbs wouldn't respond anymore. The scream became a howl of rage.

"We'll have to tie his hands next time," Morrigan said, her voice almost bored as she yawned.

"I don't think we need to—"

"You're so willing to let him get back to her?" Morrigan's voice was low and sharp.

"No," Sera whispered.

"Bring him back," Morrigan spat.

Finn tried to fight the pull, but it was fruitless. He felt Seraphina direct his limbs like puppets on wire and he mechanically pushed himself up and rejoined them in the clearing. He sat beside her, spine straight. She smiled at him as if to reassure him, but she didn't force him to smile back. If she had, he would have fought it.

Morrigan dug in her pack and retrieved a length of ragged rope. She tossed it into Seraphina's lap. Sera's eyes were downcast as she sat on her knees and bound his hands.

"We need to keep moving," Morrigan said as she stared up at the gray dawn sky.

"Can we eat first?" Sera asked.

Morrigan scoffed. "We have to hunt in order to eat."

Seraphina blanched, but said nothing. Sera didn't eat meat for the same reasons Erilyn didn't, but if Morrigan knew that, she didn't seem to care.

"I'll find something on the way and we can stop to cook it," Morrigan said. She pulled a water skin from her bag and took a long drink. "Drink some water from the pond and let's go."

Seraphina took one last long, sad look at Finn, then nodded. Unable to respond, he watched as she followed Morrigan's orders. Once again trapped in his stone body, he knew that his only chance to escape was gone. They would never let their guard down like that again.

Chapter 29

"Layers"

Morrigan

THE shock of seeing Finley crawling away, pulling against the nightcrawler's tether, sets your heart racing, but you hide it well. When you speak to the girl your voice is firm, but clear, and your anxiety and sudden rage are hidden behind the facade you wear so easily now.

As Finn is put back into the cocoon Seraphina has created for him, you take a moment to collect yourself. You watch him, his aura, his spirit, his energy, fighting to get free. More of Erilyn's castoff gold has joined with his green, making him strong. The girl's will to obey you, to keep him tied, is starting to wain in the face of his panic and anger. Her weakness is something you cannot abide.

A little more of your red ties her pink, but she's so focused on Finn that she doesn't notice. As the sun rises, bathing you in cool, yellow light, you fight the urge to tighten your grip on the girl even more. Her feelings for him are strong and prickle against your skin like icy rain. You could take her over completely, force her feelings away, and through her, force Finn's feelings for Erilyn away, but you worry That if you try it now, it won't work. It'st oo soon.

So instead, you just infuse her aura with a little more of your own, letting those tiny tendrils take root, and try to force your anger down where she won't sense it. Letting her drag him along on a leash allows you to conserve your energy.

"We need to move." The girl's hunger makes her a liability and you wrinkle your nose in disgust. "I'll find food for us on the way." You try to make your voice soft, to feign compassion for her needs, and she nods.

You take another drink from your waterskin. With vitium fresh in your veins, you put on your pack—one scavenged from the wylden town before you left—and leave, knowing they will both follow, because they have to. They are nothing more than wild animals you need to tame.

Leaving Erilyn's gold-stained clearing helps you calm down. You should never have gone there. You'd gone there to see if Sera could control him, but also to taunt him. Hurt him for choosing Erilyn over you. But it hadn't worked. Instead, you'd woken to him crawling away, filled with his longing for *her*.

Away from the remnants of Erilyn, your head clears.

You should have gone straight to the Dark Woods where you can hide in the twisted trees. Your grip on Seraphina is tentative, but once you're inside, the forest will help you take full control.

You lead them toward the Dark Woods but focus on finding her food—as you promised. The woods are cold and you can hear Finn's heavy footfalls behind you. Part of you thinks he might be in just enough control to do it on purpose to try and alert someone to your presence, but it doesn't matter. Out here, you are alone. The crunch of leaves beneath his boots is nothing but a lovely noise that reminds you of how far from anyone else you are.

Finally.

But the nightcrawler's hunger is starting to wear on you and you know you need to find food quickly before you lose your patience. So you let your mind expand until you find squirrels in a tree nearby.

You're preparing to call them to you so you can slit one of their throats—just the thought of it sends a thrill through you—when the girl grabs your arm. You hiss at the abrupt interruption, teeth bared, and she stumbles back.

"I don't eat animals," she squeaks, her voice barely there. She swallows heavily. "The squirrels you found, I—I can't eat them."

"That's ridiculous," you say, preparing to turn back toward them, but she grabs your arm again and you gasp as she shares a memory with you.

Desperately hungry. Eating a bite of charred meat in a dark cave. Desperation overwhelming her as she felt the animals death. The food coming back up as she cried, holding her knees to her belly and wishing for death. She had been alone—before the other children arrived.

You still think her foolish and weak—the death of each creature you ate gave you strength—but she'd shared it with you with an expectation of empathy. And so you give her that.

"I didn't know," you say, voice scratchy and low. "I'm sorry. We can try to find something else."

The girl practically glows with acceptance and you know you've made the right call. Even though it irritates you, you force your focus away from the squirrels and instead try to find any late winter berries. You aren't sure what sorts of food are safe to eat in the Dark Woods .

You've never sought out plants, but the girl is adept at it. You can't ask her to join with you, to help you search, because she might sense your tether, but you can see how she did it in her mind. You set a grueling pace to keep her distracted as she pulls Finn along and try to mimic what she'd done.

You try to *sense* the weaker auras of the plants. It's more difficult, because you've always attuned yourself so strongly to things with heartbeats, but you can do it. You can do anything.

Seeking out the plants now reminds you of when you'd first learned to use your abilities with Cillian all those months ago, after Rosemarie finally created a solution that was ingestible. A smile creeps onto your face as you remember.

It had been warm, and Cillian had agreed to take the solution with you. You'd been sleeping with him for a while, telling Finn you were working late. He'd been your secret, and you'd been his. When he had offered to take the solution with you, it had meant something more than you could put into words. It made what you were doing with him more real.

You'd gone out into the woods near the quarry where Rosemarie was being held. It had been warm and sticky outside, and he had unbuttoned his shirt and exposed his broad, pale chest. It had been sweet, the way he sat in front of you you, legs crossed, knees pressed against yours. He'd stared into your eyes as you both touched your water skins to your lips and taken that first glorious sip.

You shiver now as you remember how the vitium had washed over your tongue and down your throat. How his hand had found yours just as your *senses* exploded outward. You'd gasped and gripped his fingers and he'd gripped yours.

And then, you could *feel* him. His heartbeat was strong and loud. His attraction for you was like a musk in the air. Silvery light shone all around him, rivaling the light from the sun.

And then he was on top of you, lips and hands hungry, and you forgot about anything except the way his hard, warm body felt as it pressed yours into the soft, moldable earth.

But then the memory shifts and you trip as his heavy, warm body transforms into his corpse—skin pale, eyes empty. You breath deeply through your nose, but his lifeless face still floats there in your mind. You can't shove it away. Can't shake it. You clench fists that tremble at your sides.

"I'm sorry about Cillian," Seraphina says, suddenly at your elbow. You grit your teeth and nod, but say nothing. "He wasn't so bad," she says, wincing, and for a moment you imagine slapping her for such a pitiful attempt at consolation. But you don't. You only nod again and she falls back.

You walk awhile in silence, still picturing the ghost of Cillian's dead face in your mind. You try to distract yourself by looking for food, any pale sign of plant life, but he's there, just beyond your reach, and you can't focus.

Just you're sure you'll have to convince the girl to eat meat, you find something—beautyberries. There aren't many—a few handfuls—but the bright pinkish-purple berries catch your eye and you make a beeline toward them. Normally they're all gone by early winter, but when you sense the earth here, you feel a thick vein of vitium below the earth. That's the only reason you can think of that this bush would have survived the winter. The leaves are gone, but the berries clumped on the branches like kabobs are vivid and ripe.

As the others join you, you carefully break off the few limbs with berries.

"Beautyberry," you say as Seraphina looks at the berries skeptically. "It's safe." To prove it, you hold the stick up to your mouth and bite off a clump, each berry no bigger than a pea. The berries burst in your mouth and the unique flavor brings back other, unwanted memories.

"They're sweet and spicy," Cillian had said before he presses a clump of them to your lips. "Like you."

You take another bite, trying to ignore the flavor and the memories it carries.

Serphina takes a bite and wrinkles her nose, but finishes the berries quickly. You hand the other branch to Finn and he takes it with wooden movements.

"Eat, Finn," Seraphina says, her voice sticky-sweet. He eats, because she makes him, and she smiles as if he is doing it to please her.

"If we continue on," you say, tucking your branch of beautyberries into your pack to eat later, "we can make it to the Dark Woods by nightfall."

Sera swallows heavily and nods.

You lick the berry juice from your lips. If you let yourself, you could remember how Cillian had kissed you with lips stained magenta. But instead, you look back at Finn and see the same, dark stain on his mouth.

Cillian is dead, but Finn is not. A smile spreads across your face and you wonder if the berries have tinted your lips as they have Finn's. You imagine pressing the stains together and burning all of your memories of Cillian away.

Yes. This is enough. With thoughts of Finley firm in your mind, you turn and lead your two pets toward your inevitable future in the Dark Woods .

Chapter 30

"Waylaid"
Erilyn

RINGOL *is full of men and women wearing white lab coats. A table sites beside a building that is vaguely familiar. Two men stand on one side while people—young and old alike, all haggard and hollow—line up on the other side. When the people reach the table they are handed a small cup with two dark pills in it, along with a piece of paper.*

The image shifts, I think time has passed, and the once docile people have changed. *They're savage, biting and scratching and screaming at the people in white coats who fight and run. They scramble into big vehicles which pour rancid smoke from pipes. A few of the large machines are one fire. Not all the people in white make it and the white of their coats are stained with blood and dirt as the people of Ringol wreak havoc on their town.*

Another shift and the scene goes dark. *People in dark clothes load crates and boxes onto carts and moving through caves mouths, deep into the earth. The crates are hidden away. People hide with them as others come with weapons. Inside the boxes, pure vitium pulses.*

The people with weapons—with guns—try to fight their way to the raw vitium, but no matter how many people they kill, they can't find it. Can't find all the people hidden away in the dark. And then the wild townspeople from Ringol are there—the wylden—and their threat is too great to continue to search.

The images begin to shift rapidly, like flipping through a book, and I grow dizzy.

The wylden fight the people above for so long, the people below are forgotten.

The people below find vitium chambers and surround them, but never move inside. The crates are scattered to keep them safe, then forgotten. The people below stay there and grow pale as the vitium in the caves, hidden away in the crates, all around them, leeches into them. It's the birth of Citadel.

Another shift. The caves are gone and I'm in Sunnybrook, heart aching. *The people are confused and afraid as they use whatever is at hand to build a wall. The people of Ringgold, once their friends, have attacked them. There's no time for burials. The bodies of the dead are burned, and the wall is built with the remnants of buildings torn down for supplies.*

Through it all, I can feel so many big things—*the world outside away from here, away from Appalachia, is at war over vitium as the other sources of fuel run out. Battles rage. People die. Until there's hardly anything left. People everywhere are torn asunder.*

The breath in my chest feels tight. The memories are coming as images and feelings and a sense of knowing, so fast it's hard to keep them all straight.

Generation-upon-generation of people inside the walls of Sunnybrook, their friendship with Ringgold forgotten as their fear of the wylden grows.

In Citadel, the city grows as the people learn to chisel out new tunnels and homes. Scouts travel in the dead of night to Sunnybrook and steal food and supplies to supplement what they can't make themselves.

The wylden living in the crumbling buildings of Ringgolds, learning to scavenge as they follow trails of vitium beneath the earth like fish traveling along a stream.

The world outside, coming back to life. Appalachia, forgotten.

With excruciating effort I pulled myself back. There was so much I hadn't *seen* that was in my mind now, as if it had been implanted there.

The caves branched out all over—beneath Sunnybrook, Ringol, and the Dark Woods. Ringol was so much closer to Sunnybrook than I'd realized, but separated from it by a stretch of Dark Woods. Below the Dark Woods were vitium caves along with the forgotten crates from so long ago. There was so much vitium, along with other things the people in white had been stored away, and it had all twisted the earth above it.

It was all there in my mind like a giant, living tapestry and it was so much I wasn't sure I would be able to hold it all. But little by little, I sorted through it.

I sat for a long time, holding these memories. The glowworm-light dulled a little with the passing of time. I felt each wylden wake with a clarity I'd never experienced before now. They quickly sensed the change in me— distress, confusion, new power.

I opened my mind to them and shared what I'd learned from the earth, thought I parceled it out so they wouldn't as overwhelmed as I had been. I let them see it all, knowing in part it was about where they came from.

"Us," Fia said into the quiet, after everything had been shared. She laid her hand on her chest and tears welled in her vitium-blue eyes. "We were made." Her voice cracked and Dill slipped his muscled arm around her shoulders.

"I was too," I said as I shared my own memories— lying in a vitium cave, absorbing the substance just as the wylden had so many generations ago. We had taken different paths to get here, but in the end we were the same. All of us shaped by the teal stone that had changed the face of the whole world.

Renewed, event though I hadn't slept, I shouldered my pack and faced my companions. "There used to be peace. And if we try, we can have that again." I swallowed hard and thought of Bala and Alder in Citadel, already working toward this goal. "We need to get to Sunnybrook."

My friends followed behind me as I led us toward my home, the path clear now. The glowworms that had been stars for our night crawled back into their crevices, but new glowworms appeared along the tunnel wall as we walked, moving with us to keep the path lit.

As a baby, these tiny creatures had given me hope and comfort. As a girl, they'd been the impetus to my escape from the dark. And now they were guiding me home.

Our group moved in silence, but we moved quickly. As the path we took gradually inclined, we all moved with more urgency. It was full daylight when we stepped outside. The light was bright, and I turned my face toward the sun with a deep sigh. I had never been meant for a life below ground.

We had exited the caves into the quarry behind Sunnybrook. My heart stuttered a staccato rhythm inside my chest. At the top of his rocky hill were a patch of woods, and within those woods was Finn's workshop. It took all of my self control not to run there. That's where he would be waiting for me. But I couldn't do that. Not yet.

If we went in the back way, and a Patrolman spotted us, it would seem like we were sneaking in. Everything had to be done the proper way if this was going to work, so we had to walk up to the gates and hope we weren't shot on sight.

Instead of heading up the quarry trail toward the woods, we headed away, past a large, green pond, then hiked up a different hill through scraggly foliage. We crested the ridge and came out in the woods on the outside of the wall around Sunnybrook.

"We'll go in through the main gate," I said, my throat suddenly dry. "We need to meet with the council and—"

My voice cut off as I felt a surge of joy in my chest that was not my own. It was coming fast, a vivid purple aura pulsing with need.

I looked up as Luna appeared on top of the wall and leapt down, landing nimbly on her feet before pouncing on me, knocking me to my knees. I had to catch myself and smiled as she butted her head against my chin, purring loudly, her large, rough paws on my shoulders. I wrapped my arms around her and watered her fur with my tears.

"Luna," I whispered, voice warbling. She chirped in that way that reminded me of a small bird and then licked my cheek with her coarse tongue. I laughed and hugged her thick neck as the relief that she was alive poured over and through me like warm water.

When Luna had leapt at me, Dill and Zeke had drawn long knives from rough leather sheaths at their waists. They slowly replaced them as they *listened* and watched, confused.

"She's my friend," I said, looking at them over my shoulder, then back into Luna's icy blue eyes. I rubbed her cheek and she leaned into my hand with a deep, rumbling meow. I stood after a moment, knees soaked from the damp ground, but kept my hand on her head as she leaned against my leg. One piece of my heart was back where it was supposed to be. If I could get back to Rosemarie and the children, back to Finn, I would be whole.

"We need to go to the gate," I said with more confidence now that Luna was with me. I showed them the gate, the guards, the danger they presented. "I'll do the talking. I'll keep you safe."

Luna at my side, we made our way around the wall. I wanted to reach out to the children, let them know we were here, but I was afraid the wylden minds entwined with mine would frighten them. So before I did I gently pulled my mind away from my companions, like shutting a door to a room. Alone for the first time in so many days, I *searched* for the children.

I'd expected it to take some time, but as soon as I *looked*, they were there. I could feel each one individually— Asa was arguing with someone, Noah was content, Jubal was playing a game with string, and Galen was laughing. Never had I felt them so carefree. I didn't *feel* Sera, but before I could look for her, the other four registered my presence in their minds with sparks of joy.

I picked up the pace, eager to see them. This was almost over. Soon I would be back with the children. I would be back with Rosemarie—my grandmother. I would be back with Finn.

The gate was almost within sight. Inside the walls, the children movd toward us. The gate was closed tight when we reached it, but I'd expected that. Two guards were posted and when they saw us, they froze. Their fear was oily and thick in the air—I'd expected that too.

"Hello." I cleared my throat, still not good at talking with people. "I'm here on behalf of the wylden." I motioned toward Zeke, my voice shaking. "This is Zeke, their leader." The guards reached for weapons as their fear spiked. I threw up my hands in supplication, panic for my new friends in my chest like a fresh wound. "No, wait. Please. We're here to—"

One of the guards loosed an arrow. It was wobbly, shot from shaking hands, and it went past us and into the woods.

I felt relief, then confusion, followed by a wash of anger that wasn't mine. The guards were looking past past us and I followed their gaze. My own anger joined theirs as all hell broke loose.

Chapter 31

"Sinking"

Finn

THE medicinal taste of beautyberries was still on Finn's tongue, making him feel sick, but he didn't have enough control of his body to take a sip of water from the water skins Sera filled and put in his pack before they left Erilyn's clearing.

He wanted to to scream, but all he could do was stare out of eyes that no longer felt like his own and observe the passing scenery. He tried to look for paths on the off chance he could escape and find his way back to Sunnybrook, but even when he was clear-headed, Finn had never been good at maneuvering through unknown woods.

Morrigan and Seraphina said very little as they walked and Finn was grateful. Every time he heard Morrigan's voice, anger surged inside his chest so strongly, it burned. Seraphina doused every surge of anger. He thought she might be trying to soothe him, but it just left him feeling lost in the fog. If he stayed calm, Seraphina didn't pull his leash quite so tight. He thought about trying to talk to Sera in his mind, to persuade her to let him go, but it wasn't worth risking being put fully under again.

Birds were beginning to chirp in the trees as the earth warmed and Finn got lost in his memories. His feet would go where they needed without his attention. He thought of Sunnybrook, and days spent whittling and carving things for the market. He thought of Lucy. He htought of the children. Of Luna.

Of Erilyn.

Her face, surrounded by a halo of golden light, popped into his mind, giving him that smile she saved for him, and he stumbled. Seraphina looked back at him over her shoulder, her eyebrows knitted together. He felt her start to *press* inside his mind, so instead he made himself focus on his workshop. He pictured his chisels, wood shavings, the feel of a freshly finished piece in his hands. He didn't let himself think of the ring he'd made for Erilyn or how much more at home he'd felt there when she was there with him. Seraphina seemed satisfied and turned away again.

The only person that seemed to be offlimits was Erilyn, so Finn returned his thoughts to Seraphina's siblings. He thought back to the day they'd taken him to play hide and seek to try and teach him to *hide*. They had told him to *think of trees*. He hadn't been able to do it then, but maybe he could now.

He tried to keep his thoughts general—the children playing in the last bits of snow, laughing, how much he missed them—but he was also doing as they'd taught him.

He started by observing the trees they passed through. Seraphina kept her eyes forward, as did Morrigan, so he pushed a little. He let his mind stray from the children and focus solely on the trees around them. In his mind he added more with thick, concealing leaves—only a few at a time—until Seraphina and Morrigan vanished.

When he'd tried this the first time, one thought of Erilyn had destroyed the sanctuary in his mind. His his desire for her to be there with him had fractured his focus. But he was ready this time. He made sure to keep the trees firmly in his mind, made sure he had a firm grasp on the illusion, before he thought of her again.

And then she was there alongside him, standing in a ray of sunlight, gray-blue eyes shining. He smiled at her and she smiled back. He waited for Seraphina to turn or Morrigan to stop, but hey kept walking. He'd hidden her from him. He'd made a safe place in his mind.

Relief poured through him as he retreated fully into the trees, knowing Seraphina would kep his feet moving. Serpahina and Morrigan faded away until it was just Erilyn and the trees. He held his hand out and she took it. He pulled her close, and she tucked against him, head under his chin. He couldn't feel her breath or her heartbeat, but he could remember what they felt like. He may not have her here—he may never have her here again—but he would always have these memories, and he would never let them go.

Chapter 32

"Return to the Dark Woods"
Morrigan

THE moment Finn retreats into his mind, you feel it. You may not be in control of him, but you are *watching* and *listening* through the girl's leash, but as long as he's docile, you can't worry about that right now. You have to put all of your attention on the nightcrawler. The closer you draw to the Dark Woods , the more curious, more hesitant, she becomes. Your hold on her isn't complete yet, and you work to keep it tight, but hidden. The girl is more powerful than she knows, and even though you're stronger that she is—you're stronger than anyone—you don't want to have to waste your energy fighting her. Besides, if you lose her, you lose your ability to conrol Finn.

"Why the Dark Woods ?" Seraphina asks, and you sigh. She's asked before and you've told her it's the only place you'll be safe—a half-truth—but she senses the lie. You take a calming breath before you answer.

You have to find a truth that she will buy into. "It's our best place to hide where no one will come for us." No one will follow you in. It would be too dangerous for them. "I can hide us. And the animals there will protect us." Because you'll make them. "It's the only place I can truly keep us safe."

Seraphina nods woodenly. You feel her acceptance as a trickle through your tether and you wonder how many more times you'll have to do this before you're in the woods where your control over her will be easier to maintain. The woods, the vitium there, will sustain you.

"We'll be there soon," she says, a tremble in her voice.

You feel it too. The vitium pooled beneath the ground there calls to you. The girl is pulling back against her leash, and you tighten it just enough to get her to comply. Behind you, Finn walks—eyes vacant. You glance into his mind, but all you see are trees. He is probably imagining Erilyn inside his imaginary sanctuary, but you don't care. The woods ahead are calling.

At the edge of the Dark Woods , the nightcrawler hesitates. You bite back a comment about her cowardice, about how she should be used to the dark, and instead put your hands on her shoulders.

"I won't let anything happen to you. To *either* of you." You lean toward her and give her shoulders a squeeze. She's afraid—still a child—so your reassurance is enough.

As soon as you cross the threshold into the forest your senses come alive. This place feels like an extension of yourself. The vitium below the ground sings in welcome and you sigh.

You connect with your beasts, hiding it from Seraphina. The birds have retreated back to the pond—useless creatures—but the cat and the wolves come when you call.

You trek deeper into the woods, looking for a place to camp. The darkness caused by the tangle of branches overhead makes you feel safe.

Finn hasn't realized where you are. He's still hiding in the forest he's created in his mind, which is good, because you're pretty certain he would fight the girl's hold if he knew he was back in these woods. The girl is hesitant, still afraid, and you try to reassure her, but you're too excited to do much. The power of the forest tingles as it fills you up and you tight the girl more securely to you, using her distraction to your advantage.

The starlings' lake is nearby, but you don't want to camp there. It's full of bad memories for the girl and you want to maintain an illusion of her wellbeing and happiness for as long as you can. Besides, the water is rank. But you can find somewhere else. Unlike the woods outside, this forest is an open book to you. There's a small stream that runs near the pond, but not into it, and you head there, calling your roped animals to you with every step.

You reach the stream and are struck by how similar this place is to Erilyn's clearing, except there's no gold stain. There are large trees with roots that break the ground's surface, a few pines around one side—though their needles are too sparse to offer shelter—and the stream, like her pond, is off to one side. Something about finding this space, so like hers, makes you feel like you have a secret.

"We'll camp here." Your gritty voice surprises you, but you don't show it.

"Alright," the girl whispers. "Is it safe to build a fire?"

You nod, smiling to reassure her, but it feels like you're showing too much teeth. When she shies away, you turn and try to contain this giddiness that's filled you up. The power from these woods is intoxicating. You clear your throat and say, "Collect the wood, please."

The girl's eyes go wide at the thought of going into the trees alone, but you give her a little *push* and she agrees. You watch her, never straying from your line of sight, as she collects bits of twisted, dark wood from the forest floor. She returns quickly with hardly anything in her arms, but you take it with a smile—softer this time. The animals you've called are close, and having a fire will be comforting for her when she sees them for the first time.

Finn stands off to the side, face still blank. Part of you is grateful that he's compliant, so you don't have to worry about him trying to escape again, and part of you is furious that he's hiding like he is. That he *isn't* fighting. Then again, he was never much of a fighter.

Not like Cillian was.

Unwilling to fall into memories again—soft lips, warm, hands, ragged breaths—you focus on building your small fire. Once it catches flame, the nightcrawler girl moves beside it and crouches, holding her hands up as if she were freezing, though the air here is warmer than outside the woods.

In the shadows, the animals wait, hiding until you call them into the light.

"Seraphina," you say, your voice raspy. "Make Finley sit, please."

She does as you command, though she looks confused—you never say please to her, and now you've said it twice in a matter of minutes. Finley sits beside her, legs crossed, face blank. His eyes are open, but there's no awareness behind his gaze. You want to slap him.

"When I was here last," you say, crouching beside the girl, trying to sound gentle, "I made some friends."

"Friends?" she asks, eyes wide. "People?"

"No." You shake your head and smile just a little. "Animals. Like—" you swallow the bile that rises up with the thought. "Like Erilyn's cat."

"Luna," she says, softening. "You—you met a cat?" she asks hopefully.

"And some wolves," you say, and she tenses again. "But they won't hurt you. They're my friends. And I thought—" you *listen* to her desires, and then continue, "I thought having them might make you a little less lonely." You glance to the side where they wait in the shadows.

Realizing they're nearby, the girl starts looking around, then stops when she *senses* them. Only after she finds them does she see them, and she shrinks away, but you put a hand on her shoulder to hold her in place.

"Like this forest, they look dar, but they're not evil." You squeeze her shoulder. "Okay?"

She looks at you, her eyes going fuzzy for a moment as you *push* her to accept what you're saying. She shakes her head, as if trying to rid herself of an annoying bug, then nods. You tighten your tether again and she quits fighting you.

Seraphina gasps as the joined wolves appear. Their fur is matted and too thick, but other than that and the fact that they are connected, they don't look so different from a normal wolf. It's the cat—huge, black, hairless with thick ropey muscles—that causes the fear in Seraphina to bloom. The great, grotesque beast ducks its head and curls its shoulders forward as if it senses her disapproval.

You open your mouth to speak, to tell her that it's alright, but before you can she moves away from your hand on her and walks toward the beasts. Her trust in your is almost implicit. The Dark Woods have helped you control her.

Seraphina approaches the wolves first with her hand outstretched and her palm up. The wolves growl low in their throats, but it quickly turns to whines as they take turns sniffing her fingers. Tentatively, she runs her hand up one of their noses and scratches between its ears. The other, jealous, nudges its counterpart aside and Seraphina rubs it's fur as well.

After that, the wolves relax. They take turns licking her palm, then lay down at the edge of the firelight, heads on their respective paws.

Seraphina then turns to the cat. It's larger than Erilyn's little white monster by at least double. It's head is blocky and large and its fangs protrude over the bottom lip, giving it a constant, gruesome smile. Seraphina looks at it for a long moment, her forehead creased, and the beast ducks its head further.

The girl looks down at her hand, turning it over, then glances back at you. In her mind, you see the comparison—her whiteness in stark contrast to your sun-kissed skin. She looks back to the cat and takes a steadying breath, then extends her trembling hand toward the beast. The cat doesn't move, so Seraphina takes another small step forward.

"It's okay," she says, and you can feel how she's sharing calming feelings with the beast, even though her own emotions are anything but. "It's alright," she whispers.

With movements so slow they are hard to see, the cat approaches, crouched low. It sniffs her hand, then pulls back. The way its muscles shift beneath its inky skin in the flickering firelight disgusts you, but the girl doesn't seem to notice.

One step at a time, she gets close enough for the cat to easily hurt her if it wanted to, but it doesn't. Instead, Seraphina gets down on her knees and waits. There are long moments where the only sound is the crackling fire. Seraphina doesn't move, and the cat stares at her through its dark eyes. Then the cat's muscles soften and it lays its head on its paws just beside her.

With a hand that no longer trembles, Seraphina reaches out and lays her fingers flat on the large cat's blocky, furless head. It's dark eyes go wide and then soften before a soft, broken-sounding purr begins to emanate from the beast's chest.

Seraphina looks at you, a brilliant smile stretching across her face, as she continues to pet the creature. "What did you name him?" she asks, as she runs the tips of her fingers over slick skin.

"I haven't," you say, watching with caution.

"Can we call him Ebb?" she asks and you nod as she turns back to it.

"He's your friend, too," you say. Sera continues to stroke the cat's head—her hand obscenely pale against the black. While she basks in her accomplishment of taming the beast, you look into the animals' minds to see if they accomplished the task you set for them.

You're grateful the girl isn't paying attention, because when you see that Erilyn and a group of wylden escaped the woods, that they were almost completely unharmed, fury flames hot and wild in your chest. You clench your fists and feel your nails dig into your palms.

If Erilyn escaped, I means that sooner or later, she'll come for Finn and the girl.

Chapter 33

"Balance"

Erilyn

I didn't sense the attack coming until it was too late. I turned, following the guard's line of sight, just in time to see one of the twins flung into the air. She screamed until her back hit a tree, then her yell ended with a choked sound. My heart stuttered, but she was up and crouching in a moment.

"Keep the gates closed!" I yelled up at the guards, who looked at us with fear, bows and arrows in their arms almost useless with lack of practice.

It was the group of wylden that Zeke had cast out of Ringol. When they'd left, there had been about five of them, but their numbers had grown. They must have gone back to Ringol after we left and found more wylden sympathetic to their cause.

I sent a quick image to my sweet Luna—*keeping the children safe inside the walls*—and off she went, climbing the wall as if it were a tree and disappearing behind it.

Nico, the man who Zeke had cast out came at me, fist raised. Heat welled in my gut as I prepared to throw him back, but Dill jumped between us and punched him with a massive fist. My attacker was up, intent on attacking Dill. I let my power well, prepared to explode, but then I heard Fia scream and my concentration was shattered.

She was pinned on the ground by a man twice her size, a broken knife pressed against her throat. Blood trickled from where the knife's edge had started to slice into the soft skin beneath her chin and with my hands outstretched, I screamed. The man was thrown off and his half-knife flew away and landed somewhere in the grass.

Fia jumped up. There wasn't as much blood as I'd feared. She wiped it from her neck and onto her pants. She nodded at me in thanks before she leapt and attacked the man who'd had her pinned—wild and uninhibited, using her body as much as her abilities.

We fought fiercely, but there were only six of us. Their numbers were at least double ours. So far, our only protection from the full force of the onslaught was the fact that we'd been clumped together when they arrived and only so many of them could attack us at once. But they were strategizing—easing us away from one another to pick us off one at a time. Zeke had been drawn off and was fighting two men. The twins were back to back fighting a person apiece. Dill alone fought three.

We weren't going to make it. Sunnybrook was *right there,* so close I could touch it, and we weren't going to make it.

Heat birthed from anger and fear welled in my belly. It roared forth and exploded outward from my hands, from my chest, from everywhere.

Everyone, including my friends, went flying back, tumbling limb over limb. I had enough werewithal to cushion my friends, and they were up and regrouped with me quickly. We stood, shoulder to shoulder, our backs to the gate.

The savage wylden regroups as well and approached us, auras crackling with murderous intent.

We were outnumbered. All we could do now was hope to stop as many of them as we could before we died. I wasn't ever going to see Finn again, but by this last act, I could do my part to keep him and the rest of my family safe.

The six of us were jittery and tired—from the fight, from our journey, from all the days before this—but we were ready.

I called my power up and into my hands, but movement in my periphery caught my eye. I looked up toward one of the small balconies at the top of the wall where the patrol often kept watch and my stomach bottomed out. There stood Aiyanna, Galen on her hip, along with Asa, Noah, and Jubal.

No. I wanted to scream at them to run, to hide, to get as far away as they could, but then I *felt* them. The four children and Aiyanna joined my mind and it was like a blast of cool air on a hot day. I was still connected to Zeke and the others and I let these two connections blend so that we were all joined. Never had I felt such power racing through my veins. I felt invincible.

We can hold them still, keep them from attacking, Aiyanna's voice, lavendar and sweet, said in my mind. *Help is coming.*

I didn't question. I trusted Aiyanna. Together, my friends—cave dwellers and wylden—and I reached out and wrapped our auras around the shadowed wylden. The wylden struggled, fighting against our invisible hold with screams and roars, but they stopped advancing. Our rope-light held.

Almost there, came Asa's small voice, and we all doubled our efforts.

I felt frantic movement behind the gate just before it opened. It was taking all of my attention to hold the wylden in place. I was shocked when members of the patrol alongside other townspeople came out, armed with knives and gardening tools. I could taste their fear bitter on my tongue, but also their fierce determination to protect their home.

"They can't move!" I yelled, sweat trickling down my forehead. "But they're strong. We can't hold them much longer."

The patrol members moved first, and even though they were young, they led the others toward the wylden. I could feel our bonds starting to loosen as the wylden's used their own auras to try and break our chains. The captured wylden screamed, trying to frighten the people away until they could fully escape our grasp, but the people of Sunnybrook stood firm.

The people of Sunnybrook surrounded the wylden just as the first attacker broke free. Like a chain reaction, the rest followed and the the battle raged again, except this time we outnumbered them.

Aiyanna ushered the children off the balcony as the first blood was spilled. I heard the attacking wylden scream as a knife slashed through the flesh of his upper arm. First blood caused a frenzy.

Bodies collided.

Weapons clashed.

Men and women—upworlders and wylden alike— wailed in anger and in pain.

A patrolman was thrown down, weapon knocked from his hand, and with a grunt I tackled the wylden about to land on him. We both went down, my shoulder aching from the impact. I rolled away and the wylden tried to grab me, but the patrolman I'd helped was there and kicked him in the face. Without time for a thank you, I ran to where one of the twins was being held against a tree, a hand gripping her throat.

The scent of sweat and blood permeated the air as I used my abilities to rip him away from her. As soon as he was donw, I fell to my knees, exhausted. The wylden had been mostly fighting with their bodies, and now I knew why. I hadn't slept and the energy the earth had shared with me were fading.

Distracted, I didn't realize someone was coming up on my side until their arms were locked around me. I hit the ground with a thud, all the air leaving my lungs in a painful whoosh.

I gasped and coughed into the dirt as I tried to break free, but they were too strong. Too big. His breath against my cheek was rancid and hot as he rolled us so that he was holding me against his belly. I kicked and bucked, trying to free myself, but he was so much stronger than me. Only when he tried to right us, pushing himself to his knees, was I able to throw my head back and connect with his nose. He screamed and released me as blood gushed over his mouth. I jumped up, woozy, and kicked him in the face as hard as I could. He fell backward, still clutching his nose, and I darted away, unsteady on my feet.

Near the wall, a wylden man had two townspeople cornered. The metal rakes they'd brought as weapons lay in the dirt a few yards away. I started to run to them, but lilted to the side as the earth seemed to shift beneath my feet. I stopped to find my balance, so dizzy I thought I might vomit. The wylden gripped two long, rusted blades. I could *feel* his joy—he was taunting them with an impending death.

I tried to stand, but my knees wouldn't support my weight. I wasn't going to make it. But then Dill was there, running in from the trees with a roar in his throat. He grabbed the other wylden by the hair and jerked him back as if he weighed nothing. The man, flat on his back, tried to get up, but Dill pressed his foot into the wylden's throat. He dropped his knives and tried to pry Dill's foot off, but Dill was too strong. The citizens of Sunnybrook picked up their weapons along with the knives. The attacker finally threw Dill's foot off and stood, eyes wild. He looked at Dill, then at the two upworlders with his knives, and with a final scream ran off into the woods.

The two people—barely older than me—nodded at Dill. He nodded back, a grim expression on his face that caused his long, pink scar to pull tight, and together they rejoined the fray, Dill's long, matted hair swinging wildly.

Hope burned bright. An alliance between the upworlders of Sunnybrook and the wylden of Ringol was possible, but we had to make sure we won this fight first. I dug deep, reaching down into the earth for help, and found a reserve of energy to fight for our new, fragile alliance.

After the first wylden ran into the woods, others followed. The people of Sunnybrook kept fighting alongside my friends until the only attackers left were the original few, including. He stood, blood dripping from a gash on his forehead, weapons hanging down by his sides.

"No more," Zeke growled. Even though all the assembled wylden could feel what Zeke wanted, he spoke for the people of Sunnybroo.

"You can pledge to join what we're doing here," I said, trying to speak clearly, past my racing heart and shaking limbs, "or you can leave and never return." Along with my words, Zeke showed him what would happen if he returend—death and destruction, but not ours.

Nico looked at me for a long moment, a scowl on his bloodied face, then lookback back to Zeke and growled. His hatred of both of us was thick like smoke. I tensed, ready for one last fight, but it never came. Nico looked at all of us gathered. His shadowy aura darkened, and he and his companion darted back into the woods. I tracked them, relieved when they kept moving further and further away.

And just like that, it was over. The last of my borrowed energy seeped away and I wanted to do nothing more than find a place to rest, but we still had much to do.

First, I checked to make sure my friends were ok. Zeke's arm was cut, but not terribly, and the bleeding had stopped on its own. Fia had a cut on her neck and a bruise showing on her cheek. The twins had it the worst—one of them had a broken arm, the other a wound in her side—but they were both standing. Only Dill was relatively unscathed.

I looked at them, relieved that they'd all made it through, then looked at the people of Sunnybrook. We hadn't lost anyone and we hadn't killed any of our attackers. I felt awash with relief that there'd been no loss of life this time.

"We need to talk to someone in charge," I said, my voice wavering with exhaustion. "These wylden are my friends." They huddled around me. "They're here with me to—"

The gate opened, interrupting me, and out bolted Luna, followed by the children, Aiyanna, Lucy, and Rosemarie. The children swarmed around me, their tiny arms grabbing onto my legs. Their auras touched mine and it was like stepping into a ray of sunshine. I fell to my knees and soaked up their love. I touched their hair, their cheeks, overwhelmed with gratitude that they were here and whole. But I didn't see Seraphina or Finn.

"Let them in," Lucy said, walking through the patrol with a confidence and maturity I hadn't ever seen in her. "All of them."

"Ma'am," one of the patrolmen said, "with all due respect, they're wylden. Shouldn't we—"

"They just helped you defend our town," Lucy said, her voice firm and clear. "This is what we've been talking about since we got back. A truce."

Zeke stepped to my right, Fia to my left. I got to my feet, the children still clinging to me. I tried to stand tall, but I was weary down to my bones.

The patrolman looked at her, then back at us. After an tense moment of silence, one of the two men that Dill had saved spoke up. "This one—" he said, gesturing to Dill, who stood behind us all. "I mean, this man saved my life." He took a step closer to Dill, though I could sense his fear. "If he hadn't been there, I'd be dead." A man nearby nodded in agreement.

The patrolman who'd disagreed at first sighed, then looked directly at me. "Morrigan said you were leading them," he said, eyes narrowed. "She said you were the reason they attacked our wall."

"I can explain everything," I said, swaying where I stood. "But I give you my word, these people mean you no harm."

The patrolman still wasn't convinced, and I could feel a good portion of the gathered crowd begin to agree with him. With the battle over, all they saw were their enemies. I was at a loss.

But then the children came to our rescue. One by one they released my legs and went to the wylden. Asa took Fia's hand. Noah and Jubal went to the twins, careful to avoid their injured sides, and offered their hands. But it was tiny Galen who made the biggest impact. He had gotten taller, I noted, but he was still small for his age. He walked through us, even pushing past Zeke with his little hand, to get to Dill. Dill, the giant wylden with a scarred face. The one man of all of them who looked frightening without trying. The man who could crush Galen like a bug if he wanted. Galen looked up at him with a quizzical look, then raised his arms, asking to be held.

Dill looked down at him in confusion, then a smile spread across his wide mouth, stretching his pink scar. He plucked Galen up gently and sat him on one of his massive shoulders. Galen grinned as he wobbled. He gripped Dill's hair in his tiny fingers, but the large man didn't seem to mind. Dill reached up with one hand and gently held Galen's feet against his chest so the tiny boy wouldn't fall.

I turned back to the guard and waited. I could feel his, and the others', reluctant acceptance. I wasn't surprised that these sweet children had won them over.

"They can stay in the library," Lucy said, relieved, and the guard nodded his head once.

Asa led all of us, gently pulling Fia behind her. Noah, Jubal, and the twins followed, with Dill, Galen, and Zeke bringing up the rear. Rosemarie and a woman I didn't recognize followed them, but not before Rosemarie caught my eye and smiled.

Seeing them all together reminded me of the word, the concept, Zeke had taught me. *Lacing.* I understood now what it meant to be laced together. To be willingly tied to someone, as Finn and I had been before. The pieces didn't have to fit perfectly for them to still fit together. Love and patience could fill in any gaps.

Almost everyone had gone back inside the games, and I was so tired, but still there was no Finn. Where was he?

I swayed, but Lucy and Aiyanna were there to catch me, each taking an arm and draping it over their shoulders. I wanted to ask where he was, where Sera was, but they led me and it took all that I had to put one foot in front of the other. I'd used more energy than I'd realized.

"Are you okay?" Rosemarie asked, doubling back to join us once she was sure the children were safe. She stopped in front of me and cupped my face in her cool hands. I could see her still in my memory, rocking me to sleep as an infnat, and a deep longing filled me up. But that conversation deserved time and energy I didn't have yet.

"I'm okay," I said, even as Aiyanna and Lucy supported most of my body weight. "Where are Finn and Seraphina?"

The others exchanged a look—tight expressions that were supposed to appear neutral—and dread prickled through my body like dribbles of icy water.

"Let's get inside and get you some food, then we'll talk," Rosemarie said as she stroked my cheek again.

I wanted to demand answers, but I was too tired to do anything except agree. I knew whatever they were going to tell me was going to be bad and I steeled myself to hear it as they helped me limp into the Sunnybrook, the gate closing behind us.

Chapter 34

"Clarity"

Finn

FINN lay in the sun dappled shade with Erilyn in his arms. It felt so real, he could almost convince himself that ther est had been a bad dream.

But when he pulled her close, he couldn't quite feel her against him. The trees around him were thick and dense, but their color wasn't quite right—too green, too bright. The grass was too soft. The sky too blue. Only the girl in his arms looked exactly as she could. Hers was a face he could picture precisely without even trying.

If this was to be his fate—imprisoned by Sera in his own mind—at least here he didn't have to look into Seraphina's eyes, knowing she'd betrayed him. At least here, he could be with Erilyn instead of being trapped and alone.

As he lay in the grass, Erilyn in his arms, some part of his mind registered that his body had stopped and sat down. He was tempted to leave his trees, to see where they were, but it wouldn't do any good. Wherever they were, he was still powerless. And so he stayed here with the girl he loved.

He leaned back and looked into her gray-blue eyes, so like riverstone. She smiled up at him and his heart fluttered. One day he would make it back to her. He was trapped for now, but he would get away. He had to.

Like an insect buzzing too close to his ear, somethig nagged at him from ouside the trees. He didn't want to leave here, didn't want to leave Erilyn, but the buzzing grew more and more insistent. As it grew, the forest grew hazier. He looked down, horrified as Erilyn's form faded away like smoke.

As the trees vanished, the fog went with them. It took him a few seconds to process what he was seeing, almost like he was waking up from a very intense sleep, but once he did his hear thundered with the need to run.

Before him was a small fire. Dark, twisted trees. Air that was too warm. And Seraphina, sitting next to some large, black creature with dark eyes and slick-looking skin.

"Sera," he tried to yell in warning, but his voice was barely a scratchy whisper. She turned, a soft smile on her face. The beast beside her lifted its head. It's ears went back as it stared at Finn, but Sera just lifted her hand and rested it between it's stubby ears—bright white skin vivid against the black. It's muscles rippled as it shifted its position, catching the firelight, and Finn couldn't help but think it looked like foul, dark water.

"Finn," Sera said, her voice soft. "It's alright. They're my friends."

The invisible bonds he wore loosened and his muscles were once again his own. She was giving him a measure of freedom. He hadn't been able to move this freely since his failed attempt to get away. He rolled his shoulders and neck, both stiff, and looked around. Two wolves lay with their heads on their paws, shoulders pressed tightly together, on Sera's other side. He returned his attention to the giant beast at her side.

He wet his lips and swallowed. "Are we in the Dark Woods ?"

"Yes," Morrigan answered and he snapped his head toward her. She was standing on the other side of the fire, fully lit, but she seemed to blend in with the forest behind her. "You're finally safe."

Her voice rasped and set the hairs on the back of his neck at attention. He tried to see the girl he'd loved, but he couldn't find her in the woman who stood before him. Her eyes now were too wild. The lines in her face, too hard.

"Safe." He ground his teeth and scoffed. "I'm in the Dark Woods as your prisoner. There's nothing safe about that."

The big animal beside Seraphina growled low in his throat. The sound was deeper than Luna's growl, but it was definitely a big cat, though it was unlike any cat Finn had ever seen.

"Sssh," Seraphina said as she stroked the hairless skin between its ears, and it settled. "You're not a prisoner, Finn," she said, her voice sad. "We just wanted—" she looked at Morrigan and her expression went blank, then became confused. Morrigan sighed in irritation and Seraphina's face cleared. She turned back to Finn with that same soft, airy smile. "We just wanted you to be safe away from Erilyn's influence."

"Her influence?" he asked, anger simmering in his chest. "All she's ever done is love me. She never forced me to do anything. Never dragged me along like an animal on a leash."

Seraphina's expression grew perplexed again. She absently stroked the monstrous black cat, which inched closer to her.

"He's confused, Seraphina," Morrigan said, her voice deep. "Her influence will wear off eventually, lbut ike ridding a body of fever, it will take time. Until then, *we* have to keep him safe."

Seraphina winced and the inky cat at her side meowed in a gravelly voice as it pressed its head into her side.

"Erilyn's not influen—" The words in Finn's throat choked off as Sera turned toward him, expression hardMorrigan stepped to her side, a sly smile on her dirty face.

"How do you know it will happen soon?" Seraphina asked, her voice pitiful with longing.

Morrigan pursed her lips and let her head fall forward. Her long, dark hair was no longer shiny as it fell over her shoulder in tangles. When she looked up, the dim firelight playing on her features, she almost looked sad.

"The animals showed me something when they arrived," she said, her voice gruff. She looked at Finn and narrowed her eyes. It was an expression she wore often when they were together—when she said she had to work late or when she said she wasn't upset about something he'd done—but then he'd been too trusting and naive to realize that's what was happening at the time. But not now. Now he saw her for who she truly was. She was about to lie.

"What?" Sera's eyes went unfocused as she leaned toward Morrigan.

"Erilyn came into the Dark Woods a day or so ago," she said, voice soft. "But—" she turned to face Sera fully, "the starlings got her. Drove her into their pond." Seraphina gasped and covered her mouth. "She didn't make it out."

"You're lying," he was able to force out between clenched teeth.

Morrigan's head snapped toward him, her hair flying out, eyes flashing dangerously.

"He's in shock," Morrigan said, never taking her eyes off him. "Help him rest again."

"She's dead?" Sera asked, pale eyes filling with tears. "Erilyn is—"

Sera's words cut off as Morrigan put her hand on her shoulder. Sera's eyes went wide, the tears falling, before a placid smile graced her features.

"Finn, please rest," Seraphina said, her voice airy and flat.

He didn't want to. He wanted to scream. To shake Seraphina. He could see it so clearly now. Morrigan was controlling her. Sera hadn't betrayed him, Morrigan had tethered her.

But ther was nothing he could do as Sera's command for rest invaded his mind. He wobbled, fighting it, but he wasn't strong enough. As he fell backward into the dirt, he caught a brief flash of light around Sera—brilliant pink, surrounded by a thin line of red that trailed back to Morrigan.

He tried to *tell* Sera, to *show* her, but her command took hold and everything went black.

Chapter 35

"Preparations"
Morrigan

AS Finn sleeps and Seraphina dotes on the dark creatures, you take a few moments to yourself. The black cat has failed you. Under normal circumstances, you would kill it, but the girl has bonded with it—you can see it's pulsing aura blending with hers. Better to leave it alive to distract her than risk alienating her now.

Somehow, Finn knew you were lying about Erilyn's death. If only you hadn't been so weak after Cillian's death, so distracted by your emotions, you could have killed her then.

Erilyn will not stop searching until she finds Finn, and in turn, finds you. The Dark Woods offer protection, but it isn't enough. You need more.

When Sunnybrook's wall was built generations ago, it was to keep the wylden out, but it was also to keep the people of the city within. You can't build a wall, but it gives you an idea.

"Seraphina," you say. Your voice shocks you with how scratchy and low it is, but the girl doesn't seem to notice and you clear your throat. "I have to leave for a little while."

She spins toward you, white hair flying out in an arc. Nightcrawlers disgust you as much as the cat-creature does, but in this moment you can't help but notice how striking she is—her paleness within the darkness of the forest.

"Why?" she asks, voice laced with panic. "Where are you going?"

You *push* her to be calm. You need compliance. Obedience. The forest's energy bleeds into yours and you tighten your tether more than you've dared so far. It's almost complete. Just a little more and she'll be completely yoursl

"Erilyn's gone," you say as you move around the fire toward her. "But others will still come for him. The ones she corrupted before her death." You crouch beside her and place your hand on her shoulder. "I need to make sure that when they do, the forest will protect us."

She sits silently, trying to *read* you, but you're always one step ahead and only let her see what you want her to.

"But you'll be back soon," she whispers, eyes large. "I will."

She nods and the lumpy black cat, Ebb, crawls on its belly until it is pressed against her leg. She drapes her arm over its massive shoulders and hugs it to her. It could tear her apart in moments, but she isn't afraid. You aren't sure if that makes her brave or stupid.

"If Finn wakes up—" she starts.

"I trust you," you say, though you don't. You push her to keep him asleep, a compulsion she has to obey.

You smile, though you know it doesn't reach your eyes, but she accepts it. She's so desparate. So alone.

The two wolves stand when you call them in your mind. They aren't as strong or as vicious as the cat, but you don't dare try to take him with you now that he's bonded with the girl. It will make her feel safe, which will help her aobey your commands. Without another word for her, you leave the circle of firelight.

The darkness of the woods feels like a warm blanket slipping around you. You take a hearty drink of the vitium solution in your water skin, but you're running low. You'll have to go back to the quarry for more or figure out how to take the vitium from the forest itself. It supplements you, but without vitium already in your system, you don't think you'll be able to use it as a source.

The teal liquid coats your tongue and slips down your throat, sharpening your vision. With the canines following you, you head toward the pond and the rogue starlings, but halfway there, something stops you. Your senses are sharper than they've ever been—a combination of the vitium and the forest—so finding the cave opening hidden inside a tangle of roots feels like it is meant to be.

Your plan comes into crystal clear focus as you stop, the wolves cowering at your feet. You had meant to go to the birds, but with so much power thrumming in your veins, you don't have to go to them. All you have to do is think. With vitium singing in your blood, you reach out to the swirling black voids and show them what they must do when the time comes. Then, to the wolves, you give a single command—*watch*. They whine, wanting to go back to the girl, but they cannot disobey you.

You look down the tunnel, past the tangle of roots, into the darkness beyond. You can *feel* nightcrawlers below, roiling beneath the surface like so many ants. Ants are disgusting, but useful. They just need instructions to follow.

You are sure the ones left behind in Sunnybrook have turned the town against you, so you can't return there. The wylden are Erilyn's little puppets. There's only one course left for you to take. If you are going to win this, you ned an army. It is time for you to go introduce yourself to the cavedwellers of Citadel.

Chapter 36

"Last Stand"

Erilyn

IT felt wrong to be in Cillian's office, but this was where Lucy had brought me. She told me I had to eat some soup and drink some tea before she'd tell me anything, but I knew it was bad.

Finn wasn't here. Seraphina wasn't here.

It was frustrating to be kept in the dark, but I was so tired, and my friends' concern for my wellbeing permeated the room. So I did ask I was askd to doI tried to *listen*, to figure out where Finn and Sera were, but Aiyanna kept those thoughts blocked from me. That could only mean it was very, very bad.

I sat in front of the fireplace where Cillian and I used to take our lunches together and ate bites of rich, vegetable soup made from thick leafy greens and roots. The children played in the floor with little stuffed dolls. Asa told me that a woman named Mehri had made them. I hadn't met her properly yet, but she was currently tending to the wounds of my wylden friends, which made me like her.

The soup filled my belly quickly, but I didn't really taste it. Luna lay alongside my leg where it was stretched in front of the fire, to get the most of the heat. Aiyanna, Lucy, and Rosemarie were off to the side making tea and whispering, which only set my nerves on edge. I couldn't *hear* them, thanks to Aiyanna, and I ground my teeth in frustration.

Galen, always so sensitive to those around him, put his tiny hand on my arm. He tried to soothe me and I smiled. I set the empty soup bowl down and he crawled into my lap. I hugged him, pressed a kiss to his soft curls, and closed my eyes.

Since I'd left the children, I'd been in a constant state of searching for the next move, the next thing. With Galen grounding me, I let myself just be, at least for a moment, and it felt better than I could articulate. Eyes closed, I was unsurprised when three additional sets of arms wrapped around me. Through their touch, I *felt* their love, rich and warm like summer rain.

And then I was crying. Not quietly. Not softly. But sobbing from deep in my belly, a deep well of emotion I carried inside pouring out. I carried so much—not knowing where Finn and Sera were, Cillian's death, learning the truth about my parents—and it all poured out of me. I had the thought that I should shield the children from the brunt of this, but they just hugged me tighter.

"We see," Asa murmured before kissing my cheek.

"It's okay, Eri," Jubal said, his voice gentle.

"You aren't alone," Noah whispered.

Galen hugged my neck.

"Are you okay?" Rosemarie asked into the aftermath of my breakdown. She, Lucy, and Aiyanna were all staring at me and I wondered how I was supposed to share all of this with them with only words. How I could put voice to so much pain. Lucy's brother was dead. Aiyanna's people were in a revolution. Rosemarie was my grandmother. And then there was the centuries' old knowledge the earth had shown me—how the wylden and cave dwellers, all of us, came from the same people. The vitium experiments. The scientists fleeing into he earth. The vitium changing them. Changing us. Changing everything.

It was too much.

I squeezed my eyes shut, feeling like the world was caving in around me. I felt the echoes of sharp stones piercing my skin and the earth trembling beneath my hands and knees. My chest was too tight.

"We can help," Asa said, her little voice sounding so grown up. "We can help you bear it."

It was selfish, but I nodded, tears still pouring unfettered down my cheeks. The children hugged me tighter and then helped me ease the emotions back. They didn't erase them, they didn't take control, but they helped me breathe past them. Helped me shoulder the weight of so much until I was in control again.

"Erilyn?" Rosemarie asked softly.

"I have a lot to tell you," I said as the children disentangled themselves from me and sat in various spots around the room, taking advantage of the warmth of the fire. Luna had moved aside when the children came, but she returned to me now and laid her head in my lap. I let my fingers get lost in her fur as I braced myself. "To tell all of you."

"Cillian's dead, isn't he?" Lucy asked, her voice hollow. Her aura—which was so often minty green when she was with Aiyanna—slowly shifted until it was a deep, burnt orange.

I met her eyes and nodded, feeling my heart crack along with hers. Aiyanna slipped her hand into Lucy's and I saw some of the strong facade Lucy wore chip away.

"Was it Morrigan?" she breathed.

"I think it was a cave dweller during the attack on Ringol," I said. Aiyanna's eyes opened wide and she tried to pull her hand away, but Lucy held on tight. "Your father led them," I said to Aiyanna. I hated the pain this caused her, but I had to be truthful. They needed to know everything that I knew. "He survived, but the wylden won. There were losses on both sides, and—"

"I thought Cillian was going to hide," Lucy said before biting her lips together. "With Morrigan."

"He was." I tensed. Luna lifted one of her big paws onto my leg beside her head. "When I found him, Morrigan was gone. I think they were trying to run. To get away during the fight." I forced a breath into lungs that suddenly felt like stone. "If I hadn't made them stay behind—"

Lucy just shook her head, lips pressed tightly together. "If he ran, it's because she convinced him to." She sniffed once and lifted her chin. "If this is anyone's fault, it's Morrigan's. Not yours."

"What about my father?" Aiyanna asked, her voice sounding so much like it had when we were young. "If the wylden won, he will try to retaliate."

"He tried," I said. "But your people were angry. They've taken power from him."

"That's—" Aiyanna smiled. "That's unbelievable," she breathed.

Lucy turned toward Aiyanna and some of the cool-mint returned to her auralight. Her green reached for Aiyanna's purple and some of the burden I carried lightened.

Off to the side, Rosemarie watched me with a shrewd expression. Her hands were clasped over her stomach, but her knuckles were white. "You called the people of Citadel *her* people." She wet her lips with the tip of her tongue. "Not yours. Hers."

"I did," I said, swallowing hard past a lump in my throat. I felt Aiyanna's eyes land on me, but I kept my gaze locked on Rosemarie. "On my way here I learned—well, I grew up in Citadel, but I'm not from there." I swallowed again, my mouth dry. "I learned my parents were from here. From Sunnybrook."

Other than the crackling fire, the room was silent. I stared up at Rosemarie, my heart thundering, and with shaking hands I reached into my pack. From it I pulled the tattered, stained bit of blanket I'd taken from the cave and offered it to her.

She took the scrap of fabric, her fingers brushing mine. She ran one hand over the cloth, over and over. Her aura flared bright purple and tears filled her eyes.

"Erilyn," she warbled. "When I found you, when I learned your name, I didn't let myself dare hope that you were her." She dropped to her knees in front of me. "You looked so much like my Roselyn, but there was no way for me to know if you were really her." She gripped my fingers and squeezed. "I always hoped, but I couldn't know. And so I decided I would love you no matter what. She stared at me for a moment and then I pulled her to me and felt silent sobs wrack her body.

After a few moments, Rosemarie pulled back. She wiped the tears from beneath her eyes and sat back, beside me. She turned to the others, still sniffling. "My daughter—my sweet Roselyn—was a part of the council. They hypothesized a connection between vitium and the wylden." She adjusted her grip on my hand. "She and her husband, Eddan, often went on scouting trips. When her little girl was just under a year old, the three of them went out on one of these trips." Rosemarie squeezed my hand. "It stormed that day. I waited for them, but they never came back." Her voice cracked.

"I saw them," I said. "Memories of them."

Rosemarie squeezed her eyes shut as fresh tears fell. I feel her longing and sadness, but I don't push them away, because all those feelings already exist in me.

"How are the wylden connected to vitium?" Lucy interjected, her voice raw. She'd been crying too and her grip on Aiyanna's hand was iron tight.

"We had theories," Rosemarie said as she covered our joined hands with her other. "We discovered thick veins of vitium along their seasonal paths. It was the only thing we could find that would explain why they traveled the way they did. It was that discovery that led to my original experiments on vitium." She squeezed my hand firmly.

The room went quiet and I knew it was time to share the rest. "You were right," I said, grateful for a break in the emotion. "The wylden are tied to vitium, but so are the cavedwellers."

"How do you know?" Aiyanna asked, curious but not upset.

"The wyden and I traveled here through the caves. When we were down there, I *saw* it," I said. "They were memories stored in the earth. In the vitium."

The children understood, but the others were all confused.

"When a moment is strong enough, it leaves a mark on things. An imprint. When I touched the baby blanket, I saw my parents. I saw them die—" My voice broke and Rosemarie's hand squeezed my fingers to comfort me. "Later, I also saw older memories. Before Sunnybrook had a wall. Before Citadel even existed." I bit the inside of my lip. They all watched me with rapt attention.

"The Vitium War happened because of experiments on it. They used it as a fuel source, and wanted to weaponize it. They also used it as a drug—like Morrigan." I felt a spike of anger and fear from somewhere in the room, but it was quickly tamped down. "The people in Ringol were given little pills, but something went wrong. It turned those people into the wylden."

All eyes were one me now.

"Was that what caused the war?" Lucy asked. I shook my head.

"No, the war started somwhere else. Far away from here, but it started because of vitium." I pressed my lips together. "But here, after the wylden were created, other people came for the rest of the pills. Except a group of upworlders had already taken the pills, along with the raw vitium they'd been using to make the pills, and hidden underground. The war started shortly after, and our area of the world was forgotten."

Noah handed me a cooled cup of pine tea and I pulled my hand from Rosemarie's to accept it with a tight smile. She remained sitting by my side. "After that, Sunnybrook put up a wall and Citadel was built and the wylden grew more wild." I sighed and took a sip of tea.

"What happened to the rest of the world?" Lucy asked. She'd moved the edge of her brother's desk and Aiyanna leaned beside her, her head on Lucy's shoulder.

"The war broke it," I said and Lucy nodded. Sharing all of this had made me fel better, so I kept going. "The Dark Woods are where really dense pockets of vitium are. I think the caves where those original people hid the pills and the raw vitium they'd harvested are below the forest, or at least part of it. Plus, there's a lot of natural vitium there as well. There's too much and it's twisted the plants and aniamls there."

Lucy and Rosemarie exchanged a glance with my mention of the Dark Woods and ice settled in my gut.

"Now it's your turn," I said, sitting forward, muscles coiled tight. "Where are Finn and Sera?"

Aiyanna stood straight, arms crossed over her belly, and looked at the childrenl. Lucy stared at the floor as Rosemarie slipped her arm around my shoulder as if in comfort.

"Where are they?" I whispered.

It was Asa who spoke, her usually confident voice quiet and unsure. "Morrigan took them," she said and I thought my heart might stop. "They went to the Dark Woods ."

I pushed Rosemarie's arm off and was on my feet before I'd even fully registered what she'd said, Luna up with me.

The door to the office flew open and Fia walked in, eyes wild. "Alright?" she asked. In the doorway, Dill appeared, and behind him, was Zeke.

"I have to go back to the Dark Woods ," I said, panic making my thoughts choppy. "Finn's there. And Sera." I let the wylden *feel* and *see*.

"We will go," Fia said as Dill and Zeke pushed through the doorway to join her. They were both so big, and being in this office made them seem larger. The three of them together was quiet a sight to behold.

"No," I said as I shoved the water skin that had been refilled inside my pack. "No, I need you to stay here in case those other wylden come back." My eyes darted all over as if the answers lay somewhere in this room. "To protect Sunnybrook." I wet my lips.

Rosemarie took me by the shoulders and turned me toward her. "Breathe," she said, and I took a gulp of air. My body trembled. "You don't have to do this alone."

"We'll go with you," Lucy said, standing up tall. Beside her, Aiyanna nodded. "Rosemarie, you can hold down the fort here. Right?" Rosemarie nodded.

"We're a team," Lucy said, and I my panic lessened a tiny bit.

"How will we get there?" Aiyanna asked as she picked up some bread and cheese that had been cut and laid on a wooden board and wrapped it in some cloth. She packed it in her own pack, then set to refilling their water skins from a pitcher. "The Dark Woods are far."

"They're not as far as you think," I said as I clenched and unclenched my bands. "We can go through the caves," I said, a waver in my voice.

Lucy scribbled something on a piece of paper. "Here," she said, giving it to Rosemarie. "It's my written consent that you're standing in for me until I get back." She squeezed Rosemarie's hand. "The people trust you and the children," she said, giving Asa a smile as she ruffled Galen's hair.

THINGS moved quickly after that. Fia and the other wylden, fed and given fresh clothes, were taken to the wall to stand guard with the patrol. It was what they'd volunteered to do, and I was happy they were fitting in.

Before I left, I kissed each of the children with a silent promise to bring Sera and Finn home. They lent me bits of encouragement and strength. Finally, I hugged Rosemarie as tightly as I could. She didn't say anything other than a soft, I love you, but it was enough. As long as I had her, it would alwayss be enough.

I wanted Luna to stay with the children, but she refused, growling low in her throat. In my mind I saw her at my side, and while I wanted her to be safe, I was grateful she would be with me.

Mehri joined Rosemarie and the children, and then Lucy, Aiyanna, Luna and I were off, half-running through the woods, back toward Finn's cabin and the quarry that rested behind it.

During my time in the earth, I'd felt the layout of the tunnels. I could still see them in my mind. I could see how they connected and where I needed to go to make it to the Dark Woods quickly. This time, I didn't hesitate when we came to the cave opening. With Lucy and Aiyanna just behind me, I entered the earth again.

Chapter 37

"Sanity"
Finn

FINN fell through blackness without body or thought. Seraphina had pushed him into sleep so abruptly that he felt disconnected from everything. Alone and adrift.

But then, slowly, his senses woke. He smelled rich earth and felt soft, freshly fallen pine needles beneath his back. The sun warmed his face and turned the backs of his eyelids red. And then, his heart skipping with joy, he felt the girl in his arms, her breath warm and soft against his neck. Everything before this moment was fuzzy, but he knew that if he had to choose one place to stay for the rest of his life, it would be right here with Erilyn.

Finn tightened his arms around the girl he held and sighed. He pressed his lips to her hair, but it didn't quite feel right. It was too thick. Too coarse.

He could feel her body, warm against his, but something wasn't right. His skin didn't tingle like it did when she was close. And her body against his felt too long, too muscled.

He kissed her hair again, hoping to *feel* her, to *sense* her, like he had in his cell in Ringol. But instead, the smell of sweat and blood invaded his nose and he pulled back.

With each second, his mind cleared. He was back in the trees he'd crated in his mind. He shouldn't be able to feel her here. He shifted where he lay on the ground and a stick dug painfully into his side. *Pain.* That shouldn't be here either.

He opened his eyes, blinking into the bright sunlight, and looked toward Erilyn, hoping at least seeing her would help calm his anxiety. He yelled and scrambled away as his eyes landed on Morrigan instead, face clean, hair silky and long as it had been before all this started.

A dark red summer dress was draped over her curves and her hair lay in waves across the pine needle-covered floor, but her eyes still had that mad look vitium had given her.

"Finley," she said, her voice echoing around the clearing so loudly he winced. "What's wrong?" She sat up, her hair falling across her shoulder as the strap of her dress slipped down.

"Why are you here?" Unlike Morrigan's voice, his was swallowed up by the clearing as if the air were too thick.

"Why wouldn't I be here?" She stood and he followed suit so that he could keep distance between them. Her eyes were too green and her lips were painted the color of fresh blood. She stepped forward and he stepped back, holding his hands up as if that might keep her away from him.

"You're not supposed to be here," he said, his voice still hollow and thin.

"Of course I am," Morrigan replied, a predatory smile stretching across her face.

Finn watched, horrified, as she slowly transformed. The soft, red dress swirled away until she was once again in the dirty, green shirt and pants that he knew she was wearing in the real world. Her hair grew tangled and wild. The paint on her lips faded away, only to be replaced with a smattering of blood as if she'd kissed it away from something else. "I'm here, because *you* want me to be," she said, voice oppressive. "You called me."

"No," he said. He squeezed his eyes shut tight and tried to focus—on the woods, on Erilyn, on keeping Morrigan out, but when he opened his eyes again, she was still there. "No!" he yelled. He felt like he was back in the closet with no way out.

His heart beat painfully in his throat and his vision started to go fuzzy. He remembered what it had felt like to leave his body in Ringol, to somehow travel to his friends, to see their auras and *feel* them so clearly. He looked at Morrigan again and could *now see* her aura—red, crackling light that surrounded her.

She wasn't a figment of his imagination. She was real. Somehow, she'd broken into the sanctuary in his mind.

But it was *his* sanctuary, and he refused to let her stay. Her smile faltered as he processed all this, but before she could say anything else, he ran at her, hands out, a scream pouring from between his lips. His hands connected with her shoulders, firm and real beneath his palms, and he shoved her as hard as he could. Shocked, she fell back and hit the hard-packed earth, falling through it and vanishing as if she'd been made of smoke

Finn ran his fingers through his hair and spun in a tight circle. The trees and sun were back to how they were supposed to be—the same trees and sun and sky he'd created to hide from Morrigan and Seraphina. But if Morrigan could get in this wasn't a sanctuary, it was a prison.

Finn paced and pulled at his hair.

Erilyn. He pictured her face, the way her nose crinkled when she was thinking, the way her eyes reflected the gray-blue sky. But she didn't appear. He squeezed his eyes shut and thought of her and only her—how her body softened against his when he kissed her, how she could look at him and he knew what she was thinking. But when he opened his eyes, the clearing was still empty.

This is where he normally panicked, where he normally tried something thoughtless and brash. But that wouldn't do any good, and he knew it.

He took deep breaths to keep the panic at bay. He'd seen Morrigan's aura. And days ago, he had left his body and seen Erilyn's. He didn't know how he'd done it, but he was sure it had been real.

He'd done it before. He could do it again.

Back in his closet prison, he'd been desperate. Just as desperate as he was now. He'd only wanted was to see Erilyn. To know that she was at least okay. So he closed his eyes, and let that same desperation take over.

There was a beat of nothing and then he was moving, carried along at an unthinkable speed. Twisted branches and tree trunks whipped by, but he wasn't afraid. He kept Erilyn's face in his mind and focused on his need to find her.

He expected to leave the woods, but instead dove down into a tunnel and everything went dark. The ground was emanating a pale white light that he knew wouldn't be visible to his eyes. He flrew through tunnels and passages, though he could feel no wind, no movement.

And then Finn stopped, his vision swimming for a moment with the sudden shift in perspective.

He was in a tunnel that was dotted with glowing teal light, like the worms Erilyn had shown him so many weeks ago. And beneath that light, beneath him, he saw them—Erilyn, Lucy, Aiyanna, and Luna, each glowing with their own unique color. Lucy and Aiyanna looked to Erilyn, confused, because she had stopped abruptly. She was looking up, right at him as if she could see him, her stormy eyes bright in the aqua light.

"Finn," she whispered, the golden light that surrounded her pulsing with the beat of her strong heart. She took a step forward, eyes still up toward him. "Finn," she said again, her fingers reaching out as if she could touch him. He wanted nothing more than to reach for her hand, but he didn't have a body here.

Something in the tunnel behind her made her auralight flare as if in warning. She looked behind her and Finn felt a spike of her fear before she looked back to him, her eyes wide. Her voice broke as she said, "We're coming."

Like a taut rope being cut, Finn was suddenly jerked back to his body. He didn't travel tether like before, but instead it was like he'd been standing and suddenly he'd been shoved back onto his behind. He opened his eyes and expected to see the circle of trees, the unnaturally bright sun, but instead he was looking up at a canopy of tangled branches. Beside him, Seraphina sat, her face a mask of worry. He was back in the real world.

With a groan he sat up, his head pounding, his mouth dry.

"Where did you go?" she asked as she handed him a skin of water. Beside her, the large black cat that had so disturbed Finn at first sat and watched him, it's long, shiny tail flicking back and forth in the dirt.

"What do you mean?" Finn asked, his voice hoarse with disuse.

"Just now," she said, brow creased. "You were—"

Morrigan chose that moment to materialize from the shadows like a wraith, a scowl marring her once lovely face, and cut off whatever Seraphina was going to say.

"We have to prepare," Morrigan said, staring daggers at Finn. "I've gotten us some help," she paused, her nostrils flaring, "but sitting here as we are is no good." She gathered up her things. "We have to get to the starling pond."

"Prepare for what?" Seraphina asked as she stood and dusted off the back of her tunic. The cat followed and pressed itself against her side. The creature was so tall that Sera had to stand on her tiptoes to lay her arm across its massive shoulders. Her small pale fingers were splayed against the ropey muscle.

Morrigan exhaled through her nose. He could still see the faint outline of red around her and the small stream of red light connecting her to Seraphina.

Pulling her water skin from where she'd tied it to her belt, Morrigan took a long drought. Finn saw the red light around her pulse and brighten with the drink. She looked at Seraphina, her eyes narrowed, and the tiny rope of light that connected them grew larger.

Seraphina jerked, her eyes wide. Finn was powerless to do anything but watch as she threw up her hands as if to shove Morrigan away, but Morrigan flicked her fingers and Sera's hands dropped to her side as her face went blank.

The big cat beside Seraphina whined and pressed against her, but Sera was motionless.

"We have to get to the pond, Seraphina," Morrigan said as her eyes traveled to Finn. "You have to keep Finn under control."

Seraphina nodded once, and the large cat whined again, it's large, ropey muscles trembling slightly as sit shrank lower toward the ground.

"Erilyn's on her way," Morrigan said, her voice soft as she kicked dirt over their small campfire, "and when she arrives we have to be ready to kill her."

Seraphina didn't look at Finn as she pulled her own leash against him taut—so tight it hurt. His muscles no longer his own, his voice once again locked away, he could do nothing except scream in his head as he followed woodenly behind them, back into the woods toward the starlings' pond.

Chapter 38

"Starlings"
Morrigan

YOU set a brutal pace toward the starlings' pond. Your journey to the nightcrawlers' hole in the earth was only moderately successful. Since their attack on Ringol, their leader—Roark—had been arrested, so instead of finding him and appealing to his baser instincts to come to your aid, you'd had to sneak and hide like a rodent until you found who you needed. There were two wylden there as well, working with the nightcrawlers, so you'd had to be even more careful. You couldn't get close to Roark, but you'd found nightcrawlers loyal to him—those who had been taking their vitium and preparing for battle, as instructed. They were ready for a fight, so it was easy to convince them to help you. There weren't many, but there should be enough—to fight Erilyn off, to act as a human wall around what was yours.

You'd been on your way back to Finn and the girl when you'd *felt* Erilyn in the caves. Her friends were with her—the older nightcrawler girl had been hiding them. It wasn't until Finn found them—his emerald essence flying through the forest and tunnels like a panicked bird—that you saw them, crawling through the earth like the worms they were.

They are coming for you. Or for Finn and the girl. You aren't sure, can't *sense* them like you should, but it doesn't matter. You know where they are now. You have the upper hand.

As you dash through the Dark Woods , the starlings' pond comes into view and you breathe a little easier, even as the noxious fumes from the water's surface burn your lungs. Unlike everything else in these woods, this pond was not shaped by vitium. It doesn't *feel* right. If you *look*, you can see large, corroded metal pipes at the back of the pond. Beyond the pipes, you see rubble that may have once been a building. Whatever had poured from those pipes, now filled with holes, had madet his pond what it was.

You break into the clearing and smile, assaulted by the water's unnatural heat. From the tangld branches above, the giant starlings look down at you, waiting. You'd sent them instructions before your journey into the caves, and you are please to see they are still with you. They're harder to control than the wolves and the cat, but are more willing to follow you here.

"Is it safe?" Seraphina asks, gasping in the toxic air. Finn stumbles into the clearing behind her, sweat on his expressionless face. The cat—Ebb—brings up the rear, shoulders curled and tail low as it flicks from side to side. The wolves are still back at the cave entrance, there to keep Erilyn from leaving the earth.

You don't answer. You don't have to now. Instead, you set about finding a space close to the pond for Finn to hide, and for the girl to stay with him so that he stays still and quiet. Until you can control Finn yourself, you need her.

Off to the side, near the water, is the hollow tree that Finn and Erilyn hid in the last time you were all here. It's mostly uprooted and with a shove you knock it on its side, leaving a deep gouge in the dirt.

"Here," you growl. Now that you know they're coming, know what to *look* and *feel* for even if they're hiding themselves, you can sense that they're close. You cock your head to one side—at least Erilyn is. You can't feel the other two. But it doesn't matter, because Erilyn is all you care about.

Seraphina woodenly walks to the upturned shell of a tree and sits in the hollowed space. Finn follows, teeth ground together. Through your hold on the girl you can feel how hard he's fighting her. He shouldn't be able to do that.

He'd felt her coming. Somehow, he'd learned how to *find* her, and that was giving him the strength now to fight.

He'd never fought like that for you. If only you'd killed her in Ringol.

But as hard as he fights, Seraphina's control is stronger. When she and Finn settle and quiet, you take a drink of your vitium—the last drink in the skin. You'll have to go get more after this is over, but this last bit along with the energy of the forest is enough. Your fingers tingle as you toss the water skin aside.

You can feel her—Erilyn has left the caves and is making her way right for you. You don't bother to *look* for the wolves. If she's out of the caves, they're dead. They couldn't disobey your commands. But it's no matter.

Behind you, Ebb huddles beside the girl, dwarfing her even as it curls in on itself. You *pull* hard on its tether and though it tenses and whines, wanting to stay with her, it comes to you. The girl reaches for the creature with pale hands, her eyes wide, but a *nudge* from you stops her. If Erilyn's little beast is with her, this cat will ensure it doesn't last long.

With a forced casualness, you sit on top of the log, hoping that by being so close to Finn, she won't think to look for him there. Besides, the closer you are to the two of them, the more easily you can help the girl hide them. In his mind, Finn is screaming for Erilyn, and you worry that you and Sera won't be able to hide him for long.

Eyes closed, you reach out to the birds. You don't need them to fight—you want to be the one who drains Erilyn's life from her—you need them to make sure that Finn stays hidden. They ruffle their feathers and settle more securely on their branches. Their swirling, black auras expand and cover Finn behind you. You *look* for him and smile. If you didn't know where he was, you wouldn't be able to find him, either.

Perfect.

Erilyn is moving swiftly. You wait, foot tapping the earth, as you clench your fists and get ready to end this once and for all.

Chapter 39

"Inevitable"

Erilyn

CITADEL was in upheaval. We'd bypassed the city center, hiding as we went, but cave dwellers, powered by vitium, were waiting for us. They'd been ready to attack, ready to kill me until they'd seen Aiyanna.

Morrigan had been here. She'd convinced these people that if they stopped me, they could have Sunnybrook. If it weren't for Aiyanna's presence with me, I would have been outnumbered. She convinced them that a truce with Sunnybrook was better than trying to take it by force.

I could feel Lucy's indecision—to stay with Aiyanna and help broker peace or to come with me and get her own revenge on Morrigan—but in the end, she stayed with Aiyanna. It felt right, somehow, to be going up against Morrigan alone, but I had to admit was a little bit afraid.

The only thing that kept me moving forward without hesitation was knowing that I was going toward Finn, the boy who'd broken into the quiet of my life and become the most important person in it.

Ready to get to him, I pushed my way up through old tunnels and emerged, exhausted, into the dark forest. I climbed through roots that vaulted overhead like a dome, Luna right on my heels, into the muggy air.

I had only taken a couple of steps when Luna stopped, a growl deep in her throat. Her ears were pinned back as she stared into the dark. There, just out of the pale light that filtered in from above, I saw four eyes. I could *see* their auras—blending together, surrounded by a haze of Morrigan's red—and recognized them as the wolves who'd chased me the last time I was here.

Luna was scrappy and strong, but she was no match for wolves. I only had one chance.

Animals had always been easy for me to connect with, and I trusted my instincts with these wolves like I would with any others. I pictured Finn, letting them *see*, and shared my desire to find and protect him. Recognition flittered in their minds and wet my lips as I tried again. I pictured Sera this time and one of them whimpered. The red light around their auras flickered and I *felt* their desire to go to her.

"I want to keep her safe," I whispered, letting my love for both of them fill up the pace between us. I squatted low and held my hand out, picturing Sera's face the whole time. Luna stayed beside me, posture alert and ready. The wolves whimpered again, and I held Seraphina firmly in my mind.

Paws shuffled in the underbrush, tails swished, one of their whines turned into a cry, and their shared auras started to brighten, the red around the edges fading away. It was long moments later that the red was completely gone, driven away by their love for Sera, and they stepped out of the shadows.

The two wolves were attached at the shoulder. They stepped toward me, heads low, a pitiful whine in their two throats as if they were afraid I might hurt them.

"It's okay," I said, hand still outstretched. They sniffed my fingers, then looked at Luna, ears back and tails tucked. She studied them for a moment, then sat back on her haunches, ears perky and normal, and the wolves relaxed. I let myself take a relieved breath.

I showed them Sera again, then Finn. "I need to find them," I said, hoping they would understand. One of them panted lightly as they stood up in tandem. The other licked my hand, then pressed its cold nose into my palm. Images bloomed in my mind and icy fear settled in my gut.

She had taken them to the starlings' pond—the place where I'd used Finn like kindling for a fire, I'd realized how easy it would be to kill him if I wasn't careful. I hated that place more than I hated anywhere else in the world. I wondered if she chose it because somehow she knew that.

My hands shook as I stood and tightened my pack on my shoulders. I nodded at the wolves and tried to feel grateful, then followed them as they led me deeper into the woods.

IT didn't take long to reach the pond. We stopped when the odor grew thick. I closed my eyes and put my hand on Luna's head to help me focus, just like I'd always done in the woods before I even realized what I was doing. Together, we *looked* into the clearing and found the swirling, black auras I knew belonged to starlings, but nothing else. No Finn. No Sera. No Morrigan. But the wolves were sure they were here. They were as despearte to get to Sera as I was. I took a deep breath, ignoring how the fumes from the pond made my throat itch, and focused on Finn—on his deep green auralight that shone like dew-wet grass in the spring.

Finn, I called, heart aching. *Where are you?*

Like fog dissipating in sunlight, the mass of swirling black voids started to swirl away and behind the cloud they'd created, for a fraction of a moment, I saw it— a flash of green along with his voice saying my name in my mind. *Erilyn.* It was gone as quickly as it happened, but it was enough. Morrigan was hiding him from me, but he was here.

Heart ricocheting against my ribs, I patted the wolves' heads. Morrigan would most likely kill them for helping me, so with a gentle thought I thanked them, showed them I would take care of Seraphina, and encouraged them to leave. One of them licked my hand

and nuzzled my palm, then off they ran to hide until it was safe.

I stood straight and took a deep breath, trying not to gag on the stink of the pond, then pulled the knife I'd brought and gripped the handle. I'd never been much of a fighter, though. Some part of me hoped I would be able to talk her out of this, convince her to let htem go. I could still feel the weight and heat of being trapped inside her aura, but Finn had loved her once. Surely there was good in her somwhere.

With slow, steady steps, I crossed the threshold from the Dark Woods into the starlings' territory. I could see them all up in the trees, their beady eyes fixed on me. The yellowed fog swirled around my ankles, and while it didn't hurt, I knew that the water it came from would. Inside the clearing, I stopped and looked around.

At first glance, the whole area appeared empty. If the wolves hadn't brought me here, if I hadn't *heard* Finn call for me, I might have left to search somewhere else. But I knew they were here.

A massive tree had been uprooted and lay on it's side near the water's edge, but other than that and the scraggly plants dotted here and there, the space was barren. I thought it was the same tree that Finn and I had hidden inside the last time we were here, but I couldn't be sure. Every time I tried to focus on it, something in my periphery would catch my eye and draw my attention away.

Luna looked up at the birds and hissed. Her gaze fell on the fallen tree and she growled, her tail twitching in agitation. Something was there, hiden from me. I looked at the tree again, using my abilities as much as my eyes, and there, just above the top of the trunk, was the smallest bit of brown hair. My heart stuttered.

"I'm here for Finn and Sera," I said, my voice strong and loud, though the sizzling air seemed to eat up my words as soon as they left my mouth. The birds in the trees didn't so much as flinch. "Let them go and we'll all leave you alone. You never have to see me again."

There was a moment of absolute silence and stillness, movement behind the fallen tree. I'd expected Morrigan, but instead out stepped Finn. My heart leapt with joy and my breath caught as I took an involuntary step forward. I wanted to run to him, but something held me back. His expression was completely blank. His eyes were dull. His steps were wooden as he approached, hands clenched at his sides.

"Finn," I said, trying to *read* him and finding only the void that I recognized as the starlings' auralight. Sweat broke out on his brow as he walked, his movements jerky as if he were fighting each step. "Finn!" I called again, unable to stop myself from taking another step closer. The void around him flickered, revealing a hint of green, surrounded by pink, and he stumbled to a stop.

"No," he croaked, falling to his hands and knees. "I won't hurt her!" He was tethered, but not by Morrigan. It was Sera's pink light I'd seen all around him.

I stepped toward him and hit a wall of air, just like the last time we were here. I wanted to beat it, to break it down, but I knew I couldn't. Finn stared at me, eyes tear-filled and clear, but slowly they went foggy again. His shoulders hunched forward as he stood, hands and knees covered with dirt, but he didn't come forward again.

"Morrigan!" I pushed against the solid air with my hands. "Let them go!"

It was Sera's turn to step out next, a large, frightening black cat behind her. It's body bulged in strange places, like a stuffed animal with too much stuffing. It had no fur that and it's skin looked oily, like a king snake. It's head was large and boxy and it's eyes were dark. It was the cat that had chased me through the Dark Woods. The one that had almost gotten me. Before I could warn her, she put her hand on its head and it stepped against her side, its shoulders easily as tall as hers.

"Go home, Erilyn," Seraphina said, her voice quiet. She stroked the great black cat between its too-small ears. "You aren't good for Finn," she said as she stepped ahead of the cat and tilted her chin up. "You *bound* him to you," she said. "You *hurt* him." Her eyes went glassy and she smiled. "We'll never do that to him." Her smile dimmed as she said, "We love him."

"Seraphina." My voice cracked as I watched her. "This isn't you. Morrigan. She's doing this." I tried to step forward, but the wall of air stopped me again. The birds watched from their barren perches, still as stone. Beside me, Luna crouched and growled, her eyes on the black cat.

"Go home," she said, her voice heated. "Please, Erilyn. We don't want to hurt you."

I looked at the little girl who I saw so much of myself in—into her eyes and into her aura. I could see how Morrigan had gotten her claws into Sera, how Seraphina's own anger and jealousy had given Morrigan the opening she needed.

My voice wobbled as I spoke, but it wasn't fear for me that frightened me. "What about your sisters and brothers? They need you."

She laughed darkly. "Why would they need me when they have you?" she asked as she wiped away a tear I hadn't seen fall. "You go back and take care of them and I'll take care of Finn." The dark cat growled at her side.

"Seraphina," Morrigan said as she seemed to materialize from beside the fallen tree just feet from where Finn still stood, motionless. "I told you she would never listen. Never understand." She looked at me and smiled, showing her teeth. A shiver chased down my spine. "You know what must be done."

"Kill her?" Seraphina asked, her eyes clearing a little and going wide as she turned to Morrigan. "But I—"

"You're so much stronger than you know," Morrigan crooned, stepping around the tree trunk to stand beside Finn. "You can do this. Together, you and I can protect him. Love him."

I could see Morrigan's aura like an invasive vine, crawling its way into Seraphina's beautiful pink, and I knew I twould keep crawling and growing until the pink light was snuffed out.

Sera turned to me with tear trails through the dirt on her cheeks. The cat beside her crouched and looked up at her. It shrunk back, no longer menacing. If anything, it looked afraid.

The wall of air in front of me vanished and I stumbled forward. The knife in my hand was pointed toward them from my fall and Seraphina looked at it in anger, and then fear.

I dropped the blade into the dirt and fell to my knees. She might attack me, but it didn't matter because I could never hurt her. I loved her too much.

"See?" Morrigan said, her voice a dark whisper. "She's given up. She sees that we're stronger than she will ever be. Go ahead, Seraphina. Protect Finn." Morrigan stayed where she was, but her voice seemed to creep closer as she said, "Let's end this."

Sera stepped toward me and tears flowed freely down her cheeks. She clenched her jaw, hands in fists at her sides. The black cat followed her.

Luna crouched low beside me and growled, her eyes tracked the other cat.

"Ebb, please don't hurt Luna," Seraphina said. The black cat meowed back like a kitten. Barely a foot from me,

Sera stopped. "I don't want to hurt you," she said, her voice thick with tears. "Just agree to go, to leave us alone, and she'll let you leave." She wiped her nose on the back of her hand. "I don't want to hurt you," she repeated, her voice wavering.

"I can't," I said. "I love you, Sera. And I love Finn." A combination of anger and pain flashed across her face, her auralight flaring brightly. "I can't leave either of you with her."

"Seraphina." Morrigan's voice was sharp like a whip and the younger girl started.

The cat at Seraphina's side whined as Seraphina shuffled closer to me. I *watched* her vivid pink aura pulse, surrounded by red, infused with veins of it. Her eyes on me were desperately sad, but still she gathered power to her, the light near her chest glowing so brightly it was almost white. I'd always known Sera was stronger that me. She was stronger than Morrigan, too, but she didn't seem to realize it.

I stared up at her, at the light growing like a small sun in her chest, and did the only thing I could. I tore down any wall I'd ever built to keep people out, walls I still held in place without meaning to after living with them for so long, and let my love for her go free. She blinked and shook her head, confused, and the light in her chest dimmed. Just past her I could see Finn, shaking his head too. They were both trying to break free.

"Eri," Sera whispered, tears hot and fat on her cheeks. "I can't—" her confusion shifted to panic and she took a step away from me. She turned to Morrigan and crossed her arms over her stomach. "This is wrong," she breathed.

Morrigan's nostrils flared. There was a beat of nothing, then quick as lightning Morrigan's arm flashed to her waist. Her knife flew through the air toward Seraphina before I could fully register the movement. The black cat beside her tried to knock her aside with its massive shoulder, but even it was too slow. The knife found its mark with a dull thud.

Finn darted to Seraphina's side, her tether broken. The black cat lay flat against the earth and meowed brokenly. Beside me, Luna joined the other cat in a chorus of misery, her ears pressed against her head. Somewhere out in the woods, the wolves took up the call, all of them echoing the feeling of agony that burned my chest.

Finn looked at me, his face a mask of fear as his hands hovered over the knife handle. I could *feel* her life seeping out of her, her blood trickling into the dirt. The unnatural fog from the pond swirled around her, making her already pale skin look sick. I didn't move from where I knelt, frozen, and dove into her aura, aiming straight for the wound where her pink auralight pulsed with each panicked beat of her heart. Where her body was injured, her auralight pulsed and darkened. I *grabbed hold* of the wound and squeezed, closing the wound, not caring if I left any gold behind. It didn't matter, as long as she lived.

In the few heartbeats that this took, Morrigan had drawn her other knife. Part of my aura with Sera, helping her cling to life, I lunged to my feet and threw myself at Morrigan, grabbing my own knife from the dirt as I went. Because of my time with the wylden, it was simple to separate my mind as I focused on keeping Morrigan away.

Her red aura crackled around her like a lightning storm. I could *feel* Seraphina's tenuous hold on life and an anger unlike any I'd known before welled up hot inside me.

Teeth gritted, muscles trembling, I slashed at Morrigan with my knife. She was faster and physically stronger than me. She'd trained for this. She dodged my attack and slashed at my arm. Blood and pain bloomed, leaving a twin mark to the healed scar on my other arm.

I rolled away, blood soaking the fabric of my sweater. It wasn't deeep, so I ignored it. I couldn't beat her like this.

Chest heaving, I let a long-familiar heat well in my gut. I pulled from the vitium all around us I thought I might burst with how much power held. I spread my feet apart to stabilize myself and threw my hands out toward her, putting all of my anger into my *shove*. Morrigan flew back, tangled hair flying in front of her face as her back cracked against the hollow tree. She screamed in rage and looked up at the birds. Behind her, the toxic pond chopped in a sudden gust of wind.

The starlings regarded her with the beady eyes. They ruffled their feathers, but stayed on their branches. Her aura flared hot in anger. Her green eyes were bright with madness when she looked at me again, teeth bared.

Finn—deep and green and entirely himself again— had pulled Seraphina to the edge of the clearing. I glanced over and saw him cradling Sera to his chest, his shirt dark with her blood. Luna and the cat Sera had called Ebb were in front of them, crouched low, ears back.

Sera's bleeding had stopped, so I pulled all of my energy back into myself. I met Finn's eyes—so beautifully blue—and felt a surge of love mingled with fear. In his arms, Sera was unnaturally pale.

I turned back as Morrigan threw her body at me. I dodged her, barely, as she slashed the air viciously with her knife. I fell to the side, my own knife falling into the dirt. I grabbed for it, but she kicked my hand and snatched up the blade. I jumped ot my feet, hands stretched out toward her. We attacked at the same time—her with knives, me with a blast of air—and we both once again tumbled into the dirt.

In our struggle, she had maneuvered me closer to the pond. I coughed, eyes watering, as the thick yellow fog seeped around me. I looked at Morrigan, now between me and them. Behind her, Finn said something, but I couldn't hear him. I focused on Morrigan as she forced me back toward the water.

"It was always going to end this way," she said as my foot sank into the mud beside the pond's edge. Toxic water lapped at my boot and I fought the urge to gag at the rotten-sweet smell. "You ruined *everything*." Her scratchy voice is too loud as it slips from between chapped lips. "You stole Finn from me. You killed—" she stopped, brow creased in confusion, then shook her head. "If it weren't for you, Cillian would still be alive." Her voice wavered with his name.

"I didn't want any of this," I said, hands outstretched as my heels sank deeper into the mud. I wished Finn would pick up Seraphina and run. If I died, they needed to be far away. "I just wanted—"

"This is all your fault!" she growled and lunged at me, blades out.

Erilyn.

Time slowed as Finn's quiet voice sounded in my head. I could *feel* his love, as brilliant and pure as sunlight after a storm, and it gave me the strength I needed.

Time sped up again and I dodged one of Morrigan's knives. Her aura brushed against mine, prickly and sharp, and she roared in rage. Being near her felt lik being too close to a fire and I needed to put it out before I was burned up. She slashed at me again and the water behind me chopped. It splashed my arm, soaking my sweater and seeping into my knife wound. I screamed as it burned. Her knives moved in a blur and I felt her *pushing* me toward the water. If my boots hadn't been so thick, the water would have already reached my toes.

My boots sank deeper into the mud and the only thing that kept me from toppling in is the air I used to keep Morrigan from me, but the water is splashing higher now, almost as if it's reaching for me. I can't hold her off much longer.

Erilyn! Finn's voice screamed is in my mind again, his love and desperation as vivid as my own for him.

Morrigan slashed at me again, both knives flashing, and I do the only thing I can—I pull my feet from the mud and spin, hands outstretched, then *push* as hard as I can. Her knives fly from her hands as she flies backwards and lands with a splash in the choppy yellow-green water.

Chapter 40

"Burn"

Morrigan

RAGE and the forest's vitium burn inside you, making you invincible as you fight her. You want to laugh as your knives cut through the air, hungry for the tang of blood that means you sliced her again.

It's almost over when she turns. *Shoves* you into the water.

No.

Your mouth is open in shock as the yellow fog around you. It cushions you and for a moment you think you'll be alright. This forest accepted you. It's going to protect you just as you'd told Seraphina it would.

But the fog doesn't hold you and you splash into the water. You sink beneath the surface and the caustic liquid fills your open mouth and scalds your throat. Your skin is on fire. You struggle toward the air, pain lancing through to your bones, and scream as soon as you break through to the surface.

All you know is pain as the water—too thick, too warm—splashes all around you. On the shore you see Erilyn stands with her hands out and you think you feel a *tug,* as if she might pull you back to shore. Behind her Finn, but you can't see if he's coming to help you.

You follow the *tug* like a rope and try to swim back to the shore when the starlings begin to swarm. They swirl above you, a black cyclone, their void-like auras pulling at your own, and whatever it was that was helping you breaks.

All you know is pain as the birds keep anyone from reaching you. You can't see Erilyn anymore beyond the splashing water, the black birds, the agony, but within the midst of so much darness you *feel* her aura reach for yours. Her gold, warm like sunlight, connects with your red. You feel her taking some of the pain from you, suffering it so that you don't have to. You don't have time to think about why as the starlings close in, their swirling black voids forcing you beneath the surface.

Even with Erilyn shielding you from some of the pain from the shore, everything hurts. Your lungs scream for air. You skin feels as if it is being flayed from your body. Your bones ache as if they might break and your muscles clench and spasm. If it weren't for Erilyn, the girl you hate more than anything, this would be unbearable.

The edges of your awareness blacken as water fills your lungs, but the darker things get, the less you notice the pain.

This is it.

You thought things would be different.

In the last seconds, when the darkness starts to feel soft and warm, when the pain is nothing more than a distant echo, you see Cillian.

His eyes are bright and a live and his smile is joyful as he reaches for you. With your last conscious thought and beat of your heart, you reach for him, too.

Chapter 41

"Broken Things"

Finn

THE starlings swirled in a cyclone over the water, and when they retreated to their branches, the water was still.

"Erilyn!" but she didn't seem to hear him. Her eyes were glued to the pond where Morrigan had been. He'd seen her fall in, seen her struggle, and Erilyn had stayed rooted where she was.

He didn't have to be able to *see* or *feel* to know that Morrigan was dead, but he would have to deal with exactly how that made him feel later. Right now, Seraphina was dying in his arms "Erilyn!" he called again, voice breaking, calling for her with every part of himself.

Erilyn jerked with a gasp and stumbled to where he was, her face a mask of misery. Ebb moved aside as Erilyn approached, a low whine in his throat. Luna laid beside him, shoulder to shoulder, her ears flat to her head. Off to the side, the wolves watched from the shadows.

"Sera," Erilyn choked out as she fell to her knees in the dirt beside them. Her hands hovered over the knife that had lodged itself neatly between her ribs. Seraphina's breaths were shallow and her oversized sweater was stained crimson. "No, no, no," Erilyn sobbed before pressing her hands over Finn's where he held the wound around the knife.

"Can you heal it?" Finn asked as he pulled Sera a little higher on his chest. "Like you did for me?"

Erilyn closed her eyes and this time Finn had no trouble seeing her aura glow around her skin. It was deep, warm gold and it flowed from her hands into the frail girl in his arms. Her face crumpled and fresh tears poured over her cheeks.

"What do you see?" Finn asked, heart aching.

"I don't know—" She grimaced and Finn saw the halo of light, golden like a rising sun, grow. "It's complicated," she said, voice breaking as tears leaked from her eyes. "The knife is deep, but more than that, her aura is damaged from Morrigan's tether. I don't think I can—" Her words choked off as she opened her eyes and stared at the treeline just as Aiyanna and Lucy burst through.

"Sera!" Aiyanna cried as she fell to her knees beside Erilyn. Her hands shook as she cupped Seraphina's pale face.

Lucy stopped near Luna and Ebb, hand over her mouth, as still as one of the trees.

"Help her," Aiyanna hissed at Erilyn as she took Seraphina's limp hand tightly in her own.

"I can't," Erilyn said, voice still broken. "I'm not—" she hiccuped a sob. "It's too much!"

"Do it together," Finn said as he adjusted his grip on Seraphina, hating how fragile her breaths were becoming. "Just help her."

"I don't know how." Aiyanna's voice sounded like a frightened child, but Erilyn's nodded.

"We can lace," she said, voice breaking. Erilyn took Aiyanna's other hand. "We can lace our auras to help her. You just have to be with me, okay?" Erilyn looked back at Finn. "You too. I promise I won't take too much," she said, her voice cracking as her expression crumpled. "I promise I won't—"

"Take whatever you need," he said, his voice gruff.

Erilyn closed her eyes, touching both Finn and Aiyanna, and the clearing grew silent. Finn met Lucy's gaze, which was as wild as his felt, then he looked back to the little girl he held in his arms.

The air warmed around them. From Erilyn's hand, bright golden light seeped into Seraphina's chest and she started to glow. Holding her felt like sunlight against his skin. Eyes wide, Finn watched as brilliant purple light surrounded Aiyanna's hand and followed the gold, making Seraphina glow even brighter.

Finn held his breath as the purple and gold light soaked into Seraphina. Her cheeks—far too pale before— grew a little pinker, but she remained limp in his arms.

Erilyn's hand over his tightened and he felt a pull in his chest. He watched, transfixed, as green light passed from their joined hands into Sera's chest as well. Finn couldn't take his eyes off the beautiful swirling lights—gold, purple, and green.

"Finn." Erilyn's voice was barely a whisper. He looked away from Seraphina's blood soaked chest, coated in brilliant light, toward the girl he loved. Erilyn's eyes were still closed and her cheeks were shiny with tears that continued to fall. "I need you to take the knife out."

"Okay," he rasped, voice hoarse as if he'd been screaming.

"Do it quickly," she said and he nodded, his mouth dry.

Erilyn and Aiyanna pulled their hands away and Finn stiffly gripped the knife's handle, his hands covered in Seraphina'sblood. Ebb and Luna had gone completely still and silent beside them. He took a quick breath, then pulled the knife straight out, grateful it wasn't serrated.

Seraphina jerked in pain and he threw the knife aside to put pressure on the wound again, his hand warming with the new flow of blood.

Erilyn and Aiyanna's hands rejoined his and fresh tri-colored light poured into the girl.

"Please, Sera," Finn said, wanting her to hear him, to *feel* what he was feeling. "Please fight. Stay with us." He stared at their hands and was surprised to see a surge of green. It wasn't being pulld from him, but given freely, fueled by his despire for Seraphina to live. "Please," he whispered again.

He stared down at their joined hands. He felt Sera's bleeding slow, then stop. Gold, purple and green poured into the small girl and ever so slowly, pink joined it.

When Erilyn and Aiyanna pulled way, Finn looked down at the little girl in his arms. Her cheeks were pink. Her chest was rising and falling. Her shirt was soaked in blood, but the wound beneath the rip in her sweater had been healed.

"Is she—"

"She's okay," Erilyn said, falling back on her heels. Her expression held none of the relief Finn felt, but Aiyanna's did. She reached forward and pulled Erilyn into a crushing hug, whispering something into her hair, before she sat back and held out her arms.

Gingerly, muscles shaking with fatigue, Finn transferred Seraphina's sleeping form to Aiyanna. Lucy slipped next to her and lay her hand flat on Aiyanna's back as Aiyanna held Seraphina rocked and shushed Seraphina like a baby.

Erilyn watched them for a moment, her face blank, then stood and walked back toward the pond. Finn used water from one of the skins to rinse his hands, then, stiff and sore, he stod and followed her. When he reached her, he wanted to grab her, to hold her tight to his chest, but her shoulders were curled forward and she held her arms around her stomach as if she might be sick, so he stayed back.

She stared out over the green-yellow water, which was as still as glass. "Morrigan's dead," she said, her voice as stiff as the rest of her. "I killed her." Her voice like broken glass.

There were no words that would ease the pain she felt, so instead Finn reached out and took her hand. Erilyn looked up at him, her eyes wide and disbelieving, and then collapsed against his chest.

Finn pulled her tight to him, folding around her as if he could sponge her pain away. He pressed his lips against her hair and left them there, grateful that she was alive.

She sobbed without sound into his chest and tentatively gripped the fabric of his sweater in blood-caked fingers. "I'm sorry," she whispered into his sweater, her words thick and wet with tears. "I never wanted this. I didn't want to hurt anyone."

Finns kissed her hair again and again. He tighted his grip around her. "I know," he whispered. "It's okay. I've got you."

She cried into his sweater for a long time, but just like he had been willing to hold Seraphina for as long as it took to get her back, he would do the same for Erilyn. Until he was sure she could come back from this precipice of despair, he wouldn't let her go.

Her tears slowed and her shudders dissipated. Her tight muscles loosened along with her grip on his shirt. Her ragged breaths lengthened and evened.

"Erilyn," he said, his lips brushing against her forehead. She looked up into his eyes, her expression trusting and broken, like an animal that had been beaten but wanted only to be loved. He kissed her forehead again. "Let's go home."

She looked back at the pond one more time and Finn tightened his grip on her a little more. Her sigh was deep and pained as she nodded, and with his arms around her shoulders, Finn led her back to the others.

Chapter 42

"The Lacing"

Erilyn

WE made it back to Sunnybrook without any complications, but I barely remembered the trip. Aiyanna and Lucy shared the task of carrying Seraphina, and Finn had stayed with me, his arm around my shoulders. We'd had to leave Ebb behind—the sun outside the Dark Woods was too much for him—and his pain as we walked away with Seraphina had only added to my own.

In the month since, things had slowly gone back to normal. Sera recovered, and each day she came out of the shell she'd woken up in a little bit more. She was afraid that we all blamed her for what she'd done to Finn, but of course we didn't. She wasn't the monster here. I was.

My wylden friends traveled back to Ringol after our return, but the lines of communication were now open. Cave dwellers, wylden, and upworlders had been working together for weeks now. Lucy still spoke for Sunnybrook while Aiyanna served as a spokesperson for the cavedwellers. They'd tried to talk her into taking her father's seat, but she'd declined, and now Citadel was being governed by an elected council. The children were taking lessons with Rosemarie and Mehri, even Seraphina, and Finn was working in town to help tear down the wall that was no longer necessary.

But as everyone else healed and moved forward, I couldn't forget what had happened at the starling's pond. Morrigan's final feelings, her final pain, were still felt fresh in my mind. At night I found myself rolling away from Finn's warm embrace after he fell asleep so that I could hold her pain deep in my bones to try and pay for what I'd done.

The only time I interacted with the others was when the wylden needed a voice. Fia did her best, but when they needed someone to translate further, I was brought in. It mostly consisted of me sitting between Zeke and Aiyanna, Dill behind us like a guard, while Lucy, Aiyanna, and the others appointed to each council debated.

It was during one of these moments, watching Fia speak to our strange assembly, that Zeke leaned over to me and whispered, "Lacing." I opened up my *sight*— something I rarely did since Morrigan's death—and *saw* the auras of all of our peoples dancing together in near harmony. It was a balm for the constant pain I carried, hidden behind fresh walls in my mind.

When I wasn't in council meetings, I was in Finn's apartment. He'd insisted we not go back to the workshop, but wouldn't tell me why. I assumed it was so that I would still socialize with our friends—Rosemarie and the children vissited each day, all except Seraphina. Rosemarie had made a new sun cream—one that didn't darken their skin—and it was so lovely to see them all exactly as they were meant to be. But no matter how sweet the children were, how loving Rosemarie was, I still felt apart from them. Like when Morrigan died, part of me had died as well.

Most of my days were spent alone. Finn left each morning to help tear down the wall, and came back each evening with something for supper.

We didn't talk much, but that was okay. I didn't have much to say. But I looked forward to this part of each day because the moments just before we fell asleep was the only time I ever felt settled anymore. Wrapped in his arms, which had grown stronger from all the hard labor, Luna stretched out beside us or on the floor in front of the small fire, I could convince myself that everything was okay. But then he would fall asleep, Luna would fall asleep, and I was left alone with only my memories.

I spent most nights curled around my knees, *watching* Morrigan's red light be snuffed out beneath putrid green water.

Finn noticed, but he never pushed me to talk about it. He was just there with me. When I finally did fall asleep each night, I was plagued with nightmares. Sometimes the nightmares were just memories, and in others I was the one beneath the waves. But each morning I woke to Finn holding me, his arms strong and gentle all at once.

Only on the one day a week that Finn took to rest did I feel almost normal. We would spend the whole day wrapped up together in his apartment, talking about the children, about the weather, anything but the things that plagued me. Sometimes I would just lay my ear on his chest and let the sound of his heart lull me. Often, I woke up after drifting off only to find tha thours had passed. They were the only times I slept dream-free.

But then he would go back to his work, tearing down the wall, and the cycle would begin again. I went through the motions of each day, trying to hide how I felt from my friends, my family, then guiltily taking solace in the comfort Finn offered each evening until I was alone again and could relive Morrigan's death.

My penance was too light.

THE first day of spring arrived on a rest day. I woke with sun on my face and had the brief, joyful thought of getting out in the woods with Luna for a bit. But no sooner than the thought entered my head, it transformed and I was back in the Dark Woods, and any desire to get outside vanished.

Finn kissed my temple and wrapped me more securely in his arms, unknowingly bringing me back to the present. He'd done this back in my clearing, too—kept my bad dreams at bay.

My only joy came from Finn and the love that he shared with me—love that wasn't prompted by a tether, love that was given freely and without expectations. Love I didn't deserve, but was selfishly unwilling to let go of.

"It's spring," I whispered and he smiled and nodded against my cheek, his stubble scratching my skin. His arms were warm as he held me and I took a deep breath to try and just exist in this moment with him for as long as I could. Caged in his arms I could pretend like everything was fine.

Luna stretched from her spot on the floor and chirped once before pushing the window open with one paw. She often left to visit the others—the children, Rosemarie, Lucy—and while I missed her while she was away, I was glad that her family had grown when mine did.

"Want some breakfast?" he asked, his lips brushing my earlobe. Chills chased down my spine, but I tried to ignore them. Since we'd found each other in the Dark Woods , this was as far as we'd gotten. Even a small kiss felt like too much, something I no longer deserved. Every time his lips brushed mine, I saw Finn with Morrigan, and remembered that his lips had once pressed against hers. Then I saw her fall into the lake, over and over again. So with every attempted kiss, I pulled away, and he let me.

"Sure," I said, rolling away from his heat and leaving the comfort of our shared bed to stoke a little more life back into our fire. Now that spring was finally, fully here, we wouldn't need it anymore.

Lucy made sure we were stocked in food—fresh bread, goat cheese, and dried fruits. But this morning we were running low with only a bit of stale bread and a half-empty jar of pine needles. "We don't have much," I said, a nervous edge to my voice. We'd eaten in the dining hall a few times, but it was almost always stoo much for me—all the thoughts and feelings, crammed in one place.

Finn jumped out of bed, a wide grin on his face. "I'll go get us something and bring it back," he said, eyes bright. I was taken aback by his sudden energy. He typically woke slowly, needing to be coaxed from bed on a rest day.

I shook my head, hating the thought of him going to any extra trouble for me. "No, it's alright. We can—"

"I'll be back soon," he said as he slipped boots on over the thick wool socks Rosemarie had made for him. He crossed the small room in two long strides and kissed my cheek, right beside my mouth. "Wait here," he added, his eyes sparkling. I nodded and he kissed my cheek againhis lips lingering for just a moment, then he was out the door.

Alone with my thoughts again, I pushed Luna's window almost closed to keep the draft away, then mechanically poured water from a pitcher into our metal tea tin and hung it over the fire. When it boiled, I added pine needles and waited. The minutes ticked on in silence. From the food shelf I retrieved the old, dented, metal cup that had come from my clearing. The images on the side— the children playing, the man holding a jug that said XXX on the side, the broken letters spelling LUEGRASS—had faded a little more after our travels over the winter, but were still intact. I shook my head as I took it down, strangely comforted by this ugly relic. The tea was weak—the result of using old pine needles instead of fresh—but the flavor reminded me of a simpler time and it calmed me.

I stared into my mug of weak tea, lost in my own thoughts as I waited for Finn to return. When the door opened, I was more than a little bit surprised to see Seraphina instead of Finn. I sat my ugly mug on the small table beside the bed and stood, filled with nervous energy. She closed the door behind her, eyes on her feet.

"Sera," I said, my voice cracking. Since we'd returned from the Dark Woods , we hadn't spoken. I'd seen her with the others, had been in the same room, but we hadn't so much as made eye contact before this moment.

She looked up at me now, her eyes wide. I was taken back to that day we'd talked in the woods, before we ever made it to Ringol. It felt like a lifetime since then.

For long moments, we stared at each other, silence thick between us.

"I'm sorry," she finally said, breaking the silence. The anger and hostility she'd shown me before I left to find the wylden was gone and had been replaced with a palpable sadness that I didn't need abilities to sense. "I'm sorry I—" Tears welled in her eyes, her hands shook, and I couldn't stop myself from crossing the room and pulling her into a hug.

As soon as I touched her, she dissolved into tears, her thin arms circling my waist, her cheek laying against my chest. Without trying, her remorse poured into me like water from a burst pipe and I did my best to catch it all, to hold it, even though it ached in my chest.

I *felt* how sorry she was for being angry with me, for being jealous of me, for hating me because Finn loved me. Her arms around me tightened and I felt a fresh wave of feeling that would have brought me to my knees if I hadn't been ready for it. She was sorry, most of all, for allowing Morrigan any control of her life at all.

As I held her to me, I also held her pain. I experienced all of her feelings, one at a time, and then like removing a stopper from a bottle, I let it all go. For both of us.

"It's okay," I whispered as I stroked her hair, which lay smooth and long down her back. "Everything's okay."

After a long moment, she loosened her grip on me and I let her go, but she only stepped back a little. "You forgive me?" she asked, her voice small and so terribly young. After all we'd gone through together, it was easy to forget that she was just a child.

I smiled and cupped her cheek, something Rosemarie did when I was feeling particularly low. "Of course I do," I said, meaning it with my whole heart. "You're my family."

She sniffed once and I *felt* her emotions settle. As she accepted my forgiveness, I felt some of the weight I'd been carrying lift as well—like sunlight after long, old days of nothing but gray clouds.

"I wasn't supposed to do that," she said, wiping a tear from beneath her eye. "I was supposed to just come and get you," she said as she stepped back toward the door.

"We *all* are," Asa said as she pushed the door open and stepped inside, bumping Sera playfully as she did so. Behind Asa were the other three children, all smiling.

"Right. We all are," Seraphina repeated with a roll of her eyes, which made Asa smile broadly. Another piece of my broken heart settled into place as I saw Sera with her siblings, every bit the loving, annoyed older sister

"Finn told me to wait for him here." My stomach clenched and my eyes darted to Sera. Her love for him had been the door through which Morrigan had gotten in, but she didn't get angry when I mentioned him now.

"He told us to come get you," Sera said, her cheeks pink. "I promise."

If for no other reason than to show her I trusted her again, that I would always forgive her no matter what, I nodded. I slipped my soft, worn leather boots on—Rosemarie had been able to salvage them after their exposure to the starling pond, though they were scarred and worn now, just like me. I grabbed a sweater and followed the five of them out into the cool spring air.

Once outside, Seraphina took one of my hands and it made my heart stutter with joy. Galen took the other, his white curls particularly bouncy today, and with a soft laugh I followed them into the sunlight.

We walked away from town, and once I realized we were heading into the woods toward Finn's workshop, I sped up. I hadn't been here since we returned. I'd asked a few times, but Finn had always had a reason not to go, and after a while, I'd stopped asking. Morrigan had built it for him, and I worried that he didn't want me there because of what I'd done.

But now we were headed there and I felt lighter than I had in a while. The birds sang, having returned with the warmth, and I inhaled the smell of budding plants. Sera and Galen's hands were soft and warm and I couldn't help but smile as the others pointed out the animals they could *see*, hiding in the brush, ready to emerge from their winter rest.

I was distracted by the children, and in retrospect that had probably been their doing, so when we reached our destination, I stopped and stared around dumbly. We must have gone the wrong way, because Finn's workshop was gone. Instead, we stood in front of a full cabin, large enough for an entire family to live in. Smoke streamed from the chimney and on the porch were two wooden rocking chairs.

Asa, Noah, and Jubal raced ahead, full of giggles, while Sera and Galen pulled me up the steps. We stepped inside and I was struck by how lovely it was—a table with chairs stood in one corner of a kitchen area, next to a wood-burning stove. Through one doorway I saw a room with bookshelves and chairs covered with plush cushions. Galen let go of my hand and Sera led me through the building one room at a time, a secretive smile on her face. There was a room with a large bed and table with an unlit oil lamp, a room with a tub and water basin, and a room that was empty, but felt filled with possibilities. When we came back to the first room, I had no answers for this beautiful place, but both Lucy and Aiyanna were there wearing matching smiles.

"What's going on?" I asked. The children were sitting at the small dining table, waiting for their sister. Sera squeezed my hand, then joined them, all of them giggling softly as they ate sweets that Lucy must have brought for them.

"It's time to get you ready," Lucy said. She had the same gleam in her eye that I'd seen so often when I first met her and another piece of my broken heart mended.

"Ready for what?" I asked, eyes narrowed.

Lucy only shrugged and dragged me into the bathing room. With a laugh and a smile, she pushed me down onto a stool and started brushing my hair with a wooden comb. Aiyanna followed, arms crossed over her chest. In the next room, the children talked quietly, their voices like wind chimes.

"You're telling her nothing?" Aiyanna asked, an amused smile on her face. "Nothing at all?"

Lucy scoffed before she pressed a kiss to Aiyanna's lips. "Of course I'm not," Lucy said. I looked up in time to see her waggle her eyebrows, but she turned my head and started working on my hair again.

I laughed without meaning to—it had been a long time since that had hapened. "Lucy, what is going on?"

"Just trust me," she said, giving my shoulder a squeeze. "Have I ever led you wrong?"

I laughed again and shook my head. This all felt like a strange dream, but I wasn't willing to wake up yet if it was.

I chewed on my lip as Lucy brushed my hair, then braided it back. Aiyanna offered her a basket full of baby spring flowers, and Lucy's clever fingers tucked them into the braid.

"Perfect," Aiyanna said when Lucy was done. A shiny piece of metal served as a mirror and I could see that, just like at the winter gala so very long ago, Lucy had made me beautiful.

I opened my mouth to ask another question, but Lucy just shook her head and tugged me out of the room before I could say anything. I found Rosemarie waiting in the small bedroom I'd seen when I first arrived, a dress laid flat on the bed beside her. Lucy gave me a gentle shove int the room, then waggled her fingers at me and followed Aiyanna to where the children still giggled and whispered.

"I made this for your mother," Rosemarie said as she took my hand and pulled me closer to the bed. "She wore it the day she joined with your father." She swallowed past her emotions and smiled at me. "Let's get you into it, okay?" she asked.

I nodded. I didn't know what was happening, still unsure if this was real or a dream, but if Rosemarie wanted me to wear my mother's dress, I would.

Rosemarie helped me get undressed, then slip the dress on. It was a soft, pale yellow with tiny white and green flowers embroidered along the neckline and scattered across the skirt. I felt like I had been wrapped in a spring field. She fastened the buttons down my back and smoothed the skirt for me when she was finished. It fit perfectly.

"I had to alter it a little," she said as she stood in front of me. "Your mother was a little taller than you." She sniffed as she pulled a pair of slippers—soft and thick, dyed the same light green as the leaves on the dress—from a basket beside the bed.

"It's beautiful," I said, voice soft as I ran my hands over the rich fabric. Rosemarie smiled and cupped my cheek and I leaned into her touch. I hadn't let myself be touched much since we returned and it felt better than I had words to express.

She looked at me for a long moment, then glanced out the small window. It was nearly midday. "Are you ready?" she asked me, her smile light. "We should really be on our way."

"Where are we going?" I asked nervously, but Rosemarie just smiled befor she kissed my cheek. I slipped the shoes on, then followed her back out into the main living area where the others waited.

"We'll all be here when you get back," Seraphina said. She was holding Galen on her lap while the other children played with some knitted stuffed animals that had been in a chest beside the door.

"No one is going to tell me what's going on, are they?" I asked, but they all just smiled, the children whispering again, their cheeks pink. Aiyanna kissed my cheek, Lucy gave me a hug, and Rosemarie led me outside.

After all that had happened so far today, I wasn't really surprised to see Fia waiting with Zeke and Dill. "Beauty," Fia said, a smile on her lips as she embraced me, her aura gently touching mine in greeting. Behind them was a wagon hitched to a single horse.

"A gift," Zeke said, his voice gruff and warm. Beside him, Dill smiled, his pink scar stretching tight. They all wore new, tidy clothes, and had recently bathed, but other than that, they hadn't changed. "For you."

"A gift?" I asked, looking between the three of them. Fia stepped to Dill's side and I couldn't help but look at their auras—navy and maroon—tangled together. "Why?"

"For the lacing," Dill said, his smile broadening.

My mouth went dry. The cabin. The dress. All of it had clicked into place and I felt foolish that I hadn't figured it out before.

"Finn and Luna are waiting for you," Rosemarie said with a soft smile. "If you're ready, I'll come with you."

"Alright," I breathed, heart racing. I turned to the wylden, then back toward the cabin where the others had stepped out onto the porch. Cave dwellers. Wylden. Upworlders. All my friends and family were here. I felt a sudden surge of joy—something I hadn't felt since long before I left in search of the wylden.

But it was short lived as the image of Morrigan falling backward into the water invaded my mind, her pain echoing in my bones. I started to succumb to it, but others were there with me——Fia's, Sera's, Aiyanna's— blocking the memory and soothing the ache in my soul. I felt their understanding, their love, and I choked out a sob as for the first itme in weeks that horrible memory was held at bay.

I took a shaky breath and met the eyes of my family, all smiling. Then Dill helped me step up into the wagon while Zeke helped Rosemarie on the other side. At the house, Lucy and Aiyanna had ushered the children inside, but they were all crowded around two windows smiling at me through the glass. Rosemarie took the reins and clucked her tongue and the horse—a lovely dappled gray mare—responded easily. Fia waved, her hand in Dill's, as Rosemarie drove the wagon toward a newly made gap in the wall.

We followed an old wylden trail, but it didn't take long for me to realize which direction we were traveling. What normally would have taken a day or longer only took a couple of hours in the wagon. Rosemarie's hand found mine as we bounced over the rough ground and I let her presence soothe my nerves.

When we entered a part of woods that was familiar to me, my heart beat a painful cadence against my ribs.

"He's a good man," Rosemarie said into the silence. My grip on her hand was iron tight.

"He is," I agreed as the wagon rolled to a stop. "A very good man." I wet my lips and held back what I really wanted to say, which was that he was too good for me. That I had thought he didn't want this anymore. That what I had done was too terrible to deserve this—to deserve him.

Rosemarie stepped down, then helped me, making sure my beautiful dress didn't tear. She cupped my cheek and rubbed her thumb over my cheekbone. "And you're a good woman," she said, before leaning forward and kissing my forehead. I bit my bottom lip and let her feelings wash over me like summer rain. I didn't feel like a good woman, but her love overpowered those negative thoughts and I felt a little more of my heart heal.

Rosemarie kissed my cheek, then took my hand and walked me through the trees. I saw my maple first—I would know it's sprawling branches and wide trunk anywhere. My heart felt like a hummingbird in my chest as we moved toward my clearing.

Heart in my throat, we rounded the maple with it's massive aerial roots and I stopped as tears threatened to choke me. The ground had been swept clean and my garden had been pruned and tilled, ready to plat. The pond sparkled in the evening sunlight and beside it, the firepit was ringd with fresh stones and held a small fire. And there in the middle of it all stood Finn, Luna at his side, in front of the pine tree that had been my home for so long.

The healed branches, still dotted with tiny white flowers, had matured quickly. The needles were the same dark blue-green as they had been the last time I was here, but the branches were thick and heavy like the unburned side. It wasn't the same tree as it had been, but even the scarred part was beautiful.

But what drew my eyes the most was Finn. It felt like my heart might stop at the mere sight of him. His face was clean shaven and he wore new forest green pants and a burnt yellow shirt that I knew had been made to compliment my dress. His dark, wavy hair was brushed back out of his face and his beautiful blue eyes sparkled. Beside him, Luna sat proudly, her fur brushed smooth.

Rosemarie led me toward them. My legs felt like a sapling in the wind. "I love you," she said as she kissed my cheek.

"I love you too," I said, smiling as a single tear dripped down my cheek. She wiped it away with her thumb, then setpped away as I turned to face Finn.

"Is all this okay?" Finn asked, his eyes big and round. I felt a smile spread across my face as I laughed and nodded, a little more of that pain I'd carried for the last month fading away. I'd been so afraid that he didn't want this—didn't want me. This was perfect.

"Good," he said, smiling broadly. He reached for my hands and I took both of this, relishing in his calluses, the warmth of his skin. He rubbed comforting circles into the skin on the back of my hands with his thumbs. "When I met you," he started, his voice quiet, "I thought you were the most unusual girl I'd ever met. You were kind simply for the sake of being kind. You were selfless and risked your life for mine on more than one occasion. You were so strong, but also so soft, and I found myself wanting to tell you everything, all the time." Like when he held me in the night, I let mysel just be in this moment and the love he was sharing with me blocked out everything else. "you and I, we've been through a lot." He adjusted his grip again, which was the only sign he gave that he was nervous, and let all that we'd been through hang in the air. "But each day that I've known you, I've become more and more sure of one single thing, one truth—I love you, Eri. Of my own free will—" he added with a smile, "and with my whole heart, I love you. Before I left you in Ringol, you promised me that after everything was said and done, we would marry me. I want us to spend the rest of our lives together. No matter what."

A tear fell like a single raindrop down my cheek, but I didn't move to wipe it away.

I bit the inside of my lip and stared up into his sky blue eyes as I searched for the right words. "Before I met you, I thought I was meant to be alone." I swallowed heavily and glanced at Rosemarie whose eyes were bright with her own tears. "I'd lost everything." Luna chirped as if in accusation and I laughed lightly as she nudged my hip with her nose. "Except Luna," I amended. "And then you crashed headfirst into my life and everything changed. You flipped my whole world on its head and I can't imagine what my life would be like if you hadn't." Fresh tears welled in my eyes, but I pushed through, holding his fingers even tighter. "I met you and for the first time in a long time, I felt like I mattered."

My voice broke as I thought back over the last month. He stroked the back of my hands with his calloused thumbs and I raised his hands to mylips to press a kiss to his knuckles.

"I'm sorry for anything I've done to cause you pain, but if you'll let me, I'll spend every day from now on trying to show you how I feel. I love you. So much." I looked up at him through eyes bleary with tears that had yet to fall.

Finn smiled down at me and it was like sunlight breaking through clouds. Beside him, from a pocket of her dress, Rosemarie produced two metal rings. They were made of shiny silver that had been braided into a circle. Finn let go of my left hand to take the smaller one from her and she handed me the larger one.

With steady hands, he slipped the braided ring onto the same finger that wore the wooden band he'd made for me so long ago. I followed and slipped the ring I held onto his finger. His smile was bright as he took my hands again. "I will love you for the rest of my life," he said, and I felt my hands warm.

"And I'll love you," I said, the smile on my own face mirroring his. "Forever."

The sunlight was warm, but staring into his eyes made me feel even warmer. All day I'd felt pieces of my heart healing, but this moment felt different. Finn's eyes darted to my lips and my belly warmed with the promise his expression held. When he leaned forward, I tilted my head up to meet him. His lips pressed against mine and that final piece of brokenheartedness melted away.

As he kissed me, his lips soft and sweet, I felt a stirring in my chest. The sensation was subtle at first, but it grew quickly. It was my aura—growing, changing. I opened up my awareness and looked. His green and my gold reached for one another. As he kissed me, his arms around me, strong and warm, our auras blended together. There were no ties, no tethers, just two people becoming one.

Lacing—an act the wylden had talked to me about, had tried to explain, but that I only now understood.

Our kiss slowed after a few moments and he pulled back enough to rest his forehead against mine. I couldn't keep the smile from my face as I felt the weight of his hands on my waist mixed with his auralight dancing along the edges of mine, featherlight.

"That's better," he said, a soft smile on his face and relief evident in his voice. "This is exactly how it's supposed to be."

Beside us, Luna meowed and pushed against me, and my fingers found her fur. Rosemarie laughed and joined us as well, wrapping us both in a hug, tears flowing freely down her face. Beside me, the flowered-half of the pine swayed in the gentle spring wind.

My heart felt so full I was afraid it might burst. This was more perfect than any dream I'd ever dared have and for the first time in weeks, I didn't question if I deserved it.

Once all our tears were spent, Rosemarie and Finn headed back to the wagon. I took a moment, alone, too look around my clearing. The aerial roots that had sheltered me from storms and danger stood strong and if I *looked* into the pond, I could see the little brilliant spots of minnow light that had comforted me so often in lonely summers.

Finn appeared behind me, his arms slipping around my waist as he rested his chin on my shoulder. "We can come back as often as you want," he said, and I nodded gainst his cheek. Luna circled my ankles and chirped, then headbutted me toward the wagon. "I think she knows Lucy is planning to fill the cabin with food to celebrate with us," he said with a laugh, and I couldn't help but laugh in return.

Rosemarie was already seated and waiting, and after Finn helped me into my seat, he slipped in beside me, his arm going around my waist. I lay my head on Finn's shoulder and took a long look back at my clearing. Finn pressed his lips to my hair and I sighed, content for the first time in as long as I could remember.

With a small smile, Rosemarie flicked the reins once and off we headed, back toward Sunnybrook, the home Finn had built, and the family that waited for us there.

Epilogue

Erilyn

The late summer sun was high in the sky as I walked, Finn's hand in mine, through the market in Sunnybrook's town square. This was my first summer in Sunnybrook—at least my first that I could remember—and I'd loved every moment of the heat, the lively stalls that were set up each week, the comradery. But what I loved most were the new stalls—wylden working alongside upworlders to learn various trades, and cave dwellers there trading rarities from the caves—precious stones and dark seaweed—for things like sweet cakes and richly colored fabrics

It had been nearly six months since Finn and I had laced our auras, had joined our souls, and things had only gotten better since. I still had moments where I was overcome with grief and guilt for those we'd lost, especially for my hand in Morrigan's death, but when I sank into that quagmire of grief and self loathing, Finn was always there to hold me and pull me back out. No matter how often it hapeend, he was there on the other side, waiting for me. Loving me.

But those moments were becoming fewer and far between and for now I contentedly walked with his hand in mine as we browsed stalls of handwoven fabrics, knitted jumpers, baked goods, and fresh juices. Asa, Galen, Noah, and Jubal ran ahead of us, trailing Rosemarie, who was browsing fresh herbs. She ran the library again—with my help—but she had decided to use her experience working with vitium to start working with medicinal salves. She'd made the solution that the cave dwellers had used to attack the wylden, and even though it wasn't her fault, I thought this might be her way of making amends for all the lives that had been lost.

Seraphina had gone back to the Dark Woods after days after Finn and I laced. At first I'd worried it was because of that, but she'd convinced me that it was because she missed Ebb and the wolves. I'd been against her going—all of my memories there were full of pain and suffering—but she'd convinced me that the woods weren't bad. They were just different. Like any woods, they had dangerous places to be avoided—like the toxic lake—but there was safety there too. It had been Morrigan that had taught her that. Where no one else could hear or see, she showed me how conflicted she felt about that, and about Morrigan's death. By going back, she could find some closure.

After she settled there, other cave dwellers had joined her. The woods were dark enough that they didn't need any cream to be upworld during the day. To me it was frightening, but to them it was like a bridge between the caves and the sun. What once had been a place that was avoided was now a place to meet and trade as the cave dwellers discovered more and more hidden treasures within those woods. Roark had always said the people of Citadel deserved more and now, without his leadership, they'd gotten it. And it was all thanks to little, powerful Seraphina.

Over the last few months, Ringol's buildings had been repaired and gardens had been planted with the guidance of people from Sunnybrook. The wylden learned to tend them quickly and a regular route between our town and theirs had been established. The other wylden— Nico and the others—were still out there, but with the upworlders, wylden, and cave dwellers all working together, they hadn't approached us again.

Nico wasn't the only one who wasn't happy about ournewfound peace. There were people in all three towns that were against the truce, against us working together. I could only hope that, over itme, they would see how much better this was.

But right now, all I saw were cave dwellers and wylden working alongside upworlders and my heart felt so full I thought It might burst.

Finn and I walked past a stall of beautiful, hand-knitted blankets and I stopped to look at them, one hand cradling on my stomach. As I touched a particularly soft blanket—woven with strands in nearly every color of the rainbow—and felt a stirring in my abdomen. It felt like a gentle wave inside my belly. I'd known I was pregnant for weeks, but this was the first time I'd felt it move inside me. I closed my eyes, Finn's hand moving to my lower back, and *looked*. Warmth and excitement filled me up as I saw not one, but two points of light nestled inside my belly. Both tiny auralights shimmered with all the colors of the rainbow, unsure of what they were going to be. I smiled and bit the inside of my lip.

"Is it the baby? Is everything alright?" Finn asked, his voice by my ear full of concern. Ever since we'd realized I was carrying a tiny life inside me, he'd been extra attentive. It wasn't until we'd figured it out that he told me so very shyly that he could see auras now, too. He told me all about how he'd seen my aura in Ringol, and again when I'd come to get him from the Dark Woods. Rosemarie thought it might be because of his connection to me, but regardless of how or why he could do it, since he realized we were going to have a baby, he'd been monitoring my aura as if my life depended on it.

I opened my eyes and turned to press a kiss against his lips, glad he'd let his beard grow in again.

"Everything's fine," I whispered and pressed my lips into a smile to keep the joy I felt from overflowing. "I was just checking the babies." His eyes went wide and placed his hand over mine. "They're *both* okay."

"Both?" he asked, his eyes so blue in the evening light. I felt the babies move again and he closed his eyes to *look* for them. Maybe they'd just been too small before now, but I witnessed the moment he *saw* them a smile lit up his face.

"Well then," he said, clearing his throat as he turned to the women running the stall—a wylden and an upworlder—with a smile. "We'd like to buy this one—" he handed them the rainbow hued blanket I'd touched before. "And this one," he said after a moment, picking up a blanket woven in alternating stripes of brilliant gold and deep, forest green.

The women smiled, at ease together, as Finn traded some handcrafted tools that were perfect for spooling fibers and knitting.

"Two babies," he murmured with a chuckle as he tucked the blankets into a basket hanging from his arm. "I better get started on a second crib."

I laughed as his arm went around my waist and I laid my cheek against his shoulder. He kissed my hair before he gently pulled his arm away to lace his fingers with mine.

Up ahead of us, the children found Lucy and Aiyanna's stall, which was always a favorite as it was overflowing with warm bread and sweet cakes. I could hear Lucy's stern but playful voice as she admonished them not to eat them all at once and then their giggles as Aiyanna snuck them extras while Lucy pretended not to notice.

After receiving a bit of goat cheese from Lucy and Aiyanna, Luna doubled back to join us and I let my hand rest on her head.

Birds chirped from the rooftops around us and the sun sank toward the horizon, making everything look golden. Tomorrow we would travel to the Dark Woods to meet up with Sera and share the spoils of market day. Even if they weren't all right here, right now, I was surroudned by my family, and they were thriving.

As Finn and I joined the others, the summer sun warming my skin, his hand in mine, I couldn't help but think that there was nothing in the world quite as perfect as this.

Author's Note

IT'S BEEN A WILD RIDE. When I started writing the original version of *The Upworld,* I dreamed of a magical, mystical day where Erilyn's whole story would somehow be out in the world. And now it is. Erilyn has been with me for so long, much longer than the other characters, and it's a bittersweet feeling to know that this part of her story is complete.

I initially imagined Erilyn many, many years ago while reading a novel about warriors and wizards. There was a woman–a side character–with that name and I was captured by it. So I started imagining what a girl like Erilyn might be like. At first, she was an elf and she had a little dragon that perched on her shoulder and went everywhere with her. Then, she was just a girl who got pulled from our world into one filled with magic and danger. (But she still had her dragon.) And eventually, she just became Erilyn–a girl who was flawed and damaged, who was powerful and often afraid, who was loving and wanted to be loved. And of course, her dragon became Luna (the real star of the show).

Erilyn and I have been through a lot together, and while I'm not sure if I'll ever write anything in her world again, it is a possibility. It feels too final to say, "never again." And so, for now, this is the end to Erilyn's story. Thank you for reading it and for being a part of this journey with her and with me. Writing this series has been a life long dream and it feels magical to have accomplished this much.

Made in the USA
Columbia, SC
10 May 2024